MW00877179

Thirteen Chocolates

By Agatha Chocolats

Copyright © 2017 by Agatha Chocolats
All rights reserved. This book or any portion thereof
may not be reproduced or used in any manner whatsoever
without the express written permission of the publisher
except for the use of brief quotations in a book review or
article.

Printed in the United States of America
First Printing, 2017

This is a work of fiction. Names, characters, businesses,
places, events, and incidents are either the products of the
author's imagination or used in a fictitious manner. Any
resemblance to actual persons, living or dead, or actual
events or places is purely coincidental.

www.AgathaChocolats.com

ISBN 9781973203070

Dedication

❧❦❧

To my loving husband, for standing by my side, holding the umbrella, while I weathered through countless dark and stormy editing nights.

To my children—
My son, with his tireless voice of encouraging words,
and my daughter, whose expertise has landed her a role as my junior editor.

To my parents, for always believing in me.

And to my entire family, for your endless support...and for feeding me chocolate.

Table of Contents

Message to Reader

Dear sweet-toothed sleuth,

The following list of confections represent each of the thirteen victims, er, *guests* in the mystery of *Thirteen Chocolates*.

The lucky heirs will be arriving shortly at the mansion in the mountains. Only one by one, our unsuspecting guests will disappear. Coincidence, or murder?

Before the chapters dwindle down to one, see if you can solve whodunit. Dim the lights, snuggle into a comfy chair, and prepare your taste buds for chocolate indulgence. And relax, it's only murder— sweet, decadent murder.

Yours in crimes of cocoa passion,
Agatha Chocolats

Million Heir Collection

Thirteen Chocolates

✧❀ ❀✧

Chandler's Classic
Flaky Hawaiian Nut
Fruity Cream Puff
Ginger Snapped
Old Fashioned Whiskey Ball
Rocky Shaded Road
Slow-as-Molasses Turtle
Solid Heart
Southern Peach Cordial
Sugar-Free Thin Mint
The Bar
Toasted Joker
Tuxedo Truffle

Score Card

Play along and guess whodunit! Use this card to keep track of the eliminated chocolates at chapter ends. Last chocolate left...reveals the killer.

≈⊙≙ ⊚≙≈

Good luck, sleuths!

Life Before Chocolate

When I was little, the thought of earning pockets full of quarters while serving pie all day sounded like a dream job. But the grown-up truth is that quarters don't pay the bills, and pie makes your butt fat, *not that me and the dessert menu are exactly enemies.*

I swirled peaks of whipped cream over a mountain of peanut butter mousse, finished it off with a shower of crushed chocolate covered pretzels, and miraculously forgot all about carbs. I crowned the pie with a glass dome, shielding it from the layer of grease infiltrating the atmosphere. It sparkled like a diamond at Tiffany's sitting next to the three-day-old Bear Claws rendezvousing with the flies.

"Hey toots," yelped a voice from the bar.

I glanced down at my worthless name tag. Yep, it still read Anna, yet all day long I was expected to come, sit, and stay to the title of *babe, missy, darlin', cupcake,* and some, well, more imaginative names. Ironically, most of the patrons of the Plumview Brew diner were regulars, and in fact knew my name. The counter was reserved for the crud of the crop. Dirty old men. Dirty young men. Drinking dirty old dishwater labeled as coffee.

Mr. Kimble, with stashes of Sweet n' Lo bulging through his plaid pockets, flagged me down, waving his liver-spotted arm through the air. For the record, he doesn't tip me in quarters; he prefers nickels and dimes.

I held his glass while tipping a pitcher of ice water over it. "How are we doing this evening, Mr. Kimble?"

"Blech," he responded, sounding like my cat hacking up a tube sock, as his dentures propelled into the glass.

"Guess that means you decided on your usual." I called, "Give me a Greasy Lumberjack, make it squeal, use a hatchet, hold the logs— and drown 'em."

Now for something more edible. I plated him a generous slice of peanut butter pie. Yes, Mr. Kimble was the filthiest of the dirty old men. Dropped his flatware at every meal, just to watch a waitress bend over to pick it up. But, I had no intentions of letting someone shrivel up and die on my watch. This was the South after all.

Jimbo, my boss, yelled out to me, "Yo, Clementine. What's that fancy stuff on top of that there pie? It don't look like no pie from Jed's."

I told him, "They're just pretzels. And people don't like pies from bait shops."

"The Plumview Brew customers only eat Jed's pie. And them fancy pretzels are coming out of your paycheck. Now ya gonna grab this food outta the window? Cause it ain't gonna walk itself outta here."

I'd challenge that one.

"Hey shug, grab me a couple slices while yer at it," Willie said, under blonde ringlets, making her way to the coffee station.

Willie and I were the Ernie and Bert of best friends. Willie was the short, adorably-stout charming one, seeing the world as bubble bath half-full. I was quite taller, a bit thinner, and tended to see the bathtub drained with a ring of scum around it.

I mumbled to her, "This job stinks."

"Not today," she said, pointing to the counter. "Quick, get yer tips."

Cause seventeen cents was going to land me an apartment. I had been working this pathetic job since I became a single mom three years ago. Here I was, two months from thirty and still hadn't scraped up enough to move out of my uncle's basement.

Willie gave me a shove from behind. I trudged over the sticky linoleum, reluctantly scooping up the coins from the counter. My open palm revealed odd change. And a key? Now I've gotten some strange tips over the years. Phone numbers written on Heinz bottles, blinding photos (thank you Mr. Kimble), and a pack of Chicklets once, but this was a new one. The key looked like an ordinary door key, only it was tied off with a gold satin ribbon.

Willie quick stepped over to me. "Why Miss Clementine, I reckon today's yer lucky day."

Mr. Kimble's eyebrows danced as he gave me a gummy smile in approval.

My eyes bulged like a goldfish in a shark tank. "Willomeana Eloise, stop messing with me." I backed my steps, bouncing off a mattress of a torso. The 30-something man was tall, dark, and handsome in a stealthy body guard kind of way, and oddly, smelt of freshly baked cookies.

Willie said, "Told ya gal. This here fancy fella is taken ya to Paris, France."

The clean-shaven man, adorned in a walnut colored vest with gold buttons, complete with a chauffeur's cap and brown leather gloves, glared down at Willie through dark shades. "Paris *Falls*. Tennessee."

Willie's eyelashes applauded. "Ooh. Folks say that's the Hollywood of the South." In Willie's defense, we don't get out much.

The man said to me, "Miss Clementine, I assume?"

My scrunched eyes traveled up and up until they met my distorted reflection mirrored on his dark shades.

The man pulled an envelope from his vest and handed it to me, "Miss Clementine, I'm Frankie Ziti, your chauffeur."

"Mister, you've got yourself the wrong gal," I said.

"Perhaps you should read the letter. But, please keep the contents to yourself."

I wordlessly took the letter and hightailed it to the backroom, never taking my eyes off it.

The envelope was aged and yellowed. My fingertip swirled over the faint imprint of my typed name. Curious, indeed. I flipped it over. The envelope sealed with a perfect cursive 'C', centered on a splotch of melted brown wax, which looked and smelt like cocoa.

The letter was stamped, *CONFIDENTIAL.*

"If you are reading this, it means that I, Ulysses Chandler have died. I had no wife and no children left to speak of, just a lifelong love affair with my business. Those of you that knew me well, knew that my business was my life, from the beginning to the end. My father left it to me, his father left it to him, and now I too, must pass it on to my family. Ironically, the only family I have left, I have never met. If you are reading this, you are a stranger. And, if you are reading this, you are my grandchild. And, if you are reading this, then you are heir to the biggest chocolate factory in the world."

I took a few moments to process the contents, then reread the letter just to make sure my eyes weren't deceiving me. I never knew my grandfather, but never expected in a million years that he was the famous Chandler. I felt like I just won the lottery, or Wonka's golden ticket. And I couldn't tell a soul.

Willie jumped up and down. I wondered if she was snooping over my shoulder.

"I can't believe you're gonna be on TV," she said. "I told ya, just like Hollywood."

"Huh?" I started to correct her, realizing that I couldn't tell her the true contents of the letter, allowing her vivid imagination to fill in the blanks. It was a much better option than telling her that I had a secret.

Willie assessed me up and down. "Ain't nobody in Hollywood lookin' like this." She climbed her size 5 boots upon an over-turned stockpot, and went into make-over mode, unraveling my pony tail, sending a chestnut waterfall down my back. She licked her thumb and brought it toward my face. "You gotcha just a lil something—"

"I draw the line there," I said. And made my way toward the front of the diner.

Willie trailed behind, patting down my skirt as I walked. I scowled, "What in the world are you doing *now?*"

She whispered in my ear rather loudly, "I'm wipin' the flour off of yer hiney, so ya won't leave a bum-print in that there vehicle."

I glanced outside, past the glare of the neon coffee cup sign, at the brown Lincoln stretch with locals swarming around it. These folks would be less surprised to see a spaceship parked on Main Street. But, that's an entirely different story.

My *driver* opened the limousine door. Wanting to thank the bearer of good news, I raced towards Frankie with open arms. As his arms tightened in straight jacket position, I got the message that he wasn't the hugger-kind-of-stranger.

I stepped in the car, thanking Willie for everything.

She gave me a curtsy, upgrading my status to royalty. "If ya see Dolly, get me an autograph." Others that generally didn't give me the time of day, waved and said goodbyes like I was a celebrity. Only I wasn't going to Hollywood, or France, I was going someplace much sweeter.

Chapter Thirteen

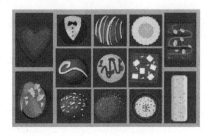

THIRTEEN chocolates teetered on the threshold of bitter and sweet.

I prayed he wasn't an axe murderer. Although if he was, I suppose I'd be riding in the trunk. *Unless,* the trunk was already occupied. But why would someone go through the expense of kidnapping me in a limousine? The psycho could have borrowed an ice cream truck and lured me just as easy.

Frankie, who looked less like a chauffeur, and more like a cement shoe salesman, lowered the partitioned window. He was still wearing those ridiculous shades as he drove us into the darkness. "We have a good two hours to Paris Falls, so make yourself at home," he told me.

Traveling two hours deeper into the desolate Smoky Mountains, where only the trees will hear my screams— yeah, I'm going to have a party back here. How could I be so naive to leave my little girl, and go off for a weekend with a stranger? I felt the bulge of the letter in my apron pocket and got my answer. Temptation.

We had lived with my Uncle Wiley since my daughter was born. In a few days, I could finally pay him back. I'd buy him a new house. A new truck. And Jillian and I could buy a place of our own. Maybe we'd even get a swimming pool.

In the meantime, I could feel the distance building between us. At least I got to see my family before I left. Frankie had given me a whopping fifteen minutes at home to pack my bags. I spent five minutes of it stuffing a suitcase with random clean clothes, a framed photo of Jillian, and an emergency box of Chocolate Chip Cookie Dough Pop-tarts. Just in case. And then I spent the other ten, squeezing the stuffing out of Jillian.

The good news was that Uncle Wiley got to meet my potential kidnapper. The bad news was that I wasn't allowed to disclose the details of my trip, not the purpose or the exact location. Not that I knew much about the mysterious Paris Falls. Just that it was a Southern style knockoff of Paris, France; complete with its own towering landmark. *The Waffle Tower.* How bad could a waffle-obsessed town be?

I fudged the truth a bit, telling my uncle that my trip was a business opportunity. Since iHOP doesn't send limousines for potential hires, Uncle Wiley went with Willie's theory. He was convinced I was going to be on one of those confounded reality TV charades that all the women were gossiping about in the beauty shop. And Shades wasn't exactly spilling his guts, or even offering any small talk for that matter. The entire time we were at my uncle's house, he stood in the doorway in parade rest, like a thug on the lookout for impromptu bullets. Definitely not rooted in the South. Southerners are born talking, aka, gossiping. The only thing that shuts us up is deep fried— well, deep fried anything.

But, now that my adrenaline had plateaued, doubt crept in its place. I was so eager to inherit the dream, I never stopped to ask myself if this was too good to be true. Perhaps, I could unravel some of the knots in my stomach by getting to know the mysterious Mr. Ziti. I lowered the partitioned window, and initiated conversation. "So Frankie, did you personally drive for Mr. Chandler?"

"Yes, mam," Frankie said, and rolled up the window.

Hmmf. I took a gander around at the back-seat space. Neon lights. An army of glistening liquor bottles in perfectly lined rows. A television/ video game system. And a car phone. I picked up the receiver. "Hi there, Frank. It's me, Anna. So, how long have you worked for Mr. Chandler?"

"Five years, mam." *click*

It was apparent, I wasn't getting anything out of Chatty Cathy. Unfortunately, I had a couple of hours to kill. No, not kill. I had to do something that would keep my mind off of anybody killing anyone. That left me with liquor or video games.

Ten minutes later... "Awe shoot, I fell into the sinking fudge pit again." *Cocoa Nuts! You have 1 life remaining.*

The window slid down. "Here's what you're going to wanna to do," Frankie spoke as if he was instructing me to take down a hit, not progress in a video game. "Find yourself a golden truffle. One of those real sparkly types. Eat it. Now you'll be flying over those fudge pits, higher than a kite. Keep your eyes open for Freddie the Filbert. You see that fella, you pop em one, right in the nut." I swallowed hard. And just that fast the window was closed again.

So much for getting my mind off of murder. I flipped off the game and eyeballed the bar. My nerves could use some liquid numbing. As motor skills were beneficial when swimming with the fishes, I opted for a little shut eye.

I awoke with a jerk, my head kissing my knees, trying to stay on the seat, as the vehicle swerved. My queasy stomach demanded that my head stay in between my legs.

The window lowered. "Deer," said Frankie. Deer. Of course. Why else would he be risking our lives, swerving on the mountainside?

There was no telling how long I slept. I had no idea where I was. Only that I was somewhere in the mountains. With a strange man. The limousine ascended up several miles of windy, gravel roads. The less traveled kind of roads. The kind of roads where brutal killers went to devour their prey, and their victim's bones not discovered till decades later. This was bad. My gut said, escape. I could jump. I could bust open the door, tuck and roll, and make a run for it. Only I wasn't a stunt man and my extent of running was to catch the elevator, so I didn't have to climb the stairs.

The car paused. Perhaps, I could actually do this. As I gave myself a pep talk, I only half believed, the vehicle came to a stop. Frankie got out of the car. Crud. I'll have to outrun him. I grabbed the door handle, and cursed. It was locked. Cement shoes, here I come.

All was still, except the sound of Frankie's shuffling footsteps scraping over the pounded dirt's surface, camouflaged by low lying fog. But, wait. He wasn't coming towards me. He was heading toward the front of the car. He followed the headlight beams that broke through the mist, illuminating a pair of iron gates. He unlocked a half dozen padlocks, then returned to the car and crept through the entrance way. And that's when I saw it. The iconic cursive *C* trademark. We were at the famous Chandler mansion.

The limo crept down a long, dimly lit driveway that

seemed to go on for miles, the view crowded by seas of pines. My heart was beating faster than hummingbird wings, while we traveled at a slug's pace deeper into the darkness, fog clouding the only sliver of light shining onto the road. At last, past another forest of trees, stood a monumental building. Only the moonlight gave hints to its brilliant structure. "Wow," I mouthed, suddenly feeling under-dressed in my powder blue, polyester uniform. I wiped down my skirt, patted the fear-sweat off of my forehead, and fixed the creases on my white collar. As if these efforts were going to make a difference.

Frankie parked in a grand circular driveway that enclosed a cement fountain large enough to bathe in. He said to me, "I'll bring your bags in through the side entry, so you go on ahead."

ᦞᦞ ᦞᦞ

My steps were slow and hesitant. A couple minutes ago, I thought I had been kidnapped by a serial killer. But here I was, standing in front of *The* Chandler mansion. Of course, the rational part of my brain fought back. People just didn't inherit multi-million-dollar companies overnight from strangers— especially, the single-mom kind of people working for minimum wage in a coffee shop kind of people.

The dim lights of the stone walkway invited me to an enormous porch. I imagined myself sitting on one of the oversized wooden rockers, sipping lemonade, while gazing at the ribbons of fuchsia roses cascading up the stone pillars of the mansion and adjoining gazebo, while my little girl tossed the crust of her sandwich to the swans in the overlooking pond. Swans. Yes, there were actual swans.

Could this really be mine? As if to seal the deal, a box, resembling a wooden jewelry box, tied off with brown and gold damask patterned ribbons, was perched in front of the

10

doorway. I knew this signature patterned ribbon anywhere. My fingertip traced over the engraved letters on the mahogany lid.

Chandler's Chocolates
Est. 1913
The Million Heir Collection
Contents: Thirteen Chocolates

Nothing said class like a box of custom-made Chandler's chocolates. Smothered in creamy coats of satiny smooth seduction, laced with nuts and flakes, sprinkles and slivers, these chocolates defined the true meaning of eye candy. My lips and taste buds united, tackling my brain's tired lectures of trans fats and threats of elastic-waisted jeans. This was no time for me to brave will power. These chocolates were my destiny. After all, chocolate was in my blood.

A few days ago, Ulysses Chandler was merely a stranger. Today I've learned that the world-famous chocolatier was also my grandfather. And he was now dead. So then, I rationalized, this masterpiece of chocolates displayed on the mansion doorstep before me, was a gift from the chocolate heavens. I nestled my new prized possession under my arm.

Okay, now for the moment of truth. I took a deep breath and poked at the doorbell, prompting a protective dog to show off its vocal chords. I waited. And waited. As the moments passed, doubts returned. Limousines. Mansions. It was all just too surreal. Like something you would see on television. Willie was right. Probably all my coworkers at the Plumview Brew were in on it, setting me up for the butt of the joke on some reality show. I surveyed the porch for the hidden camera. Ah hah. My suspicion, or paranoia, led me over to an artificial tree sitting in the corner of the porch. I frantically pawed through the web-coated leaves, only to find a butterscotch wrapper and a dead beetle.

An elder lady poked her head into to the plant. "Whatcha lookin' fer, shug?

I sprung up to a standing position. "Me? I'm not looking for anything."

The woman disregarded her crisp brown dress and ruffled white apron, getting down on all fours, her silver beehive bobbin' over the artificial dirt. "You shore enough was. Did ya lose an earring?" I'm always doin' that. But whatcha lookin' in the rubba tree for? I reckon Polly Sue Pickers once lost er one in the bushes, but you look like more of a proper lady. Ooh, and then there was that time Ethyl Rogers lost one in the loo. That poor gal got herself stuck tween the tub and toilet for eighteen hours.

Good grief. I had no idea what this woman was rambling about. But, I felt like I needed to put a stop to it. I brushed back my hair to expose my earring. "Oh, look at that, I found it." I extended my palm, and helped her to an upright position.

The old lady smoothed out wrinkles on her apron. She gave my hand a firm shake, and glanced at my name tag peeking out under my coat. "Well, heidi-doo then, Anna. I'm Tessie. Won't cha come in?"

Tessie opened up the front door, and things got real. The place was gigantic. Gigantic, as in, it could eat my home town for breakfast.

My eyes strolled down an endless marble foyer, up three flights of intricate, golden stairs, and then dropped down to greet the prodding nose of a Chocolate Standard Poodle.

"Looks like Bonbon took a liking to ya," said Tessie.

This was no coincidence, as I was modeling an assortment of grease and condiment stains. Momentarily, the dog stopped getting to know me intimately, plopping itself on my foot, its rosy red tongue hanging down long enough to mop the surrounding floor.

Tessie said, "Now then, I'm gonna go put on a kettle, while Boris here shows ya yer way to the library."

A frail butler, buried in a walnut tuxedo, shuffled me down a cathedral-like hallway. With his diminutive stature and balding head, I somehow felt I should be collecting $200 on the Monopoly board.

Boris paused at the coat closet and held out his hands. I passed him my chocolates, while I wriggled out of my jacket.

He hung the coat and continued walking. "Miss Clementine, right this way." The mansion had the bones of an ancient stranger, yet the face of a familiar friend, its intricate architecture hollowing out nooks and crannies for nostalgic knick-knacks. Aged wallpaper hosted mountain landscapes and cozy, shaded wall sconces. I followed the butler's stunted steps down the brown and white checked marble hallway to the library doorway.

"The lawyer will be here shortly for the reading of the will," he said.

I took a deep breath. This was it. My life was about to change. No more stuffing jelly doughnuts. No more paying for Pampers with pockets full of quarters. Right here before me was a chocolate kingdom, and I was about to be crowned the queen.

Boris' white gloves motioned me through the doorway. "Miss Clementine, you may join the others."

Others? And just like that, my royal title deflated like a whoopee cushion.

I stepped inside, eager to define the meaning, and more importantly, the quantity, of the others. A handful of people sat around a table. Okay, no biggie. I didn't need a gazillion dollars for myself. By my math, stinking rich divided by a half a dozen people, still equaled spoiled rotten.

The room was filled with awkward silence. Each attendee sat in an elegant winged backed chair, covered in a delicate pattern of golden leaves and cocoa pods. I wordlessly took a seat, and forced my focus beyond the circumference of faces bordering the conference table, taking in the ambience of the library— its endless shelves of meticulously stacked books that hugged the focal point of the room, a brown brick fireplace which mimicked a dark chocolate bar. How Mr. Chandler must have adored cozying up with a book in one of the leather chairs facing the blazing flames, while taking in the delightful smell of burning wood and the gentle trace of sweet pipe tobacco in the air.

The cologne-soaked guy next to me had over-styled hair and a popped denim collar, looking like he just walked off the set of the Breakfast Club. He caught me in a stare, offering his hand. "Cashmere Finch." He angled his iPad screen in my direction, displaying a feline fashion show. "I'm a designer."

Huh. Who knew? Ordinarily, this oddity would trigger a pile of questions. But at this moment, I was more anxious about getting on with the will. I put a pin in my agenda, while I did the polite thing, and oohed and awed at Trixie prancing down the catwalk in her hot pink tutu and studded pleather vest. I swallowed my pride— yes, diner dive waitresses have a smidgen of it, and began making small talk with him. I was telling him about my tubby, talentless house cat, Milton, when my attention strayed to a redhead lady standing across from me.

Shoved into a napkin ring of a dress, she stuck out like a call girl at the Ritz Carlton. I could only imagine what type of work she did at the mansion. But, her appearance wasn't my concern. She was rummaging through a box, as if she had just discovered a heap of rare jewels.

I motioned the butler over. I whispered to Boris, "I think that lady has my chocolates."

The butler pivoted his steps and marched over to the woman. With heels, the gal had a good foot on him. He showed no signs of intimidation, snatching the box from her hands. "Madam, this does not belong to you."

Wow, way to go butler. Now that's what I call service.

"The name's Kiki. And what's the big friggin' deal?" she said. "It's just a box of chocolates." She turned to the side, fluffing her wavy mane off of her shoulder. And that's when we saw her cheek puffed out like a chipmunk sucking on a golf ball.

Boris' flesh ignited to blood red, like a raging bull ready to charge her cape of crimson hair. He satisfactorily contained his butler disposition. "Quite simply, they don't belong to you. They're estate property." He set the box back on the conference table and raised a single finger at her, scolding her like a child, "Don't touch."

Hmff, so much for *my* chocolates.

Boris tugged on his coat tails and tweaked his bowtie, and Kiki lit up a cigarette.

Meanwhile, Tessie had returned with a tray full of refreshments. She set a plate of cookies on the table. "Anyone care for a cup of tea, before we get down to the nitty gritty?"

I accepted the offering, with instant regrets. While Tessie poured the tea, some hairy bafoon, smelling like a liquor store, shoved past her to grab a cookie, knocking the pot out of her hands.

The burly bearded fella let out a beastly growl from the deep pits of his furry chest, and then a hiccup. "Watch it, Granny."

Tessie's eyebrows bounced in surprise and quickly deflated into a scowl, like an inverted soufflé. "Dang nabbit! Why that man's 'bout as clumsy as an ox makin' love to a squirrel. Where in tarnation he come from anyway?"

A quick reminder of why I serve coffee for a living, and not beer. I insisted that Tessie go clean herself up, while I took care of the mess. As I squatted down to pick up the last of the tea-ware, Sasquatch said to me, "Woah, you got some on my shoe."

I glanced down to his snake skin boot. "I don't see a thing."

"Then maybe you should get a closer look." He gave my back a shove, whispering toxic fumes in my ear, "Be careful, wench. Next time you kiss the ground, you may not get back up again."

My eyes met his caterpillar eyebrow. My body did an involuntary shiver. And this would be the point I would switch my customer to decaf.

Cashmere, paused his runway video. "So, I see you've had the displeasure of meeting my brother, Caesar Marino. Don't mind him. He's drunk."

It was a bit hard to ignore somebody when they were threatening your life and drooling on your shoe. "Your brother?" My eyes squinted, searching for a resemblance in their faces. Baby-faced Cashmere and Bigfoot-ed Caesar didn't exactly look like bookends, they barely passed for the same species.

Cashmere reiterated, *"Step* brother. And you haven't heard the best part." He reached into his jacket pocket, flashing an envelope, identical to the inheritance letter that had invited me to the mansion. "This makes him— er, *us,* your cousins."

"No?" I sang in an unconvinced soprano.

"No" I belted out in a baritone of disbelief.

My whole life it was just me. I had never even considered the possibility of cousins. My mother had been adopted, so up until now I had no knowledge of my natural grandparents. Let alone that gramps was the infamous Chandler.

I scoped out the ring of faces surrounding the table, fighting to find a resemblance to any of them. I asked Cashmere, "More cousins?"

"Yep."

Wowzers.

໑ଓ ୨ଡ଼

Boris closed the doors and presented himself to the group. The butler's words filtered through his snowy mustache, "Before we begin, allow me to introduce the grandchildren. You will find that you all share a common thread. Each of you has a parent that was adopted. And this is your link to the Chandler bloodline."

While Boris mumbled text off index cards, with zero intonation, I mentally jotted down my own observations. The first being that the butler didn't want to be here, and resented every one of us that he had to wait on.

I made mental notes about each of my newfound cousins as he introduced them.

Cashmere Finch, 33, Celebrity Pet Fashion Designer

The twig-like man, obviously stuck in the 80's, watched his iPad intently as kitties draped in lace and tulle pranced down the runway to the tune of *Girls Just Wanna Have Fun*.

Caesar Marino, 38, Las Vegas Bartender, (step-brother to Cashmere)

Caesar spilt over his chair's cushion, halfway onto the lap of the redhead sitting next to him. He diligently studied her cleavage, while his pinky struggled to dig a foreign matter out of his back teeth.

Kiki, 40, Former Model/ *chocolate thief*

"Kiki", just Kiki. The redhead squeezed into a thread of a dress, which was rising higher by the minute, evidently thought her centerfold fame should grant her single name status. She dug tool after tool out of her suitcase-sized purse, applying powder and lip gloss to her over-inflated lips, filing her nails, and tweezing her eyebrows into even thinner slants.

Mrs. Ashton Hodges, 26, Perfume Sampler

The pocket-sized dirty blonde, dressed in a magenta cashmere sweater and plaid skirt, tossed a piece of bubble gum into her mouth. Within seconds, a hot pink bubble grew over her face. The gooey membrane burst, momentarily breaking the silence, like a foghorn during a church sermon. Her cheeks reddened as she stared cross-eyed at the splattered neon residue on her nose.

Mr. Brice Hodges, 28, Former Professional Quarterback (Ashton's husband)

Jock guy, who seemed to have just spruced himself up in the locker room after a big game, clean-shaven, casually dressed in a lime jersey and jeans, had his nose in the paper, no doubt checking scores from last night's game. His slightly squinted eyes, cocked smirk that raised up into a trophy of a dimple, seemed to disregard his wife's blow-out.

Harley Wellington, 27, Yacht Salesman

Harley, adorned in his glowing golden locks and dressed in spring break casuals, was a definite candidate for Ritalin. Although, I must admit he was kind of interesting to watch. For a moment, I felt like Jane Goodall observing chimpanzees in the wild. A ballpoint pen seemed to amuse the attention- challenged man. He twirled it around in his fingers like a baton, then squished it into the groove above his lip like a mustache, balanced it on its cap in his upright palm, played chicken with his left hand— stabbing the exposed ballpoint in between his fingers, and finally flicked it over to Caesar, bouncing it off his potbelly, initiating a game of table soccer.

Priscilla, 36, Director of a Ballet Company (Sister to Harley)

The definition of prim and proper, this gal seemed to stem from a different branch of the Wellington family tree, her fruits from a Calvin Klein clothed loin. I never saw anybody sit upright so straight; you could measure her right angled back with a protractor. Her head hung high, as if her whole lanky-being was being sucked up into the headband that sat upon her platinum blonde hair. Her head never flinched to the others and their immature behaviors; her eyes astutely focused straight ahead.

After the introductions, one thing was for certain. My cousins were all successful, and loaded. I was the ugly blue-polyester duckling in the flock of rich swans. For now.

The grand mahogany doors creaked open behind us. An older man, wearing an expensive navy blue pinstriped suit, which was cheapened by his greased-down silver comb-over and button-challenged potbelly, entered the room. Followed by members of the staff.

Tessie squeezed past the others with a fresh pot of tea. "Good golly, look at all these kin. Looks like Ol' Chandler was as busy as a rooster in a hen house. I reckon them girls knew how to ruffle his feathers, and then some. No wonder we got us a whole coop full—"

The cantaloupe-headed man, with thick blotchy rind-skin, took command of the room, interrupting Tessie. "Good evening, folks," he said. "I am Mortimer Winston, lawyer and estate trustee manager for Mr. Chandler's will." For a lawyer, he appeared uneasy. Like a weasel in a walrus body. "We are here today to—"

"Hey, what are they doing here?" asked Caesar, the drunk, pointing to the employees. "This is personal family business."

"Everyone in the room has been requested to be here," said the lawyer. He pointed to each employee while introducing them. "You've all already met Boris, the butler, and Tessie, our kitchen maid. And to my left is Frankie, Chandler's personal chauffeur, and Jasper, the head gardener. The gardener, chewing on a toothpick, tipped his ten-gallon hat.

Okay, a few more heirs. Still, plenty of will to go around.

Caesar folded his unruly primate arm, over his exposed hairy chest. "As long as the old farts are just here to wait on me. Those losers better not think they're getting a cent of my money." This led others to vocalize the same.

The redhead honked at the apparent absurdity. "Share? I'm not sharing with anyone." Not a surprising statement coming from the woman who stole my chocolates.

I tried to tactfully spell out the situation to her. "Kiki, we were all under the impression that we were sole heirs. But as you can see, Chandler had multiple grandchildren and employees."

She took a puff of her cigarette, allowing the smoke to drift in my direction. "Who are you again?" she asked me.

"Anna. From Plumview, North Carolina."

"Well Anna from Plumview, I decided that I didn't want to share my money with anybody. Including hillbillies, no matter how desperately they needed new clothes."

Like her clothes were so wonderful? I glanced again at her designer red dress, revealing her bare tan legs pouring into scarlet steel-tipped stilettos. I revisited my own legs covered in support stockings in the shade of suntan that ran into clunky black rubber soled work shoes. Bonbon gazed deep into my eyes to let me know she was on my side. I fed her a tea biscuit just in case.

Winston pounded a stapler on the table like a gavel. The lawyer's face flushed to eggplant purple and he began to sputter nonsense. "Oh, flibber flabber, poppycock." Oddly that silenced the group. He took in a breath and spoke with a forced calmness, "None of you have yet earned a penny."

Earned?

Winston continued, "Mr. Chandler wanted to be sure that the person taking over his factory gained expert status about every aspect of his chocolate enterprise."

Caesar said, "This is chocolate we're talking about here. You unwrap it. You eat it." He held out his pudgy palm for payment.

Winston sighed. "The person taking over Chandler's empire will need to be familiar with the hundreds of Chandler products, as well as the properties. The factory, the mail order company, the store front, not to mention the new amusement park and hotel. The person who wins this inheritance should be a Chandler expert."

Whoa. "Did you say *person?*" I asked.

"That is correct. On the thirteenth hour of the thirteenth day, a notary will arrive by boat and deliver an exam to all the heirs. The person that receives the highest score will become the sole heir of Mr. Chandler's chocolate factory and estate."

And there was the bombshell I'd been waiting for. It was a competition. All or nothing. And right now, I had nothing. Evidently, I wasn't the only one upset.

Harley, the yacht salesman, waved a tan arm in the air. "This is bogus. Nobody ever mentioned a test."

Winston once again banged his mock gavel. "Bogus-shmogus. Mr. Wellington. You, and anyone else who finds this opportunity to gain a multi-million-dollar factory to be unworthy of your time, are welcome to leave. However, please be aware, that anyone that departs, will automatically be eliminated from the competition."

My brain tried to wrap around the craziness of the situation, while calculating possibilities. What in the world did I know about this company? If it was based on chocolate consumption, I'd have it in the bag. But company history was a whole different story. I gazed around at my competition, realizing that the grandkids were all in the same boat. The real threats were the employees. The people living and breathing the company every day.

I asked, "Do we at least get a study guide?"

"Consider every moment of your stay, your study guide. Everything branded Chandler's is fair game."

So that would make my odds slimmer. But, not impossible. If there was any chance of this being mine, I had to take it. I owed that to my family.

The lawyer slid *my* wooden box of chocolates to the center of the table. "As a bonus, the late Mr. Chandler himself, custom designed these chocolates representing each of the thirteen heirs. The winner will also be awarded this priceless, one of a kind box of Chandler's chocolates."

Okay, so maybe the box didn't belong to me— yet. I had found it on the doorstep and assumed it was meant for me as a welcoming gift. Of course, that was before I realized that there were a dozen other heirs.

Winston opened the lid on the mahogany wooden chest.

My lips tugged down to a grimace noting the empty square, like looking at a puzzle with one piece missing.

Boris directed his pristine white butler glove in Kiki's direction. "You can thank that redhead sucking down her fourth glass of '74 Cheval Blanc for that. Kiki, or Cuckoo, or whatever rubbish she goes by."

"Well this is a problem," said Winston. He flipped through his papers. "Section 17b. The consequence of stealing or defacing Chandler property is immediate disqualification and ejection from the property."

"You've got to be freakin' kidding me," said Kiki. "You think I'm giving up millions of dollars over a crappy piece of candy?"

Winston cleared his throat. He looked around to the rest of us. "Unless, they are willing to make an amendment."

Kiki mustered up pouty eyes, and a sad pity story, *and* flashed some cleavage to the men. As much as I wanted to see her leave, I wasn't going to be the lone bad guy.

Winston scribbled up an amendment. "Well then, it appears we will be enforcing a new rule. Anyone who ingests, steals, hides, mutilates, or manipulates the chocolates from this point further, will be disqualified. No exceptions. All in favor?"

The group choral response put the new rule into motion.

Winston filled us in on the itinerary for the next two weeks, including visits to the chocolate factory, Chandler's amusement park, and its new partnering restaurants and shops. Besides the fact that I was separated from my family, this sounded like a dream vacation.

"Lastly, the use of cell phones and other electronic devices will not be permitted during the training," said the lawyer. "I must emphasize to you, that the matters of this will must remain confidential. The public, including the authorities, have not yet been notified of Chandler's death, and when they do, there will be heirs popping up out of the woodwork. Headache for me, and lots of wasted time before you or anyone else, can even get close to their inheritance."

I fought back the lump in my throat. "We can't even talk to family?"

"A house phone is available to you all for your convenience. However, your conversations will be monitored. Now, good luck to all of you that decide to stay."

Winston and the other staff left the meeting, and the room exploded in chaos.

Caesar's pudgy fingers flicked his golden key across the table, making a landing on Kiki's lap. "What a load of crap. I didn't come here for a competition."

Drunk or not, I had to agree with him. When people compete for money, things get ugly. And family, or not, I had a feeling these people were going to play to win. Gloves off.

Kiki dug a key out of the shallow depths of her dress and compared it to Caesar's key. "The teeth are different. Maybe only one key opens up the door to the chocolate factory. She took a drag of her cigarette. "Hey hillbilly girl, let's see yours."

I forced myself to bite my tongue, as I seemed to be making more enemies than friends in this house.

"Come on, we don't have all day, she persisted. "Let's see it."

I felt my head, taking a moment to mentally retrace the key's whereabouts. "I just need to find my apron. I think I left it in the limo."

Kiki laughed, "Good luck with that; your driver just left.

Caesar, with excessive spray, imitated the sound of a bomb explosion. "One down."

They weren't going to get rid of me that easy. Not on a technicality over a piece of metal. And something told me Kiki wouldn't be as compassionate to return the favor, and pardon me. Not with this kind of money on the table.

Unfortunately, Frankie was nowhere to be found inside. But, I don't think he could've left that quickly. I started the haul down to the driveway, piloting my steps into the darkness, instantly isolated in the boundless black air, vulnerable to the moonlit shadows and chattering trees. I told my paranoia, "Relax. It's just a stinking key."

Clink clonk clink clonk I tried to ignore the echoing sounds of my lone footsteps pounding on the cement, the wind whistling through the leaves, and the distant howls of some animal who I forced myself to believe was a vegetarian, and was only on the prowl for a friendly face to lick. My arms hugged around my body, protecting it from nothing.

At last, I could hear the gentle cascades of water flowing into the driveway's fountain. Shoot. No car. This meant that the vehicle was either parked, or I was too late.

I followed a narrow drive running along the side of the building. After a small hike, my calves were appreciative to have found the parking area. And hallelujah, my limousine. The only obstacle now was getting into the car, which was sandwiched in between a larger, stretch limousine and a delivery truck. I paused for a moment, taking in the whispers of the mountain air, allowing a wave of willies to travel up my spine. I had the sudden sense that I was not alone. Focus. Get your bag, then run like the dickens back to the mansion.

My body shimmied in between my limo and the truck. I pulled up the door handle on the limo. Locked. I wiggled the lever up and down. Heaven help me, I was going to get into this car. I leaned my back onto the truck, planted both feet onto the limo door, and shook the handle like a crazy woman, sending both vehicles into a rocking tremor. *Beeeeeep.* Awe, seriously? I set off the alarm on the delivery truck.

I squeezed myself through the narrow passageway between the vehicles, just about making my way to the truck's open-aired door. With all my might, I just couldn't fit. I made a mental note. Starting on tomorrow, I would go on a diet. Maybe. Definitely, the day after that. Since my body wouldn't budge forward, I jostled it backwards. It was at this moment that I realized it would have been much easier to go around to the other side of the truck. The other side, which wouldn't pancake me in between two pieces of metal. Mmm, pancakes. My irresponsible thoughts drifted to rich, warm syrup oozing down stacks of buttery browned cakes. My calorie-excessive thoughts turned against me, instantly expanding my hips. I was stuck.

The horn blared in my brain. I searched down deep for my inner-Hulk, exploding forward. Going nowhere. My outer Hulk-thighs made it impossible to squeeze into the doorway of the truck. I leaned my upper body forward, and now was close enough to stretch my arm into the opening. My fingers randomly searched for a phone, keys, a plunger, jaws-of-life, something…uh oh…something fleshy and long… and hairy. Something long and hairy-that connected to a fleshy and hairy hand. Yeeks. I shoved my inner-Hulk aside, and embraced my inner-sniveling scaredy-cat, victoriously pushing my body to the driver's door. My feet maneuvered up the steel steps, finding the hand's owner asleep at the wheel. I took hold of his shoulders and gave them a good wiggle. "Wake up. Wake up, gosh darn it." I shook him again, as if my prodding was going to be more effective than the blazing horn currently busting the sound barrier. I gave his chest a good shove, causing his head to spring backwards. The horn he had his forehead pressed upon, stopped. And now there was only one thing in between me and that mansion doorstep. A dead guy.

This wasn't happening. I panicked. I offered my condolences. And, I panicked some more. I had to get out of here. As in, right now. I pondered my options. Either I climbed over Dudley-dead guy, or I spent the night wedged in between the two vehicles.

I took in a deep breath. And did absolutely nothing. I took in another deep breath and tugged again at my inner scaredy-cat, now laced with a heavy dose of paranoia. What if the man was murdered, and the killer was lurking in the shadows? Yes, that was just the exact motivation I needed. Within seconds, I had a steering wheel in my crotch and my rear-end in the poor chap's face. I realized my current position wasn't appropriate, but it wasn't my fault his bulging belly was taking up most of the seat. I'm thinking he had indulged in his own fair share of pound-packing pancakes. Ugh. I couldn't gain any leverage from this position. I twisted my body around, my face now crunched into his life-less, stiff chest, that reeked of Ben-Gay. Yes, think gay, happy thoughts. I managed to get one leg up on the stick shift. My head lifted in an effort to follow my leg's lead, then pounced right back to the cold ribcage. My stinkin' earring was caught on the man's tie. Seriously? Why couldn't I have lost my earring like Ethyl Rogers in the toilet?

A light flashed over my face. Thank goodness.

"Anna, is that you?" asked a voice.

My peripheral vision caught a glimpse of a popped jacket collar. It was the cat-diva, Cashmere. "Yes, yes, yes," I yelled out. "Thank the heavens. I could kiss you right now."

The light flickered over the dead man's face, then back on to my face.

"Oops," said Cashmere. "Sorry, gal. My bad. I'll leave you guys to it."

"No, don't leave me. The driver underneath me is dead, my foot is stuck on his stick shift, and my ear is attached to his ascot."

༺◎ ◎༻

An hour or three later, my heart was back in my chest, my words in prayer for the dead, and my dignity still floating around somewhere in the parking lot. After a lengthy Q&A, mostly directed at me, the authorities theorized that the driver died of a heart attack. Under normal circumstances, natural causes would be unquestionable. But, this night was far from normal.

I smuggled any doubting thoughts, submersing myself into my new surroundings. The Raspberry Room. It was instantly apparent that I should have explored my room, before taking my moonlit stroll. I removed my apron off the bed and retrieved the key from its pocket. The key was inscribed with a serial number and the letters JB on it. But nothing noteworthy. It looked just like the others' keys. And I would bet, that none of them were going to be fitting into a master lock on Grandpa's factory. The key was probably meant as a mere symbol of the prize.

I sprawled over the king bed, where cherry posts stood elegantly, ever so delicately carved, like wooden vines sprouting from a bed of luscious pink blooms. The walls were covered with a combination of light and dark pink stripes, detailed with trails of budding berries. In the center of the wall was an oil painting of a glistening ripe raspberry, nestled in rigged chunks of mouth-watering chocolate. Each little groove and bump on the berry seemed to be bursting with juice. As I lay there admiring the painting, I noted a subtle hint of raspberry fragrance in the air. Mr. Chandler had thought of it all.

A shimmer of gold caught the corner of my eye. Chocolates on the pillow? I adoringly unwrapped the pink and gold shiny foil, unveiling a dark chocolate sphere. The chocolate crumbled in my mouth, exploding creamy raspberry heaven onto my tongue. This, this, I could get used to.

My lips mouthed goodnight to the framed photo of my precious girl, Jillian, which I displayed upon the mantel. The photo froze my toddler in mid-puddle jump, her magenta umbrella shielding her sparse ponytail from the drizzling rain.

I had no idea how I'd survive thirteen days away from her. Homesickness had already set in. I was under the impression that I'd be gone for the weekend, not half of a month. It was a good thing that I had shoved extra clothes in my suitcase, not that that was even a worry right now.

I forced my attention off of the photo and allowed the flames in the fireplace below to lull me to sleep. And then was quickly woke by voices in the hallway.

Boris, the butler, said, "Mrs. Hodges, I'm afraid that all of the king beds have been taken."

Newlyweds. Ugh. I pulled the covers over my head, unsuccessfully extinguishing Ashton's pesky little voice.

"Certainly, there has to be another king-sized bed," said Ashton.

"Just the Master's suite, on the third floor, madam."

"Great, "Ashton said. "Brice and I will take it."

"But madam, the Master's room is strictly off limits," said Boris.

"Mister, the *Master* is d-e-a-d. He won't be needing the bed tonight."

Dead. The word screamed in my brain, the image of the truck driver echoed around it. And my dampened spooked soul was quickly drenched in fear. I tried to console my doubts. It was a heart attack. People die from heart attacks every day. A person could have a heart attack at any time, at any place. Even in a parked truck. And then I realized what was bothering me. Before the driver died, he had made his final delivery. Yes, come to think of it, he had delivered a very desirable, one-of-a-kind box of chocolates.

꧁ ꧂

Old Fashioned Whiskey Ball: Milk chocolate ball with an aged whiskey infused prune ganache center, finished off with a strikingly tangy kumquat drizzle.

Chapter Twelve

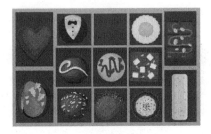

TWELVE chocolatiers-in-training found themselves in deep cocoa.

*A*fter a slim night's sleep, the intoxicating aroma of coffee, widened my bloodshot eyes and lifted me downstairs. The step-brothers, Cashmere and Caesar, were the only ones sitting at the massive table covered with mountains of assorted muffins, pastries, and fresh fruit. I decided to go with the *keep your enemies close, and your enemies that threaten your life closer* philosophy, offering Caesar a pained, pretentious smile. He groaned, so I opted to take a seat next to Cashmere.

Cashmere was dressed to the nines, er the eighties, in a turquoise sequin t-shirt and white silk jacket that would make Don Johnson proud.

"How'd you sleep?" he asked me.

"As good as expected after discovering a dead body. I'm just thankful you showed up when you did." I assessed his face for any hints of deceit. Never know. Perhaps he was in cahoots with his brother. His guiltless eyes stared back at me, with a heavy dollop of suspicion. Well shoot, that back-fired. Before he could return the interrogating comments, I directed my conversation to the other end of the table, where the butler and maid stood side by side, like diminutive salt and pepper shakers. "Good morning, Tessie. Boris."

Tessie smiled and brought over a steaming pot. "Anna, would ya care for some coffee, hun?"

"Yes, please. Hey Tess, did you know that delivery guy that passed away last night?"

She set the teapot on the table. "Shore enough did. Poor soul." She settled into the seat next to mine. "Paulie. Paulie Parker. We weren't mighty close. Though, he worked for Chandler fer quite some time." Her pupils rose up in thought. "Forty some odd years. Used to hang out in the parlor and hit the bottle. Then a few years back, he retired and went off on some cocka mangy Senior's bowling tour." She whispered, "Meanwhile, I heard he left his wife and was swappin' spit with the tour bus driver, Miss Betty. But, ya didn't hear that from me. Any who, I reckon that didn't all pan out, on account of he pulled his groin and went back to drivin' fer Chandler."

Boris monitoring the space from the corner, forced a cough. Tessie acknowledged the butler and got back to pouring coffee. As petite as they may be, it was a clear sign of who wore the trousers in the hierarchy of command around here.

A break in Caesar's eating frenzy announced the arrival of Kiki. For the first time this morning, he was chewing his food. He stared at Kiki falling out of a snug, shiny pink satin night gown and chewed for a long, long time.

Tessie said, "Oh lawdy, looks like someone's been tryin' to squeeze a hawg into a girdle."

31

Kiki squealed, "Are you implying that I'm a pig?"

Tessie nodded her head. "Oh, no mam. Just a Southern expression."

Kiki snarled. "Watch it lady. You're not careful, you'll be the first one kicked to the curb when I inherit this spook house." She mumbled to herself, "I swear there was a ghost clawing at my window last night."

Harley, the so-called yacht salesman, appeared in the doorway. Somehow, I expected him to be wearing a sailor cap, boat shoes, and speaking with a fancy millionaire accent. Just like they do on television. But he was quite a disappointment, the care-free fella came across as nothing more than a beach brat.

While Kiki was still going on about the ghost nonsense, Harley snuck up behind her, "Boo," he shouted, giving her shoulders a squeeze.

Kiki's body twisted and flinched in a blink, knocking Harley in the nose with her elbow. "What's wrong with you, moron?"

"The name's Harley."

Kiki's eyes veered up and down the man's Ron Jon attire. "You don't look like a biker."

"Yacht salesman." Harley sang, "I ride the waves, baby." He held a napkin to his bloody face. "And no worries about the nose, it's not the first time it's been broken."

Kiki took a seat and tore into a chocolate muffin. Something told me she wasn't worried about the man's well-being.

Meanwhile, the second shift for breakfast had arrived. The newlyweds. Brice, clean shaven, wearing his million-dollar smile, richened with irresistible dimples, wore a lime jersey and jeans. He pulled out the chair for his petite blonde wife, who was once again smothered in pink, from her fuchsia tinged wispy hair, down to her pink fuzzy Uggs.

Before Brice had a chance to sit down, he too was greeted by the yacht salesman. Harley said to Brice, "Why if it isn't my man, Hodges." He switched the blood-soaked napkin to the other hand and offered his empty palm. "Let me shake your hand, Mr. Quarter backer Dude."

Brice eye-balled the bloody cloth, and casually slid his hands into his pockets.

I was impressed that he was famous enough to be recognized. I said to him, "Wow Brice, you actually play professional ball?"

Kiki laughed obnoxiously. "Seriously, you don't know who he is?"

In my head, I echoed her in an exaggerated voice. Big Red was really starting to get under my skin. I shrugged my shoulders. "Sorry, I don't watch much football." In my defense, I was never home on Monday night with it being *Butcher's Night* at the diner, aka, all you can eat mystery meatloaf.

Kiki rolled her eyes. "Oh my gosh, are you kidding me?" she asked again, as if I was dumber than a cornflake. "This is Brice Hodges. As in quarterback of the Waves. As in three-time MVP last year."

I said to Brice, "That's amazing. I can't believe my cousin is a celebrity."

Ashton put a hand on her husband's thigh. "Only Brice doesn't play ball anymore."

Harley, with zero-class, slapped Brice's jersey, "That's right, you're finished, huh? I remember watching that game. Dude, you got knocked on your butt so hard, they had to carry your carcass off the field." He laughed as if they were reminiscing good times. "What was it, your right arm? Ooof. Tough break, man."

Something told me Surf n' Turf weren't going to be best buds.

Brice took a seat and ignored the comment. If I were him, broken nose or not, I would've socked surfer boy one in the gut.

Ashton grinning from ear to ear, said to me, "My husband is a famous actor now." Brice shaded her twinkling eyes with a somber gaze.

The man did have a familiarity about him. I recalled, "Brice, you're from those diaper commercials. Oh my gosh, you're Deputy Dude."

Ashton sang the commercial jingle, "*Deputy Dude rescues baby's bootie—*"

The rest of the table chimed in, *"... he's the Poopy Patrol's officer on doody."*

And that would be enough to kill our appetites.

⋆⊷ ⊶⋆

I stacked up the breakfast plates and carried them into the kitchen.

Tessie was cracking eggs into a bowl of batter. "How nice of you hun."

"What are you making now?"

"Chocolate Chip Oatmeal Filbert Bars— fer high tea." I don't think that the Queen of England herself partook in such occasional teas.

"Wow Tessie, you are an amazing baker."

"Oh, don't ya be fooled." She held up a shiny foiled package from *Chandler's Pantry.* I knew of the brand. The gourmet catalog, a bit out of my budget, offered mixes, spreads, dips, and really anything and everything chocolate. They even offered cocoa-enhanced meat rubs. It was mostly mail order, but they were opening an actual store front in Paris Falls.

"You'll be samplin' quite a few of these during your stay," she said. "Might do you well to try as many of them as you can. Don't know what's gonna be on that test." Tessie poured the dry mix in a bowl. "This one here, you just add eggs, milk, and butter. Then, I add some toasted filberts for a lil' more crunch."

"Sounds heavenly. How about I finish these dishes, so you can work on that?"

"Thanks, hun. But don't want anyone cusin' me of not doin' my job. Couple of these folks have it in for me."

"Ah, don't worry about them, you don't work for them."

"Not yet. But, I feel a storm a comin'."

"If you won't let me wash the dishes, how about I bake something for tea?"

"Well bless yer heart, you just go on and help yerself to whatever fixins' ya need."

I blended butter, flour, sugar, eggs, salt, and vanilla in a large bowl, then spread the batter onto a cookie sheet. While the toffee bars baked, I created a double boiler on the stove and melted a large Chandler's dark chocolate bar.

Kiki barged into the kitchen. "I'm bored." She nodded in my direction. "Why are *you* cooking?"

"I like to bake." I removed the large cookie out of the oven. *mmm.* Instant air freshener.

Kiki hovered over me as I spread glistening dark chocolate over the toffee bars. Her eyes seemed hypnotized by the spatula, swirling from one side of the tray to the other. A sprinkling of chopped pistachios and mini chocolate chips adhered to the sea of melted chocolate. She licked the rubber spatula while I cut the bars and placed them on a cooling rack.

"Woo wee," said Tessie. "Looks mighty fine." She snagged the spatula from Kiki's grip and dropped it in the sink. "We'll be havin' tea shortly, mam."

"Kiki, it's Ki-ki. What's wrong with you, woman? And I don't do tea," she said while nibbling on the remnants leftover on the cookie tray. She may not *do* tea, but she manages to suck up more crumbs than a Hoover.

I filled the sink with hot, sudsy water, and as luck would have it, Kiki sniffed out work and left the room.

Tessie shook her head, sending her frizzy bunned tower into a slight tremor. "That girl's flakier than my Aunt Elma's pork belly pot pie crust. Just as smart as it, too."

I shrugged my shoulders. "I think the poor girl is just starving for attention."

"And 'tention is just what she's gettin' from those boys, when she's hangin' out of her duds like over-risen dough in a quiche pan. Back in my day, we had words for gals that dressed like that."

"Yeah, we still have words for gals that dress like that."

Tessie smiled to herself. "Ya know back when I was a youngin' in Georgia, I was quite the looker myself. Earned me the crown of Miss Pe-Can Pie and everythang. But, don't ya be fooled. This Betty didn't add any extra Crocker to her dish."

We spent the next half hour washing dishes, and colorfully dishing the naturally dyed redheaded species, until voices raised through the kitchen walls.

Tessie and I scurried to the kitchen window to check out who was making all the commotion. Kiki was stomping her feet along the front path, hollering at Jasper, the gardener. Only Jasper wasn't giving her the time of day.

The leather-faced man pulled his neck handkerchief over his face, then pulled a nozzle from his side holster, like drawing a pistol at a showdown.

While the man methodically pressure washed the sidewalk, inch by inch, the spray of water blocked Kiki's path to the porch.

Tessie shook her head and laughed. "That gal ain't gettin' ol' Jasper to move now. She mine as well be stuck at the train tracks. Cause he ain't movin' his caboose till he's done."

She was right. He wasn't budging, and Kiki was in crazy-girl-mode, throwing a tantrum behind his back. I bit my lip. "I can't watch. He's going so slow, she's going to blow."

"That's Jasper for ya. That man's got as much oomf as a slug in honey."

Kiki eventually forfeited. She scuttled around the gardener, navigating on tiptoes through the garden patches. And quickly sank ankle deep into the mud.

Tessie yelled out the window, "Take the hose to 'er!"

⁕⁕⁕

After we finished in the kitchen, I retreated upstairs for some alone time. Between finding poor Parker last night, and coming to terms with my new extended family, I had no idea how I was going to keep my sanity for the next twelve days. But with this whole inheritance holding some merit, I had to stick it out. This was one competition I could actually win. I smiled to myself. Who would have thought that my lifelong dedication to chocolate would pay off? In the meantime, I had some phone calls to make. I decided to go with the less painful call first.

"Hi Willie."

Willie squealed in delight. "Oh my gosh, tell me everything, gal. Absolutely everything. Did they put you up in some fancy smancy place? Are you there right this very second?"

"Yeah, but—"

"I just knew it. Nobody in Plumview believed it. But I shore enough did. I told ya you was going to be a celebrity. Next thing you know you gonna be interviewed by Oprah, and rubbin' elbows with Dolly. Nobody's more famous than Dolly."

Good grief. The gal has bubbles bursting like a bottle of soda pop somebody shook way too hard. "Yes, it's nice and all. But, I need—"

"Have ya checked out the can yet? I heard celebrities use tissue as thick as oven gloves. But that gets me wondering; how do they get it to suck down the hole? I reckon they must have some heavy powered commodes. Cause you never see plungers in rich folk baths. Never."

"The bathrooms are just fine Willie, but I was calling because I need you to tell Jimbo that I'm going to need more time off."

A few moments later, she said, "Jimbo said 'no problem'."

"Whewf." I didn't want to burn any bridges just yet.

"He said you can have all the time off you want, on account of yer fired. Sorry, hun."

Super, just super. Two days in, and I'm already unemployed. To top things off, I have to break it to my four-year-old that she won't have a mommy for the next two weeks.

I tried to hold back my tears. "...Jillian, I will see you soon, June Bug. Mamma loves you with all her heart." I crunched up my body on the velvet chair in the hallway, and had myself a good cry.

ᨀᧁ ᧁᨀ

Eventually, I got myself together, wiped my eyes, and caught up with the others downstairs for the film.

Boris escorted the group to Chandler's Grand Theatre. It was hard to believe that this space could be incorporated into a home. The walls were splashed with shades of muted gold, embraced between intricate gold moldings that traced the ceiling and floor. Framed vintage chocolate advertisements nestled in between the pillars on the ascending stairs. *Chocolish Licorice, Penny Doodles, Chandler's Chunkies*— many of the products I didn't recognize. Probably before my time.

We took our seats in the first couple of rows, giving clear sight to the sumptuous regal brown and bronze embroidered tapestries on either side of a shimmering curtain. Chandeliers dimmed, as golden curtains rose in front of us, unveiling an antiqued movie screen.

I sat in between Harley and his sister, Priscilla. And instantly regretted it. Harley was antsier than my four-year-old, rocking in his chair. "Anna Banana, what's up

38

chickadoo?"

He spoke as well as my four-year-old too. I tried to calm the man with small talk. "So Harley, you sell yachts?"

Before he could respond, his sister, Priscilla answered for him. "It's Daddy's business. Harley pretends to work for him, so he doesn't have to get a real job."

Harley yelled back at her, his spray shooting across my lap. "Who asked you, Miss Priss? And for your information, I sold my first yacht last month."

Priscilla laughed pretentiously. "You sold it to Daddy's business partner. He felt sorry for you."

Things were getting awkward, and potentially dangerous, as their bodies were closing in on me. "I'm sorry, I didn't mean to get in the middle of things," I said aloud, but was speaking to myself.

Harley tapped his flip flops in a drumroll on the seat in front of him. "When's this stupid thing going to start?"

Meanwhile his sister, Priscilla, had pulled a bed sheet out of her purse and was re-covering her chair with it.

"Is there something on your seat?" I asked her. "We could move down."

Priscilla rolled her eyes. "If you only knew what you're sitting on. I bet these seats haven't been cleaned in forty years. Can you imagine the thousands of dust mites breeding within the upholstery?"

Oh. Well okay then, I'll just mind my own business. Over here. Just me and my swarm of dust mites infiltrating the seat below me. Now thanks to Miss Priss planting the seed, I had a thousand itches on my bum. I nonchalantly readjusted myself in my seat, back and forth, side to side, trying to scratch with friction. With zero luck.

Thankfully, the film was starting, giving my active imagination a rest. Flashing circled numbers appeared on the yellowed screen. 3, 2, 1 … The song, *That's Entertainment*, began playing, with the clicking of the old projector reel spinning in the background. Black and white old commercials showcasing early Chandler packages blinked in front of us.

Harley cupped his hands over his mouth. "This blows!"

The others followed suit, their rude hackles drowning out the sound to the vintage film. I admit this isn't what I anticipated as the introduction of training for a multi-million-dollar company. But, I was sure it was there for a purpose, and if I was going to be tested on it, I wanted to absorb every bit as possible. I struggled to listen, pen and waitress pad in hand to take notes.

The next nostalgic advertisements stirred up childhood memories. Sweet Bitter Bonker Bars. I smiled to myself, and whispered to Priscilla, "When I was a little girl, I would save up my allowance for them and buy them out of the quarter jar at the gas station."

Priscilla huffed, "And how many cavities did you get from them?"

I ignored her insensitivity as I relived my childhood through chocolate products. The next clip featured the Chandler Chew. I recalled the commercial where the little train chugged along through the chocolate land. Choo Choo loved to chew, chew Chandler's chocolate chews. "I used to love those," I awed.

Priscilla snickered sarcastically, "It's amazing you're still alive."

I glared into her eyes, but no words came out of my mouth. A million comments wanted to charge out and attack her perfect headband crown, sitting on her perfect shiny hair, all atop her sugar-is-poison-so-I-have-zero-percent-body-fat-being. But, her hatred of chocolate had frozen my tongue in shock. In all my life, I'd never encountered such a creature. Chocolate consumption is just part of human nature. Dumb alien girl.

My focus veered back to the film which was walking us through an outdated factory, showing the basic chocolate making procedure. I was amazed by the numerous steps the cocoa beans had to go through before becoming the chocolate that we salivated over. The audience didn't let up, as they hackled like immature teenagers. The film stopped abruptly, and the lights came on.

Fifteen minutes of nostalgic chocolate making— minus the sound, thanks to my ignorant cousins, didn't exactly make me feel confident on the process. I peered down at my notepad. *blank.* Cripes.

Winston, the lawyer, marched to the front of the theatre. He loosened his tie and nervously cleared his throat. "First off, let me inform you that due to last night's unfortunate event, the chocolate factory tour will be postponed until tomorrow. Secondly, and more importantly, let me remind you all that you are not here to be entertained. Any of you who find this training to be beneath you, are encouraged to leave." He tugged on the bottom of the old screen and seemed pleased as the room finally came to a hush. But, it was the disturbing kind of hush you hear after the sound of a car crash. It was then I realized that it wasn't his words that silenced the audience, it was those words painted recklessly on the curtain behind him. The words that were dripping red-blood paint into puddles of threats, "*Win, or die trying.*"

⋆⋅☾ ☽⋅⋆

The crowd had mixed reactions to the blunt threat. Some screamed. Some laughed. And most yelled at poor Winston, who reciprocated with strings of muttered nonsense. The old man threw up his arms in defeat and quickly shuffled us out of the theatre.

What was going on here? I went from thinking I was the magical sole heir to a famous fortune, to having my life threatened. I wasn't sure if this was a serious matter, or if someone was just trying to scare us out of the competition. The painting on the curtain had the penmanship of a toddler, leading me to wonder if it was the work of a drunken man. Perhaps, the same one threatening me last night.

I spent a good couple hours in my room debating the painter's intentions, and then spent another hour in the shower scrubbing the imaginary dust mites off my body. After a call to Jillian, afternoon tea with Tessie, and a good cry in place of dinner, I sought out some company. I heeded caution to the painted warning, not allowing myself to be alone. Since Cashmere dedicated his evening to design sketching, this left me joining the other cousins for poker. Besides, as long as I knew where Caesar was, he couldn't sneak up on me or anyone else. And as a bonus, I could check for any red-handed pranksters. I took the farthest seat from Caesar, settling in next to the newlyweds.

∽◉ ◉∾

Caesar nibbled from his personal table-side buffet, inhaling handfuls of pork rinds and beef jerky. His head jerked in the direction of Boris. "Hey butler, how about some beers?"

Boris paused his game of tug of war with Bonbon and looked blankly at Caesar. Only it was deeper than a blank look. It was more of a *if I had laser eyes, you'd be bursting into flames right now*, kind of look. The butler flanked towards the doorway and spoke in a monotone, yet raised voice. "Tessie, the freeloaders require malt beverages for this evening's intoxication."

Caesar folded his fingers and cracked his knuckles. "Woah, I'm missing a ring," he said. "Hey butler, you or your little maid have sticky fingers?"

Boris stood table-side, "What are you implying, sir?"

"What I'm implying little man, is that somebody stole my poker tournament ring." He held up his ornamented fingers. "See, I'm missing one."

"So, we're to believe the thief slid it off your finger?"

"Don't be a moron. I keep them in a box. I just hadn't realized I was one short until now."

"I'm sure you will find it sir. Now then, the maid will be back shortly with your beverages," he told him, and left the room.

Brice held his wife's hand, "That's odd, Ashton lost her bracelet earlier today, too. Huh, maybe just a coincidence."

Caesar punched a fist in his palm. "I find out somebody stole my ring, they're gonna get a batta bing, batta boom up the gazoo."

Thankfully, Tessie was back and everyone's gazoo went unharmed. For now. She distributed frosted mugs to the boys. She nodded to me. "Anything for you, hun?"

"I'm fine," I said. "Hey Tess, why don't you join us?"

"I couldn't possibly—"

Caesar removed a half-eaten jerky from his mouth and took a long slug of beer. "You got money, lady?"

Tessie pulled a coin purse from her apron pocket.

Caesar burped toxic fumes in delight. "I say, welcome to the table, Granny."

Brice scooted his chair closer to his wife, Ashton, who was only there to watch, making room for Tessie.

"So, what are we playin' here?" Tessie asked him.

"Texas Hold'em. You know how to play?"

She shrugged her shoulders. "I reckon I'll catch on."

"Okay then, ante up," Brice said while dealing the cards.

In just a half an hour, Tessie had caught on to the game rather nicely. She showed her winning hand proudly. "I got me a full pond."

Caesar scratched his head. "Huh?"

"A full pond. See, I got me three floatin' lilies and two toads in the hole." Tessie's chip stacks grew, and Caesar's chip bowl dwindled. Mesquite potato chips crumbled out of his mouth like an avalanche, spewing flakes onto his mountainous belly, filtering into the grooves of its hills and valleys.

Tessie said in my ear, "Why that man has more rolls than the Pillsbury Doughboy."

Caesar glared at Tessie. "Don't you need to go to bed, or take your medicine or something?"

"You kiddin' me? I'm on a winnin' streak."

"Well then, go get us more beers." Tessie reluctantly took the orders.

"Hurry," Caesar said. "Deal the cards before she gets back."

Why it appeared to me as if these sharks were scared of a little minnow.

Caesar took the opportunity to make his big move. "I'm all in."

Harley slid his chips to the center. "Me too. Mano a mano."

Kiki's long fake nails struggled to lift the chips off the table. "Sorry to ruin your date boys, but I'm in too." She smirked at Brice and I. "Anybody else? Or, are you little girls going to go knit a potholder with Granny?"

Unaware to her, *Granny* had returned with chilled mugs of beer. Tessie bumped into Kiki, dribbling some spirits down her back. "Oh, hawg-wash. Sorry, 'bout that *bare mam.*"

Kiki's spine straightened, and her eyes cursed the woman. She held her tongue while she climbed back up on her pedestal, trying to not lose the momentum of her pending victory. She spread out her cards. "Read 'em and weep boys. A flush."

The boys tossed in their cards and Kiki hugged her arms around the pile of chips, pulling them to her chest.

"Just a sec," I said.

She rolled her eyes and sighed. "Go fish, Anna."

Tessie grinned at me. "Whatcha got, girl?"

"I got wenches on deck, with a One-eyed Willie on the plank."

Caesar's eyebrows scrunched, "Your whos, did a what?"

Tessie's cheeks raised up to her eyes. "Why she's got her a heart flush, Jack high. I do declare, this gal has smoked your chimney and swept out yer flute."

Kiki smacked down the towers of chips. Her eyes rounded the table, as if searching for weak prey. "So Ashton, when did you and Brice get married?"

Her words sounded accusatory, as if she caught Ashton with a hand in her cellulite scrub.

Ashton's cheeks blended into her fuchsia cardigan. "Just a couple weeks ago."

"The date?"

Ashton hesitated, but before she could answer, Kiki called her out, "Morons, these guys have been playing us. She doesn't even have a ring on her finger."

Brice said, "Fine. You're right, Ashton and I aren't married yet." He put his arms around Ashton's slumped shoulders. "But, we're going to do it real soon. I'm the heir, so I was the only one invited. She just wanted to come for a weekend getaway. So relax, nobody is trying to take anybody else's money."

"That reminds me," said Kiki. "Anna, who's Jillian? I heard you whimpering on the phone."

My stare met her tarantula-legged lashes. "My daughter. Why?"

She honked at my apparent absurdity. "I'll tell you why. Because you're trying to hoard the inheritance too. Probably some fine print."

Brice combed fingers through his hair. "Get over it, Kiki. Nobody is trying to take your precious money."

Kiki leaned in toward Ashton, "We'll see about that. In the meantime, *she* has no business being here."

Caesar snorted, "Sure she does. Eye candy." He placed his palm on Ashton's thigh, pushing up on her skirt.

Ashton sprang up and headed toward the door. "I'm outta here."

Brice shoved the table toward Caesar. "Seriously man, you didn't just put your filthy mitts on her." He got in Caesar's face. "Stay away from Ashton."

"Ooh, and what are you going to do, tough guy?"

Brice grasped Caesar's gold chain. "Do you want to find out?"

"Pansy, you ever put your hands on me again, and I'll have you done for. I got some friends back in Vegas that owe me some favors, if ya know what I mean."

I convinced Brice to leave the room before things got ugly. And somebody's gazoo got injured. We walked over to the parlor, Bonbon tagging along.

"I'm sorry," he said. "Those jerks know how to get me riled up. Ashton is my weak spot. Heck, I don't like it when another guy even looks at her."

"Well, I think she's lucky to have someone that cares about her so much."

"I guess." He hit his palm on his forehead, "Man, that whole marriage thing was dumb."

I pursed my lips to the side, as if confirming the stupidity, but not wanting to verbalize it.

"It was Ashton's idea. She hates to be alone. She couldn't come with me, if she wasn't family. The crazier part is that I don't even want to be here."

We took a seat on the couch. "Why not?"

Bonbon made herself available for scratching and Brice took the bait, stroking her along her back. "Not to sound conceited, but I don't exactly need the money. Football was good to me. The money, not so much. Trust me, it brings out the worst in people. I considered not even coming."

My eyebrows sprung up. "Really?"

"Ashton wouldn't let me turn it down though. But don't think badly of her. She's not greedy like those moneybags in there, she's just afraid of being poor. Rough childhood."

"You're talking to a single mom living with her uncle. Rough adulthood."

"Just wait," said Brice. "Things are going to get ugly around here."

Unfortunately, I think he was right. We may be long lost relatives, but more than that we were competitors.

Bonbon rolled over, prompting Brice to scratch her belly. "But for me, coming here wasn't about the money, he said. "Sure, the money could be put to good use. Investments, charity, ... He smirked devilishly, "DNA testing."

I laughed. "No kidding. How in the world can we be related to these people? One is weirder— and hairier than the next. Makes you wonder what our Grandmother looked like." My face involuntarily scrunched, trying to force visions of old lady Sasquatch out of my brain. "So, what changed your mind about coming?" I asked.

"Guess I was curious if I had other family. Growing up, it was only me and my dad."

"Sounds familiar. My mom died when I was little girl."

"I'm sorry. At least you had a mother though. Mine took off when I was a baby. Guess I never really knew what I was missing, but part of me always wanted siblings."

Brice got down on his knees to give Bonbon's underside the royal treatment. "It's still hard to grasp the concept that our grandfather was the famous Chandler. I wish we had gotten to know him. Bet he was an amazing guy."

"No doubt. I'm just glad you decided to come. Otherwise, I would have never known I had a normal cousin."

Bonbon stood and shook her fur out. Brice, now face to face with the dog, scratched her behind the ears and talked in a baby voice, "You're such a pretty girl. Oh yes you are." He laughed. "So much for the normal theory."

Yes, normal. I felt kind of bad for labeling him in my mind as a stereo-typical jock. After some down time with Bonbon, Brice escorted me back to my room. I locked the door and collapsed on my bed. The day's events exploded in my mind.

Good grief. How would I manage two weeks with this family of wackos? The training had just begun, and I already felt physically and mentally inept.

I unwrapped the dark chocolate truffle resting on my pillow. And felt better for the five seconds it took me to wolf it down. Even chocolate couldn't cure homesickness. I searched the mantel for inspiration. What's this? My picture of Jillian was gone. I walked over to the fireplace to see if it had slipped off the wooden shelf and inadvertently got wounded by my answer. Tiny fragments of glass scattered over the wood floor, but no signs of the frame or photo. I thought of the mad accusations at poker tonight. Goosebumps sprouted over my skin. Why would somebody want a picture of my baby girl?

∞♊♋∞

It was day three, and thankfully, we were back on schedule, touring Chandler's chocolate factory. I was glad to be in a public place, away from the mansion. These crazy cousins were really starting to give me the creeps. Winston, without the aid of a magical golden key, pushed in a numeric code at the door's entrance and welcomed us all inside.

I was having a Charlie moment, sinking my senses into room after room of industrial-sized machinery producing conveyors of precious confections traveling about miniature intertwining highways.

My training group included Tessie, Cashmere, and the fake newlyweds. We followed our factory guide, Vivian, into a huge warehouse. Vivian wore a white shower cap thingy that struggled to contain her orange Ronald McDonald styled hair. She reached into her lab pocket. "Almost forgot to give you all your souvenirs."

I reached out my palm anxiously accepting her offering. "It's not chocolate," I said, tugging a plastic hair net over my head. I observed Cashmere gingerly gliding the plastic over his gelled masterpiece, finding some comfort knowing that he was more miserable than me.

Below us, workers on forklifts, stacked endless bags of cocoa beans. Others were tossing the sacks onto large conveyor belts that reminded me of the moving walkways at the airport. I kept my eyes open for passing Oompa Loompas.

We followed the parade of sacks to another room. Here we found larger conveyor belts with loose cocoa beans rattling about.

Vivian pointed towards the contraption. "And over here, we have a winnower," she said. "As the beans are rattling along, they lose their shells and extra debris."

"Hey, Brice," yelled Caesar, leaning over the rails on the metal catwalk above us. "Great vibrating action down there; you gonna buy one of those machines for the Mrs.?" Like a little boy's secret handshake, Harley banged knuckles with Caesar.

This resulted in obnoxious honking from Kiki. That horrific sound sent goose-welts down my spine. I was starting to feel like one of Pavlov's experiments every time I heard it, only it wasn't a bell I was hearing, and it wasn't saliva forming in the shallow pit of my stomach.

"Good heavens," said Tessie. "I'm shore glad we didn't get stuck with that bunch of clowns."

Cashmere glanced up at the group. "Yep, Bozo, Bongo, Bimbo—"

"And poor Jasper," said Tessie. "Poor fella looks miserable draggin' behind them dang yahoos."

My eyes raised up to see the trio chasing each other about, in midst of Mission Wedgie. Poor fella, indeed.

We followed our guide past a series of boisterous steel monsters, thankfully ridding ourselves temporarily of the three-ring circus. Our new location, The Roasting Room.

"This particular machine is where we roast almonds," announced Vivian. Thousands of nuts scooted into illuminating ovens, then toppled out the other end, dawning their new copper-toned tans.

Tessie's mouth opened in awe. "Oh my southern stars. I could meet my maker in here."

"The smell is heavenly," I said to her, taking in a large breath of ecstasy. "Makes me want to bake something warm and nutty."

Tessie smiled widely. "Like a toasted fudgy praline pie?"

My stomach savored the suggestion. "With a warm, caramel butterscotch sauce on the side?"

"Don't forget the home made whipped cream on top," Tessie added.

Goodness gracious. Someone in this world gets me. All of that chocolate talk had made us famished. We nonchalantly lost our guide, wandering off to the vending machines in the employee break room.

I had a seat at a table and dug into a little sack of sugary goodness. My pupils rose to meet Vivian's scolding glare. Busted. My easy to blush cheeks, currently being packed with Mint Melt-Aways, glowed in the hue of guilt. I swallowed hard. "Sorry, we were just taking a break."

She waved it off. "Awe, no worries. But, we need to gather up our group and finish the tour. That guy that escorted you here this morning, gave me strict orders on what you were to observe today. Going to make me sign off on it and everything."

"Oh, you must be referring to Mr. Winston, the lawyer."

Her face lit up like a peg punched into a Lite-Brite hole. "The lawyer? So, the rumor is true, one of you *is* trying to buy this factory?"

"Um no, er—" I pointed to the coffee station. "Hey, there's the rest of the group. We should get going."

"Okay, lady. I get it, top secret stuff. Your secret is safe with me."

Priscilla's nose strolled up to our conversation, sniffing out gossip. "Secrets? Who's telling secrets?"

Vivian took a few moments to glance up and down the pompous-poised suited ballerina, and then apparently found it in her best interest to part ways.

The tall, frail woman sat her perfectly-postured body down, like a vase on a pedestal, taking the seat next to mine. Between her God-given height and her neck's exaggerated altitude, her presence made me uncomfortable. I suppose looking up at someone's nostrils made me a bit intimidated.

"So, what's this about secrets?" Priscilla asked.

"Awe nothing," I told her. "Hey, where have you been? I haven't seen you all day."

"That's because I've been in hiding back here, avoiding that disgusting factory. Just coping with the scoundrels that have been traipsing in and out of this break room has been dreadful enough." She fanned the air around us.

"The workers, disgust you?"

"Most certainly. Snacking on their Ho-Ho's and Kool-Aid."

"Kool-Aid?"

"Oh, whatever those neon colas are in those machines," she said. "And grown women, all sitting in a cluster, gossiping like school girls. *Public* school girls, mind you. Most of them talk like that maid back at the house."

"You mean, Tessie?" I said. "She's wonderful."

"Wonderful, says you. Back where I come from, the help is proper. They speak proper, and that's only when they are spoken to. If you ask me, that lady is out of line. When I take over, I will see that changes are made. The help will know what is expected of them, and will do it without any lip. Furthermore, the butler will not be playing fetch with the mutt inside of the house. *And* the gardener will prune the Crepe Myrtles before they look like blooming chaos on sticks. Why, have you seen the hydrangea bushes?

Atrocious. I think the whole staff needs to be replaced. Don't you agree?"

"Well no, I *quite* like them."

She gasped in a squeal, at my apparent absurdity. "You better not let the others hear that you're getting friendly with the staff. And you should know that once you become friends with them, they'll never respect you. You have to be the boss. Give them orders and penalize them when they disobey. That's the only way to properly train them."

Train them? Does she think they're working for peanuts at the zoo? Her nose did that pointy up thing that it does, actually prompting me to look to see if there was something on the ceiling.

I attempted to change the subject, shoving my Mint Melt-Aways' box in her direction. "Care for a chocolate?"

Priscilla jerked her body back, as if the box was covered with molded manure. "Certainly not. I don't do carbs, and I don't do fats, and I most definitely do not do chocolate."

My eyes widened like Oreos. "Really? I don't think I could live without it."

"You won't live long with it." She glared. "Oh shoot, that silly maid has spotted me. I have to get out of here before they try sticking one of those plastic rain caps on my head again."

Tessie joined me at the table. "Who does that gal think she's hidin' from? Why she sticks out like a butterfly in a hornet's nest. Although, I bet she stings like the latter."

"Evidently, Miss Priss is afraid of the factory grunts breathing cooties on her."

Tessie's forehead scrunched in puzzlement. "Piece of work, I say. Didn't know he made 'em that way."

"I'm guessing she's had lots of lessons from Mummy."

Back on our tour, we soon found ourselves floating in heaven's kitchen. There in front of me, stood a shiny miracle. This one machine, equipped with dozens of magical mechanical nozzles, squirted rich melted chocolate into molds, creating a gazillion bars a second. It was mesmerizing. I couldn't stop watching.

Cashmere snapped his fingers in front of my face. "Anna, it's just a machine."

"Only the most magnificent machine ever," I said to him.

"Girl, you're obsessed."

"So. Better chocolate, than hair product."

"No. Better off looking stylin', than having to rip out the seams in your Levi's."

We caught back up with our group, now observing rows of chocolate filled steel vats as far as the eye could see. Each vat was connected to a series of pipes, which led to molding stations, where various confections popped out onto moving conveyor belts. After traveling through a cooling tunnel, workers stood along the continuously moving candy, checking for inconsistencies in the products.

Vivian grabbed a square of chocolate off of the belt and spoke to our group, "At this point in the process, our food scientists take samples of the final product to be examined in the lab. We want to make sure that each chocolate is made at the highest quality and at the proper weight."

Cashmere said, "You mean, you want to be sure no roach legs are in it?"

Vivian gave him the scorn of a teacher catching their spit-ball assailant in mid-attack. She rewarded the rest of us obedient students. "I don't suppose any of you would like a sample?"

My mouth watered, as I reached out my upright palm. No sooner did I feel the sugary goodness on my hand, somebody swiped it. I turned around to see Harley. He raised my chocolate into the air and quickly jerked it lower. "Too high, too low." And then ate it one greedy bite. "Too slow."

It was that defining moment, someone finally felt like family. Harley was like that mean, rotten brother that taunted and tormented his sister. But right now, his ugliness was overshadowed by a bigger problem.

Buzzers sounded. Lights flashed. Workers scrambled, like a colony retreating from its ambushed anthill. The well-oiled machine, had come to an abrupt stop.

We looked to Vivian for guidance. "Everyone remain calm," she said, straining to speak over the humming of the alarms.

"What's going on?" I asked her.

"In the sixteen years I've been here, we've never had a full lockdown. From time to time, there's a problem with an isolated machine." Vivian laid a palm on her chest. "But, this here is major. Something has stopped the entire production."

I followed the bulk of the crowd gathering in front of a section of steel vats. The machines' flashing red lights indicated that the problem was nearby. We were like kids playing, colder/hotter, and we were headed right towards boiling.

Caesar, bulging out of a buttoned white lab coat, two sizes too small, came bustling down the aisle, resembling the Stay Puft Marshmallow Man. "Hey you guys, come quick. It's Priscilla." He put his hands on his thighs in between deep breaths.

We raced behind him, weaving through resting conching machines. A crowd of workers surrounded the wailing sound of panic. Caesar pushed his way to the center, creating a path for us.

I was afraid of what we might discover. Priscilla wasn't the most kind-hearted of gals, but I certainly didn't wish harm upon her.

She was sitting on the cement floor, tears pouring down her cheeks. She didn't appear to be injured. I squatted down next to her. "Priscilla, are you okay?"

"Oh, it was just awful," she said.

I put my hands on her shoulders, forcing her stare into my eyes. "What, what was so awful?"

Priscilla pointed a trembling finger toward the steel drum in front of her. "It was a hand— actually an arm, all covered with chocolate, hanging over the side of that machine. Like a zombie digging itself out of a muddy grave. It was just dreadful."

Harley wrapped his arm around his sister's shoulders. "That's ridiculous, sis. I'm sure you imagined it. Come on, let's go get you some fresh air."

Workers tightened in around the massive cylinder Priscilla had identified.

Boris' stern voice bellowed, "Step back, people."

A forklift made its way through the crowd, lifting two workers up onto a flat. They submerged their arms into the brown thickness. "There's a large mass in this canister," said one of the men.

They worked their way through the chocolate pool with their hands and extendable tools. "I got something," said a worker. He struggled to pull an article from the mass. "Oh crap, it's a boot."

Boris took charge of the spectators. "Let's move on people. Let these men deal with the situation."

Not everyone was willing to listen to the elder man, but I for one, wasn't sure I wanted to see what, or worse, who, they were going to pull out of that container. Unfortunately, the crowd wasn't budging. They weren't moving. In fact, they suddenly became quiet and still. Against my better judgment, my gaze rose back up to the forklift, only to see a limp body being pulled from the canister. One of the men rubbed a cloth over the soiled face.

"No," cried Tessie. "That's Jasper James."

⚬ᯭ☙ ❧ᯭ⚬

Slow-as-Molasses Turtle: Lightly roasted pecans with a candied molasses coating, smothered in caramel and dunked into a heavy milk chocolate coating.

Chapter Eleven

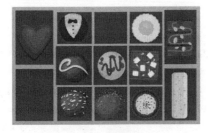

ELEVEN orderly tourists dangled over the edge of sweet chaos.

Although nobody had an appetite for dinner, Tessie was in the kitchen anyway. I pleaded with her, "Tessie, let me make dinner tonight. You don't need to be cooking."

"Oh yes, I shore enough do. There's nothin' else in the world I can do right now to get my mind off this horrible day. How in tarnation does a grown man uppin' die in a tub of chocolate?"

We worked in the kitchen in silence. Tessie tossed chicken quarters into a seasoned flour mixture, then into a pot of sizzling oil, while I did what I do best. Dessert. I could only think of one way to lift Tessie's spirits. Fudgy

Praline Pie. I whisked together butter, sugars, corn syrup, eggs and vanilla. Then, folded chocolate chips and pecans into the mixture.

Meanwhile, Tessie plucked golden brown drumsticks out of the spitting oil. "This was Jasper's favorite. This, this, he plumb adored."

The prom king and queen joined us in the kitchen. Brice rolled up his sleeves and tied on an apron, forfeiting his crown, while his queen cowered behind him.

Tessie's eyes got watery. "Well bless yer hearts. I'm 'posed to be cookin' for yawl."

"Never mind that," said Brice. "Just put us to work."

"Okay, hun. How 'bout you goin' to fix the table, and Ashton dear, you use that there pan over yonder fer the pig's feet." By the twinge in Ashton's face, I reckon she wasn't from the South.

Tessie's face cracked a smile. "Honey, yer face turned as white as a buttermilk biscuit. Maybe you'd get along better with the cornbread?" Tessie warmed up pig feet, garlic, and bacon in a pan. "Mmm hmmm. This will do nicely in the collards." It wasn't long before the kitchen smelt like the church hall on Pancake Sunday.

As if on cue, Kiki swung open the kitchen door. "Where's dinner?" She asked, while picking crumbs from the cornbread pan.

Tessie smiled mischievously. "Oh gal, you're gettin' hungry. You must have smelt the hawg's feet cookin'."

Cashmere and I plated the food, then Brice stacked the sizzling dishes on his arm, waiter-style.

Tessie scanned the food as it made its way out the kitchen. "Brice, did ya get yerself a burn?" She reached into her apron pocket, pulling out some salve. "Slap a hunk of this on, and you'll be good as new."

The skin on his wrist was raised and pink. He twisted his upright wrist. "This old thing? Got this scar from a skateboarding wreck when I was kid."

Tessie nodded her head. "Boys will be boys."

We transferred the remaining food to the dining room and filled the seats at the table. This was the first time Tessie and Boris had joined us for a meal. Under ordinary circumstances, it would have been a treat to have a home-cooked Southern meal. But, two people had died. Appetites were scarce. The normally boisterous group, was quiet as they picked at their food and threw back their drinks. Either upset by the loss of Jasper, or perhaps just bored of arguing with one another.

I had the misfortune of sitting across from Sasquatch. This one's appetite was just fine. With the table silenced, Caesar's heavy breathing, and salivary glands diligently working through a chicken thigh, were unbearable.

Priscilla's face appeared even more disgusted than mine. She hadn't put one speck of food on her plate. "Is this all you people do around here, is eat?" Granted Southern food wasn't the frail gal's favored cuisine. Nor, was anything fried in a gallon of grease, but I had yet to see Priscilla eat two full bites at a meal.

Tessie shook her head. "Don't yawl have any heart? Just go on and eat up. This one's fer Jasper."

Priscilla stared down the fried feast in front of her. "Do you have any idea how much cholesterol is in this meal?"

Uh oh, now she did it. I had the sudden urge to duck and cover.

Tessie stood up and placed her hands on her stout hips. "Heavens to Betsy, mercy me. Girl, you just done put a beaver in my bonnet."

Harley, having his usual maturity of a ten-year-old, giggled. "She said beaver."

Tessie continued the lashing to Priscilla. "Dang nabbit. You just eat up, ballerina. A man died today for no 'parent reason and you're gonna complain about havin' to eat a lil' piece of chicken? Now you goin' get yerself an extra greasy drumstick, and stick it in that perdy lil'—"

"Now, now, Tessie," Boris interrupted. "Sit down. Scolding that child will not bring back Jasper. But, you did bring up a valid question," said the butler. "Did the man, in fact, die for *no* reason? I'm starting to wonder if there was foul play."

Caesar with a mouthful of food, puckered his lips and individually slid his greasy digits in and out of his mouth. "Don't beat around the bush, old man. You accusing somebody of something?"

"I'll be blunt," said Boris. "I don't believe Jasper's death was accidental."

Caesar piled some collard greens and pork onto his plate. "Do you have proof? You know, *before* you start pointing fingers at innocent people."

This would probably be a good time to bring up Caesar's threats, but I was pretty sure that would end with Caesar flinging fried chicken at my head. And in truth, I didn't believe he had anything to do with the Jasper's accident. Tragic events often cause mourners to seek a source for blame. At least this theory convinced me to keep my trap shut momentarily.

"Nobody is pointing any greasy fingers at anyone, sir," Boris said to Caesar. "I'm just inviting you all to survey the facts. Seeing that there were railings on the walkways, I find it unreasonable to accept Mr. James *fell* over the edge."

Tessie plopped a hefty scoop of collards onto Priscilla's plate. "Come now, Boris. Yer talkin' plain gibberish. Why Jasper didn't have an enemy to speak of."

"Oh, I disagree," said Cashmere.

I kicked Cashmere under the table. But, apparently my friend didn't know the universal code for shut up.

He stood up, circled the table, planting his feet in front of Kiki. "I heard you were screaming at Jasper yesterday."

Kiki told him, "I don't know what you're talking about, fruitcake."

"Anna says different."

Thanks for throwing me under the bus, pal.

Kiki shot me Medusa eyes. "Well then, Anna should just mind her own little hillbilly gal business."

My fork froze midway to my mouth. This girl was really starting to push my buttons. You wanna dance Big Red? I put down my fork, to keep it from jolting out of my hand. "So Kiki, why were you yelling at Jasper?"

"I don't have to answer to you."

"Okay then—" I gestured to the rest of the table. "Tell them. I'm sure they'd all like to know why you were furious with the man, so close to his death."

"Are you guys serious?" Kiki asked. "You think I had something to do with it?"

"If not, you should just be truthful with us. Otherwise, you're just looking suspicious."

"Fine. I just informed him that he over watered the gardens next to the pathway, and because of it, my $700 shoes got ruined in the mud."

"Yeah, I bet you told him just that sweet."

"You really think I'd murder someone over my Jimmy Choos?"

"If the shoe fits." How did I get in the middle of this? I had no intentions of making murder accusations at the dinner table tonight. I stuffed cornbread into my mouth, before it got me into more trouble.

The doorbell rang, giving Kiki's interrogation a rest. Boris tended to the door. A couple minutes later the butler returned, and addressed the table. "I've just had a little chat with someone from the coroner's office. If my assumptions are correct, I would gather to say that Mr. James had a few other enemies." The butler eyed Caesar, "Oh, and Mr. Marino, I believe this may very well provide the proof you were seeking." He held up a thick envelope. "The coroner sent over Jasper's personal belongings." He tore open the envelope and dumped random items onto the table.

"My ring," said Caesar, scooping up an obnoxious ornamented gold band. "That no good thief."

Brice retrieved Ashton's bracelet from the pile, and Priscilla recognized some earrings she didn't even know were missing. That only left a gold-plated pipe.

Tessie reached out and took hold of the smoke piece that looked like an artifact. She looked to Boris. "This here belonged to Chandler. A gift from his granddaddy. It was under lock and key."

Boris patted his bald brow with a napkin. "So then, everyone still think the thief's death was an accident? Or is it possible, somebody here wanted revenge? Ladies and gentlemen, it is in my opinion, that someone at this very table is a cold-blooded killer."

⋯⊙⊙⋯

The next morning, aka, day four, we found ourselves back at the round table. Winston stood before us. The lawyer cleared his throat and as usual, read off of his index cards. "As you can see, everyone is not in attendance. Due to yesterday's unfortunate events, the employees have been given the day off to grieve."

Caesar slid his Mr. T style ring back and forth over his finger. "Grieving, or plotting more ways to chase us off? I'm not buying this *gardener/thief* theory Boris is selling us. That greedy midget thinks he's going to scare me away, he's got another thing coming."

Winston scratched at red blotches sprouting on his neck. His forehead scrunched, while he muttered, "N-n-non-sense. Mr. Marino, as always, if you don't find life here in the mansion satisfactory, you may leave. Now then, I will see you all tomorrow." He recklessly stacked up his papers, and scurried out the door. Frankly, I think these kids were scaring the poppycock out of him.

I said to Caesar. "So you think Boris stole personal items, planted them on the gardener, and then knocked the poor man off, all in an effort to get us to leave?"

"What, are you dense? That's what I just said."

As Caesar's dragon breath invaded my space, I realized conversing with him, wouldn't end well. Point blank, his accusations were ludicrous.

Cashmere strolled over to the area where Winston was standing. "Hey, Winston forgot his briefcase. I'll see if I can catch him."

Caesar pointed his sausage finger at his brother. "Move, and I'll squash you like a little dainty ladybug." He flung the leather case onto the table.

"You can't go through the man's stuff," I said.

Caesar ignored me, springing open the lid with one push of a button. "Bet he's got that stupid test in here." He thumbed through the papers. "Newspaper? Like anyone reads those anymore. A stack of business cards for the Nut House. Sounds fitting." He rifled through the man's things quicker, tossing items to the side. "Boring. Stupid. In-ter-est-ing. Well, well, well, what do we have here?" he sang.

In my best goodie-two-shoes voice, I said, "You can't look at the test. That would be cheating."

"Nope, this is something far more interesting. Seems like our friend Mr. Wellington has been busy."

"Dude, mind your own business," said Harley, in his typical surfer tone.

"I thought we were friends," Caesar said to him. "It would have been nice to know there were business opportunities."

Harley paced back and forth next to the table. "It's not like that. I mean, I wasn't supposed to say anything."

Kiki sat up straight and put out her cigarette. "This sounds juicy."

Harley paused his steps and pushed both hands through his glowing yellow locks, his guilty face looking like he just devoured three bowls of porridge. "All right, I overheard Winston on the phone talking about Chandler's stocks. Bottom line, when this business becomes one of ours, we'll have the opportunity to purchase shares in the company."

I interrupted, "I'm confused. So why would he let you buy shares now?"

"Because I caught him in a loophole. The property doesn't legally become any of ours until we complete the training and take the test. But then, if it doesn't belong to us, who does it belong to? The dead guy can't claim it anymore. You see, Winston didn't cover his holes in the will. He said if I kept it to myself, he'd make it happen."

It appeared as though the boy had a couple more marbles bouncing around in between his ears than I gave him credit for. But it smelt illegal and reeked of greed.

"Don't you guys get it? Mr. Chandler of the world's most famous chocolate factory is dead," said Harley. "He's an American icon. When the public finds out about his death, sales are going to sky rocket. I'm diving in while the tides are low, if you get my drift."

Caesar slapped Harley's back. "Hell, I'm getting a piece of that action."

Harley smirked. "Man, you'd never miss an opportunity to get a piece of any action."

Winston didn't come off to me as someone that would be in the middle of illegal business transactions. But, he did come off to me as a coward. And that would allow these selfish jerks to get away with anything.

Caesar rummaged through the briefcase. "Look, it's the loser's cell phone." He pushed *office,* then he and Kiki took turns leaving the lawyer harassing messages.

❦

Later in the day, Cashmere, Brice, and I formed a study group. We spent the afternoon scouting the mansion for study materials, examining anything found with the Chandler's logo. The problem was we had no idea what material the test would cover.

I eventually veered my focus to Chandler snacks, raiding the kitchen for samples. It had nothing to do with the fact that I was stressed, and needed chocolate. Purely educational.

After filling up on study materials, I decided to turn in early. Since we would be visiting the amusement park tomorrow, and I was emotionally exhausted; I could use the extra rest. I turned down my bed, disappointed not to find a shiny jewel on my pillow. But it wasn't about the chocolate, it was the reminder of the gruesome details of the past two days. My body rolled up into the goose-down duvet, trying to find comfort in its warmth. I couldn't help but think of poor Jasper and the suspicions surrounding his death. Not to mention, I was still perplexed over Parker's alleged heart attack and the painted threat on the theatre curtain. Unanswered questions were piling high.

And what about these other grandkids? I couldn't comprehend how they could just move on after such trauma, like nothing ever happened. How human compassion had been pushed aside and replaced by money and greed.

My thoughts veered to home. I abandoned my daughter to be here. It must feel like a lifetime to her in her toddler mind. I suppose greed is what brought me to this mansion, as well. Perhaps, I'm no better than the rest of them. I threw myself a couple more punches, then wept my swollen eyes to sleep.

An odd noise woke me up. Like something screeching across the floor. Paranoia was once again setting in. The only way I was getting any sleep tonight was to disprove my imagination.

I slipped into my robe and headed to the bedroom door, feeling a piece of paper sticking to my foot. I rescued the paper from my sole, identifying it as a recipe clipped from a magazine page. *Death by Chocolate*. Mmmm. With a name like that, I'm guessing it would whip up one doozie of a cake. I pocketed my treasure, licking my lips. Thank you, Chocolate Fairy.

Screech! I heard again, as I fumbled into my slippers. I opened up my door and tip-toed through the dark and lifeless hallway, down the grand staircase. Like with all the racket down below, it was going to be *me* that was going to wake somebody up. A scratching noise was coming from the kitchen. I scurried over to the dimly moonlit parlor, tripping over a bumpy thing and stubbing my toe on a hard something. Anybody ever hear of night lights? I managed to find a poker next to the fireplace.

Thundering beats vibrated in my chest, as I creaked opened the kitchen door, only to be introduced to total blackness. My hand smoothed over the wall, failing to locate the light switch. I stayed against the wall, frozen in fear, as something screeched across the floor in front of me. Ghosts. Please don't be ghosts. With every ounce of my being, I clinched the poker in both hands and rose it up above my head like a golf club. I closed my eyes and, the lights flashed on.

"What in the name of Boy George are you doing here, girl?" said Cashmere.

And that's when I saw Bonbon's metal dog bowl at my feet. The eager dog sitting behind it.

"She's only wagging her tail because she doesn't know you were about to make a shish-ka-pup out of her."

I dropped to the ground and hugged the dog. "Poor puppy. She was hungry." I scooped dog food into the metal pan. "And what are you doing here?" I asked.

"I heard a noise."

I noted his arms behind his back, so I circled behind him, identifying his weapon of choice. "Oh, you were going to take somebody down with that umbrella. A little Mary Poppin's action, huh?"

"Okay then, so I guess we're both a little paranoid."

I placed the umbrella on the island, and discovered the prize box of chocolates on the counter. "I wonder what the box is doing here." I inventoried the wide-open box. "Somebody has been having a midnight snack. There are two missing chocolates now."

Cashmere's eyebrows bounced up and down. "Ooh, midnight snack. Neither of us are going to sleep anytime soon, so what shall we have?"

I grinned. "That's easy." I plated two slices of Fudgy Praline Pie.

Cashmere followed me to the dining room with two glasses of milk. He pulled the candy box from his robe. "And for dessert—"

"No way. I'm not eating any of those sacred chocolates. You heard the lawyer. You shouldn't even be touching it."

"Well, somebody else has been eating them."

"My bet is Kiki. That girl can't help herself."

Cashmere inspected the box. He read, "The Million Heir Collection."

"Million heirs," I repeated. "Winston said these chocolates were designed for us." I studied each of the candies with wide-eyes. "Do you really think two of these were created specifically for us?"

Cashmere bit his lip. "Assuming Kiki didn't eat ours."

"Let's see which ones she ate." I pointed to the empty spaces in the box and read, "*Slow-as-Molasses Turtle* and *Old-Fashioned Whiskey Ball.* Sound like anybody we know?" Heat rose to my forehead. "Or, *knew?*" I swallowed hard. "Oh my gosh. These sound like Jasper. And Paulie."

Cashmere looked at me through eyes full of worry. "Anna, I don't think it's a coincidence that the same two missing candies happen to belong to the two dead guys."

My brain crossed its t's, dotted its i's, and connected the dots. "So, you're saying, these guys were—"

"Murdered," said Cashmere.

That single word sent a trickle of heebie jeebies down my vertebrae. My fingers wrapped around the wrinkled paper in my pocket. Suddenly that recipe for death wasn't sounding so appetizing. I wiped my mouth with my napkin and shoved my plate away, putting my full attention on the box of deadly chocolates staring back at me. My brain had tried so hard to stifle this suspicion, but there was the evidence sitting right there in front of me. Paulie Parker, the delivery guy, was the thirteenth chocolate, not Ashton— the fake newlywed.

"We need to call the police," I said. "And then we need to get the heck out of here."

"Anna, don't be ridiculous. If we leave, or contact the authorities, we'll be disqualified."

"The money isn't going to do us any good if we're dead."

"Listen. I'm scared, too. We just need to stick together and keep our eyes open."

"We don't even know what, or who we are searching for. Who could do such a thing?"

He nodded his head towards the candy box. "My guess is Kiki. We know she ate the first piece."

"All right, so she's certainly no June Cleaver. But, a murderer?"

"So then, who?" he asked.

"Well, if we're going on the chocolates, we can add Boris to the list."

"The butler?" he asked, surprised.

"You should have seen his face when he was prying the box out of Kiki's hands. And don't forget, he was the one who brought up all those suspicions at the dinner table tonight."

Cashmere scratched his head. "Then there's the people seeking revenge for their stolen jewelry." My mental list scribbled Caesar's name in big red letters, but I didn't have the heart to make the accusation of his brother out loud. Besides, killing someone over one ring seemed extreme. Killing someone over millions? A bit more plausible.

"My gut still says Kiki," said Cashmere. "I overheard Ashton telling Brice that she found some suspicious papers with background information on the grandkids. Seeing that there are no computers here, someone had to do the research before we arrived."

I slugged down the rest of my milk like it was 80 proof whiskey. "We need to get our hands on those papers. It's our only clue right now."

"No can do. Dumbbell returned the papers, so that nobody would know she was snooping. And guess whose room she found them in?"

I clinched my lower lip. "Kiki's."

"Bingo." He pointed down to the floor by the door that led to a side hallway, "Hey, I don't remember seeing a light on over there. Do you?"

"I hadn't noticed. But, I didn't think anybody else was awake."

"Let's go check it out," Cashmere said, like a little kid wanting to peek inside his birthday presents.

"What if it's the killer?"

"Then, we'll catch 'em off guard."

Darn dog. If she didn't wake me, I'd be sound asleep right now in Chocolate Dreamland. Instead I was in spy mode, trying to intercept a murderer.

We armed ourselves with our impromptu weapons. Cashmere twisted the doorknob and smiled back at me in satisfaction. He glanced down the lit staircase. "The coast is clear."

I felt like I should be wearing all black and a cat mask, rather than a Hello Kitty robe and polka dotted scrunchy.

He called from the bottom of the stairs, "Holy cow, are you serious?"

"Shhhhh," I hissed. So much for our cover. I raced down the last couple of steps, leaving the historic mansion behind. Below in the basement was a modern-day, grown ups' playground. The space was filled with a row of self-standing video arcade machines, an electronic football tossing game and a cool bench attached to the wall, made from the backend of a Chandler's limousine.

A trio of oil paintings hung on the walls behind a dark oak pool table. The enormous replicas of nostalgic advertisements were spotlighted with individual copper lamps. The first one, was a milkman carrying glass milk bottles in one hand and a box of Chandler Chip cookies in the other, while a girl peeked at him through a window. Clever, I thought. The middle painting featured the backside of a boy and his dog, sitting next to a man who was fishing on the end of a dock. The man was showing off the catch of the day, an empty fish basket, while the boy was eating a Chandler's milk chocolate bar. The caption read, *The Best Fishing Trip Ever.*

The final painting, on the connecting wall, was a precious pigtailed girl sitting on a tree swing. She was eyeing a paper candy sack nestled in her hands, her white tennies pointing inwards, awkwardly crossing over each other. Each shoe was topped with a shimmering bell. The caption read, *Bells, pure Bliss.* The painting was all in black and white, except for the glittering silver bells on her shoes and the chocolate Bells scattered randomly across the text and Chandler's logo. My fingers traced along the artist's initials scribbled in the corner. A.H. I vaguely recalled the advertisement from my childhood. I used to eat the candies with my uncle when we went to the movies.

I hollered to Cashmere, "Hey, do you remember *Chandler's Bells?*"

"Huh?" I heard from the adjoining room.

"*Chandler's Bells.* They were bell shaped candies filled with malt chocolate and caramel. I was so bummed when they stopped making them."

"Uh, I don't know. But, you're *not* going to be bummed when you see this."

I followed his voice to an adjoining space.

Cashmere cheered, "Come on baby," as he tossed a gold speckled ball down the alley.

"Seriously?" I gasped. Six pins fell down.

"Anna, see if you can pick up the spare."

"Shoot, I haven't bowled in years." I flung a glittered fuchsia ball. It swerved into the gutter.

"Okay, maybe not your game."

We headed back to the pool room, pausing in front of the bar. I plopped myself down on a stool with a bronzed pretzel-shaped back, spinning myself around on its swivel seat.

My fingertips couldn't resist gliding over the glazed counter before me that looked good enough to eat. The bar itself was a high-glossed wood carving of a Chandler's chocolate bar, minus the wrapper. Endless shelves behind it, held a spectrum of Chandler's liqueurs and wines. We unscrewed the assorted sweet bottles, sniffing, and sampling the flavors, like kids in an adult candy store.

I licked my lips. "The Black Forest Cordial is divine."

"Can't be as good as the Crème de Caramel Corn." Cashmere poured another shot of the buttery liquid and smoothly swigged it down.

I moved on to a refrigerated cabinet, helping myself to a sparkling pink bottle. "Oh, we've got to try this. It's a Cotton Candy Cooler." I tilted the bottle, while Cashmere popped opened the lid with a bottle opener. He yanked a bit too hard, and the neon liquid splashed all over me.

I made a beeline to the bathroom and rinsed my hands off in the sink. After my hands were dripping, I realized that the towel rack was bare, so I helped myself to the linen closet. Oddly, it was empty, with the exception of a chocolate brown robe. As I was covered in a sticky mess, smelling like a carnival, I didn't see the harm in borrowing it. As I yanked the robe off of the hanger, I noticed a hint of a glimmer at the closet's rear. After bundling up in the clean robe, I squatted down to investigate. Whoa. A door knob.

Of course, my common sense couldn't squash my curiosity. Besides, after discovering this fun house attraction of a basement, there was no telling what I might find in the connecting secret space. I turned the knob, and peeked through the open crack of the doorway.

The adjoining large space was dark, except for dim lights above. I pushed open the door further, tracing the glow up to recessed lights in the ceiling. Their luminescence cast view upon a series of framed pictures and glass shelves of meticulously arranged sports memorabilia. It reminded me of something you would see in an upscale sports bar. The room appeared to be lifeless, but I couldn't be positive in the dark. I stepped quietly out of the closet, scurrying my body behind a bulky leather couch.

A voice out of the darkness surprised me. I corked my startled squeal with my palm.

"Hee hee. Do it again, Brice."

Oh boy, that voice I knew. Suddenly, the entire wall in front of me lit up and went into motion. Holy smokes, this was one honker of a television screen. I knelt back down behind the couch, the humungo screen still in view. It was difficult to identify the player at first, with his brown wavy hair squished into a helmet, but his jersey gave him away. There was Brice bigger than life, running along the football field, some big burley guys on his trail. He passed the thirty, did a fake out, then threw the ball into the end zone, his team mate scoring a touchdown. The crowd cheered, and my heart throbbed.

Ashton said, "I can't believe we have this whole place down here to ourselves."

Brice said to her, "For once, your snooping paid off. Just don't mention it to anybody else."

While they continued watching sports' clips, I did more poking around. I focused in on a framed picture on the wall. The leopard green eyes. The smirk-y dimple. Yep, it was Brice. Chandler was obsessed with his career. This room was some sort of shrine. I suppose that wasn't an odd thing, seeing that his grandson was a famous football player. And I suppose if I had done something grander than stuffing Long Johns, he may have had a place devoted to me, as well.

I had myself another gander at the photos, studying an earlier college photo taken randomly along the sidelines of the field. A younger Boris was off to the side, standing in the background. So, Boris and Chandler were friends. That explains why the butler's so cranky. I can't imagine the resentment he must feel towards all of us strangers coming here to take over his house and his life-long friend's belongings.

The room roared as the life-sized crowd on the screen cheered. Ashton squealed, "Brice, you look so sexy running down the field in your tight pants." The picture froze on a close-up picture of Brice.

"Okay, you can take it off pause now," he told her.

She giggled. "Just admiring the view." She ran the tape in slow motion. As Brice's arm cocked back to throw the football, I got a larger than life look at his wrist. That's curious. No scar. Guess Brice wasn't a fan of Mabel's Pickled Possum Jam. Not sure I blamed him.

Ashton continued to pause Brice's every move, focusing up on attributes a cousin did not want to see. Meanwhile, the sultry comments were getting R-rated. Ashton's gag talk, combined with my stomach acids churning milk and alcohol into rancid juices, left me feeling more than queasy.

What was I doing here? I was eavesdropping in on Brice and Ashton's date, that's what I was doing. I was a peeping Tom. And if I didn't get out of here quickly, I would be a sick Sally.

I crawled back toward the door. Only in the dark space I couldn't find it. I reached my arms sporadically in front of me, searching for the doorknob— and finding a leg. I yelped. The lights came on. And I, on all fours, was greeted by Boris' ankles.

"Can you kindly let go of me, child?" he said, not the least bit amused, still dressed in his butler uniform. Good golly, does the man sleep in these clothes?

Before Brice and Ashton got to interrogate me, Bonbon pranced into the room. And when I say pranced, I mean pranced like an eighties' designed diva-kitty with a name like Trixie. Cashmere smiled proudly at the pooch dressed in violet sequined leg warmers and a matching headband.

Boris grabbed hold of his forehead, as if we induced an instant migraine. "What kind of twisted party is going on down here? And what in heaven's creation is the dog wearing?" He didn't give time for a response. "This was the Master's private space. None of you have any business being down here. So, if you hoodlums would kindly stop disrespecting it, and move your sick games upstairs, I'd be most obliged."

"Sorry, Boris." I pointed to the photo of him on the wall. "We realize now that Chandler was your friend. I wish I had gotten a chance to meet him."

He paused, as if offering a moment of silence. "Well, he's gone now. Which, to be clear, does not give anybody the right to take ownership of his personal belongings. If you require a robe, Ms. Clementine, kindly ask the maid."

I looked at him with dumbfounded expression. He pointed to the monogram, UBC, embroidered on the robe's pocket. To be fair, I hadn't noticed that little detail before. Not that that made me feel like any less of a schmuck right now.

Boris continued, "Now, you kids get out of here. And somebody, get that ridiculous ensemble off the dog."

We filtered to our rooms. I invited Bonbon into my room. Otherwise, there was no telling how she would dress for breakfast. Not to mention, she would make a good watch dog. I locked my door and tucked the dog into her side of the bed. And then I nestled in for a long night of— not sleeping. Which wasn't helped with the fact that the 'Footloose" song was jammed on the replay button in my brain. Thanks, Cashmere.

After an hour or two, I fell into a deep coma. I was so exhausted, nobody could wake me up. Except, a baby? Once again letting my imagination get the best of me. Goofy dog sounded like a crying baby. I nudged Bonbon with my foot. Crud. The dog was looking back at me, wagging her tail. And the baby, which didn't exist in the mansion, was still crying its head off.

I stepped out of bed, my feet struggling to navigate into slippers. And the crying stopped. I stood silently for a few moments, convincing myself that I had heard the noises. Then, slipped into bed, convincing myself that the crying was something I dreamt up.

The next morning, I found the dining room unusually quiet. Perhaps I wasn't the only one not getting any rest. I helped myself to a shiny silver chafing dish. As I lifted the lid, sweet steam lifted off the chocolate sauna, revealing cocoa crepes stuffed with a ricotta cheese filling and topped with a heavy-handed drizzle of luscious thick blueberry sauce. Tessie was indeed a magical being.

With cheeks full of calorie-filled glory, I ignored Priscilla, who was being her typical health-nut enthusiast, sprinkling wheat germ onto a tub of tasteless, fat-free yogurt. Did anybody tell the dumb girl that she was at the famous Chandler's chocolate mansion? How could we possibly share the same blood?

Brice and Ashton had a seat at the table. Making eye contact with them, made me feel like a schmuck all over again.

"Sorry about last night," I said to them.

"No worries," said Brice. "Guess Boris didn't care too much for us being in the basement either."

Tessie took a seat next to me and sipped her tea. "Ya know, all the years I've been workin' here, I didn't know that room existed. I used to have to go down the street for my guilty pleasure."

Right in mid-swig of my coffee, the woman makes me choke. "We don't need to be filled in on your personal life, Tess."

"Oh there, there. Get yerself out of the gutter, gal. I go just a hoot an' holler down the street to Gert's house every Tuesday to watch Dixie Hicks."

"Dixie Hicks, the television cook, is your guilty pleasure?"

"Honey, have you ever seen how much butter that woman cooks with? Guilty pleasure, indeed. Dottie's son got her one of them humungous sets. In all my days, I never saw such a big stick of butter."

Since I was already looking like a nut job to some, I decided to wait until the others left to ask Tessie about the baby. Or, the ghost. Or, the ghost-baby.

"Oh lawdy," said Tessie. "I got some tonic that will clear that right up fer ya."

I added another crepe to my plate. "I'm not losing it. I swear, I heard a baby crying."

Tessie waved it off. "Ah, probably a cat."

I raised an eyebrow.

"Probably a cat, giving birth to a whole litter. Of babies. Baby cats." She shook her head. "Nah. Reckon you should try the tonic."

After my crazy-lady-diagnosis and three more crepes, I went upstairs to get dressed. It took a bit of effort to squeeze into my jeans. Perhaps, I'd been stress-eating a tad too much.

I grabbed my waitress pad for notes, and jotted down the creepy baby encounter as it was fresh in my mind. *Before* it was washed away with tonic. As I sucked in my stomach, I managed to squish my waitress pad into my pocket. And then retrieved it again, recalling a key piece of information. Last night, somebody went out of their way to send me a message. I scribbled in big letters. The recipe. *Death by Chocolate*. It was at this moment, I realized my role had changed. I was no longer just trying to ace a test, I was trying to catch a killer.

I finished making myself presentable. Swiped on some lip-gloss, pulled my hair back in a ponytail, and I was good to go.

Next stop, day five's itinerary, Chandler's Chocolate Mountain. Even though the park hadn't officially opened to the public, employees and their families were invited to a soft opening, while training took place and kinks were smoothed out.

Frankie dropped us off at the entrance of the amusement park. My plan was simple, I was keeping my eyes open and staying clear of Caesar. After the incident at the chocolate factory, no location was safe. We walked in as a crowd through the front gate, down the main street's shop-lined road, then scattered like roaches in the middle of the night upon reaching the replicate town hall. And just like that, I lost track of Caesar.

But that worry was quickly replaced with infatuation. "Oh, sweet heaven on earth," I said to Cashmere, taking in the smells of chocolate covered, chocolate dipped, chocolate fried, and chocolate everything consuming the air. We were taking a sneak peek at the most anticipated theme park ever. Really, this was mandatory training? I wanted to spend eternity here. Which I was careful not to verbalize, just in case someone took me literally.

Our steps paused in front of the park's famous landmark, Mt. Chandler. Every hour, on the hour, the volcano would erupt with a chocolate explosion. Brown liquid spewed out the peak, while the scent of chocolate drifted through the air.

We expanded our exploration of the town, Cashmere and I skipping down the brown brick road like Dorothy and

Scarecrow, past endless gold lampposts, each capped off with a mock Chandler's iconic foiled truffle. Our stroll continued down Chandler's Trail. This was the most alive I felt since this whole training hoopla had begun.

Although, most of the stores weren't yet open, a lit shop with a glittery pink sign stole my attention. We squished our faces into the front window of *Soufflé*. Heaven, to a girl like me. Meaning a girl that chooses her lip tint based on its flavor. Pink satin material draped over French inspired striped hat boxes, creating a display for assorted bottles. *Raspberry Ripple Body Wash. Marshmallow Fluff Lotion.*

"I guess smelling like the stuff would be the next best thing to eating it," I told Cashmere.

"Are you kidding? You wouldn't be able to stand yourself."

I was distracted by a jovial tune coming from a carousel in the middle of the town center. "Listen. Do you hear that song?"

"You're passing on smelling like a human candy bar for *Peter Cottontail?* I have to hear the story behind this."

My steps steered towards the music. "That song is in Jillian's rabbit that she got from the Easter Bunny last year. She adored that toy. Well, that was before she brought it over to Toby Stilskin's house for a playdate. Evidently, Toby didn't care much for the Easter Bunny's previous offerings, and yanked the cute button eyes out of its wee little eye sockets. Jillian was devastated, until my uncle brought the patient into his hospital, aka the tool shed in the backyard. He performed a miracle that day. Basically, he super-glued a pair of fishing bobs to its face, and scribbled on some pupils with a Sharpie. Bob the bunny now looked like he could hang in the ping pong-eyed company of Elmo, only Bob's eyes always appeared a bit bloodshot."

Cashmere squinted one eye. "So, Jillian's looking forward to *Bob* visiting your house next month?"

I smiled. The carousel was the most gorgeous one I had ever seen. Chocolate bunnies chased marshmallow yellow chicks, while silver and lilac foiled butterflies frolicked over tulips and daffodils. The ride magically glowed with endless rows of pastel lights flashing in time to the music. I imagined Jillian's face lighting up as I propped her on the toddler sized chick. Boy, do I miss her.

"You good?" asked Cashmere.

"Yeah, just getting sappy."

"Let's go find something to cheer you up."

"Anna, wait up," hollered Tessie. She trotted up to us, out of breath.

"I'm sorry, Tess. I thought you were going off with Boris."

"Nah, Boris insists on goin' to watch after them boys. Me, I'd rather have some fun, than babysittin' trouble."

The three of us wordlessly walked down Rocky Road, overloading our senses. Whiffs of chocolate caramel empanadas, a breeze of freshly baked biscotti, the fragrance of fried funnel cocoa cake overflowing with bananas. Two words, Aroma Therapy.

We strolled past a ride scrambling in and out, back and forth, to the tune of *I Want Candy*. "Check it out," said Cashmere, pointing to the *Truffle Shuffle* as it started to slow.

Tessie said, "Well, I'll be a tadpole's tush. Boris is on that ride, sittin' next to what's his face. Ya know that furry-faced fella that passes more gas than a Hess truck."

"That would be Caesar," I said, comforted to know he was staying out of mischief. "And I'm afraid Boris is rather green."

"Serves him right for carryin' on like a youngster. Why, he looks like he's fixin' to march off to the marble orchards."

The old man staggered off the ride. As much grief that she gave him, Tessie was right there to meet him with an extended arm. She said to him, "Let's drag these ol' bones to the bench. We need to gel your jam, before you done get yerself preserved."

The others got off the ride and took off deeper into the park. Caesar called back to us, "You girls want to ride *Sugar High?*"

My face gleamed like a sparkler on the Fourth of July. "Oh Cashmere, I heard of that one. Goes 0 to 80 in three seconds."

"That explains why Caesar asked us," said Cashmere. "He knows I don't do roller coasters. He forced me on one when we were little. All I have to say is that it wasn't pretty, and he still owes me a new Members Only jacket. Anna, go on. I'm going to get myself a snack."

I ran off and joined the others in line for the roller coaster.

Harley, in typical surfer mode, gave me a hang ten sign. "Oh gnarly, Annie's joining the cool crowd."

How did I lose Caesar that fast? The guy stands out of a crowd like a Weeble Wobble in a Lego land. I asked Kiki, "What happened to Caesar? He's been following you around like a greasy puppy dog."

"I can't help it," she said while fluffing her mane. "I just have that effect on men."

"I give her an A for attitude," said Harley.

I'd give her a B, and it wouldn't stand for Best buddy.

Harley pushed past us. "Later chickettes, it's time to ride." He sprawled out in the first row and left us to share a seat in the back.

"Perfect," I mumbled.

The roller coaster started its climb up the steep tracks.

"What's your problem, Anna? I can't help it if you're jealous of me."

"Jealous, not in a million years," I said.

We continued at a slow pace up the steel hill, the clinking of the tracks intensifying.

"Oh, you are so jealous," said Kiki. "Jealous that I can get any guy I want, and therefore, get anything I want."

I hollered over the pounding on the tracks, not realizing we were reaching the top. "You're crazy, I'm not jealous of... *woooo!*" The roller coaster car shot out and sped down the steep mountain. I caught my breath. "I'm not jealous of your fake hair—" we took a sharp turn, "your eyes that are a different color every day—", we did a loop de loop, "your fake lashes—," our bodies banged side to side as we did a series of spirals, "or your tan in a can." The track curved and started to drag up another hill. "Not of your inflated puffy lips, or your Botox—," the coaster reached to the top and raced through a tube of white flashing lights, simulating sugar, "and certainly not of your face that has been pulled more times than a piece of taffy, your silicone-stuffed body, and your fancy trashy clothes covering your phony bologna body."

Our cart came to an abrupt stop and our bodies jerked back.

"Whewf," I said.

Kiki climbed out of the car. "Feel better now, Anna?"

"Yes." Truth is, I felt horrible. I can usually control my temper, but that girl had been pushing my buttons for days. I guess with my adrenaline racing, I just exploded.

Our walk back to the bench was a silent one. Was I jealous of her? Had this really been the fuel of my fire? I had to admit, she was a good ten years older than me and certainly in much better shape. But, her physical attributes by themselves was not what angered me. It was more the payoffs that she got from all those fake butcher-shopped pieces. But then again, it wasn't all her fault. We lived in a society that worshipped artificial beauty. If your beauty lied within, well then, you better be in the market for a plastic surgeon that was willing to dig it out for you.

I met up with the others back at the park benches.

Caesar had a turkey leg in one hand and a chocolate covered candy apple in the other. "How was it?" he managed to spit out, in between inhaling chunks of meat.

"Dude, you missed it," said Harley. He clawed his fingers into the air. "Cat fight!"

"Really?" said Caesar. "I'd put my money on Kiki. Heck, I think she could kick my butt."

"Nobody hit anybody," I said.

"Not yet," said Kiki.

"Oh, I sense another match coming on," Caesar said waving his smoked drumstick in the air, chanting, "Go, go, go!"

"Yeah Anna, let's go. Let's show everybody just how pathetic you are."

"We're done," I told her, looking like a big fat chicken.

"Sure, you can dish it out, but you can't take it."

How could these guys manage to squash the fun out of an amusement park? A chocolate-themed one, nonetheless.

Priscilla's voice was heard in the distance. "Hello. A little help here." Good grief, another country heard from.

I moved in front of a twinkling tree to find Miss Priss, stuck in the road? "What in the world are you doing?" I said to her.

"My heel is stuck in between the bricks." Who wears heels to an amusement park?

Harley was quick to come to his sister's rescue, kneeling beside her. "And people say that you're the brains of the family. Go figure. Step out of the shoe, woman." Priscilla stood on one leg, hugging his head for balance. He twisted the shoe and with one considerable tug, cracked it right off the heel. "Seriously, sis. What would you do without me?"

"You just busted my shoe, you moron." Priscilla smacked him in the back of the head with her heel-less pump. She returned the broken shoe to her foot and then, pulled hand sanitizer from her purse. "I just spent the last couple hours complaining to the so-called guest services. Where's the health department when you need them? Most of the park's real restaurants are closed, leaving these disgusting snack sheds for us to feed off of like wild animals grazing in troughs. The only passable dining available is clear on the other side of the park, and you have to take some filthy trolley pulled by animals to get there. The foolish thing was about to leave, so I hurried, and slipped in a pile of," she whispered, "horse poo."

I imagine every soul in her presence was biting down harshly on their tittering tongue.

"Now I'm going to have to march myself back to that office and tell them about the toxic feces and faulty brick work. This place is a law suit ready to happen."

Priscilla cleansed her hands, then offered the bottle to her brother.

Harley disregarded the offering, wiping his hands on his jeans. "Where's that Officer Doody when you need him?"

Caesar high-fived his turkey leg to Harley's knuckles.

Priscilla narrowed in on Caesar's greasy turkey, his beard showing clues of the cotton candy he ate before we arrived. "You know, that stuff is going to kill you."

I waved over familiar faces in the crowd, thankfully giving Priscilla's whining session a break. Winston and Frankie together, exemplified the Ying and Yang of body types. The girth of the lawyer's belly, matched the width of Frankie's muscular shoulders.

"Where have you guys been hiding out at?" I asked them, relieved to be in the company of some sane people.

Winston pushed down his comb-over blowing in the wind, resembling a cockscomb atop of his bald pate. "We went on this delightful trolley ride that passed through a luxury hotel under construction. Then, to our pleasant surprise, we were transported to this most outstanding seafood restaurant. I had Alaskan salmon with a spinach salad tossed with a light raspberry vinaigrette. After eating so much heavy food lately, it sure hit the spot."

Priscilla started to breathe heavy, like a kid about to have a tantrum. It wouldn't surprise me in the least if she went back to customer service and held her breath until she turned blue.

Frankie pulled a golden box from a gift bag and showed it to me. "Miss Clementine, in case you find yourself sinking in a pit of fudge—"

I looked around my feet. "Huh?"

"It was a joke. You know, *Cocoa Nuts*, the video game?" he explained, without cracking a hint of a smile. Frankie removed the lid, exposing neat rows of golden truffles.

It would be rude to decline. "Thanks, Frank." Good guy, but a bit cocoa nuts.

Winston said, "We ran into Brice and Ashton over by Chocolate Lover's Land. Brice has something to show us, by the Soda Fountain."

Caesar's eyelids jolted open, revealing a set of gleaming eyes, like cherries on a slot machine. "Hey maybe they're giving out food samples."

With curiosity and hunger lingering over logic, our misfit group hiked over to Chocolate Lover's Land. Caesar lagged behind the crowd, making stops at every chow wagon along the way, while Priscilla wobbled behind him huffing muffled curse words no proper lady would ever articulate.

We discovered the couple sitting at a picnic table, in front of a brightly hued animated soda shop. The parking lot, filled with antique cars, and carhops delivering nostalgic trays of treats, transported us back into the fifties. In the center of the mock parking lot was a literal soda fountain, aka, a gigantic root beer bottle spraying water into cement mugs below.

We found Brice and Ashton sitting under a red and white striped umbrella, sipping one shake with two straws.

Caesar's amphibious tongue glossed over his lips. "Whatcha drinking?" he asked them, as if he was famished.

Ashton closed her eyelids and took a long sip, no doubt teasing the ravenous man. She spoke in a euphoric tone, "It's called *Love Potion*."

Of course it is.

Brice rolled his eyes. "It's just a cherry milk shake with chocolate chips."

Ashton corrected, "Actually they're little chocolate hearts bursting with passion fruit flavor."

Caesar ogled each of the roller skating waitresses gliding by, from the top of their heart-shaped candy box hat, down to their puffy scarlet sequined miniskirts. He smiled in satisfaction. "Nice scenery, but where are the friggin' samples?"

Brice shrugged his shoulders.

"Well then, why did you guys drag us over here?"

Ashton slurped up the final bit of liquid love, then enthusiastically led the procession, bouncing across the lane like Tigger in the Hundred Acre Woods. Us followers, not so elated, painfully groaned all the way, like a parade of depressed Eeyores being sent off the side of a cliff. Her prance paused in front of a river adorned with everything Ashton. Sugar and spice, and everything…glitter. It was the fantasy world where fuzzy-bottomed bunnies licked lollipops, and frilly gowned princesses rode periwinkle ponies under glistening waterfalls. Sweethearts floated down the flowing electric blue river into the *Tunnel of Love*.

Ashton said to us, "This is it. We're all going to ride it together."

Seemed a little twisted to me. I understood that Brice's loyalties stood with Ashton, but this was sinking a little deep. *Titanic-ish* deep.

Caesar briskly shook his head, sending the loose skin on his neck into a turkey-like tremor. "Sometimes, don't you just want to dribble that gal and hope to make a basket?"

Brice stared the fowl fella right in the eyes. "Don't start with me again, Caesar."

I stepped in between the repelling testosterone forces, "Hey, why don't we all just give this ride a try? Oh, and Caesar, I heard that there are free chocolates at the end of it."

Brice whispered to me, "Thanks, Anna. You'll see. It will be worth it."

It was worth it, just for me to keep tabs on Caesar.

"Let's get this over with," Kiki said to Caesar, climbing into a heart-shaped chocolate box. "This is like a Valentine's Day gone totally wrong."

Caesar licked his chops, as she bent over to sit in an empty candy cup. "I don't know, seems pretty yummy from my view." They sat in the sweetheart-shaped gondola like a pair of dressed up candies, Kiki probably feeling less like a confection, and more like a piece of meat.

Boris offered his arm to Tessie. She shook a finger at him. "No funny business," and clung onto his arm.

Cashmere and I grabbed the next candy box, leaning our backs onto the heart shaped lid. I totally felt like a chocolate goober. The boat began its float past a lawn of candy heart flowers, suggesting that love was in bloom. *XoXo, Hot Stuff, Be Mine.* Then, it drifted into the chocolate heart-shaped entrance.

We floated through a trail of lit heart-shaped arches that flashed to the sound of a heartbeat. And then pushed along through a dark wind chamber, forcing our nasal sensory to take the lead. Sweet smells consumed the air, providing an olfactory feast for our inner child.

Now with relaxed mind and soul, we were immersed into the heart of the ride, magnificently surrounded by a literal tunnel of chocolate confections in 3-D. To my side, was a clip of the chocolate factory, showcasing shiny tempered chocolate, squishing out of nozzles into miniature molds. You felt like you could just reach out a finger and take a swipe at the rich goodness.

Over Cashmere's shoulder, I could see magnified bowls of chocolate being stirred in slow motion. Tiny divers jumped off of the sides, sinking their bodies into the perfectly swirled chocolate. You couldn't help but lick your lips. I took a deep breath taking in the sweet chocolate aroma, while the candy lid seat of the boat gently tilted us backwards forcing our view up to the ceiling.

Up above was an aquarium of dark, smooth chocolate with various Chandler confections swimming about. Chocolate caramels— turned to darkness? The ride came to an abrupt stop, the projections and music stopped, and we found ourselves in the pitch dark. As in, I couldn't see the bangs in front of my eyes. Note to park, install emergency lights.

Cashmere must have sensed my fear, or heard my heartbeat, or felt the boat tremble with my terror. "It's okay, Anna. It's just a glitch."

Howls echoed through the tunnel.

"I'm sure it's just Caesar or Harley goofing around," he assured me.

A body scampered by us. Although the ride was on water, I assumed there was a running board along the side for employees.

"I'm going to go check it out," said Cashmere.

"No, don't get out," I realized I was saying to myself, as I jet my arm out to his empty seat.

I focused on the sound of my own breathing, burying myself in deep meditation, finding an island of tranquility. My peaceful inner waves drowned out the groans. Hushed the monstrous howls. And silenced the moans of a deep cackling demon. I opened my eyes. My peaceful inner self was a liar. I had heard every horrid sound.

But, it didn't matter. I was over-reacting. Nobody was going to hurt anybody. Those guys were just up to their usual immature shenanigans.

And then there it was. A scream. A long, screechy, scary-as-all-the-dickens blood-boiling scream. I thought about climbing out of the boat to escape, but decided that that would probably result in me drowning. Even with my golden truffle. I slumped down as low as I could in the seat, doing my best to hide in the darkness.

And then, as quickly as the ride had stopped, it started back up again, right where it left off. Chocolate caramels were stretching apart in slow motion, ruby red lips biting into a juicy chocolate covered strawberry, pretzels being dipped into pools of chocolate, droplets dripping off their sides. This ride surely earned its name as the *Tunnel of Love*. Unfortunately, I wasn't in the mood. I just wanted off the darn thing.

I exited the ride onto a platform, greeted by Cashmere.

"Thank goodness you're okay," I said while hugging him, my body still trembling. "What happened?"

"It was just those morons." He pointed to Caesar who was suspiciously dripping wet, his shirt splattered with bright red stains.

I gasped.

"Strawberry slooshie." Somebody threw it at him.

"And the scream?"

"That would be Kiki. Some slooshie splashed on her pinky toe."

I let out a sigh of relief. If I had a chocolate for every time I asked myself how any of these people could possibly be related to me, I'd need new jeans.

Boris helped a flushed Tessie out of the boat. "Well if that don't beat all," she said. "That was more fun than straddlin' a mechanical mule at the county fair."

Boris forcefully cleared his throat. Guess there was a lot I had to learn about mountain life.

Everyone was off of the ride except Brice and Ashton.

The ride attendant, a high pitched, freckled teenager who looked like he was drowning in his father's clothes, said robotically, "Please exit to your right. The ride is now complete."

"Just give us a second, kid," said Brice, winking at the lad.

"Please exit to your right," said the attendant in a now slightly cracked voice.

Brice stepped out of the boat and got down on one knee. The ride attendant took the opportunity to flash a picture.

Brice gazed into Ashton's now squinty, blinded eyes. "My sweet, darling, love of my life, will you marry me?"

Ashton squealed, "Yes!"

Brice slid a ring on her finger, and she sprang out of the boat and jumped on him, wrapping her legs around his body, like a possum's tail coiled on a tree limb.

"Congratulations," said the attendant, wiping a tear off his cheek. "You people are what makes this job so meaningful."

"That's what we came to see?" said Harley. "Bogus."

Caesar turned back to the ride exit, sinking his chubby fingers into the free sample basket. He mumbled with satisfied stuffed cheeks, "Er, was okay. What's next?"

"For goodness sakes, the couple just got engaged," I said to Harley.

"Yeah, yippy skippy. So now what?"

Winston addressed the group, "I hate to burst anybody's bubble, but we will be leaving shortly. So, if there's anything you would like to see, now is the time to do it."

Cashmere rubbed his hands together briskly. "Who's up for Rolling Pin-ball?"

Caesar chuckled, "That's a sissy ride; anybody who's got any will ride the Fondue Fun-do. It looks wicked."

I motioned to Cashmere, Tessie and Boris. "I guess it's just the four of us."

"Count me out," said Boris. "I've had enough swinging in circles for one night. Besides, those boys could use some inconspicuous chaperoning."

"Okay then," I clasped the arms of Cashmere and Tessie and led them through Cupcake Country's valleys of sprinkles and gumdrops.

We found our place at the end of the line of the Rolling Pin-ball attraction and watched human balls being flung into the whopping larger-than-life pinball machine. The passengers' pinballs mimicked bumper cars, bouncing off other cars, off of obstacles, and through a flour tornado water mist. And for an extra bonus, when the cars veered towards the lower end of the attraction, they were slammed back up into the pinball machine by giant rolling pin paddles. Yes, it was a fantastic amount of bouncing around.

Cashmere gaped at the attraction, his complexion turning the shade of the Wicked Witch of the West's skin. "I just had an idea. I'll meet back up with you at the limo."

I don't think Tessie or I believed his excuse, but neither one of us would dare call out the coward-like behavior of our friend. Meanwhile, our attention was grabbed back to the screaming riders, horrifically being jerked around in bouncing caged cars. "Rain check?" I offered.

"Whewf. Bless yer heart darlin'. Those carts were spinnin' round like bloomers in the rinse cycle. I'm not sure these ol' limbs can twist like that anymore."

"It's okay, Tess. It will be more fun watching the Three Stooges on that bungee drop ride."

We paused on top of a chocolate covered cherry lined bridge walkway, giving a clear shot of the Black Forest. This section of the park showcased fruit themed, adrenaline-packed attractions. An illuminating sign flashed atop of a rather skimpy bungee-type ride, *The Fondue Fun-do.*

This was one ride you could count me out of. "There's not really much to it," I said, examining the ride's apparatus. Strawberry-shaped bucket seats hanging onto translucent ropes, faded into the night sky, giving the illusion that they were floating in mid-air. Below was a pond of water, which reflected off the brown tile walls, simulating a pool of chocolate.

Tessie's palm wrapped over her open mouth. "Oh, lawdy. Someone's actually goin' to get on that there contraption."

I squinted my eyes. "I can't make out who it is."

"Oh my stars," she said. "I gotta get me a closer look."

We walked toward the attraction, never taking our eyes off of it.

Kiki and Caesar were buckled into the seats, with their hands clinching ropes and legs dangling underneath, reminding me of the kiddie swings at the park. Only the kiddie swings at the park weren't death traps. Without warning, the berries plunged down towards the earth.

Tessie laughed. "Woo wee, sounds like our swine's a squealin'."

They bolted down so fast, I found myself bracing the rail in front of me. Inches above the water, the berries paused, bouncing the passengers up and down wildly through the air like yo-yos.

I held my queasy stomach, trying to yield it from reaching up to my throat. "No, thank you."

Tessie laid a palm on her chest. "Goodness gracious. I would have had a stroke by now. The girl has guts goin' for er." She smiled wickedly. "I wonder if she bought those, too."

Waiting, as the buckets climbed back to the top, I scanned the ride's warning sign, a lengthy paragraph long. My heart froze when I got to the bottom. "Closed." In big letters. Not just any old big letters. Letters scripted in a very familiar blood-red paint.

"Tessie, we need to warn them," I said, pointing to the sign. We scurried through the ride's entryway to the boarding platform. Harley was grinning ear to ear behind the control desk, while Boris stood there, face in palm.

"We got to get them off," Tessie said to Boris.

"I told them not to go, said Boris. "But, they wouldn't listen."

I shoved my body next to Harley, taking in the rows of buttons on the control panel. "How does this work?" I asked in a panic.

Without explanation, he slammed a red button. "It's just this one little magical button." The berries that had rested at the top, plummeted down rapidly toward the ground. The passengers cheered. The audience gasped.

Watching the berries so intently, slowed time. Farther and farther they raced. My eyes didn't blink, my pupils plastered on the flying fruits, expecting them to spring back up in the air at any moment. One berry bounced up. As the other berry hit the bottom point, a rope snapped. Caesar was tousled upside down, all his weight bouncing vigorously up and down on a single rope.

"We have to get him off," I cried.

Harley slowly pushed up on the lever. "I got this," he said. The berry began its climb back up to the platform. We all took turns yelling out to Caesar, "Hang on!"

As Harley pushed up on the lever, there was another snap. Poor Caesar was left hanging by a thread. The berry was only half way back to the platform. Harley was sweating. His hands were shaking. "I've got ya big guy." He inched the lever up. Higher and higher. Yes, it was working. Caesar was almost to the top.

"Stay with it Harley. You're doing great," I said. The others were at the platform ready to grab him. "Just a little bit more," I said. "You're almost there—" *Snap!*

Just inches from safety, the rope snapped, and the berry dropped, horrifically crashing down into the shallow cement-lined cocoa abyss, never to rise again.

⊱⊰ ⊱⊰

The rusty twangs of a classical melody invited me into the library. *Oh My Darling Clementine.* Yes, way before my time. But, I recalled learning it at a Bumblebee Jamboree in the company of *Oh Susanna* and *She'll Be Coming Around The Mountain.* I traced the tune to a gramophone next to the fireplace. The words forced into my brain, *you are lost and gone forever, dreadful sorry, Clementine.* Now that the brassy melody was complete, I noted that I didn't have the only watery eyes in the room. "There you are, Cashmere. I've been searching for you everywhere."

He stared off distantly into the crackling flames. "I figured that most of the people here were too ignorant to read, so I figured this would be the best place to be alone." His eyes met mine. "No, of course I wasn't talking about you, Anna. Please sit with me. I could use a friend right now."

I sunk into the leather seat next to his, taking in the warmth from the hearth. We sat in silence for several long moments. He undoubtedly soaking in sorrow, and me in guilt. I had convinced myself that Caesar was a ruthless killer, but he was only a victim. I took in a deep breath, then attempted to swallow the lump in my throat.

Cashmere's glazed over eyes penetrated the illuminated logs before us. "I just can't believe Caesar is gone. Why did he have to go on that stupid ride?"

I kept a quiet tongue, being an ear to my hurting cousin, who had become my friend.

"Damn, that idiot." He punched a fist to the chair. "The ride was closed. Closed means you don't get on the ride. Why didn't he listen to Boris?" He combed his fingers through his hair and squeezed his scalp with his palm. "I know why. Because he was just plain stupid, and ignorant, and selfish, and cared about nobody in this world, but himself." He burst into tears. "But, you know what? That imbecile was my brother. The only family I had left, and we treated each other like crap."

Cashmere continued his lashing. "I should have been there to stop him." He sunk his head into his bent arm and wailed.

I squeezed his other hand. "Don't do this to yourself. It wouldn't have mattered if you were there or not. Caesar had a mind of his own."

Tessie entered the room, presenting a tray of refreshments to Cashmere.

"No thank you," said Cashmere wiping his eyes.

She handed him a cloth napkin, and he dabbed his cheeks.

"I won't take no for an answer," she said. "Now then, I've fixed ya a fresh pot of Chamomile. It's medicinal." She handed him a cup, then filled it with fragrant tea.

Cashmere and I disregarded the offerings. For a change, I didn't have an appetite.

Kiki called out from the entranceway. "You guys having a party in there?"

Tessie hollered back, "No mam, just a lil' tea time fare."

Cashmere smirked. "You know, she hates it when you call her *mam*."

Tessie grinned like the Cheshire cat. "Is that right?"

Kiki walked up behind me. "I don't do tea." Meanwhile, her arm reached over my head to the cookie platter. Once she had the cookie shoved into her cheek, she reached for another.

"I thought ya didn't *do* tea," said Tessie.

"I don't, but I'm really depressed right now." She forced another biscuit into her mouth. "I was right there next to him. I've never seen anything so horrific in all my life."

"Kiki please," I said, discreetly pointing to Cashmere. "Show some compassion."

"Are you going to start with me again, Anna? Didn't you tear me apart enough last night?"

I pursed my lips for a moment, then decided to take the high road. My head turned around to face hers. Her face was so full of cookies, she looked like a pelican with a bulging beak. But, I resisted all urges, and took that high road. I managed a compassionate demeanor. "About that, I'm sorry. I didn't mean any of those things. I was just upset."

Her hand clung onto her hip and her neck tilted up as if she was trying to swallow a school of snapper. "So, you *are* jealous of me?"

Oh brother. The high road is for the birds. "Kiki, this really isn't the time for this."

She aggressively wiped her palms onto her skirt, leaving powdered sugar clouds behind. "I see how it is. Everybody can console poor little Cashmere and his fragile little wuss feelings, and the hell with the rest of us."

"Kiki, his brother just died in a tragic accident."

"Duh, Anna. I was there. Remember? Next to the man. You know the one dangling on a string. But the question is, where was he?" She looked over to Cashmere. "I'm starting to wonder if you sabotaged that ride before we got there."

I gasped.

"Oh, don't act surprised. I'm sure you were thinking it too."

Cashmere screamed out, "How dare you. That was my brother."

"Oh yeah, pull the brother card out. Like you really treated him like one."

"We weren't the closest of brothers, but heaven strike me down, I didn't kill him. Now please, get the hell out of here and leave me alone."

"You're not the boss of me," Kiki said to him. "I'll stay here as long as I like."

"Great. You stay here and feed your fat face with cookies, and when you're done with that, why don't you finish off that stupid box of chocolates you want so badly." He nodded to the table. "Put us all out of our misery."

The box of confections was displayed behind the gramophone. And just as expected, a third chocolate had been removed. One less chocolate. One less heir.

ოლე ელოი

Toasted Joker: A rich and chunky chocolate, filled with liquor, rolled in dough, and toasted.

Chapter 10

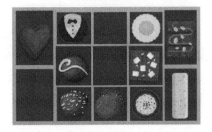

TEN dinner guests prepared their appetites for a heaping helping of murder.

E veryone went their separate ways for the rest of the day. I prepared for a hopeful night's rest. As water sprayed into the porcelain sink, I cupped it into my hands and rinsed my face. My mind raced with all the accusations ricocheting through the house. Maybe Caesar's death was really an accident.

I stared at my mirrored reflection, seeing a little girl terrified of the monsters in her closet. I wasn't fooling myself. I was scared. The competition was dwindling, one life at a time.

Now that Caesar had died, my suspicions had too. Somebody else was behind the missing chocolates. And the threat on the theater curtains. And the deaths.

At the end of the day, everyone here had the same motive. Money. *But, who needed the money the most?*

I took out my waitress pad and jotted down some notes.

The Wellington siblings: Priscilla and Harley didn't need the money, but never seemed to have enough of it.
Kiki: ditto
Mr. and Mrs. Hodges-to-be: Ashton had a minimum wage job, but once she married Brice, she would be well taken care of.
The service personnel could all use the money.
So, then the bigger question was— Need or Greed?

Bang! Something pounded against the wall. I hugged my ear to the wallpaper. There was rattling about in the room next door. The vacant room.

I stuck my head out into the hallway. Empty. I could see light shining underneath the door. So what? Why was I getting myself all worked up? Just because nobody was staying in this room, didn't mean nobody could be inside of it.

I knocked on the door, just to make peace with my doubts. And I was greeted with a crashing sound within the room. I called out, "Hello? Who's in there?"

No answer. How could somebody pretend to not be there with all that racket going on? I tried the doorknob. Locked.

It wasn't a big deal. So, someone was in the room. It didn't mean it was the killer. Or, the ghost-baby. Just some random soul, locked in a room, possibly plotting murder number four.

The thought of being alone tonight, just wasn't an option. This gave me three choices; Tessie, who was probably already asleep; Brice, who probably wouldn't appreciate me crawling in the middle of the bed between him and his fiancée; and ol' faithful, Cashmere. The only problem now was getting to his room. I viewed the counter full of cosmetics and grabbed a bottle of hairspray.

Anybody messes with me, I'm spraying them in the eye sockets.

I put on my robe, grabbed a pillow, and stuffed the pillowcase with my emergency Pop-tarts. Perhaps, I was an emotional eater. But, this was no time to scold myself. The chocolate would get my mind off of the killer, allowing my heart to beat properly, saving my life. Hence, chocolate was saving my life.

I dashed down the hallway, like a rat being chased by a rolling pin, to Cashmere's room, all the while checking my back. My fist knocked repeatedly on the door. Come on, open.

Cashmere opened the door and I pushed my way into the room.

"Woah. What's going on?" he asked me.

I closed the door and locked it. "I was hoping I could bunk on your floor."

Cashmere glanced at my hands. "Uh, sure. But what's with the extra hold hair spray?"

"Defense."

"In case you ran into Bazooka-Beehive in the hallway?" He unlocked the door. "I was just going to go for a snack. I haven't eaten all day."

"You don't want to go out there." I pulled the Pop-tarts from the pillow case. "Here, eat these."

He pointed to a bag of marshmallows by the fire. "Looks like we're having S'mores."

While I relocked the door, Cashmere got an extra blanket from the closet and spread it out on the carpet in front of the stone-stacked fireplace that uniquely cornered the wall. Ordinarily, this setting would set the stage for a romantic evening. But with Cashmere, it felt more like hanging out with a best friend at a slumber party.

We poked marshmallows onto the end of homemade hanger skewers and held them over the fire.

Cashmere said, "So tell me what's going on."

I told him all about the mysterious room next door, meanwhile finding serenity watching my marshmallow turn golden brown.

"It's done," he said. "Take it out."

I caught the marshmallow on fire and then blew out the flame. "This is how you toast a marshmallow."

"No, that's how you burn down a historic mansion."

The marshmallow stretched as I pulled it off the skewer. I tilted my head back and let the strings of sugar lead the marshmallow fluff to my tongue.

Cashmere's nose wrinkled in disgust. "It's scorched. Speaking of which, did you see the name of the missing chocolate in the box?"

I nodded. "*Toasted Joker.*"

"Nobody would have hurt my brother. It was an accident, right?"

I looked into his eyes. "You know it wasn't. That stupid chocolate box is proof."

"But, how's that even possible? Caesar got on the ride with his own free will." Cashmere rubbed his forehead. "To top things off, Kiki is trying to convince everyone that I'm behind it." His eyes bulged. "Behind my own brother's murder."

Cashmere sprung up. "We need a drink." He grabbed a bottle of chocolate wine off of his nightstand, and then went into the bathroom. "It's the best that I can do," he said, holding up two paper Dixie cups for my consideration. "Unless you want to go brave the kitchen."

"Dixies sound delightful."

He poured the murky liquid into the cups and raised his into the air, "To Caesar, my brother."

"To Caesar."

Cashmere rubbed his hands together briskly. "Okay then, enough about my brother for now."

We sat in silence for a while, sipping on wine, staring into flames. My brain latched onto thoughts of home. I didn't want to be here anymore. I was scared, and I missed my daughter.

"What in the world are we doing here?" I said. "We're in the middle of nowhere, putting our lives on the line. Meanwhile, my child is at home without her mother. What, for money?"

"Yeah, for money," said Cashmere. "There's no way I'm walking out of here, and handing this competition to my brother's killer." He took a swig of his drink. "And you need to remind yourself what you're here for— your future. Come on, it must be hard being a single mom."

"Sure, life would be easier if I didn't have to worry about money. I could move out of my uncle's basement and get my own place. Not to mention, I wouldn't have to worry about begging for my job back at the diner."

Cashmere smiled in satisfaction. I felt like I was under his care, making a breakthrough in my therapy session. "So then, what would you do with your life?"

Wow. Now that was a loaded question. I hadn't really put much thought into that. I kept thinking about this inheritance as a chance to rescue me. "Maybe I'd do something crazy, like open my own bakery, or have another go at a party business."

"If you don't mind me asking, what happened to Jillian's father?"

"The curse of a small town."

He looked confused.

"I grew up in a place where everyone knew everyone else's business. Same folks at church, at the grocer, from elementary to high school. You get to a point where you want to escape. You feel like you're missing out on the rest of the world. My uncle never had much money. Worked at the lumber factory. We never traveled out of the state. So, after high school, I met this man from the city. Todd. You have no idea how foreign he was to me. A date in Plumview consists of nachos and root beer at the bowling alley. This fella came along wining and dining me. I was swept off my little small-town gal feet, and moved to Charlotte."

I shoved a half of dozen marshmallows on the skewer, mainly because it was a stressful topic. "Long story short, I met Todd in February, got married that fall, and was pregnant by winter. Things happened way too fast, and he got scared and ran— while I was in labor."

"No way."

"Yep. Todd said he needed some fresh air. And evidently, the nurse that escorted him out of the delivery room, knew just where to find some."

"You poor thing."

I broke off a square of chocolate. "It's my own fault for not getting to know him better before I married him."

"We all get clouded in the area of romance. But, one thing's for sure. Don't you dare blame yourself. He's the jerk, taking off leaving his family. He's the one missing out. You're sweet and funny. And pretty. Definitely, a notch above the rest of the Chandler blood."

I raised my paper cup. "To being prettier and smarter than the other Chandler grandkids."

Cashmere clinked my cup. "All right, here's the plan. We stick together, keep each other safe, and go into Chandler's test with two chances. When one of us gets the top score, we split the inheritance."

As his plan was making me nervous, I skipped the flames, shoving chocolate in my cheek. "In the meantime, we have to take the bull's eye off your back," I said. "You need to let everyone know where you were last night. Kiki's going to spread rumors faster than she could choke down a Snickers bar. What made you run off so suddenly anyway?"

"Don't tell me that you're suspecting me now, too?"

"Of course not."

Cashmere walked over to the nightstand. "I remembered seeing the ride attendant taking a picture of the proposal. I went back to buy the photos for them."

He tossed a stack of heart-shaped photographs onto the blanket. "I also got some of the rest of the gang. Then, on my way back to the limo, I stopped at Chandler's Pantry."

I backhanded his arm. "Without me?"

"Sorry. That's where I got the wine. I got a bottle for Brice and Ashton, too." He gestured back to the nightstand.

I held up a picture of Priscilla and Frankie, the driver. "This one's a keeper."

Cashmere studied the photo and snickered. "Frankie isn't wearing his trademark shades."

I took a closer look. "Yeah and Priscilla's making body contact, without crinkling her nose. Not even a disinfectant wipe in sight."

"Ooh, maybe she's sweet on him."

"Maybe. But, she couldn't have a chauffeur as a boyfriend. Mummy would never approve."

⚬෴ ෴⚬

I started day six, waking up with my cheek stuck to my pillow. Nothing worse than a marshmallow hangover.

"Good morning, sunshine," chirped Cashmere. "Nice do."

I glanced at my reflection in the dresser mirror, noting one side of my hair mimicking a nest. "Ick," I felt the sticky strands. "Why Cashmere, I think I found your secret hair product."

"You wish." He combed through his dark, slick hair with satisfaction.

"I'm going down for coffee," I said. "Do you want me to wait for you?"

"No thanks. I'll be down in just a bit."

In the hallway I found Tessie clutching an overflowing laundry basket.

"Morning, Tess."

She peeked over the dirty heap of towels. "Hi, shug."

I grabbed the basket. "Let me take that for you."

"Well, bless yer heart. This ain't even part of my job, but that lawyer fella went and kicked all the other help outta the house."

"You poor thing. Having to attend to all of us has put a lot of extra work on you."

"I'm fine. And Boris helps me out when those kids aren't lurkin' 'round."

I followed her down to the end of the hall, into the farthest bedroom. My eyes took in the space. "This is my kind of room." I drew in the invigorating scent of rich chocolate and peanut butter in the air. The heart of the room was a brick fireplace with yet another oil painting hanging above it, this one fittingly showcasing dark chocolate chunks surrounded by peanuts in shells and delicately carved chocolate scrolls. The king bed had a masculine feel, dominating the room, with its nutty tan bedspread standing out against the dark chocolate walls. Round and rectangular pillows in shades of beige accented the bed.

The morning sun beamed into the window, shining upon a gleaming bite-sized cobalt package, which rested majestically on the pillow sham, like a glass slipper on its regal pillow. Goosebumps sprouted on my arms. "This is Caesar's room, isn't it?"

Tessie frowned. "Yes, it *was*."

I placed the chocolate on the dresser, while Tessie threw pillows onto the floor.

"I still don't understand why they got on that ride," I said, while tugging the sheets off of the bed and tossing them into a pile.

"I'll tell you why. Cordin' to Boris, Kiki was tauntin' him, and then of course Harley joined right in. You know those kids. If one of 'em got a tattoo of a donkey on their rear end, they'd all follow suit."

"Seriously? Kiki was taunting him to ride, and now she has the audacity to point fingers at Cashmere?" I mumbled, "I gotta get my hands on those papers."

Tessie raised an eyebrow. "What papers?"

"Ashton," I put my fingers in quotes, "*found* some papers inside Kiki's room. Papers with personal information about the grandkids."

"Well let's go get 'em."

"We can't just traipse into Kiki's room in broad daylight."

"The heck we can't. I'll go in for the beddin', while you stand guard outside."

Tessie led me down the hallway. She pointed to the adjacent door. "Okay, this one is Kiki's room. The one next to it is Priscilla's. I've already seen both them gals this mornin' in the kitchen."

I stood in front of the doorway with hands in my pockets, trying not to appear suspicious. Failing miserably. I cocked my head toward Tessie. "How will I let you know if somebody is coming?"

Tessie whispered in my ear, "How 'bout ya imitate the matin' call for an Appalachian Horned Billed Bullfrog?"

"You're messing with me, aren't you?"

She chuckled. "Just make some small talk. I'll hear ya."

I assumed my guard position. "All right then, coast is clear. Roger, Roger. Or, whatever I'm supposed to say."

Tessie left the door wide open, so she could hear me. I peeked inside the mint green room. Wow, one room was more magnificent than the next in this place. The walls were wallpapered with an elegant emerald scalloped pattern that offset the mint green layer underneath. Intricate gold molding bordered the ceiling, matching the doorframe of the connecting bathroom. A golden framed mirror hung on the opposite wall from the bed, stretching over a lit fireplace. How Kiki must relish waking up each morning greeted by her reflection. She had desecrated the beauty of the mirror with selfless graffiti, decade-old magazine centerfolds of herself, contouring her body disgracefully over various hotrods. My eyes retreated to the other side of the room, where Tessie was in Bond-mode. She hastily rummaged through dresser drawers and suitcases.

Bonbon galloped down the hall, pausing at my feet. She sat down, tail wagging like a metronome, and gave me a friendly howl.

Tessie said, "What in tarnation er ya doin'? The crazy toad call?"

"It's Bonbon."

"Just keep er quiet." Bonbon followed Tessie's voice.

"Bonbon, come back here," I whispered. "Here girl." But, she went off sniffing some dirty clothes on the other side of the bed.

Tessie slipped open the bottom of the nightstand. "I think I found them," she said, holding up a large envelope.

My attention diverted to the stairs. I peered over the balcony rail. *Harley, oh shoot.* Before I could motion to Tessie, I heard her screech. *Horrifically.* I rushed inside, where Tessie stood motionless, pointing at the heap of dirty clothes. Meanwhile, Harley had joined us.

The three of us watched, as Bonbon pranced out of the clothes' pile proudly, as if retrieving a fresh catch for her hunter. Clumps of woman's hair hung limply outside of the dog's mouth. Red hair.

I gasped. "Oh my gosh, Kiki."

Tessie fit her hand over her gaping mouth.

I pointed a firm finger at the dog. "Bonbon, drop it," I commanded, as Harley sporadically toed at the pile of laundry.

The bathroom door bust open. "What in the hell is going on out here?" said the very much alive, Kiki, her hair dripping onto the wood panels, clasping a terry towel around her body

Tessie's face turned pale as if she had just seen a ghost.

Harley's expression was more of bafflement. He yanked the clump of soggy hair out of the dog's mouth. And I think all our eyes rose to Kiki's head, scanning it for a bald spot. No bald spots, but her hair was noticeably shorter. I shouldn't have been surprised to learn, that her hair was purchased too.

Kiki wrenched the detachable locks from his fingers. "Do you mind?"

His eyebrows scrunched. "Gnarly. Why's the pooch snacking on your hair?"

"Don't worry about it Harley, just get out of my freaking room. All of you, get out."

We scrambled to the door.

"Wait," said Kiki. "How did that stupid dog even get into my room? My door was closed."

"I don't know," said Harley. "I just came when I heard the scream. I figured somebody else bit it."

Her glare moved on to me, and then over to Tessie. "What's your story, Granny?"

"Well, I was just gettin' the beddin'," Tessie explained, nonchalantly slipping the envelope behind her.

"What are you hiding?"

"Nothin'."

Kiki jerked the envelope out of Tessie's hand and tore it open. "Well, well. What have we got here?" She read aloud, "Ronald Caesar Marino. Born in Raleigh, NC. Half-brother to Cashmere blah, blah, blah. Let me jump to the yellow highlighted stuff. Dropped out of high school sophomore year; DUI Clark County, Nevada; charged with assault in Vegas club; served two of five years for check forgery; most recent winnings 3.5 million dollars."

She continued, "Brice Hodges. Drafted to pro ball, salary 2+ million; bum arm (hand written, *right* arm) ended football career; earns over 100k month for commercial residuals, contract with Dudley Diapers."

Harley snorted. "Talk about crap. Get it *crap*, like in diapers?"

Listening to the others' personal dirt, was like driving by the aftermath of an accident. You don't want to look, but you just can't help yourself. Meanwhile, I didn't want to hear what the papers said about me.

"Woah," said Kiki. "It says here that Harley and Priscilla have no blood relation to Chandler."

Harley grabbed the papers from her. "Let me see that." He skimmed through the page, and discarded the stack in the fireplace. "That's a load of garbage. Where'd you get that bogus information, Kiki?"

"They aren't mine," she told him.

"That's funny, cause they're in your room," he said. "I see what's going on here, you're making up lies, trying to force me and my sister out of here."

"I told you, I've never even seen them before. Now can you all get the bloody heck out of my room?" She shoved into the bathroom, slamming the door behind her.

As Tessie and I went into the hallway, Harley said, "Don't let her lies fool you. My sister and I have every right to be here."

Once he was out of earshot, I told Tessie, "At least we have a little bit to go on. Kiki and Harley just went to the top of my radar." I patted her on the back. "Good work, gal."

"Yeah, not too bad for an old lady, except for that little hissy fit. What in heaven's creation was that rat-haired doohickey thang-a-ma-jig?"

"Those would be Kiki's hair extensions."

"Good golly, my first thought was that the dog drug in somethang dead it been keepin' under the porch.

꒰ఎ ꒱

Tessie and I decided that we needed to uplift the spirits in the house. This was Brice and Ashton's last night together in the mansion. With all the drama in the house, Winston thought it best for her to leave.

We met Cashmere in the kitchen and the three of us collaborated to design the perfect engagement cake for Mr. and Mrs. Smoogey-Woogums-to-be. Meanwhile, we filled in Cashmere about the papers.

I sketched the cake plan on a napkin. "I'm not sure if Kiki is lying about the papers," I said. "Regardless, if Harley and Priscilla aren't heirs, they have no business being here."

Cashmere's eyes squinted in thought. "It doesn't make sense. All of us grandkids have the same story. Before we got the invite to come here, no one knew who their natural grandparents were. So, why would Harley and Priscilla be invited to a will reading, if they had no relation to Chandler?"

"They wouldn't," I said.

"My thoughts exactly," said Cashmere. "If you ask me, Kiki is trying to narrow the odds."

"But she couldn't expect that we'd all take her word for it. Not with so much money at stake."

"Are you kidding," said Cashmere. "These greedy people will take any opportunity to eliminate someone from the competition."

"I'd trust a hog with a Ho-Ho before I'd trust that gal." Tessie circled the kitchen, gathering baking supplies and rambling non-stop about the whole escapade in Kiki's room. She would deny enjoying Kiki's company, but the truth of the matter was that the redhead's antics entertained her. "...and do you know what else was in that girl's drawer, next to the papers?" she said. "A jar of red paint."

Cashmere and I looked at each other.

I raised my eyebrows. "And you didn't think to tell us this?"

"Well I shore enough just did." Tessie nodded to Cashmere who was blending butter in the mixer. "I reckon *you* heard me?"

"Tess, that means that Kiki was the one that painted the threat on the theatre curtain," I said, stating what I thought was the obvious.

"Humf. Well, so it does. Nice work, hun."

Could Kiki really be the one behind all of this terror? She did have an argument with Jasper on the day that he died. And she was in his tour group at the factory. She was also with Caesar when he had his so-called accident. And now we find this evidence in her room. But, even with all of that, something seemed out of sorts. I venture to say that this family of strangers had a lot of secrets. And I was going to do my best to dig them out.

The three of us made a pact to keep our suspicions of Kiki to ourselves so we could keep an eye on her without her being aware. In the meantime, we'd try to keep the rest of the heirs calm, and more importantly together. Safety in numbers.

Cashmere and I invited Tessie to join our plan to share the inheritance. We all agreed that we'd rather share the fortune, than have the famous factory get into the wrong hands. And three heads were better than one.

After the cake was baked and cool, I volunteered to do the decorating. I molded two cartoon-like birds in a nest. The larger was mustard yellow with big gushing green eyes, the other bright pink with a Tweetie shaped head, big blue dreamy eyes and elongated curled lashes. The boy bird hid a half cracked eggshell under its wing. It held in place a sugared diamond ring, that wasn't much exaggerated from the size of Ashton's actual rock. The pedestal below the nest read, "Will you canary me?"

Cake decorating was therapeutic. Before I was married, I had spent summers at my Aunt Libby's house in Orlando taking pastry classes. I hadn't taken any since I became pregnant with Jillian. But I had picked up quite a knack for cake decorating. I actually took my trade and turned it into a kids' party planning business last year. I had the determination and the skill to run a successful business, but evidently not the luck. Something always went wrong. Majorly wrong. Like the teddy bear picnic at Mayor Stilskin's house. It started off as a classy affair with guests lounging on white blankets over manicured lawns, while children sipped honey suckle snow cones, and an orchestra lulled *Teddy Bear's Picnic* in the background. Then a graceful bumble bee fairy rose out of a field of helium flower balloons, carrying a cake, making a beeline to the birthday boy. Only the bumble bee fairy was me, and perhaps I wasn't so graceful. Because next thing I knew, the orchestra's tune changed to *Flight of the Bumblebee*. The sprinklers burst on, which prompted the birthday boy's dog to sprint out of who-knows-where, taking me down— wings and all, and devouring the fudge-filled, hive-shaped cake. The day ended with my stinger stuck up Toby's nose and Skippy having his stomach pumped. Good times. A normal person would have quit at that moment. But, I was determined and gave it one more shot. One more stupid shot. I showed up at the mayor's nephew's party in a material lacking, Zula the warrior princess ensemble. What I didn't know was that his nephew was twenty-five, and expected me to be arriving *inside* of the cake. And that was the end of my party planning business.

After that, a project like this was a mere, well, piece of cake.

"I need to go grab something," said Cashmere. "I'll meet you guys up at their room."

The moment the kitchen door closed, Tessie pulled a folded paper from her apron pocket. "Good, he's gone," said Tessie.

My eyes squinted in confusion. Cashmere was our ally.

"I've been waitin' to getcha alone," she said. "Member all the hoopla in Kiki's room 'bout them papers?"

I nodded.

"Well, one of them made its way under the bed."

"Please don't tell me it's something horrible about Cashmere."

She unfolded the paper and handed it to me. It was a photocopy of an old check. *Old*, as in twenty-five years old. The check was made out for one hundred thousand dollars, signed by Chandler himself. "I don't understand," I said. "What does this have to do with anything?"

"Take a gander at the name."

I stared at the print several seconds. "It's made out to Rusty Clementine." I swallowed. "My father. But, why? How?"

"Can't say I rightly know."

I rubbed my temples. "I lost my mom when I was four, then went to live with my father, Rusty. A couple weeks later, Rusty brought me over to my Uncle Wiley's house. Uncle Wiley was supposed to babysit me for a few hours. Only, Rusty never came back. I've always kept a story in the back of my head about him having an accident. The concept of him dead, was easier to take than abandonment. But the truth was, I didn't know if the man was dead or alive." I calculated years in my head. Damn. I didn't want to admit it aloud, or at all, but odds were Rusty Clementine didn't die twenty-five years ago. Nope, my father had abandoned me with 100k stuffed in his pockets.

I wasn't sure if I was happy or mad at the prospect of my father being alive. As a parent, I couldn't comprehend how he could walk away from his child. And to add fuel to the fire, he must have known about our connection to the Chandler family. My life could have been totally different. But why would Chandler pay him that kind of money? Maybe he was an awful person, and Chandler was paying him to stay away from me. Or, maybe it was an investment of some sorts. Or, a payment. Nothing really added up, except the fact that he had left me.

Cashmere cracked open the kitchen door. "Hey, you guys coming?"

Tessie rummaged through a drawer, pulling out dainty floral cloth napkins. I held the cake, while the three of us marched up to the third floor.

Cashmere knocked on the double door. "Anybody home?"

The door opened, exposing a creamy white chocolate wonderland.

Brice greeted us, then turned his head to holler to Ashton. "Babe, we've got company."

Ashton bounced out of the closet, sprinting to Cashmere. "Oh sweetie, how are you hanging in there?"

"I'm fine," Cashmere said to her. "But, we're not here to mourn, we're here for you guys." He held out a bottle of Chandler's Chocolate Port. "We never properly celebrated your engagement." I presented the cake and we wished our congratulations.

"OMG," said Ashton. "That's like the cutest cake ever." She placed the cake on a coffee table in front of a white velvet couch in the adjoining room. "Come on you guys, have a seat."

Tessie and Cashmere sunk into the couch. I enthralled by the decor, had a look around. It didn't feel like I was in a room in the antiqued mansion, more like the presidential suite in a luxury hotel.

I stepped through the exterior French doors to the balcony. The view overlooked the pool, with tranquil mountain peaks in the distance. I got sucked up in its beauty, watching a bird escape into the clouds. Free from terror. Free from monetary attachments.

Tessie probably nearing her Ashton-tolerance-meter, tore me away from my momentary peace. She hollered, "Well, we gonna eat this thang, or what?"

I joined the others in the sitting area. Tessie already had the cake sliced and plated.

"Cashmere, I still can't believe what happened to your brother," Ashton said, in between bites. "Are you going home?"

Brice interrupted, "I think we should all high tail it out of here. Everyone keeps saying these deaths have been accidents. Three since we've been here. I don't like the odds."

Ashton worked her puppy dog eyes. "Brice, they could be accidents. The others were right there with Caesar. And the driver died of a heart attack. We can't throw away this opportunity on a hunch. I can only imagine what Chandler's worth."

Cashmere tossed his plate on the table. "I don't know how they did it, but somebody is responsible for my brother's death. So, no. I'm not leaving. What, and leave the inheritance to my brother's murderer?"

"I get what you're saying, man," said Brice. "But, someone is out for blood. Our blood." He put his hand on Ashton's thigh, "I don't want to see anyone else get hurt. And rumors are going around that some of these people aren't even real heirs."

I scraped icing and crumb remnants off my plate. "Maybe that's our first step, weeding out the people that shouldn't be here."

"We can't prove anything," said Brice.

I raised my eyebrows. "But, a blood test can."

Tessie piled up the cake plates. "I'll talk to Winston."

"Alright," said Cashmere. "Sounds like a plan. Now let's change the subject. Have you guys thought about your wedding at all?"

Ashton pounced on the conversation, like a tiger on a T-Bone. She tossed a pile of periodicals ornamented with pastel Post-It notes and folded corners onto the coffee table.

"Holy cow, where did you get all of these bridal magazines?" I asked.

"I've been dreaming about my wedding since I was five."

Sure, this was a common fantasy for little girls, but I had yet to meet one that subscribed to *Obsessed Imaginary Bride Today.*

"I figured Brice was going to be busy with all the legal will stuff, so I brought them in case I got bored."

Cashmere glanced over at Brice who was stepping on the stair climber in the connecting room, not even breaking a sweat. "Did you know about her hobby?"

"It doesn't surprise me. She's been talking about our wedding for years. The bigger, the better."

"You better believe it," she said with eyes as big as her diamond ring. "I want something extravagant. The kind of wedding that would be featured in one of these magazines." She thumbed to a dog-eared page. "Now this is a wedding nobody could ever forget. This couple got married in an ice hotel."

"These penguin ice sculptures are gorgeous," I said.

Brice, shook his head. "No penguins. I'm not waddling up the aisle."

"You should pick a location that's special to you both," said Cashmere.

Ashton pursed her lips. "We both like the beach."

I noted a colorful macaw on the honeymoon pages of a magazine. "How about taking it up a notch, and making it more of a tropical paradise?"

Her eyebrows danced up and down. "*Paradise.* Now you've got my attention."

Cashmere obviously just as excited, flopped on the bed in between us.

"What do you think, babe?" Ashton said to Brice, who was now at a slow jog on the treadmill.

"Sure."

She drew a heart around the bird. "Love Birds."

"If you really wanted to focus on the bird theme, you could have grand plume-filled arrangements and sounds of tropical birds chirping in the background," I offered.

Cashmere kept running with the idea. "And for a real show stopper, release some live birds at the end of the ceremony."

Ashton tried to jump right in, "Oh yeah, and I could wear some exotic feathered hat on my head. How cute would that be?"

We all stared at her with vacant expressions, as if she just put a tack in the soccer ball we were kicking around.

"You'd look like a showgirl," said Cashmere.

"Or, something from Dr. Seuss," I added.

Tessie looked at her blankly, "You'd just look plumb *stupid.*"

༄༅ ༄༅

Whewf. Socializing with Ashton was exhausting. Tessie and I unwound in the parlor with a cup of tea. And scones. And dark chocolate dipped cookies. I could get use to this daily indulgence. Afterwards, we split ways. She sought out Winston, while I did some studying in the pantry. The more Chandler products I could learn about, the better. And putting my focus on chocolate, got my mind off of fear.

Later that evening, we revisited our positions around the meeting table. It was hard to believe we had been here a week, but even harder to fathom the idea of another week to go. Although I was eager for the days to dwindle, I wasn't feeling prepared for a test. On mystery material.

Winston called the meeting to order. But before he could speak, Cashmere took a step in front of him, fulfilling his own agenda. "Someone here killed my brother. My first instinct was to get the hell out of here, but my sadness has transformed into rage. So, I'm not going anywhere. There's no way I'm letting my brother's murderer become one of the wealthiest people in the world."

The others mumbled to one another. Cashmere continued, "We're all here for the same thing. To win Chandler's factory. But the reality is that only one of us will walk away with it. I propose we take the competition out of this." He raised up a paper that he, Tessie, and I had already signed. "By signing this paper, you will agree to share the inheritance equally with the others. If everyone signs, the killer's motive is gone, and nobody else gets hurt."

With some skepticism, most were in agreement. The Wellington siblings, Harley and Priscilla, were not. Guess they were willing to take their chances. Their greed seemed a bit skewed, especially since the house had been questioning their bloodline today. Not to mention, neither of them had superior knowledge of chocolate— particularly the girl that had a phobia of it. Their loss.

Winston took back the meeting. "It has come to my attention that documents have surfaced discrediting some of our guests as qualified heirs. Therefore, all potential bloodline-heirs will be required to provide a blood sample. I urge everyone to cooperate, to alleviate all the rumors bouncing around the house.

⊷◈ ◈⊶

Day seven began with the discovery of a perfectly penned invitation, scripted in calligraphy, tucked halfway underneath my door.

*TEN dinner guests are cordially invited
to an engagement dinner
in honor of the lovebirds,
Brice and Ashton*

Meet in the foyer at 6pm
Dinner Attire Requested

We all got gussied up in our mansion best, following our dazzling host to his top-secret dinner party location. I trailed behind the group, following the lingering scent of Cashmere's aftershave. As we strolled through the winding walkway lined with manicured bushes, I scoped out the others ahead of me, realizing we all had a different interpretation of the phrase, *dinner attire.* Priscilla's patent sling backs, Kiki's peep-toe pumps, and Ashton's satin fuchsia, rhinestone trimmed sandals strutted themselves up the flagstone pathway. Meanwhile, I not so gracefully, held up the bottom of my cotton peach and brown potato-sack of a dress, exposing my sensible leather sandals, feeling like Holly Hobby on a catwalk. I certainly hadn't packed for any formal affairs. And that was the only excuse I was providing anyone for my style woes.

If I was going to be honest with myself, my closet was filled by my favorite stock boy, Clearance. I couldn't imagine walking into a store and buying an outfit just because I liked it. These cousins reminded me of some of the gals I grew up with, their mamas dressing them in all the latest trends. My uncle surely didn't have a clue about fashion, nor the wallet for the mall, so took me shopping at the downtown thrift shop. I didn't mind it so much, as most of the things were almost new. But, my attitude changed at Myrtle Washington's funeral, when I showed up in a long, lace black dress with matching hat and gloves. My arch-rival, Bitsy Barker, was quick to spread rumors that I had returned from the dead, rising as local legend, *The Weeping Witch of the Willows.* Not the most respectful outfits to wear to the funeral of the town's oldest citizen. How was I supposed to know it was someone's retired Halloween costume?

We made our way up the stone stairways that led to a landing, offering a postcard view of the Smoky

Mountains. Directly below was a lake, where satin waters blushed under the setting sun. Not a soul in sight for miles. So tranquil. Yet, so alone. No cars passing by to hear a cry for help. No snooping neighbors next door to observe suspicious activity. No witnesses.

I took a deep breath. I had to stop inventing paranoia. There were enough natural occurrences to fill my emotions. I would enjoy the dinner, the stellar scenery, and the conversation of relatives.

Our host had created a table-scape that would make Martha Stewart flush. A fanciful table of fine china and silver was nestled in a blooming arbor, setting the ambience for a night of mountain-side elegance. A ceiling of lavender wisteria flourished above us, sure to transpose Ashton's already fantasy-filled head into a lavender cloud.

Cashmere insisted that the evening would be hosted by him, and him alone. The plan was simple, we were going to keep all the heirs together, and therefore safe, while keeping an eye on all of them, especially Kiki. And none of us were going to sputter the word, "murder". We would learn more about the killer's playbook, under natural conditions.

Our host held out a wicker chair at the head of the table for the guest of honor and pushed her taffeta pink draped knees under the lilac tablecloth. Only Ashton could get away with a Pink Panther colored strapless dress, cinched at the waist with a bow the size of Texas. It was the bridesmaid dress from hell that no woman in her sober mind would ever purposefully wear. But, somehow Ashton with her Polly Pocket figure, managed to get away with it. Ashton's face glowed in the reflection of the silver candelabras, most likely gazing in delight at the thoughtfully arranged baskets of fresh flowers, no doubt cut directly from the garden and arranged by our host himself.

Kiki pulled out the vacant seat in between Frankie and Harley.

"Priscilla was going to sit there," Frankie told her.

Harley interrupted, "Nope, afraid not. Because I was saving this seat for Kiki."

Kiki's smile rose almost as high as the slit on her dress. While she shimmied into the chair, Priscilla backhanded her brother in the back of the head.

After everyone was seated, grandkids and employees alike, Cashmere assumed the role of the waiter. Smashingly dressed in a black jacket with a satin plum skinny tie, he circled the table, distributing frozen cocktails to his guests. Afterwards, he raised his own pink-filled glass, trimmed with glittering rosy sugar, into the air. "Tonight is about love and new beginnings. It's not about the last couple horrific days filled with these gruesome accidents. Tonight is about this gorgeous couple." He addressed the pair, "Brice and Ashton, in honor of you two lovebirds, I present to you a *Frozen Flamingo*. May your lives together, always be *tweet*."

I slurped up the frothy concoction, ready to buy whatever Cashmere was selling. First off, the drink, which kind of tasted like a Bubblicious flavored Margarita. Surely, right up Ashton's alley.

Cashmere moved behind me. "I gave Kiki a triple. If we get her zonkered, maybe she'll talk."

Brice stood up. "Awe thanks, man. This is awesome," he said, quite stylish in a white button-down shirt and navy blazer. He added, acknowledging the rest of the guests, "And thank you all for sharing this special occasion with us."

Tessie sat next to me, in a purple floral dress, matching hat, and white gloves (which promoted her dressy clothes to Sunday best status). "That gal is gainin' herself a good man. Good golly, have you had a look at that boy's choppers?"

"Pardon me?" I asked not attempting to translate the women's self-defined southern language.

"My mama always told me when choosin' a man to take a goosed-eyed gander at his teeth. Sort of like buyin' a horse. You can tell by those perfectly lined milky slabs, that he's a good catch."

"Yes, the man's teeth naturally sparkle as if he's doing an ongoing toothpaste commercial, but it's not like he's competing at the Westminster Kennel show."

Tessie ignored my words, savoring the pampered attention of the temporary help. Cashmere unraveled her swan-shaped purple napkin in one swift fling and delicately laid it over her lap. Why if I didn't know better, I thought her cheeks were getting a wee bit flushed. Either from the attention, or perhaps the booze.

Her words gushed, "Well isn't this just a lovely affair? Our boy really knows how to throw one humdinger of a shindig." Tessie helped herself to a linen-lined basket, pulling out a partridge-shaped, hard crusted wheat roll. She inspected it for a few seconds. "Hmm, freckled bread. Mighty interestin'. Shug, you see the butter?" she said to me.

I glanced around the table and passed her a miniature porcelain plate. "Here, try this. It's an olive spread."

She crinkled her nose. "Looks like beetle poop."

I swear, sometimes this woman was more difficult than my four-year old. I scooped some on her spoon to give her a better look. "It's just olives, capers, lemon juice—maybe some anchovy paste."

"I don't eat beetle poop and I don't eat squashed goldfish."

"Anchovies," I corrected her.

"Whatever fancy name ya want to give it. It's ground up fish guts, and I'm not eatin' it."

"Seriously, this coming from the woman who eats pig feet?"

Tessie's eyes plastered to Kiki. "Speaking of pigs, anything suspicious goin' on with the ol' gal?"

Kiki sat across the table from us, falling out of yet another tube-sock of clothing. "You talking about me again, Granny?"

Tessie flicked the spoon of black mush off of her spoon, making its landing in Harley's crystal water glass. "I was just sayin' that this here fancy dinner reminded me of you dear," she said, while eyeing the grainy glob now floating in the oblivious man's beverage.

Kiki diverted her attention to the man sitting next to her, cleverly avoiding a slander in disguise. Poor Frankie was in the wrong seat. The man had the physique of a linebacker, yet viewing his round baby face, which was usually hidden behind his Men in Black shades, he eluded an innocent presence about him. As big as he was, his head and appendages didn't seem to scale with his over-grown hands and feet. Kind of like a puppy that hasn't quite grown into its big floppy ears yet.

Kiki dropped her pole into the water. "So Frankie, you seem to have a very important job. Tell me, have you ever chauffeured around any celebrities?" She stared deep into his pupils with glassy-eyes, as if attempting to hypnotize him.

I believe the cocktail was kicking in.

Frankie seemed a bit uncomfortable. "No. Um, well, Chandler— I suppose he was a celebrity."

She put some bait on the hook, slanting her body in his direction, showing off her Jessica Rabbit red number, undoubtedly trying to get the naive boy's attention. She gave a flirtatious laugh. I could tell it was fake because it was the first time she laughed and didn't sound like a tuba player falling into a pothole.

"A candy man isn't a celebrity, silly," she said to him.

"You mean, chocolatier. That would be the correct term," he said to her, presumably un-phased by her flirting.

I wasn't sure of Kiki's ultimate motive. Was Frankie her next boy toy, or her next victim? I tossed him a life raft.

"Hey Frankie. Thanks again for helping me out with that *Cocoa Nuts* game. I couldn't have gotten past level three without you."

Frankie went directly into video game mode. "Now remember, when you get inside the chocolate factory, you want to collect all the Sweet Bitter Bonker Bars. If you collect one hundred of them, you'll get a free life."

In this mansion, a free life could come in handy. I smiled and nodded as Shades rambled random game secrets, glancing briefly over to make eye contact with Kiki. She nodded to me, non-verbal girl talk for, *it's on*, while her palms pushed up her bra cups until her dress overflowed with vanilla scoops. Desperate. But, Good Humor.

Cashmere returned to the table to serve our first course. He whispered in my ear, "I see Kiki's not wasting anytime trying to work on Frankie. Keep your eye on her." He presented wide-trimmed white bowls centered with velvety golden steaming liquid; the combination of colors cleverly resembling a delicately peppered egg over easy. "This is Summer Squash Soup," he announced, now taking on the role of the personal chef.

It smelt divine. I peered down the table at the pack of horses with heads crouched into the watering trough. Even Priscilla was eating. She sipped in tiny droplets of soup, being ever so careful not to spill on her fashion statement of the evening. She wore a white-buttoned jacket with navy lapels and matching navy skirt. Holding up her napkin, finishing off her airline attendant style, was a puffy red plaid scarf.

Her mouth went upwards into a half smile. "Finally, some descent food," she said.

Tessie said to me, "Ah, what does that gal know? Only food good enough for her, is that in which she slurps up on a silver spoon."

I wasn't going to get in the middle of it, but Tessie did have a point. The poor girl had been so spoiled she never got to experience good ol' cholesterol-filled American food like cheeseburgers, french-fries, and chocolate malts. No doubt, as the latter is typically slurped up through a plastic straw.

I said, "So Tess, I take it you are enjoying the soup, more than the bread dip?"

"Yeah, the color and texture looks like a possum peed on an anthill, but the taste is just fine."

I shook my head, studying the woman's deceiving angelic eyes and cherub cheeks. She had the kind of cheeks you just wanted to pinch, especially when she said something inappropriate.

As if the soup course was a commercial break, Tessie and I with empty bowls, now resumed our viewing of the boob tube. The Black Widow was still spinning her web. Kiki leaned toward Frankie, in close-talker range. He bent slightly backward, clearly not a fan of squash breath.

She suggestively swirled her polished red nail over the condensation on her cocktail glass, as if writing a proposition in finger paint. She spoke to him in her best raspy Mae West voice, "Perhaps you and I can get better acquainted. You could give me a private tour of the back of the limousine sometime."

And there it was. We had to stop this little rendezvous.

Frankie leaned away from her face that was now practically resting on his lap. "I'm afraid that I'm not allowed to use the vehicle for personal usage, which would include tours, errands, and personal travel," he rattled off, as if reading his contract aloud.

Wow. Didn't see that one coming. Hook, line, and sunk.

Boris interrupted the soap opera, "Are we all going to just avoid the white elephant in the room?"

Harley glanced around as if really expecting to see an albino Dumbo.

Tessie put a napkin to her mouth. "Boris, not now."

"Don't hush me, Tessie. I'm a grown man and if I care to speak, I will do so." He spoke to the table, "Now then, which one of you arrogant, pompous, greedy self-centered children have killed three innocent people in cold blood?"

The table was so silent, you could hear a bee toot.

"Get off it old man," said Harley. "We're in the middle of a party here. Like the little dude said. We're here for the lovely couple."

And the free booze.

Boris stood. Even with his petite stature, he could be intimidating. "Who in their right mind, has a party after three people have been murdered? Are you all off your rockers?"

Bless his tick-tocking heart, our waiter, Cashmere, had perfect timing, interrupting the battle of Boris. He put on his charming table side smile. "To keep with the lovebird theme for the evening, I will now present your main entree. Please enjoy." He graciously presented silver domed dishes to his guests of honor.

Ashton trilled, "Oh, I just love surprises. This is like so much fun."

Yeah, fer sure.

Cashmere removed the lid from the plate.

Vapors rose up to Ashton's elated face. The steam evaporated, and she poured out her heart to the chef, so he would know exactly how much she appreciated his offering. "You murderer! How could you?"

"What? What did I do?" said Cashmere flinching, as if he was afraid she was going to whap him one with a candlestick.

Boris assessed the situation with raised eyebrows. Perhaps, his harsh speech was more persuasive than he anticipated.

Ashton glared down at her plate, sniffling. "How could you serve such a thing?"

"It's just a quail," Cashmere said, shrugging his shoulders.

"It's just a baby— is what it is. With its wee little wings and teeny tiny little frail quaily-legs." She wiped her frowning mouth, threw down her napkin, and left the table. "You're a monster."

Brice did his best to remedy the situation, calling after her, "Sweetie, we'll bury it. We'll give it a funeral and everything. Sweetie?" He sighed heavily, and shook his head watching her disappear down the pathway.

"Way to go, Cashmere," said Harley. "Hey, maybe for her birthday you can surprise her and barbecue Bambi on a rotisserie."

"Oh Brice, I'm totally sorry," Cashmere said to him.

Brice reassured the chef, "Don't mind him, it's not your fault, man. She'll get over it." He dug his fork into the succulent meat and said with a full mouth, "Mmm, it's delicious." Then quickly added, "And I'll kill any of you that repeat those words to Ashton."

"My, my, Mr. Hodges," said Boris. "I see you're quick to threaten people."

Brice gave the old man a mock punch in the arm. "Boris, come on now. You *know* I'm kidding. And seriously, would you want to be on her bad side? She may be tiny, but her wrath can be explosive."

"Point taken," Boris said satisfied.

"I can't believe it. More edible food," raved Priscilla. She said to her brother, "Harley, have you tried the vegetables? They're delicious."

Tessie smiled widely. "It's actually kale and okra. I'm glad you're enjoyin' it so much dear."

Priscilla's upright mouth slowly flattened. She stopped chewing her food and swallowed what was left in her mouth whole. She put down her fork. "Are you saying, *you* cooked this?"

"Just the greens."

"Well, they're— good," she said hesitantly, as if suddenly suspicious.

"The key is to use lots of lard and my old trusty Berta," Tessie said.

"Something tells me that I don't want to know who Berta is."

"Awe, Berta is my iron-skillet. I haven't washed 'er since the day I got 'er."

"Please tell me that that day, was today."

Tessie laughed. "Oh heavens, no. Berta and I go way back." She stared up into the air as if to calculate. "I reckon that the ol' gal is 'bout thirty-four years old, give er take a decade."

Priscilla's face was turning a bit pale.

"All those years of cookin' chitlins and ham hocks builds up some mighty fine flavors. There's just nothin' like it."

"I have to go now," said Priscilla with a sudden urgency, her napkin seeming to act as a cork on her parted lips.

Boris spoke up once again, presumably noting that he was rapidly losing his audience. "So, anybody going to stand up and own up to their actions?" dared the old man.

"Good heavens mister, you going to start on us again?" said Harley. "Just let us eat our dinner in peace, Dude."

"Maybe all of you *dudes* can just sit by and do nothing, and wait for the next person to be picked off. But, not me. I'm going to keep my eyes open and send one of you to prison where you belong."

Kiki said, "Maybe they really were accidents. And you're ruining our night, accusing innocent people."

The old man's eyes bulged, and I flinched. "Three." He raised boney fingers for emphasis. "Three deaths since you hoodlums arrived. Accidents? No, I think not."

Kiki threw back her wine. "Okay, let's say for a second you're right, and they were murdered. Who's to say it wasn't you?" She glanced to Tessie, "Or one of the staff?"

"That's preposterous," he said.

"Is it?" she mocked. "Because I think it's *preposterous* to accuse the grandchildren."

Boris' face turned purple.

This wasn't going well. We needed to keep everyone calm and on the same side. Which meant we needed another party to blame. "Boris, is it possible that an outsider is responsible?" I said.

"Do I look like Columbo, young lady?"

Kiki laughed, her genuine banana seat Schwinn horn honk.

"Well think about it. Is there anybody else— family, friends, old flames that would be entitled to part of the inheritance?"

Boris stroked his tidy mustache as to actually consider my question. I was just offering a distraction, but may have stumbled on something accidentally.

"Let's see," he pondered. "I really didn't know much about Chandler's family. Never even knew he had kids, let alone grandkids."

"Did he have any siblings?"

"Just one. A brother named Homer. But, they weren't on good terms. Homer's been trying to get Chandler to sell out to him for decades. There's no way Chandler would leave him a filthy penny."

"You never know. It's apparent that he wanted to leave the business in the family and this was one family member that he actually knew."

"Nah, he despised the man. I'm telling ya, count Homer out."

I heard the words, but scribbled down Homer's name on my mental list. At this point in time, nobody could be counted out.

Boris stood. "Enjoy the rest of your evening. I'm going to go lock myself in my room."

Without warning, Harley sprayed like a garden hose, releasing a stream of gritty liquid onto Brice's white oxford shirt.

"What in the heck is this?" said Harley, wiping his tongue with his napkin.

"Oops," mumbled Tessie, no doubt recalling the misfired flick of beetle poop.

Brice looked down to his shirt. "What's wrong with you, man?"

"I don't know. I think pretty boy put bird crap in my water glass, sticking with his twisted Tweety bird theme."

I was glad Cashmere didn't hear that; he would have been devastated.

Harley and Brice both decided to call it a night. The crowd was disappearing faster than Yodels in my pantry. So much for our plan of keeping everyone together. I tried to salvage what was left of the evening, soaking in the scenery. The sun resembled a symmetrical fireball, as it began its evening farewell behind rows of ridged terrains, each layer getting progressively lighter as they faded into the nectarine sky.

Kiki pursed her scarlet wide-mouth bass lips and batted dreamy eyelids at Frankie. She said to him, "So then Frankie, can't you make an exception to the rule? It's not like anybody could fire you. Plus, you seem like you could use a little bit of fun." She pulled up the slit on her dress to her mid-thigh and crossed an exposed leg over in his direction. "So, what do you say? Just this once, break the rules and give a pretty girl a ride she'll never forget."

"No can do. Sorry, *mam*." Yuh oh. Dream boy just used the *M* word.

Kiki's face went pale, her fish lips parting in an 'O'-shape. She grabbed the closest carb, shoving it into her mouth that she seemed unable to shut.

Cashmere approached the foot of the table with an over-sized covered platter. "Where did everybody go? Are they all in mourning over the stupid stuffed quails?"

"Nah, don't worry about them," I said. "Dinner was delicious."

"Bless yer heart," said Tessie. "Can hardly wait for dessert."

Cashmere fumbled around. "Shoot, where'd my lighter go? I had it right here."

Kiki sighed, as she dug into the deep valley of her sequined dress, pulling out her lighter and tossing it on the table.

Cashmere said, "Hope you saved room for chocolate cake." He placed the platter in front of Kiki and Frankie. "Kind of anti-climactic at this point." He raised the silver dome. "Dessert is served." In a quick motion he splashed dark rum over white peaks of meringue and lit his masterpiece on fire.

Before the "Oohs and awes" could escape my lips, my brain processed the scene before my eyes. A pair of angelic, pure white doves, beak to beak, sent by the heavens— were with one spark, flambéed to hell. The flames rose onto Cashmere's sleeve, traveling up his arm, onto his chest.

Like a magician, Frankie yanked the linens from the table in one swift motion. He smothered Cashmere with the cloth, tackling him to the ground. The fire was out, but my poor friend was moaning in pain.

Frankie hollered, "Call 911", as he brought an ice bucket for relief.

Twenty minutes later, Cashmere was on a stretcher, and we were all being questioned. Again.

A police officer confiscated the lighter as evidence, but marked it off as an accident. "A man douses a cake with flammable liquid. The cake bursts into flames. Sounds like user error, to me."

I wasn't buying it.

The police left. Leaving the group silent. Soot still lingering in the night air. I broke the silence, "You all know, this wasn't an accident."

Harley moaned. "Here we go. Boris recruited one."

"Good golly, Harley. Our cousin, nearly burnt up into flames."

"That's because he didn't know what he was doing. Pretty boy was trying to act all cool, and it *back-fired*." He laughed at himself.

"How can you possibly make a joke about it? I'm telling you, this was a deliberate act of violence. Just like all the others. And I'm betting, that stupid box will be showing up some time soon."

Frankie tossed it on the table. "It already has."

"What's with you guys and the dumb box of candy?" asked Harley.

"It's someone's sick way of keeping score. Every time someone leaves the house, their candy disappears."

Harley laughed. "You seriously think that?"

"See for yourself," I said.

He flicked open the lid.

"Let me guess," I said. "There are four pieces missing?"

"So?"

I pointed to the empty candy paper. "I bet this one belonged to Cashmere. Read it."

"Fruitcake. Ha, isn't that the truth?"

Idiot.

Frankie said, "Why don't we just get rid of the box?"

"You can't," Kiki told him. "These people will come after you with pitchforks. Remember when they tried to push me out the door the very first day? Ruthless."

"Unless we all agree," I offered.

"Go ahead," Harley dared me, putting the kibosh on that idea.

I spoke to the rest of the table. "You guys, we're risking our lives to be here. It's not worth it."

"Then, I guess it's time for you to leave," Harley told me.

"You know what? That's exactly what I'm going to do. And I suggest if you all value your life, you'll do the same."

◦◦◦

I threw clothes into my suitcase, in between bursts of tears. Until the tears flooded my eyes. I made my way to the shower, allowing the beams of water to strike me in the face. Numbing my skin. Numbing my soul. No more tears. Just hollowness. I stayed until the water changed from scalding, to lukewarm, to frigid. I didn't notice the temperature change so much, until icy shivers snapped me out of my trance. I dried off and hugged myself into my robe. I needed to get myself together, so I could get out of here first thing in the morning.

I scooped up the clothes in the bathroom and brought them over to my suitcase, not expecting a visitor. "Hey Bonbon. Whatcha doing here, girl?" I got to my knees and gave the dog's fur a therapeutic rub. When I got to her neck, I noticed something tied to her collar. A gift box with an envelope. I unsealed the envelope. "Bonbon, how in the world did you get this?" It was a photo of my daughter, playing on her tricycle, taken in front of my house. Handwritten words said, "I'll always be there for my precious niece."

I couldn't imagine how Uncle Wiley had found me. But, it didn't matter. It felt so good to have a connection with him right now. He didn't have to reassure me that he'd be there for Jillie. I always knew he would. But, it was comforting to read the words. I wiped the tears with my arm, noticing the words on the back. "Pinky promise." I giggled through tears. Jillie must have taught him that one.

I opened the little box. Removed the lid. Screeched. And instinctively threw the box. It sprung up into the air with

131

the release of my gasp. Everything happened in slow motion. A severed pinky finger tied off with a pink bow, flew through the air. Bonbon leaped up and chomped down on it, like a gator capturing a passing prey. "*Nooo—*" I wrestled Bonbon down, trying to negotiate with her. But, she wasn't giving up her horrid prize. Lying on top of the dog, I was finally able to pry her mouth open, only to find soggy, mushy remnants. The finger was a fake. My guess, fondant.

Why? Why would somebody play this morbid prank on me? I looked to the box for clues. There was a folded note tucked inside the lid.

"Stay, and keep our correspondence to yourself. Or leave, and go home to an empty house." The next sentence was double underlined for emphasis, "No police!"

This wasn't a prank. This was a threat. A threat I was going to take very seriously. Everyone knew that I lived with my uncle and daughter, so unfortunately, I couldn't cross anyone of my list of suspects.

I felt heat rise from my heart, up to my head. And at this moment, I needed to know my child was okay.

I picked up the phone receiver. Quickly losing patience with the rotary phone. I fumbled in the middle of the number, and had to start again. Confounded thing. Finally, Uncle Wiley.

"Is Jillian okay?" The words burst out in a panic.

"Of course she is. What's going on? It's the middle of the night."

"Sorry, I know it's late. I just had to make sure she was okay."

"She's fine. Oh, and she loved the chocolate bunny you sent her."

Heat rose back to my forehead. No, no, no. I screamed out, "Tell her not to eat it."

He laughed. "Are you kidding? The only thing left is its head."

"And she's okay? Are you sure? You should go check on her." I wanted so bad to tell my Uncle everything that was going on. I wanted to tell him to call the police and rescue me. But, the killer had me in a painful place. They were here with me, yet they still had access to my family. And there was nothing I could do about it.

☙ ❧

Fruity Cream Puff: A tastefully designed parfait, layered with white chocolate, swirls of lemon chiffon, and ribbons of lavish mango-lime meringue.

Chapter Nine

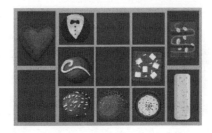

NINE forlorn passengers sought light at the end of the tunnel.

My eyes refused to open. The weight of the week's trauma forcing them shut. My body cocooned by a quilted shield of cotton and batting, rejected the day's itinerary. I would just hibernate in the false safety of my covers.

Only something stunk. As in really bad. Vapors of death smothered my breath. "What, what in the world—" My words were cut off by my gag reflex.

I fought my eyelids open, but they involuntarily retracted into a squint. A silver beehive hovered above me. Oh my gosh, I'm dead. Although, if this was some sort of angel, I had no idea where I'd crossed over to. "Tessie? What the heck are you doing on top of me?"

"Why this here is Mabel's Pickled Possum Jam," she said, as if this was a favorable thing.

I choked in a coughing frenzy causing pickled possum jam to shower its demons upon me. The resulting shriek escaping my lungs prompted her to dismount.

She stood, and tightened the lid on the jam jar. "Works every time. Takes tar off chicken feathers too."

I laid there for a few moments on my back, paralyzed by the fumes of gelled road kill. Nope, definitely not the work of an angel.

"Good golly, gal. Didn't think a freight train could wake ya. Are ya gonna sleep the day away?"

"I would, if I didn't think you'd kill me in my sleep."

Tessie handed me a mug of coffee, and drew the curtains. "Now then, let's get you fed and scrubbed. We got ourselves a busy day. Gonna take us a nice train ride on the mountainside."

"I'm done," I said. "I'm staying here today. In this room. And I'm barricading myself in," to rot. I took a sip of coffee. "And I highly recommend you getting out of here."

She had a seat on the bed. "Listen gal, I put on a shell of an armadillo, but I'm scared too. Matter of fact, I don't think there's a soul in this house, who ain't scared. But this ain't no time for a pity party. You gotta buck it up. Pull it together for Cashmere. Can't go squealin' outta the competition now. What and leave it all to the dickens?"

"But Tess, it's not safe. People have died. Cashmere was on fire for crying out loud. I don't want anything to happen to you."

Tessie let out a big breath. "Alrighty then. Let's get outta here, and let the devil take it all."

"Just you," I said.

She chuckled with sarcasm. "Then looks like we're both stayin' with the sinner."

"But—"

"But, nothin'. I don't got nowhere to go. My home is here. My family is here. And why would I let you stay?"

Crud. She was right. I wish I could tell her about the note and the threat. Without sharing that information, I would never get her to leave alone. Worst of all, it was only day eight. Just slightly over the halfway point.

I got washed and dressed and gave myself a pep talk, that I didn't believe. At least we were going away from the mansion. But, as the past couple of days proved, that didn't mean we were safe.

⋘⊙ ⊙⋙

Frankie drove us to the entrance gates of Chocolate Mountain. Only this time, we skipped the park and headed directly to the train station.

The Chandler Espresso was pristine gold metal, with enough interlocking gears and gizmos to jacket a Steampunk bestseller.

Stepping into the passenger car, was like stepping back into time. A time where one would wear dainty gloves and a large plumed hat, for a mid-day excursion. Speakers above sang Sammy Davis', *The Candy Man,* in a modern techno style.

Tessie and I took seats in chocolate velvet chairs finished off with golden fringe. In between us was a small cocktail table with a Chandler's damask patterned brown table cloth and a lamp plastered into the center of it. Golden pipes intertwined across the walls in a maze, labeled *espresso, milk*, and *chocolate.*

Frankie and Priscilla filled the seats in front of us, although Kiki tried to slither her way in. "Hey Priscilla, I was sitting there."

"No, you weren't," Priscilla told her.

"Well I was going to. So, can you please move it?"

Priscilla pulled bleach wipes from her purse and wiped down the area, like an animal claiming its territory. A very clean animal.

"Find a seat," the attendant told Kiki.

With exaggerated drama, she took a seat across from them.

Tessie whispered to me, "Frankie told me what Big Red is after."

"Oh, I know what she's after," I said.

Tessie chuckled. "Nope, more than that. Ya see, Frankie hand-delivered the test to the notary fella. Dumb gal thinks Frankie had himself a peek. Or, made a copy."

So that's her angle.

A flick to my head let me know that Harley was behind me. I cringed, peering over my shoulder at him.

"Well, well. Look who's still here," he said to me. "You were talking the talk last night. What made you change your mind?" He laughed. "Was it something I said?"

Tessie raised her eyebrows and reached for her pocket. "You want me to take care of this? This here is Mabel's pickled—."

"I know what that is. What are you going to do with it, smear him to death?"

"Heaven's no. Won't kill the lad, just blind him for a few. If you can hold him down, I can smear it under his nose. He'll tear up real good."

"No." Good heavens. Glad she's on my side.

Tessie shrugged and stuffed the ointment back into her pocket.

The train started down the tracks. Before we knew it, we were mountainside, balancing over a valley of endless trees, drifting in and out of passing clouds. Under normal circumstances, the ride would lull me to sleep. But I couldn't relax. I had this constant nagging that something was going to go wrong. And I was keeping my guard up.

After several miles, the euphoric view of the mountainside was interrupted with darkness. The train pushed forward through a tunnel. Whistling. Screeching. The dim lights of the tunnel flickered by, as if counting down to a terrible fate. My teeth clinched, my body involuntarily grasped the seat, like a cat hovering for its life over a tub of water. The darkness going on forever. And then, there it was. In the daylight, approaching at the end of the tunnel, I saw a silhouette coming towards me. Getting closer with every passing light. My heart beats took on the rhythm of the bumps in the train track. *badoom badoompa doom* My stomach fell to my knees. And then, light.

I yelped and found Tessie's hand yielding my scream, as the figure appeared right before us. The interior of the train had transformed into a golden starry sky. And the scary silhouette had transformed into my new best friend.

"Would you ladies care for a hot beverage?" asked the waiter, previously wearing brown, now dressed in a golden pinstriped vest and matching bow tie.

Tessie pursed her lips. "Better make hers a decaf."

I disregarded her, enthralled by the waiter/barista. He parked a trolley of shining, steaming beverage machines that had more gears than the inside of Big Ben. My mouth watered as he served me a Mocha Espresso. I hesitated, momentarily feeling like we were on the Polar Express, half waiting for the waiters to burst out into song and a tap dance. But, this wasn't your kid's cup of powdered cocoa. This was adult luxury. One machine spit out dark espresso, another layered thick chocolate and finished it off with sweetened foamy milk.

I settled into my seat, sipping my mocha. Dunking a fudge biscotti. Hot. Frothy. Not too sweet, but rich and smooth. I could drink this all day. Of course, I'd be a shaky hot mess, but that was becoming my normal state of being.

Twenty minutes later, the train stopped. We departed at Chandler's newest hotel. Chateau de Chandler. Sounded fancy. Sounded French. Quite fitting for a town called Paris Falls.

The surrounding shops and restaurants were representative of other chocolate consuming and producing cultures. Africa, Sweden, Belgium, South America. A tour of chocolate from around the world, right here in the South.

The hotel itself still had a long way to go. We strolled past walls of cement and steel construction, making our way to our destination, *The Cacau Cafe*.

The Brazilian restaurant could be described as chic meets rain forest. Midnight blue starry skies peeked out through layers of canopy up above. Piano lullabies harmonized with soothing rhythms of rain, filled the space. We maneuvered our way through the jungle, expecting at to see a well-dressed Tarzan beating on his chest, swinging overhead.

The group docked at the *Sandbar*. Once again, we were experiencing an attraction before the public, so there were only a handful of employees.

The enormous bar, encompassed the length of the entire room. And was spectacular. It was living. It was an aquarium that glowed a pleasant, neon sea.

We ordered lunch off touch screen menus, while the bartender took our drink orders the old-fashioned way.

I glanced over at Tessie, "What do you want to drink?"

"Well, I don't know. Guess I'll have to take a gander fer myself."

With a week's worth of stress saturating my bones, the whole list of cocktail concoctions sounded appealing. "*Coco Louco, Hammered Hula, Brazilian Shake.*"

Tessie put on her readers, punching random buttons on this foreign object of technology, refusing to take assistance from me.

"You guys going to order?" said the floral vested bartender.

"Confounded thang," Tessie said, while mashing her palm on the touch screen menu. "Yeah, yeah, don't get your britches in a—"

I interrupted, "Yes, we'll have two frozen Chocolate Double Doozies."

"Hey now, I didn't order that," said Tessie.

"It's chocolate. What's there not to like?" I whispered to the bartender, "Light on the booze on that one," I nodded in Tessie's direction, "you know, her heart." She was difficult enough to keep under tabs when sober, I didn't need Granny on a buzz.

Watching the bartender flipping around glowing bottles, was like watching a mad scientist concoct magical potions. He served up a bar full of illuminating glasses with neon froths and smoky mists of nitro.

I slid my drink off the counter. Before I could reach the straw to my lips, Tessie grabbed it out of my hand.

"I didn't fall off the turnip truck just yesterday," she said.

Boy, this gal didn't miss a wink.

I took a sip of my chocolate delight, which tasted more like a Yoo-Hoo slooshie than a cocktail, thanks to Tessie.

The bartender left, and my attention strayed behind the bar. Reptilian and amphibian homes were built within the faux stone wall, red lights illuminating through its cracks.

Harley called out to Boris, from the adjoining Billiards Room, "How about another round of brews?"

Boris grabbed a pool stick off of the wall. "How about I play you for them, son?"

Harley chuckled. "Let's see what you got, old man."

Tessie and I made ourselves comfortable at the bar.

"Sorry about Cashmere," said Frankie, who was sitting in the stool next to mine.

"Yeah, me too."

"I'll put a call in later to the hospital. See what I can find out."

Thinking of Cashmere was upsetting and reminded me why I shouldn't be here. I changed the subject, learning everything I could possibly need to know about video games.

A loud scuffling of balls and wood interrupted our chat. "No way. Bogus," said Harley. He tossed his stick to the floor.

Boris said to him, "That's how it's done young man. Now, if you wouldn't mind, I'd fashion *an Old Fashion*."

"Sounds right up your alley, old timer," said Harley.

Kiki squeezed in at the bar, standing in between me and Frankie. She helped herself to a bowl of cherries, seductively toying with the fruit on her tongue. Little by little she moved in on Frankie. Eventually, Frankie stood up and gave her his stool.

He made his way behind Priscilla, giving her shoulders a gentle massage. Kiki's face paled.

Harley stumbled behind the bar, mumbling profanities to himself. "I don't even know how to make a stinking Old Fashioned."

"My Uncle Wiley drinks them all the time," I said to him. "I can help you."

"I should just mix a shot of everything together. It would serve the old man right."

"It's no big deal," I reassured him. I dropped a sugar cube into a glass. "Now add a couple dashes of Bitters and soda water."

Harley haphazardly poured the liquids into the glass.

Kiki held out a cigarette towards Harley. "You got a light?"

As he pulled a lighter from his pocket, she moved the cigarette in front of Priscilla. If I didn't know better, I would think Kiki was trying to bring attention to his sister's new boyfriend.

Harley paused, staring at Frankie's hands that were touching his baby sister.

I dropped a cherry and orange slice into Harley's glass, trying to divert his attention. "Now mash them down," I told him.

His aqua eyes stayed fixed on Priscilla, while he smashed the fruit with the muddler, like he was hammering a nail into cement.

"Easy boy," I said.

Harley kept on smashing the fruit, while watching Frankie's hands slide down Priscilla's shoulders down to her waist.

"Hey man," Harley told him. "Keep your giant Gulliver hands to yourself."

Priscilla rolled her eyes at her brother. "Get over it, Harley."

Kiki covered her grin with a puff of smoke.

"I get it," said Frankie. "You're protective over your sister." He moved behind the bar, next to Harley, pouring bourbon into the cocktail. "So, what's your story? Anyone special in your life?"

"None of your business," Harley said.

"It's hard for him to talk about it," said Priscilla.

"That's because it's none of his business," said Harley.

Frankie added some ice and gave it a stir. "That's it," he said. "An Old Fashioned."

Harley gave the glass a swirl, took a big whiff, paused, and then chugged it down.

Kiki honked with laughter, "We must be making him nervous talking about his love life."

Harley raised his voice, "Do you really want to know?"

I swirled my straw in my drink, trying to avoid the conversation. Of course, we wanted to know, but obviously it was upsetting to him, and better left alone.

"Let's hear it," said Kiki.

"Harley, you don't have to," I said, picking up on his awkward vibes.

"No, you all want to know so badly, so here it is." He wiped his hands with a towel and tossed it on the bar. "I was married to the most wonderful woman in the world. Rebecca. Life was perfect. She was gorgeous, tall with blonde wavy hair, and sexy as hell. We had it all. We spent all our time at the beach. The sea was our home away from home. For our first anniversary, I surprised her and took her out for a sunset picnic. I borrowed a yacht and took her out in the middle of the ocean. The table was set for two, all elegant-like with fancy food, and romantic music. The whole shabang. After dinner we sat at the aft of the boat, dangling our feet over the water. As we gazed into the stars, I held her close and placed a diamond star pendant around her neck."

"It doesn't get more romantic than that," I said. This was a new side of Harley. A softer side, that was much more like-able.

Harley placed his palm over his heart and sighed. "Rebecca was shivering, so I went into the cabin to get her a blanket." His fingers sprawled out bracing his cheek bones, forming a dam for his watery eyes. "But, I never got to give it to her. When I returned," he pulled up his nose, "She was gone."

"Gone?" I repeated. "Weren't you in the middle of the ocean?"

He blew his nose with a cocktail napkin. "I guess she had too much champagne and—" he took a deep breath, "And fell into the water. I spent all night swimming around the dark ocean searching for my bride."

I walked around the bar and embraced him. "Oh Harley, I'm so sorry. That's absolutely horrible."

"It's still hard to talk about it." He wiped his nose. "And to make matters worse, they never found her body."

Frankie laid a palm on his shoulder, "I'm sorry man."

Harley jerked away. "Don't ever touch me, or my sister again."

Frankie backed off, and Harley walked outside.

The waiter spread baskets and plates of food across the bar. "When you're finished here, please take a seat in one of the party rooms for dessert."

After stuffing ourselves with an entire menu of food, Tessie and I trudged ourselves deeper into the jungle, choosing the Enchanted Rainforest Room. A treehouse was tucked into a massive lit tree in the corner of the room. We fed our childish curiosities, exploring the interactive playground.

Cocoa pods ornamented the tree trunk and branches, offering an auditory matching game. Tessie and I ran around tapping the pods adhered to the tree trunk and branches, trying to match up the tropical rhythms.

"Psst. You down there," a cartoonish, robotic voice said. Overhead, an animatronic three-toed sloth hung out of the tree. "Hi Tess-ie. Hi Ann-a. Can you help me find my friend, Cacau? He's a baby monkey. We were playing hide and seek this morning, and I can't find him anywhere."

We played along, all the while I was imagining the experience through Jillian's eyes. We took a look through the mock telescopes, spotting various rain forest animals. The object was to focus the lens on an animal. Once you saw them clearly, the animal would sound off a natural call, and then would go back into hiding. Unfortunately, we didn't find baby Cacau, as the waiter offered us dessert. Priorities.

The waiter instructed us to go to the ticket window, which served as a large interactive menu. We ordered dessert, which triggered Cacau Falls, a chocolate fountain, flowing liquid chocolate from the waterfall built into the wall.

"Glory be," said Tessie.

I pointed to a party table set in the middle of the forest. "I can't imagine having a birthday party here as a kid." I laughed to myself, the kind of laugh you make when something really isn't funny.

"I remember my tenth birthday. The week before, I had gone to a slumber party at Bitsy Barker's house. News of Bitsy's party traveled through the town, like locust. Guess

Uncle Wiley didn't want me to feel left out, so he threw me a surprise party."

"Ain't that sweet?"

"Far from it. It was the worst birthday ever." I twisted my straw wrapper into angry knots. "At Bitsy's party, we swam in her in-ground pool and had water fights. Afterwards, we played on her swing set, and camped out in tents. At my party, the closest thing we had to a pool, was an old tub my uncle used to fill for the goats. And the extent of party games was shooting cans with BB guns and toad races. Every little girl's dream. My swing set? An old tractor tire hanging from a rope. And Uncle Wiley made a castle for us to sleep in. With sheets. Over the clothesline. Yeah, I felt like a real princess surrounded by the tattered sheets that were barely fit for the mattress, let alone royal walls." I felt the resentment flowing from my mouth. It was years ago, but bottled up, it had fermented.

"Sounds like one humdinger of a shindig."

"Aren't you hearing me? Tess, my birthday present was a homemade dollhouse. With a pink outhouse!" I swore I heard the sloth giggle. I shot him a dirty gaze just in case. "Bitsy said, Barbie didn't use outdoor bathrooms. All the other girls laughed. I was so humiliated, I snuck off inside the house for the rest of the night and cried. Sure, my uncle meant well. But, he just didn't understand how difficult the struggle was for me. The other girls had everything."

"So, you were mad at your uncle because *you* were jealous of the other girls?"

For the first time, I was angry at Tessie. She just didn't understand.

Ding! Ding! A voice overhead echoed, "Please take your seats. Your dessert is now arriving." A little train pushed out of the tunnel. The Mini Espresso. It was a short train. One engine pulling two boxcars. The boxcars paused in front of us. "You may now board the train." We pulled box shaped containers of smothered sundaes from the boxcars.

And, just that quickly I forgot about being mad at Tessie.

Both of us ordered The King of the Jungle, which basically meant we built our own outrageous dessert. Mine was a chocolate brownie sundae slathered with hot fudge, plantain chips, and cocoa nibs. I wish I had skipped breakfast and lunch, because I did not want to stop eating this. Ever.

Tessie's had more of a Southern flair. Chocolate cake, with ice cream, brandied peaches, candied pecans, and caramel.

A screech in the main restaurant, paused me in mid-bite. We had made the connection to high pitched screams and horrific events. Even so, I took a second to shovel an extra bite full in my mouth, as I sprung up from my chair. Wrong, I know. I have serious chocolate issues.

Tessie and I made our way to the bar where Priscilla was squealing and carrying on like a toddler. "Put it back."

Frankie was holding a lizard looking fella, its feet paddling in the air.

"It can't hurt you. Look, no teeth." The critter's red neck bulged out like a limp balloon.

"Just get it away," she said from the far corner of the bar. Her voice was serious and stern, "Franklin, you put that away right this moment."

Franklin?

Harley pulled out a larger, foot-long lizard and placed it on the bar. "Let's race them. I've got my money on this one." Quickly followed by, "Oops."

Evidently, the lizard was quicker than anticipated. And, evidently the lizard was good at camouflaging too. It darted behind the bar and vanished. And we decided we'd better do the same.

⋆⋅☾ ☽⋅⋆

As if I wasn't stuffed enough, Winston steered us to Chandler's Chocolate Emporium. Clearly, our group wasn't going to be the only visitors to this store today, because there were enough confections in the store for hundreds of hungry shoppers. Mounds of handmade truffles and bonbons filled every corner.

The shop was more upscale than the fancy candy boutiques in the big city malls, chandeliers glowing onto glass cases of chocolate gems. Walls were splashed with a pattern of Chandler's traditional brown damask, the ceiling bordered with dripping chocolate that appeared so real, you'd think the walls were melting.

A chocolatier, wearing a tall chef hat, demonstrated the art of tempering, smearing shiny warm chocolate into satin sheets. Another, hand-dipping fresh strawberries, earned my nomination for employee of the month, as he invited us to sample trays of berries. I started with the Cookie Explosion, biting into the hard chocolate shell, coated with chunks of chocolate cookies, stuffed with a surprise filling of cookies and cream mousse. Others were filled with cheesecake, ganache, and Chandler liquors. And yes, I sampled each and every one. And yes, I was about to bust.

"How many of those things are you going to gorge yourself with?" Kiki asked me.

I ignored the stupid question. "Have you tried them?"

"I wouldn't touch them," she said with disgust. "And you've got something there," she said, pointing to a big glop of frosting on my shirt.

Who was this girl? She was usually the one packing her cheeks. I sought out some new company, and perhaps, some new chocolates. Instead, I found the source of Kiki's repulsion. Priscilla and Frankie were standing in front of a picturesque fireplace, drinking champagne and feeding each other plain strawberries. Priscilla giggled as she speared a berry on a fork and fed it to Frankie. She forced a laugh, "Chew with your mouth closed. You're chewing like a cow."

Romance at its weirdest. Poor Frankie.

I waddled back to the train, nonchalantly unbuttoned the top button of my jeans, and gave into the tranquility of the train ride back to the parking lot.

ᦆᦲᧉ ᧉᦲᦆ

Once back at the mansion, I spent the rest of the afternoon in my room, weighted down from the ten pounds of chocolate I had consumed. Meanwhile, my brain took the opportunity to torment me. There was no distraction from my thoughts. No television. No electronics. Just me alone with my memories of the past week and fears of the next.

I had zero appetite, but desperately needed company. Walking downstairs, I became self-aware that I was alone, prompting me to look over my shoulder every other step. Before opening the kitchen door, I took in whiffs of dumplings and gravy. Tessie's doing her magic again. Maybe I have a tiny bit of room left, just for a bite.

I assessed the kitchen population. Or lack of. I said to Tessie, "You're not supposed to be alone."

She looked around. "Huh. And who are you with?"

"Okay, fair enough. We both need to be more careful. What can I do to help with dinner?"

"I've got it under control. Do ya have any ideas for dessert?"

I scoped out the pantry shelf of jarred fruits and jams. "How about chocolate cherry cobbler? It's one of my popular desserts at the diner. Mr. Kimble will eat it three times a day. Mainly because he can gum the cherries. But, it's still real good."

Tessie smiled with satisfaction. "There are fresh cherries in the frig, if ya want to use those."

I gathered canisters of flour, sugar, and Chandler's cocoa, setting them on the island. "So Tess, are we stupid?"

"For makin' cobbler, dear? I reckon everyone will enjoy it just fine."

I gave her a get serious look. "No, I mean are we are crazy for staying on this property? There's a psycho on the loose. I'm a mom. I should be home with Jillie."

"That's such a darlin' name."

"Thank you. It's short for Jillian. Jillian Adeline."

Tessie's jovial rosy cheeks instantly turned pale, her skin like wallpaper paste. Her body seemed to go limp, allowing a bowl to slip out of her fingers, crashing down to the wooden floor.

"Tess, it's not a big deal. I'll sweep it up." I retrieved a broom and pushed it over the worn planks.

"Thank you, dear." She got a new bowl and carried on as if in a daze, her depthless eyes still.

I resumed making the cobbler, melting butter in a saucepan. When the pot was filled with a shallow golden liquid, I mixed in sugar and ruby, sweet cherries. I rinsed my hands and grabbed an iron skillet hanging over the sink. My steps led me past Tessie, who was still staring off into the distance. I planted myself in front of her, forcing her vision on me. "You okay, Tess?"

"Huh?"

"Something is up. I know I've only known you a short while, but I can tell that something is bothering you. Something you don't want to tell me."

Her frozen eyes melted into tears.

"What is it?" I pleaded. "Cashmere?"

"Oh dear." She sobbed harder.

I dragged over a wooden barstool, tapping on its cushion. "Have a seat." I pulled up a stool next to her. "Tessie, listen to me. We are all risking our lives to be here. So, if you know anything, anything at all, you need to confide in me."

"Oh Anna, I really can't get into it."

"Tess, people are *dead*. Don't you trust me?"

"Yeah, you're about the only one, 'specially now, tha' know—"

"Know what?"

Tessie took a deep breath, then slumped her head down. "My daughter's name was Adeline."

I forced my widened mouth shut. "I named Jillian after my mom, Adeline. Which makes you—"

"Yes. Yer grandmother."

"But, how?"

She dabbed her forehead with a dishtowel, then transformed a fly swatter into a self-propelled fan. This was not acceptable.

I got her a clean cloth and wet it in the sink. "Here, put this on your forehead."

She dropped the swatter and cooled her head. A bit of color rose back to her blank cheeks, like water colors dispersing onto a new canvas.

"Better," I said to her. "Now, take your time, and tell me how we've just become related."

"Whewf. All righty then." She continued patting her forehead rhythmically with the rag. "Well, as you know, I worked in the Chandler's mansion fer many years, since I was a teenager. The great Edward Chandler had a son about my age, Ulysses. Yep, the same Ulysses, as in yer grand-daddy. Any who, bein' in that mansion night and day, kept me away from other folks, er fellas, fer that matter. You can imagine, I became quite fond of him. Eventually, we got together, and I got me a rump in the roaster. There was no way Ulysses was gonna tell his father that he was havin' an affair with the help, let alone tell em he was havin' the maid's baby. I couldn't raise a baby in the mansion, and I couldn't afford to quit my job. It was the only thing I knew. The only job I ever had."

"So, you put my mom up for adoption?"

Her remorseful eyes connected deep into my being. "I didn't want to. It was the most painful thang I've ever done."

"I can't believe this. I'm standing here in the middle of the mountains, with my," I hesitated, "Grandma."

"Now don't you go callin' me that. I ain't no ol' biddy."

I wrapped my arms around her and squeezed. "Why didn't you want to tell me? I mean all these years, we could have been in each other's lives."

"I didn't know you existed, dear. There's a house full of kin here, anyone of them could of been my grandchild. I didn't know how many kids Adeline had. Before this ordeal, I didn't even know Ulysses had other children. It wasn't until you told me Jillie's middle name, that I was shore. Now we must keep this to ourselves."

"Why, what does it have to do with anybody else?"

"With the way these folks have been carryin' on, and a killer on the loose to boot, we don't want to give anybody any ammunition. Let's just stick together, ya hear?" And we did just that for the rest of the evening, while we caught up on a lifetime.

ംരുലൂ ളുംൽം

I headed to bed, a familiar sound pausing my steps at the foot of the darkened staircase. Faint cries. Cries flooded with creepiness, from an infant not existent in the house. I froze for a moment, focusing on the direction of the sound. It sounded like it was coming up from the second floor, my floor. I couldn't see much, only the dim light of muted hall sconces up above. I pondered my move only for a moment. Whether the baby was real, or a ghost, I was getting to the bottom of this.

As I climbed the first step, I became aware of the eerie creak in the steps. With every step, another creak, straining the brittle bones of the historic mansion. The higher I climbed, the farther away the cry. Midway up the staircase, the cries became faint. I sprinted the last of the stairs, barely able to hear the baby. As I neared the top, SLAM! A door slammed shut and the crying disappeared.

Kiki and Priscilla came out of their rooms. Cranky and even more irritable than usual, they joined forces and blamed *me* for the slamming door that woke them up.

Too tired to argue, I slammed my own door shut, and called it a night.

The strained cockle of a hoarse rooster disrupted my slumber, my eyes squinting open, taking in a slice of daylight through the rose eyelet drapes. I let out a breath of relief. Besides the appearance of ghost-baby, the remainder of the night was calm. Except for the whale mating calls ricocheting across my stomach walls. I was paying for yesterday's chocolate smorgasbord.

My path veered downstairs, initiating day nine of this nightmare. I did my usual neck-wrenching routine, intermittently checking to see if someone was sneaking up to kill me from behind. As usual, Tessie was already awake and by the smells of it, cooking breakfast for the masses. The smell of food made me nauseated. I didn't want to smell it. I didn't want to eat it. Ever again.

I fought through my queasiness, to grab a cup of coffee.

"Mornin', Grand-baby," winked Tessie. She pointed her frying pan toward the kitchen dinette. "Now have a seat, I'll fix ya right up with some vittles."

"No thanks, I'm not really hungry."

"Nonsense. Gotta keep yer strength up. We got ourselves a busy day."

Yes. A busy day of *eating.* Work staff from the new hotel would be joining us on the pool deck today, sampling menu items from the hotel restaurants.

"Now grab ya a plate."

I should have seen that coming, but I couldn't tell her I wasn't feeling well. Quite frankly, Grandma's healing methods scared me. I pulled napkins from the drawer. "I'm going to go set the dining table." I pushed the connecting door to the dining room open, and cursed to myself. The death box. Posing as our new table centerpiece. I tossed the napkins on the table, and cautiously flipped open the chocolate lid, as if it were going to detonate a bomb, then hightailed back into the kitchen.

"Have you seen anyone else this morning?"

Tessie nodded.

"Well someone's been here, and left that stinkin' box in the dining room."

Tessie placed a palm over her heart. She followed me to the dining room.

"It's different this time," I said. "There aren't any more chocolates missing." It was as if this psycho was just toying with us now. Like hurting people was some twisted game. My first thought was to toss the confounded box into the fire, or at the least hide it. But, I couldn't take a chance with a technicality. If someone saw me do it, I could be forced to leave the property. And I had a feeling there were eyes and ears everywhere.

I paced back and forth until I had a plan. "Here's the deal," I said to Tess. "No more chocolates are going to be removed from the box. We are going to babysit this box of chocolates all day, all night. How many days are left?" I tallied on my fingers. "Four days, four nights. Whatever it takes. The killer isn't going to strike without adding another notch to his or her belt. I covered the box with a silver cloche, as to not gain it attention.

Tessie rattled a rusty triangle up above. "Come en get it."

One by one, my housemates straggled into the kitchen, taking seats around the table.

Brice eyed the kettle full of steaming mush. "What have we got here?"

"This here is what I like to call Hillbilly Hash," Tessie announced proudly. "Now this will stick to yer ribs and then some. It'll do ya right when yer out there swimmin'."

"Priscilla will love it," I said.

"Ah, that gal doesn't know what she's missin' out on. She could do well with somethin'— anythang stickin' to those measly ribs." She scooped a heaping spoonful and dropped it onto my plate.

I hesitated, "Um, thanks." I had to admit it wasn't the most eye appealing food Tessie ever put in front of us, especially when my stomach felt like death.

Tessie must have noticed my hesitation. "Come on, eat up. The mornins' awastin'."

I took a small bite and to my surprise it was tasty. Bits of southern spiced potatoes and crisp bacon aroused my taste buds. But as the grease lingered on my tongue, my stomach said, abort.

Tessie came back to the table with a sizzling iron skillet, plopping a shimmering, wiggly sunny-side up egg on top of each of our plates of hash. The glassy egg stared at me like a one-eyed monster.

And I almost lost it.

While the others ate, I kept my eyes on them. Nobody seemed suspicious about the silver dome in the center of the table. If the culprit was here, they were playing it cool.

After breakfast, everyone went to change into swimsuits, except for Brice, who stayed to help with the dishes. Tessie and I told him about the hidden candy box on the table. He and I took turns helping in the kitchen and guarding the box.

My plan was working. That is, until disaster struck once again. Right in the gut. One of the caterers, a woman in a chef's coat, burst into the dining room. "Quick. We need help out by the pool."

I spoke to her calmly. "It's okay. Just tell us what's going on."

"Someone's drowning," she told me. "And I can't swim."

Cripes.

I hollered in the kitchen to Brice and Tessie. Only Tessie was in the bathroom. Great timing.

Brice followed the woman and told me to stay put.

I told myself, he could handle it. And truly, I believed he could. But, I certainly wasn't going to bet someone's life on it. I had no choice but to abandon my post.

We followed the waitress through a lush maze, through intertwining cement paths that serpentined around the exterior of the pool, like a secret tropical garden. The woman's steps accelerated into a sprint. "Over there," she hollered, pointing to the deep section.

My eyes dove below floating floral wreaths dancing on the water's surface, down to the lifeless concrete. A silhouette of a body lie still on the pool's floor. The identity was hidden in the depths of the water, under the shade of a tree. The body only a blurred image. The person's legs and arms flaring upwards. Fear, panic, and rage attacked my emotions.

Brice dove into the water, shoes and all. Seconds under the water slowed in time. We watched his descent. We watched him swim over to the body. What was taking so long? Maybe the person was stuck, like in a drain. Just as I was ready to jump in, a limp-less body sprung up out of the water like a torpedo. Brice emerged after, a couple feet away, presenting a small boulder above his head. As he approached the edge of the pool, my brain processed the scene. The boulder was holding the body down. The *dummy's* body. Relief and anger battled.

I kicked at the figure floating lifelessly on the water's surface, flinging the life-sized blow-up doll into flight. Brice caught it, and tossed it onto the pool deck.

Twisted, indeed.

The joke would be bad taste under normal circumstances, but surrounded by the aroma of lingering death, it was borderline psychotic. Brice and I inspected the doll's remnants. Beyond cheesy. Its tasteless sailor hat was duct taped on its head, a Popeye neckerchief hung limp around its plastic neck, and handwritten words scribbled across the figure's chest. The black letters read, "Hey matey, wanna buy a boat?"

I looked to Brice. "Good golly. It's supposed to be Harley."

"Harley better watch his back today," said Brice. "Seems like a threat to me."

Well that got the old adrenaline pumping this morning.

I eyed Tessie. "When did you get here?"

"Well, I followed ya out here. All that ruckus. I wasn't gonna miss out on anythang."

♾ ♈ ♾

Mild turquoise currents pulled Tessie and I to the other side of the pool, away from the drama. We followed the river bend that spouted into paradise— a two story waterfall, accentuated with vines of early blooms, rushing water onto refreshed rocks below.

We found a table in the sun. It was unusually warm for March, close to 70 degrees. Which still was a bit frigid to me for swimming, even though the pool was heated. The temperature was hitting the point of day where it was hot in the sun, but cold in the shade.

Tessie was clothed in a lemon plaid dress, shawl, stockings and matching clunky-heeled yellow patent shoes. "I best be gettin' back to the kitchen," she said, while fanning herself briskly with a tabletop menu.

"Oh no you don't, you're sticking with me."

"Whewf child, it's hotter than a pola bear in Joo-lie."

"You could take off the sweater and shoes, then you wouldn't be sweating like a—"

Her pupils narrowed. "Like a what?" she asked, if daring me to say the *K* name. I'm a proper lady. Why, I'd never show my bare shoulders and toes in public."

The woman talks about sex at the dinner table as if exchanging recipes with her lady friends, but showing her toes is improper?

156

Tessie crossed her arms and mumbled, "Can't believe you're gonna make me miss my program. Dixie's deep fryin' pickles today."

"You need to be out here, as well as I do. We may need you to beat this test. Besides, it's not safe to be alone. And you know it."

Brice joined us at the table. "Hey, did you guys move the chocolate box?"

"Oh shoot," I grasped my forehead. "With all of the excitement with that stupid doll, I forgot about it."

Brice shook his head. "Well, it's gone."

And now we wait.

An hour or two later, a team of waiters surrounded the table with platters of freshly grilled food. Beef and pineapple skewers with a cocoa rub, sweet potato wedges sprinkled with a spicy chocolate seasoning, and ribs smothered in dark chocolate barbecue sauce. They left us menus for all the hotel's restaurants. I pocketed them for study material.

"Well maybe I can stick around for a spell," said Tessie, shoving a napkin into her collar.

I was glad to have an appetite again. "Oh my. This is delicious."

Tessie smiled mischievously. "I spose the entertainment ain't too shabby either. Take a gander at who's boarded the hussy wagon."

She pointed at Priscilla, clutched in the bulging bicep of Frankie. His elbow looked like a nutcracker, as if it could squish her fragile body like a peanut with one swift bend. Priscilla, who usually tended to be more modest, was wearing a high cut, white haltered one-piece suit with a plunging neckline that went down almost to her belly button. Elaborate gold buckles mended the two halves of silk-like material centering down her chest, accentuating her protruding ribcage. Unfortunately, her pale skin was not a flattering contrast for the milky material, and the gallant style overpowered her boyish figure. It was kind of like Olive Oil flaunting a Madonna cone-corset. Frankie however, seemed as high as a bee on Posey-pollen, hanging on to her like a kid latched to his blankie. I greeted them with a smile as they joined us.

Frankie wasted no time digging into the platters of food on the table.

Priscilla giggled. "Franklin, you're obviously not going to eat that with your bare hands." She handed him a napkin. "You're not a caveman."

Frankie set the rib down and wiped off his hands.

Priscilla tied the ribbons of a white sun hat under her chin, her blonde twisted updo crowning out the hollowed center, reminding me of those white plastic collars they stick around injured dogs' necks. "It's getting hot out here," she said.

I said to her, "Why don't you go take a dip in the pool, and cool off then?"

Priscilla sat up from her lounge chair, lowering her large rimmed dark sunglasses to the bridge of her nose. I cringed as I sensed a lecture coming on.

"Now you done it," said Tessie. "I knew I should have stayed back in the house."

Priscilla raised her voice, "This bathing suit was not made for the water," she said caressing the smooth fabric with her fingers. "And furthermore, I wouldn't dip my pinky toe in that disease infested chemical pool—"

I glanced over to the sea of sparkling turquoise water, just to be sure we were both viewing the same thing.

"It's a breeding ground for germs, hairs, skin, mold, dust, sand— not to mention human and animal waste. Why anything that could drift through the air or cling to a human body, can float into the pool to make a home."

"Okay then, thanks for giving me that warm and slimy-fuzzy feeling," I said.

"Speakin' of fungus," said Tessie. "Look who's swimming over to this side." Tessie shook her head.

"Wearin' a trampy green bikini, lookin' like olives bobbin' in a martini glass."

Yep, Tessie correctly called that toddy. "Kiki doesn't leave anything to the imagination."

Tessie smirked. "Well she's gotta get er money's worth out of em."

Kiki tossed a towel over her shoulders and headed our way.

"Oh lawdy," wailed Tessie, glancing at Kiki's rear end escaping the overstretched Band-Aid sized cloth. "Looks like somebody's tryin' to squish a moon pie into a bubba gum wrapper."

Thankfully, Kiki seemed to miss that *Southern expression,* distracted by the food, instead of going at it with my rambling-mouthed grandmother who didn't know how to turn off the faucet.

Kiki pulled pieces of steak and pineapple off of a skewer. "Why didn't anyone tell me there was food out here?"

She pointed her skewer toward Priscilla. "Hey, the suit looks great."

The compliment prompted Priscilla's nose to rise up a few degrees. Her head was cocked back so far, she was starting to resemble a Pez dispenser.

Kiki assessed me up and down in my shorts and t-shirt. "Why aren't you wearing a suit?"

Priscilla paid her two cents. "Obviously because of all the junk food she consumes. All that chocolate has gone straight to her hips."

Kiki nodded her head in agreement.

Hello? I'm right here. I peered down in disgrace at my legs. I always thought they were just shapely. My naive tubby body slumped into a sigh. I wiped my mouth and shoved the crumbled napkin onto my empty plate, nonchalantly resting my arms in front of my bloated belly.

Kiki helped herself to more skewers of meat, licking her fingers in between bites. She glanced around, presumably for a napkin, but instead wiped her greasy fingers over the sides of her bikini bottom. "It's getting hot out here." She wiped a forearm over her brow.

"Hey Brice," said Kiki. "Put some lotion on my back."

He scowled.

Kiki shrugged. "What?"

"You're like my cousin or something. That's twisted."

"Good heavens. I'm just asking you to rub some oil on my back, not make out with me. Whatever. Frankie, you do it. You're not family, you're an employee. About to be mine."

Not sure if she meant that he was her employee, or hers for keeps.

Frankie stood, making a face as if he had pulled the short straw.

Priscilla folded her arms and huffed in disgust. I doubted Frankie noted her displeasure, as he waited awkwardly behind Kiki's scantly clothed body.

Kiki stood facing us, seductively gathering her hair tress by tress, to one side in front of her chest. Frankie grasped the bottle of suntan oil, then wiped his palms in his slacks, probably afraid of getting scolded for having dirty hands. He draped his hand in a hanky, twisting off the oily cap.

Kiki huffed with impatience. I could hardly wait to see how he would go about applying the lotion. Oven mitts, perhaps?

Brice let out a thunderous chuckle. He molded his fingers into a square shape, as if taking Kiki's photograph. "Here's one for your photo spread in Dogs Illustrated."

Kiki scowled and self-consciously jetted out a shoulder, jerked back a hip, as if to take on a new improved seductive pose. "And what the hell is that supposed to mean?" Before he could respond, she yelled at Frankie. "Hey, watch where your fingers are going, buddy. We've got ourselves an audience."

Frankie lifted up his hands, showing us his dry palms.

Kiki's pupils narrowed, as she sneered down to greet Bonbon nibbling on the string holding her bottoms up. She raised her hands to her ears and let out an ear-piercing squeal.

Meanwhile, Frankie had both arms flung around the pooch.

Kiki yelled, "Get that beast away from me." She jiggled her hips round about, thrusting her backside in every which way, trying to rid herself of the ravenous creature, looking like a dashboard hula dancer going over cobblestone.

Frankie was now on his knees, arms hugging the mammal's furry brown neck, as if he was fixing to ride her off into the sunset. "I'm trying to pull her back, but she's got your bikini string stuck in her mouth," he said, while losing the game of tug o' war.

Kiki gave into the animal. She grabbed the towel she was laying on, quickly draped it in front of her, and lunged with minor resistance towards the mansion. Bonbon just stood there with her tail wagging, as if nothing happened, Kiki's bottoms innocently draping out of her mouth. "Damn dog," she mumbled.

Tessie laughed to herself. "My oh my, if that don't beat all." That was worth missin' Dixie.

Harley joined us at the table. "Hey, sis." He peered over at Frankie and tossed a towel over Priscilla's bathing suit, or lack of. "You're getting burnt. You should probably go inside." He scowled at Frankie. "And you, you do work here, right? We're out of rum. You should go get some."

"Not a chance," said Priscilla. "Franklin and I were just on our way to get his and hers facials."

Frankie's elated expression, that of a puppy with his head sticking out the car window, quickly depreciated into a leashed puppy getting choked and dragged into the vet's office. I wondered if he shared my mental image of him with an avocado alien-green blobbed face and cucumber eyes. If she could talk the poor chap into a whole-body scrub, why with his physique, he would totally mimic the Jolly Green Giant.

"Oh, sorry Priscilla," said Frankie. "I should go get that rum." He stood up. "I'll catch up with you later."

Priscilla scolded him with her stare. "Just be sure to meet me at the spa at 3 o'clock. Don't be late." She awkwardly scrambled to gather her lotions, shoving them into her monogrammed tote. "Harley, I think you're right. I've had too much sun."

"Well, well," said Tessie. "That boy finally got himself a pair. He tossed her off, like a thistle on a badger."

I changed the subject quickly as to not anger Harley before he started defending his sister. "So what's with Kiki buttering up Priscilla?"

"She's up to something," said Harley. "She's the one that gave that ridiculous bathing suit to Priscilla. If you ask me, I think she's trying to make a joke of my sister."

That explained why it fit her so poorly. "I should have known, it didn't seem like her style." Putting it nicely.

"It looks plumb ridiculous," said Tessie. "Ya know what I think? Kiki's green. And ya know why?"

I shrugged.

"Frankie. On account of him choosin' Priscilla. Makin' a fool of that gal is Red's revenge."

"Could be. In any regard, I would never take fashion advice from that girl, unless I was doing a casting call for *Pretty Woman*."

Wisely, Brice changed the subject. "Hey Harley. Did you hear what we found in the pool this morning?"

Harley laughed. "Did I *hear* about it?" He threw a brochure on the table. The tagline read, *Wanna Buy a Boat?* Harley flashed his glowing salesman teeth. "Consider it my business card."

"You did that?" I asked.

"Well," he said. "It sure got your attention, didn't it?"

"Yeah, but—"

"Hilarious, right? Now Brice, you're going to want to look at the beauty on page 3. I can totally see you captain of that vessel, man." He winked. "Perfect for your honeymoon." Harley left, and Brice rolled his eyes. He flipped the page of the booklet and pointed to the photo. Harley on a yacht, surrounded by scantily clad women. "Yeah, perfect for my honeymoon, if I'm marrying a harem."

'No wonder he hasn't sold any boats,' "I said, taking a closer look. "Yeah, that will go over well with Ashton." Woah. Hold up. I pointed to a petite brunette in the photo. "See this girl? She's wearing a diamond star necklace."

Brice shrugged his shoulders. "So?"

"So, Harley bought a diamond star pendant for his wife. His tall, blonde wife. Only on the night he gave it to her, she drowned."

Brice's forehead crunched as he connected the dots.

I said, "Brice, they never found her. That necklace should be on the bottom of the ocean."

Something was wrong with his story. Deathly wrong. We debated on how to handle this information. We decided that confronting him, wasn't the most logical route. He was already a loose cannon. And if he was dangerous, we didn't want to become targets. Perhaps we could get some answers from his sister.

Brice and Tessie went to get drinks. As soon as I was alone, Harley swooped back in.

"What do you think you're doing?" he said to me.

Shoot. I hope he hadn't heard our conversation. I played dumb. "Huh?"

"I'm trying to make a sale here, and you're ruining it. I saw you flipping through the brochure. I could tell by your expression you were trying to talk him out of it."

"Harley, he has no intention of buying a boat."

"Well, not now." He stroked his fingers through his hair. "Do you have any idea how much money that guy has to throw away?" He snatched up the booklet, and got in my face, "Keep out of my business."

Since Harley went inside, I was happy to spend the afternoon out by the pool. Tessie was a bit crabby, but I tried to keep her in the shade and kept her well-fed. I didn't want her to be alone in the house. And I didn't want to miss out on any happenings by the pool. If there were any clues swimming around, I wanted to be here to soak them up.

After a couple of smoothies, Frankie was back. "Have you guys seen Priscilla?"

"Not since this morning," I said. "Aren't you supposed to meet her at the spa?"

"Yeah, a half an hour ago." He pushed fingers nervously through his hair. "She never showed. That's not like her."

"Tessie and I will go check her room. You go back to the spa in case she shows up."

Once Frankie was out of ear-shot, Tessie nodded her head. "Why couldn't we wait at the spa? If somethang happened to that gal, I don't wanna find er."

I bulged my eyes at her, translating into, "*How could you be so ridiculously cold?*" All the while, feeling the same way. I prayed we weren't walking into a deathly scenario. Surely there was a logical explanation for why the perfectionist didn't show.

We stood in front of Priscilla's door. There was no answer to our knock.

"Knock louder," I said. "If she's sleeping, she won't hear you."

"That's because she's dead," said Tessie.

"Stop that," I scolded her. "I bet she's just sleeping."

"Well then, open the door," Tessie dared.

"I don't want to wake her."

"Because you know she's dead," Tessie insisted.

"Fine. I'll open it." I turned the knob, pulled it open and winced away.

"I don't get it. Where is she?" said Tessie.

We did a search around her bedroom and bath. Nothing. Nobody.

"Let's check Frankie's room," I suggested.

A minute later, Tessie and I had landed ourselves in front of Frankie's room.

"Your turn," I told her.

"Coward."

The door was locked, but Tessie had her keys with her.

The room appeared perfectly normal. Perfectly perfect, actually. Another dead end.

"Priscilla?" I called out, just to be certain.

Tessie walked to the other side of the bed. "My, oh my," she sang.

Oh no. My heart started racing. "What did you find?"

She held up a green bikini top. "Looks like Miss Piggy has been makin' the rounds."

I joined Tessie on the other side of the bed, taking in the lovers' props. A picnic basket, flower petals, and a spilt bottle of red wine. "Somebody was having a bedside picnic. I didn't think Frankie would be one to fall for Kiki's pretentiousness."

"The boy must've taken a fall outta the dumb tree and hit his noggin on every limb on the way down."

A note was tied around the wine bottle. "Listen to this," I said. "*Meet me at 3. I have a surprise for you.*"

Tessie jiggled the bikini top in front of her chest. "Indeed she did."

"Seriously," I scolded. "Okay, let's say for the sake of crazy, Frankie and Kiki have an affair, that doesn't explain where Priscilla is."

"Listen." Tessie nodded her head to the closed bathroom door. "There's water running."

"Cripes," I said, inching over to Tessie, closer to the bathroom. I leaned my face to the door and whispered, "Priscilla, you in there?"

Tessie shook her head. "Ya think she fell asleep on the can?"

I twisted the knob with hesitation. A deep breath, along with a slight shove from Tessie, pushed me into the bathroom. Tessie flicked on the lights. The tub was completely hidden by a shower curtain. I chanted to myself, "Oh Priscilla, please don't be in there, please don't be in there." My fingers quivered as they latched onto the vinyl shower curtain. I held my breath, then tore back the curtain, like ripping off a strip of hot wax, anticipating a wave of pain. The psycho sound effect pounded in my eardrum. Legs dangled over the drain. I was never so happy to see a Daddy Long Legs in all my life. And never so angry at my grandmother for opening her mouth. "Psycho, really? Not funny."

"We haven't learned a thing," I said. "Except that Frankie is a no-good two-timer."

"Can't say I blame em," said Tessie. "Priscilla's been bossin' the lad around like he's real estate."

"But, cheating with Kiki?"

"Guess love is blind— and all that other mumbo jumbo hoo-haw that don't make a lick of sense. Reckon the wine helps too."

Tessie and I gave the room a once over, searching for any clues to Priscilla's whereabouts. While she dug through the bathroom, I tore through the picnic. I grabbed the handle of the picnic basket, and flipped open the lid. I reached my hand inside, expecting cheese or grapes, but instead got a head with beady little eyes, leading its scaly body around my forearm. My body extended away from my arm that had become the new residence for the murky tan beast, while the rest of my being was frozen in fear. I didn't take my eyes off of the snake, while I tried to speak calmly, "Tessie?" She was in maid-mode washing down the vanity. A little louder, "Uh, Tess? Little help here."

"Yes dear?"

I spoke in an unnaturally calm voice, "I need you to come over here quickly— but very calmly."

Tessie slowly walked over. She must have spotted the snake because she started screaming and trotting around in circles, while her arms flailed in the air. Kinda the opposite of calm.

"What are you panicking for woman? You grew up in Georgia for crying out loud."

"You like Disney World, don't mean you ain't 'fraid of mice."

Point taken. What I would give at this moment to change places with Minnie.

The snake's head jerked out toward her while its body coiled up tighter around my arm, feeling like a blood pressure cuff. Tessie stood on the bed. She grabbed a pillow and started bashing the snake, more like me, over the head with it. I don't think the snake liked this very much, as its jaws popped open giving a glimpse of its needle-sharp fangs. I don't know much about snakes, but I was pretty sure this fella was angry. This was bad. If this was a gift from the killer, one would assume the creature was deadly. Venomous or not, I'd rather not be part of his picnic lunch.

"Get this thing off me," I cried.

Tessie scooted off the bed, and was back in moments with ice tongs and an ice bucket lid shield. She looked like a Roman gladiator ready to slay a ferocious lion. I suppose that the snake, currently cutting off the circulation in my arm, was causing delusions. As Tessie more likely looked like an elderly stout lady in a moo-moo, dancing to a calypso band, trying to snap a pair of tongs at a man-eating snake. But, no matter how inept the woman may have appeared, I didn't give her enough credit. The brave woman grabbed the neck of the beast with the tongs. Meanwhile, I uncoiled the scaly reptile from my arm. We side-stepped together over to the table. I grabbed the ice bucket and wrestled the snake's body into it. Tessie shoved its head down in the bucket and smacked down the lid. We put the ice bucket in a pillow case, knotted the top, and placed it in the bathtub with the door closed.

"Where in tarnation did that snake even come from?" asked Tessie.

I showed her the picnic basket, which was obviously never meant to house food. No food, apart from one deadly chocolate box. I removed the empty paper. Priscilla.

I suppose it gave a shred of evidence why she was missing. But, other than that, we really weren't sure what it meant. Did Priscilla discover Frankie and Kiki's affair, get angry, and leave? Was she poisoned by a venomous snake? The one thing we were certain was that Priscilla's chocolate game was over. But, the more disturbing part, we didn't know whether she was dead or alive.

అౖౖ ౖౖ

Thin Mint: Sugar-free, milky white chocolate wafer, crowned with delicate mint pearls.

Chapter Eight

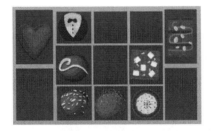

EIGHT slithering snakes told venomous lies.

On the way over to the spa, we ran into Frankie. He fired rapid questions. "Did you find her? Is she okay? Is she sick?"

We filled Frankie in on our findings, including one potentially deadly snake tied up in his bathtub. Which he may, or may not have planted in the picnic basket.

I lowered my sunglasses to get a good look into his eyes. "So then, you're seeing Kiki?"

"What are you talking about?" His words denied the accusation, but his body language sent off awkward vibes. A weird vein bulged out of his forehead. And his Adam's apple bounced up and down.

He begged us not to share any of these details with Harley, or Harley would lose it. Bad for everyone.

We questioned Kiki next, with the same oh-my-gosh-what-are-you-talking about bulgy eyes. At the end of the day, whether Frankie was having relations with Kiki wasn't the issue, Priscilla's whereabouts was. And nobody was admitting to seeing her in the past couple of hours.

Employing the buddy system, we rounded up the others, doing a wide spread search for Priscilla throughout the property. If she had been poisoned by the snake, she wouldn't venture far. Common sense tells us that she would seek out assistance from one of us. But, common sense was overrated lately.

Tessie and I took on the interior, starting with the lower level. While we searched, we theorized possible scenarios.

If Frankie and Kiki were having an affair, Priscilla could have been so mad that she just called a cab, and left her stuff behind. The less favorable option, was that Priscilla got bit by the snake. Which was most likely poisonous, as it was surely gifted by the killer. She couldn't have called an ambulance, as sirens would not go unnoticed. She could have stumbled nearby, searching for help. But then, where was she?

⋰⋱ ⋰⋱

Without clues, none of these theories really held much merit. There were too many unknown factors. And my gut was telling me that everyone involved was not sharing information.

Hours of searching later, we called it a night. I grabbed my security guard, Bonbon, and headed to bed.

My body ached. My head ached. I wanted to go to sleep forever. But, my brain refused to cooperate. It decided it was more important that I relive the past week over. And over. The fake pinky finger pointing out every awful moment.

I tossed. I turned. Alert to every creak in the house. Every branch brushing across my window. I pulled a pillow over my head, trying to suffocate my fear. Instead I became more aware of my climbing heartbeat. I took in a deep breath, removed the pillow, and jumped in surprise. Ghost-baby had returned. Taunting me with wailing cries. Louder than ever.

That's it. I wasn't hesitating this time. I was confronting this ghost, or delusion, or whatever it was.

I grabbed my trusty fire poker and called Bonbon to my side. We walked into the almost pitch-dark hallway, stray moonbeams lighting up intermittent sections of the wall.

The cries were loud. And getting louder with every step.

I whispered to the dog, "Get ready." When in honesty, I was probably talking to myself. A pathetic attempt for a pep talk, when at any moment some demon baby could sprout from the wall spewing pea soup.

A little further down the hall, and there it was. Right in front of Big Red's door. As if waiting for her to invite it inside. A doll. A doll that looked and sounded way too real, and had no business being here. My knuckles rapped on Kiki's door.

The door cracked open allowing dim light to escape. Kiki's half-closed eyes met mine, then dropped down to the crying baby doll in my arms. She rolled her eyes, and closed the door on us. Okay then.

I stood in the dark hallway, subconsciously bouncing the crying doll on my hip, while I pounded on Kiki's door. Meanwhile, I couldn't see if a killer was down the hall, down the stairs, or right in front of my face in the darkness. Chills flowed through my veins like ice water. Fine. If Big Red was going to blow me off, I'd leave the crying thing in front of her door.

I scampered off down the hall. Until my maternal instincts forced me to go back for the flippin' doll. When

Bonbon and I returned to our room, I removed the doll's batteries, and the thing finally shut up. If only parenting were so easy. I sat the toy on the chair, next to the fireplace. Now finally, Bonbon and I would get some rest. If it wasn't for the darn creepy doll's glassy zombie eyes staring at us in the glint of the moonlight. I didn't want Bonbon to have nightmares, so I shoved the doll under the bed. And would try to not let it disturb me for the next few hours.

After hours of twisting and turning, Bonbon's barking convinced me to get out of bed. At 5:00a.m.

"No, I'm not playing fetch," I told her. Sandwiched between Bonbon's jaws, the doll's crying days were over. It was now a chew toy, minus the creepy eyes. One had rolled across the floor, and I'm afraid the other was ingested.

I took the dog outside, sucking in breaths of the freshness in the new spring air. Under different circumstances, I would grab a coffee and a book, and waste the morning away in the porch's gazebo overlooking the lake. Covered with a soft blanket of fog, the scenery felt like part of a dream sequence.

Bonbon took care of her morning business, (I wasn't going to check for the doll's missing eyeball), then tugged me back toward the porch steps, back to reality, which was the tenth day in a deadly nightmare.

The smell of coffee led me to the kitchen, where I found Tessie mindlessly thumbing through magazines at the table. She didn't look so good. Her face pale, her eyes dark and sagging. This week was taking a toll on everyone. "Guess you couldn't sleep either."

She breathed a heavy sigh.

I poured a cup of coffee and topped off Tessie's cup.

"After this caffeine, neither of us are going back to bed. How about some pancakes?" When I'm stressed, I eat. That's just how it is.

Tessie gave another sigh, which I took as a firm yes to food. I united flour, baking powder, sugar, and a pinch of salt in a ceramic bowl. I welled out the middle of the batter, inserting an egg, milk, and melted butter.

Uncomfortable with someone taking over her kitchen, Tessie sprung up and took over the bowl. "Now, don't over mix it. You gotta leave some air in the batter."

I unwrapped a Chandler's milk chocolate bar, chopped it, and added it to the mixture.

She smiled. "I reckon you do know your way 'round a kitchen."

I winked at her, "Must be in our blood."

We worked together as a team, like a chef with her sous chef. Tessie was melting milk chocolate and peanut butter in a metal bowl over a double boiler, creating some sort of delectable fudge-like syrup. Meanwhile, I was flipping golden brown pancakes on the griddle.

Tessie slid the magazines out of the way, making room for the food. "Mmmm hmmm. Them cakes are smellin' scrumptious."

I inhaled a whiff of butter-infused steam before organizing the discs into tall stacks. "Those guys sleeping, don't know what they're missing," I said proudly, setting the plated pancakes on the table. "Bet we're giving them sweet dreams."

"Shore enough. Betcha Kiki added a side of bacon to hers."

I gently ladled lovely, thick syrup over my plate, licking my lips as I watched the fudgy goodness ooze over the steaming rounds. A perfect meal to accompany conversation.

I gorged my cheeks, chewing through my feelings and frustrations.

"What do we have going on here?" Boris said, behind me, prompting my skittish body to jump out of its seat.

"Good golly, you scared me, Boris."

His eyes scanned the table of food. Even in his robe and slippers, that man had the ability to draw out the guilt.

I set down my fork and pushed my plate away. "You couldn't sleep either?" I asked him.

"I'm up at this time every morning. It's my chance to clear my head. Not be bothered."

"Sorry," I muttered and started to get up.

"No, no. Sit."

And I sat, because he told me to.

"So, what are your thoughts, Miss Clementine?"

"Pardon?"

"Certainly, you have a theory on the events taken place this past week."

I patted my lips with a napkin. "I wish I knew. I can't figure out what happened to Priscilla. I mean, she didn't just disappear."

Tessie waved her fork. "I'll tell you what happened to er. That scorned gal done got her a one-way ticket to mumsyville."

Boris cleared his throat. "That's my guess, too."

"But surely, she would tell someone," I said. "At least her brother. And on top of that, she left her suitcases behind."

Boris shook his head. "Priscilla didn't appear to be one that would feel obligated to answer to anyone. And she knew she was leaving Harley behind to collect her personal belongings, and her vendetta."

"Woo wee," sang Tessie. "Poor Frankie, scorned the wrong gal." She took a long sip, emerged in thought. "Maybe it's time we call the police."

"The police aren't going to do anything but get in our hair," said Boris. "The girl has only been missing a couple of hours."

"Speaking of the police, any word on the truck driver?" I asked.

Boris leaned in, "Between us, the coroner said it was a heart attack. He shook his head. "But, I'm not buying it. These days, they can make a donkey look like a unicorn."

I pushed a fork through a puddle of chocolate. "So, who do you guys think is responsible?"

"Well, I don't rightly know," said Tessie.

"Tell me more about Frankie," I said. "Could he be capable of murder?"

"Frankie?" Tessie chuckled. "Oh heavens, no." She took careful sips from her cup. "He's nothin' more than a bashful tabby cat. Couple years back we had us a Christmas party." She looked to Boris, "Remember that?"

He shrugged.

"Any who, I 'member a gal workin' a tray of pee wees—"

My forehead scrunched. "Pee-wees?"

"Ya know, them itty-bitties that fancy people put on trays. Call 'em food, but there ain't never enough there to feed a tadpole. So then, this gal was all gussied up like an elf. I reckon you know what that is, an itty bitty—"

"Yes, yes. Go on."

"Well, that lil' elf caught our Frankie under the mistletoe. You ask me, I think she was waitin' for him. Put her tray of cheese right in the mouse's path. She planted one on him, and good. That boy turned redder than a gooseberry. Found em an exit mighty fast."

I wasn't sure how that made him innocent, except that Tessie felt comfortable with his character. "What about Winston?" I asked.

Boris frowned. "Sounds like you do have a theory after all. First, Frankie. Now Winston. You think an employee is behind this horror." His voice got in lecture tone. "This mansion was safe for 100 years— before all of you money-hungry kids showed up." He stood up. "Don't you think, young lady, that the responsible party is one of you?"

"Easy, Boris," said Tessie.

He patted her off. "I'm just getting a cup."

I said to Boris, "Okay then, who do you think it is?"

He sipped his coffee. "I'll tell you exactly who. Harley. That man is a walking time bomb."

"And he's got them demon eyes," added Tessie.

I nodded. "Just between us, I think he might have killed his wife."

"Pardon?" Boris froze his cup in mid-swig. "That's quite an accusation."

I told him about the necklace he gave his wife that reappeared on another woman.

"Peculiar indeed," said Boris. "Guilt is definitely stacking in his direction."

"But if it is him, how do you explain Priscilla?" I said.

Boris chuckled with sarcasm. "Plain and simple. She got her feelings hurt and left."

I said, "And the snake?"

Boris laughed sarcastically, "You're referring to the snake in Frankie's room. Frankie, the guy making-out with Harley's baby sister?"

"Point taken."

Tessie shook her head. "How in tarnation you gonna convince that crazy man that his sister just got up and left?"

"He's not going to believe anything we say," said Boris. "I think our best plan is to keep him happy. We are going to spend time out at the pool and spa today. So let's continue the search for her this morning, and try to keep that man on our good side."

After a half a dozen pancakes too many, the rest of the group staggered in. Big Red sat across from me, staring at me through eyes drenched with hate and disgust, but I'm guessing mostly hate. I gave Kiki a casual shrug of the shoulders, translating into, *huh? what?*

Kiki threw her napkin onto her plate and stood up. She walked around the table and leaned over me. I inadvertently ducked and squinted my eyes. She whispered in my ear, "You playing games with me, Hillbilly?"

I responded to her with a vocal, "Huh? What?"

She sat down next to me on the edge of the seat. She talked quietly. "I didn't find your little charade amusing last night."

"Woah. The doll? You think I had something to do with it?"

"Well you were the one holding it, standing in front of my bedroom door."

"That's because the dumb thing was crying and woke me up."

"For your sake, I hope you're telling me the truth."

Kiki left, and the agitated butterflies in my stomach demanded another pancake.

❧❧❧

Following breakfast, we did another once over of the property, looking for any clues to Priscilla's whereabouts, not expecting to find much. The gal was probably long gone. I know I would be, if I had the chance.

After a couple of hours of aimlessly searching the grounds, Winston gathered us up at a covered area by the pool deck. He announced to the group, "This morning we have someone here to educate you on harvesting cocoa."

I think we were all ten days beyond this training experience. But we were polite to the guest. A 50-ish old woman, peeking under an oversized straw hat, stood her rubber boots behind a wooden table and introduced herself.

"I'm Florence, one of the horticulture specialists here on property. I actually have done some field work down in Brazil, but now I do that same work here, in Chandler's greenhouse. It would be worth your while to stop by and take a peek inside. Flowers and trees a plenty. Not to mention all the beautiful birds."

Good golly, how big is this property? With all the searching we've done, we hadn't come across the greenhouse.

Florence placed some familiar flowers on the table. "If you like chocolate, you'll love these." She held out yellow daisies with brown centers and reddish-brown chocolate cosmos. "Although they're not edible, they smell delicious." She gathered the stems and placed them in a vase.

I took in a deep whiff. A chocolate garden? Yes, please.

"These are the most common cocoa fragrant flowers. If you think those smell good, you should check out the other varieties in the Cocoa Garden. You'll find chocolate vines, and a couple varieties of orchids. If it smells like chocolate, we've got it. Now I just brought those along for fun, but the focus of the demonstration is the cocoa bean." Florence presented an oval shaped cocoa pod that resembled a miniature football. She smiled, "Now back in the 18th century a brilliant Swedish botanist, renamed the cocoa tree to Theobroma Cacao."

The group's plain expressions weren't what she was going for. "That's Greek for *food of the Gods*." Florence held up the cocoa pod as if giving a gift to the kingdom.

"Awe," choral response.

Yes, brilliant indeed.

Florence continued, "Here in Chandler's greenhouse, we're doing the unthinkable. We're growing cocoa beans right here in the Smoky Mountains. Of course, that's because we're able to control the growing environment. Everything from temperature, humidity, even rainfall, mimics the natural rain forest. We've been working on this project for many years, actually able to produce an understory for the most favorable growing conditions."

Florence pulled a large machete from her sash.

My body jerked back. Guess I was a bit on edge. That's the last thing we needed lying around here. She knelt on the ground, then whacked the pod open, revealing a white mushy center. She held out the fruit to Brice.

His face transformed from a scrunch into an approval as his fingers dug into the creamy white pulp, sorting out cacao beans with his fingertips. "Cool."

"And now you know where chocolate comes from," she said.

"Well isn't this special?" said Harley, who had just joined us. "The whole family gathered around, sipping lemonade and sniffing posies. Oh wait, it's not the whole gang, because someone kidnapped my sister."

Boris put a hand on Florence's back, directing her out of the pool area, and hence, away from the mad man.

Harley took hold of the machete, cocking it back over his head. "Where's my sister, Frankie?"

Everyone gasped. Harley jerked the blade down, hacking it sporadically on a pile of firewood. His eyes were blank and full of insanity. He yelled in between swings, "Tell me. where she. is."

"Calm down, bro. I've already told you that I don't know."

Harley's eyes looked insane. "I am not your brother."

I raised my voice, very bravely standing *behind* Winston. "Priscilla went home."

Harley slowly walked over to me. He toyed with the machete, stroking it with his fingertips, while he toyed with my fear. "Nope, not buying it. Frankie did something to my sister." He looked to me, "Unless someone else knows something, and they're not telling me." I wasn't sure it was a good idea to tell the guy with a knife bigger than my head, about Frankie's possible affair, or the venomous snake.

Winston cleared his blotchy throat and spoke through quivering lips, "That's enough, young man. You can't go around threatening people with a weapon."

"Who's going to stop me?" said Harley. "I'll do whatever it takes to get my sister back. Someone here knows what happened to her." He eyeballed me, and then Frankie.

Winston shook his head. "Do you know that for sure? Yes, Mr. Wellington, someone has been up to no good. But, are we certain it's an heir?"

An outside person? Could the killer actually be someone we never even met? At this point in time, there were no clues pointing in that direction. Except for Chandler's brother, Homer. Maybe Winston knows something that the rest of us don't. Or, maybe he's just trying to divert the crazy man.

"Don't try to change the subject, old man."

I took a turn talking him down, using the calm voice technique I use when my toddler gets a hold of something she shouldn't have. "Harley, we'd gladly help you find Priscilla. But, not as long as you're threatening lives." My eyes squinted in fear of retaliation as I grasped onto the weapon. "Give me the machete."

As he held on tight, I held my breath. I said, "Everyone is watching."

He released his grasp. "Whatever. Just know, I'm going to get to the bottom of this, and one of you is going to pay." Harley left. And I breathed a blast of relief.

∽ର୧ ଗ∾

My intuition was to run away. I sprinted across the deck, tossing the knife away on a poolside table. My body didn't know how to cope with these overwhelming emotions. Maybe I was having a mental breakdown. Or a panic attack. I didn't need to label it. I just needed it to stop.

I sought out comfort in my room. I locked the door, closed the blinds, and nuzzled my face into a stack of pillows. Anger, fear, and sorrow screamed out. Sobbed out. Until a numbness took over, and I fell asleep and slept through the entire night.

The next morning, I was a bit disorientated, still in yesterday's clothes. Before I had even had a chance to open my eyes, a bad feeling swept over me. A feeling that made me want to keep my eyes closed.

I felt a warm breath on my neck.

"What did you do?" whispered a raspy voice in my ear.

I jerked up, not able to move. It took a couple of seconds to register what was going on.

Evidently, I fell asleep. Evidently, some moron broke into my room while I was sleeping.

My eyes popped open, finding Medusa-like golden coils dangling over my face. I pushed Harley's chest with all my might, with zero effect. His biceps mimicked prison bars enclosing my body. "What the heck, Harley? Get off me." But, he wasn't budging. I yelled out for help.

"Where's my sister?" he asked me.

"I don't know."

"Bull. I saw what you did."

Saw *what I did*? "I have no idea what you're talking about," I told him, while attempting to contort my body out of his hold. "Now, let go of me," I screamed and thankfully, somebody heard me.

Brice was standing behind Harley. "You starting trouble, *again*? Let go of her, man."

Harley backed off. "You think you're a hero, pretty boy. Only you're rescuing the wrong person. Go see for yourself what she did. In the kitchen."

Holy cripes. What's this moron trying to blame on me? I followed them downstairs to the kitchen, all the while pleading my case. Tessie, Frankie, and Kiki were already at the scene of the so-called crime. Tessie backed away, and there it was, right in the middle of the kitchen table, the machete forcefully speared into the wooden tabletop— right next to the infamous box of chocolates. The blade held a piece of paper in place, a message written out of clipped letters from magazines. The bumpy letters spelled out, *Revenge is Sweet*.

"Told you," said Harley. "She's crazy. And I bet she knows where my sister is." He came charging towards me. Brice and Frankie double-teamed him. Brice blocked him, while Frankie yanked his arm behind his back.

Frankie said, "Let's take this one step at a time." He nodded his head in the direction of the candy box. "Anna, count them."

I counted and recounted. Another chocolate was missing. With a quick scan of the room, I said, "Has anyone seen Boris or Winston?"

"I just brought out tea to the front porch for Boris and Florence," said Tessie.

Brice said, "Where's Winston?"

"Relax, I saw him go into the loo," said Kiki.

He motioned her to give more information.

"The one closest to the foyer. About ten minutes ago."

"I'm going to check it out," said Brice. He headed down the hallway, and the rest of us followed behind him. He paused for a second in front of the bathroom door taking in a brief listen, then nodded back toward us, signaling us with his finger on his lips, while he gently jiggled the door knob back and forth. A large bang inside the restroom signaled him, like a greyhound hearing the fire of a pistol. Without warning, he thrust his leg at the door, kicking it wide open. Woah. Perhaps he had seen one too many episodes of Cops.

Brice went no further. "Awe man," he moaned.

"Oh no, is he dead?" Tessie said, bobbing up and down, straining to see into the doorway.

Winston who was bent over in front of the toilet, sprung up to a standing position, not nearly quick enough to hide his exposed white bum with a sprawled-out magazine. "What the—" he said, his eyes bulged out, staring at his audience.

Brice's face reddened, "Oh man. Sorry. We thought you were—"

"Well, for the love of liverwurst. Are you and your peanut gallery going to just stand there?" Winston asked, with his trousers around his ankles.

My eyes scrunched. That would be an image that I'd never be able to erase from my memory. I leaned into Tessie, "I'm going to need therapy when this trip is over."

"You and me both," she said. "It's like seein' a well-hung horse. Just a gory image you can never shake."

And now I had two disturbing images in my head. I didn't want to know where my grandmother got her information from, but I knew I wouldn't be visiting our local petting zoo anytime soon.

Brice closed what was left to the bathroom door and we started down the hall.

Once in the foyer, Harley initiated a slow clap, that echoed sarcasm off the walls and ceiling. "And another great moment provided by our Officer on Doody."

Brice's eyes narrowed as he grabbed Harley's shirt in his fist. "Lay off, man. I've had just about enough of you."

"Don't even try to peg this on me." Harley forced his stare on me. "This is all her."

Brice pushed fingers through his hair. "Man, what's your deal with Anna? You were the one threatening everyone with that machete a couple hours ago."

"Yeah, and then you all saw Anna take it out of my hands."

Seriously? "I left it outside," I said. "On one of the pool tables."

Harley looked around. "Can anyone vouch for that?"

Before anyone could respond, Winston pushed through the middle of the boys, tightening his belt under his belly. "Anybody want to tell me what is the meaning of all this?"

Frankie eyeballed Harley. "We thought someone had hurt you."

"And you couldn't knock?" said Winston.

"Sorry about that," said Brice. "There was a bang inside of the bathroom. I was worried."

Harley laughed, "Yeah Brice here thought he *cracked* the case. You all get it, right?"

Winston shook his head. "If you must know, I reached for a magazine on the back of the toilet and accidentally knocked down the whole rack of the darn things. I was just trying to pick it up, when you all so peacefully checked on my well-being by breaking down the whole bathroom door."

Brice led Winston to the kitchen and showed him the chocolate box.

"See, another candy is missing from the box," he said.

"Never mind the damn box," said Winston. "What's with the mammoth knife stabbed into the tabletop?"

"It's a threat," I said. "Winston, it's your candy that is missing." I motioned to Harley. "Someone is threatening you specifically. You need to leave."

Winston's face reddened. "Awe, babble-jabber willy-nilly!" His voice raised several decibels, "Now you all listen up, and listen up closely. I've got my eyes on every one of you. I don't know what kind of stunt that was, but nobody is going to bully me out of this house." He looked at Harley and then took turns deadly staring into each pair of eyes glaring back at him. "You all should know that if you get rid of me, you might as well kiss your inheritance good bye. I'm the only one with the papers that can magically transform any one of you schmucks into a millionaire. There's one and only one copy of those papers, which I assure you is locked away for safe keeping. So, if something happens to me, the state will decide the division, and your dear old grandpa's wishes will be gone. Poof." He blew an imaginary puff of air onto his open palm.

Brice said, "Winston, given the circumstances, can't we cut the training short?"

"My recommendation is to get the bloody hell out of here, and hire a detective to weed out our guilty party," said Winston. "If all agree, we can reassemble on a later date."

"That's not going to happen," said Harley. "You bail, you lose."

"But, our lives are in jeopardy," I said. "Surely, Mr. Chandler would not want his wishes carried out this way."

"And I'm sure Winston doesn't want a call from my lawyer," said Harley.

As it was impossible for everyone to reach a consensus, we all went our separate ways for the rest of the day. Far away from Harley.

As Harley was inside, Tessie and I decided it was in our best interest to be outside. Back outside where caterers were back wining and dining us. We took the long, windy path around the pool hoping that the exercise and fresh air would relieve some adrenaline. It was day eleven. So close, yet so dangerously far from the ending.

"Harley is out of control," I told Tessie. "If Brice didn't hear me screaming for help, I don't know what he would have done to me."

Tessie nodded her head. "So then, let's get outta here."

Unfortunately, it wasn't that easy. I slid my pinky ring back and forth over my finger, remembering the threat to Jillian's life. "As much as I want to go home, I felt my lip quiver. "I just can't. Please leave it at that." I stopped walking, and looked into her sagging eyes, tired and full of fear. "But, I need you to go. I need you to be safe. Please."

Tessie shook her head. "You know I'm not leaving this house without my grand-baby I just done found."

I sighed. "I promise I'm going to get us out of here safely." I said the words, hoping I wasn't lying through my teeth.

We continued our path, now in view of workers hovering over silver chafing dishes.

Tessie whispered to me. "I got it. I'm gonna tell one of those waiters what's goin' on 'round here. They'll send the police and straighten it all out."

"No!" I said harsher than intended, staring into her eyes, "You'll just make matters worse."

Tessie paused her steps. "Gracious me. Someone's threatening you."

"I can't—"

Tessie hugged me. "We're going to make it through this. We're in this together, shug."

We left the conversation in the bushes and carried on like it never occurred. Brice was sitting at a table next to the poolside bar.

"Do you mind if we join you?" I asked.

"Please do." He pulled out a chair for Tessie.

Tessie dismissed the chair. "I'll be back. I'm doin' the orderin' this time."

A plate of grilled prawns and pancetta sat in front of Brice. "Don't let your food get cold."

"It already is. I'm not in the mood to eat."

"I understand."

He combed his fingers through his hair. "What if I never see Ashton again?"

"Don't talk like that," I said. "Maybe, you should go home."

"What, and leave everything to Harley?" He shook his head.

As I consoled him, I wondered if Harley was the root of his decision, or if he had been threatened, as well.

Tessie returned to the table with blazing drinks.

I backed up, having a flashback of Cashmere lighting up into flames. "What the heck?"

"Now this is how you order drinks," said Tessie, smiling proudly at the fiery cocktails. "This here is a Roasted Rooster. Why a swig of this will put a cockle in the ol' doo."

I could use a cockle in the doo about now.

She raised her flaming flute, "To three more days of insanity—"

We clinked glasses.

I raised my glass to my lips. "Fire in the hole." I sipped my now exhausted drink. "Holy cow, this is some potent stuff."

Tessie smiled with satisfaction, then took a slug of her own drink. And started choking. "Whewf, you ain't kiddin'. This stuff could sprout teats on a boar."

I don't think I could handle this drink on an empty stomach. I wasn't in the mood for food, but chocolate on the other hand, always made things feel better. "I'm going to go get us some dessert."

"Best thang you've muttered all day," said Tessie.

I helped myself to the dessert cart compliments of the Cacau Cafe. As the ratio of food to people was greatly overdone, I grabbed a sample of every dessert. For each of us.

"None for me," said Brice. "I'm going to go give Ashton a call."

I turned to Tessie. "Madam," I said, as I unveiled to her a sampler tray of delectable Brazilian goodies. "Señorita, may I present to you the chef's trio for your enjoyment," I spoke in my best accent, "Arroz doce, Bolo de chocolate, and Banana flambadas."

"Huh?" she scowled at me like I was wearing my underwear on my head. "Rice pudding, chocolate cake and something drenched in rum."

She smiled in approval and wasted no time digging into the confections.

Kiki paraded over to us in another material-deprived bikini, this one way too cheeky for my taste. A metallic silver bag hung over her shoulder. "I just finished up in the spa, you guys are scheduled next." She eyed the tray of goodies and helped herself to a plate.

"Thanks, but I'm really not the spa-type of gal," I said.

"*Really?*" Kiki laughed sarcastically. "Seriously though. Don't be silly. These treatments are expensive. Besides, who doesn't like being pampered?"

Wasn't she listening? I just informed her that that person was *moi.*

Kiki walked away, and Tessie spoke. "So ya trying to lose?"

"Pardon?"

"We're gettin' down to the nitty gritty. Call me stupid, but I thought you were here to win a chocolate factory."

I packed up my bag. "You're absolutely right. We need to learn everything we can for this test. Otherwise, we're sticking our necks out for nothing."

Tessie nodded in approval, and helped herself to another dessert.

I lowered my sunglasses, "Aren't you coming?"

"No need for all of this to go to waste. Let me just finish up here, and then I'll be along."

Why didn't I believe her?

⋘ ❧ ❧ ⋙

I had never actually stepped into a spa before. The place had a sterile, yet welcoming feel to it. The guest counter was empty, so I took a seat on a bamboo couch softened with plush Hawaiian-print cushions. Two frosted wall-length windows bordered the room's focal point, which I dubbed, aqua art. A coppered slate was the backdrop for water that cascaded down in one big sheet amongst the roomful of scattered potted plants, giving the feel of a mock waterfall flowing into a hygienic rain forest– no critters, no humidity, and plastic plants. The peachy-mango walls matched the tropical breeze scent in the air.

A woman welcomed me, and checked me off her log. She asked, "Will Tessie be joining you?"

"I'm afraid not." She had something less important to do.

"Okay, then. I am Mona." She held open a swinging pine door. "Right this way."

My steps were slow and hesitant down the espresso walled hallway that canvassed dancing flames rising from beige candles of variant heights. A whiff of chocolate fragrance in the air was like an old friend attempting to calm my nerves.

"Right here," she said, motioning me into a room. The ambience was relaxing, or rather romantic really, with candles scattered throughout the space. A series of chubby

188

candles in glass vases lined the back wall, while others gracefully floated in a clear bubbled liquid, perfectly arranged on a table.

Mona said to me, "You can get undressed, and I'll be back in a few minutes, madam."

Undressed? I'm perfectly comfortable in my t-shirt and shorts, thank you very much. I eyed the dual massaging cots in the center of the room. Each had a miniature pillow and a pair of precisely rolled chestnut towels topped off with a fresh gardenia, like a Christmas present. Crisp linens and a brown fuzzy robe draped over the bottom of the table. Perhaps, I could slip on the robe, they could bring me some cookies and milk, and then let me take a nap for an hour. Of course, Tessie was counting on *me* learning something.

I hurriedly took off my shirt and slipped off my shorts, not wanting Mona to open the door while I was in mid-strip. I suppose I have always been embarrassed by the scar on my back, and then there were my pie thighs and matching hips that I had never thought about before. Thanks Priscilla, for giving me yet another reason to be self-conscious in this world. I opted to keep on my britches, I wouldn't want chocolate slipping into the wrong places. I climbed up onto the table, quickly unwrapping the towels and unfolding the sheet, randomly stacking them on top of my body. My head rested on the pillow as I tried to get myself in a relaxed place. To my side, was some lava looking pit extending across the wall which illuminated coal like stones, sending steamy drifts into the air. Perhaps, this is where the aroma of smoky chocolate stemmed from. Kind of like nutty roasted S'mores at a campfire.

A gentle knock at the door. "Uh, come in," my voice said the words, but the tremble in my vocals said otherwise.

Mona entered, closing the door behind her. Her eyes traced the pile of staggered cloths from my feet, up to my hands which were clutching fabric around my neck. "This is your first time?" she asked with her lips pursed off to one side.

What gave it away?

"You will love it, madam. It's quite relaxing, and I will be gentle. If at any time you are not comfortable, you just let me know."

Okay then, I am not comfortable, I thought, but didn't have the heart to say.

"To begin, let's have you turn onto your stomach."

My body struggled to roll, getting caught up in the layers of cloth.

"Wait. Let's adjust this sheet," she said lightening my shell, then lifting the sheet in the air freeing my body, but still protecting my modesty. She rearranged the cloth, so it just covered the parts that she knew I was bashful of flashing. "Now, relax. I'm going to circulate and exfoliate your skin. It means I'm going to wake it up and get rid of all those dead skin cells."

A gentle brush traveled over my body, finally putting me physically and mentally at ease. All right, so it wasn't so torturous to be pampered. It was kind of nice.

Mona brought a big wooden bowl of glop into my view. I wondered if it was snack time. "This is mineral-rich mud, scented with the essence of cocoa oils," she said. Then, gracefully stroked the warm mixture onto the back of my legs, as if she was an artist and I was her canvas.

The cocoa scents consumed the air, as I transformed into a human candy bar. When my legs were well coated, she wrapped them up nice and secure with plastic wrap. *What gives?*

Then, she placed warmed towels over the top of them. She said, "I'll be back in twenty minutes, just relax and sip some water."

Relax, really? You just wrapped me up like last night's leftovers. I attempted to move my legs, a bit panicked by my confinement. Who could handle being so restrained? I changed my mind about any thoughts I had in the previous ten minutes. Spas were not for me. I forced my body to lie still while I focused on the illuminated, red coals. I thought back to Cashmere's room in the mansion, when we had our smorgasbord of S'mores. My heart knew he was okay. My brain hoped my heart was right.

I tried to divert my thoughts, focusing on the music. My toes wiggled to the steel drum version of *Lollipop*, piped into the overhead speakers.

A fragment of light from the real world, signaled me that the door had opened. "Mam, I'm sorry to disturb you, but do you mind if we occupy the table next to you?"

So, Tessie actually came through. "Sure, it's fine."

"Thank you, lady." She directed her new patron. "Okay, you can undress, and I will be back in a couple of minutes to begin your treatment."

I was glad to have my head facing the wall, to abolish any awkwardness.

"Thanks for coming. I feel less weird about this whole thing, knowing you're here too."

"Thanks, Anna," said a deep voice. "That means a lot."

I jerked my head and jumped up, realizing my plastered body had not followed my lead. "Winston?"

"I appreciate you sharing your room."

So much, for alleviating any awkwardness. "No prob—" I started to say as I noted him loosening his belt. I quickly turned my neck back to face the wall. My tranquility was taken over with the sound of his pants un-zippering and the jingling of his keys and coins in his pockets meeting the wooden floor. I thought it best to break the icky silence. "So, Tessie gave you her appointment?"

"All that nonsense with that confounded chocolate box, has got me all uptight. Tessie convinced me to take her place."

"How nice of her." Thankfully, he couldn't see my eyeroll.

"It didn't take a whole lot of convincing. I could use some relaxation."

Then for his sake, I hope he wasn't going to have a treatment similar to mine, being slathered with goop then wrapped up tight, like sausage meat squeezed into a casing. Bad visual. I tried to think of more conversation to save my queasy stomach. "So, any news about the blood tests?"

"Actually, yes. I've called a meeting for this evening to share the results."

"Oh."

Perhaps, he sensed the disappointment in my voice.

"I guess it wouldn't hurt to tell you. Turns out, the Wellingtons are not heirs."

"Why didn't you mention it this morning, when Harley was threatening us with a machete?"

"I just received the phone call before coming here."

Finally, some good news. Once Winston makes the announcement at the meeting, we can finally be rid of Harley. I may actually even get some sleep tonight. Then, when this whole crazy thing was over, and I have Jillian in my arms, we could get the police involved.

It got me thinking. "If Harley and Priscilla aren't heirs, what were they doing here? Aren't their names on the will?"

"Somewhere along the line, when researching the grandchildren, we must have acquired some false records. Bottom-line, since they are not legitimate relatives, they do not qualify under the category of grandchildren. Now, please keep this between us, until after the meeting."

"Of course."

The door cracked open. "All ready, sir?"

"Oh yeah," said Winston.

And now I would focus on my happy little glowing rocks on my side of the room.

"Mmmmm," he moaned.

"You are tense, Mr. Winston," said the masseuse.

"Oh boy. Ohhh," another groan.

I suddenly felt like I was eavesdropping on closed doors at the senior center. I forced my attention on the ocean sounds that replaced the steel drum island music overhead. The splashing of water seemed to purify my thoughts and drown out the sound effects of Winston's obvious deep tissue massage. I pictured the water cascading down picturesque large boulders, creating a fluid staircase, gushing down from the top flight and transforming into just a gentle trickle when it finally reached the water's glass surface. Awe crap, all this water, I've got to go. Darn Mona telling me that I had to keep hydrated. Wasn't twenty minutes over with anyway?

The quiet space next to me let me know that Winston's massage was over. I glanced over to him. Thankfully, his head was turned facing the opposite wall. Without thought, I eyeballed his candlelit, brown clumped back, forcing my eyes from going down any further, recalling the prickly full moon from the bathroom.

I scooted myself off the table, inching myself down until my feet touched the ground and then waddled myself out of the room. Thankfully there was a bathroom right outside the door.

Appreciative of high maintenance women, I helped myself to a pair of manicure scissors from a display of hair and nail supplies, arranged on a bulb-lined dressing table. I snipped my chocolate-coated self out of the plastic cocoon. After I used the facilities, I noted my mirrored reflection. Bashful Anna, standing in a public restroom, in nothing more than a pair of pink undies, a shower cap, and cocoa legs-soufflé. I thought spas were supposed to turn gals into glamour. I looked more like a risqué cafeteria lady that fell into the Salisbury steak gravy.

I contemplated my next move. Like I was really going to lie half-naked, next to Winston, while some lady's spackle knife had its way with me? I think not. That would be enough relaxation for me for the day. I tugged at the paper towel machine, tearing off a yard length piece, then wrapping it around my exposed chest. I peeked out the door. The hall was clear, so I tiptoed back into my room, grabbing my clothes off of the chair, offering a silent wave to a sleeping Winston upon my departure.

After peeling my body, like a rotten plantain, I took an extra long hot shower. Afterwards, I called my family. Even though I needed to hear Jillian's voice, it was painful hearing her ask if I could come home. And even harder, having to tell her no.

It was time for Winston's meeting. I headed to the library, where Tessie was the first to arrive.

"Thanks for ditching me at the spa," I told her.

Tessie giggled. "Ah, that old geezer needed it more than I did."

"Where is he anyway? Everyone will be here soon for the meeting."

"No, they won't," she said. "Winston left."

"I told you, I saw him at the spa."

"Well, he's gone now." She pulled a note from her apron pocket. "See for yourself."

Tessie,
I'm going to get help. Stay safe.

"He couldn't wait until after the meeting?"

"Think he was 'fraid he was running out of time."

She was right. The chocolate box was calling the shots. One less chocolate, translated into one less heir. Someone's plan was working out perfectly.

 споре

The Bar: A white chocolate bar with pieces of crumby biscotti, dotted with dried raspberries, streaked with a guilt-less charge of dark chocolate, combed over with a layer of candied pistachios.

Chapter Seven

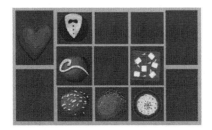

SEVEN scared sheep weeded out the wolf.

With or without the meeting, Tessie and I concurred it was safer to stick with the others. Strength, er, survival in numbers. We decided to keep Winston's departure to ourselves. It might buy us some time while the killer chased a missing target.

The sound of Kiki's laughter led us to the basement bar. Big Red's honk was an apparent mating call, as we found her once again throwing herself at Frankie. Meanwhile, Harley and Boris were having a pool rematch. I couldn't comprehend how anyone, particularly Boris, could be playing a game with Harley. On the upside, I could keep an eye on him.

Tessie and I had a seat at the bar. My body slumped over with disappointment. With Winston gone, I felt defeated.

Harley was supposed to be on his way out the door. Right now.

Instead he was here haunting me. How I just wanted to go home to my pitiful minimum wage job, sleeping in my uncle's basement.

"I spoke to Jillian. She wants me to come home," I said to Tessie, clinching the locket around my neck.

"Poor baby. Is that a picture of er?" she asked, motioning a chocolate cashew in my direction.

I opened the locket, revealing my precious girl.

Tessie squinted her eyes. "Awe, that's my great grand-baby. Why she's cuter than a freckle on a honeybee's hiney. Takes after me."

I smiled, realizing that there was one positive thing about being here. "I can't wait for you to meet her." I closed the delicate door, giving a tender peck to the golden oval. We sat in silence for a while. Probably pondering the same fear. That she may never meet her great granddaughter.

Tessie changed the subject. "Hey, don't be sour with Winston," she said. "He was scared."

"I know," I said. "And I'm relieved he got out of here safely. I was just hoping he would have shared the results from the blood tests before he left. Turns out, the Wellingtons aren't real heirs."

Tessie's mouth widened. "Why those dirty little—"

I shrugged my shoulders. "Winston wasn't sure if Harley and Priscilla were in on it. He didn't know where the false information originated from."

"Don't matter; we gotta snitch em out," said Tessie. "Get that crazy fella outta here."

"Not sure I'm the best person to kick Harley out of the mansion."

Boris joined us, positioning himself behind the bar. He leaned in towards us, speaking quietly, "Harley has been taunting Frankie again. I'm doing everything I can to keep them apart. Even tried to throw the last game. But, that man has a lousy shot."

Okay, so I now understood why people were being kind to the crazy man. I looked over to the pool table. Guess it was Brice's turn to babysit Harley.

Boris wiped down the bar. "Anna, something to drink?"

"Thanks, but you don't need to do that."

"Go head and make her a Chandler's Chocolate Bar," ordered Tessie. "She needs to relax a lil. Heck, come to think of it, I need to relax a lil too."

Who was I kidding? Chocolate. Booze. I needed all I could get right now.

Boris slammed down glasses in front of us. "Very well." He poured Chandler's Crème de Hazelnut Cacao, Kahlua, and cream into a shaker.

It felt good to finally build a rapport with Boris. I smiled at him, "Hey, thanks for letting us crash the man cave."

He shook the mixture and poured it over a pair of highball glasses filled with ice. "For the past week, this was my sanctuary of peace and quiet to get away from all of you spoiled kids. Till you all had to go snooping around, where your nose didn't belong." He topped the cocktails with a sprinkle of freshly shaved chocolate.

I didn't know how to respond. But, I don't think he was feeling the same chummy rapport.

"Awe, he's yankin' yer bonnet strangs," said Tessie.

I forced a half a smile. The man didn't crack a smile. He placed napkins and drinks in front of us.

"It looks delicious," I said to him.

Boris pulled a book from under the counter, and slapped it onto the bar in front of me. "In case you want another."

It was a Chandler's Cocktail book. I mumbled to Tessie, "In other words, make it myself."

I glanced up at the old man. "Geez, thanks." And something weird happened. Boris left, wandering into the pool area. "Tess, I think he winked at me. And kind of smirked. The odd thing, is it felt genuine."

Tessie thumbed through the book, pausing at a glossy page of Chandler liquors. "Don't cha get it gal? It's a study guide. He's trying to help ya. I can tell he's real fond of ya."

Huh? How about that? I gave my cocktail a sniff, and took a sample sip. And, went back for a gulp. "Wow. This is really good."

Tessie pointed to the shelves behind the bar. "If ya like that, ya may want to try some of those chocolate liquors back there. And the chocolate port." She got up and checked the shelves of bottles. "Now, where did those go?" She hollered to Boris, "We got any port left?"

"Two bottles came in last week," he said.

"Bet Caesar got into them," said Tessie. "You know how he liked his booze."

I put my hand over my mouth. "I don't believe it," I told her. "Cashmere was lying to me, too." I took a huge swallow of the cocktail.

"How's that?" asked Tessie.

"I asked him where he was, during Caesar's accident at the amusement park."

"And?"

I sighed. "He told me that he was at Chandler's Pantry buying two bottles of chocolate port."

"Lies indeed. That store wasn't open." Tessie nodded her head. "But, why?"

"I have no idea. Just goes to show you, you can't trust anybody."

Harley headed in our direction, on the hunt for Frankie. I bit my lip. Yuh-oh.

Boris came up behind him, patting his back. "Hey, where you off to? You owe me another drink."

"Give it up, old man," Harley said. "Make your own friggin drink."

"Better yet, I'll make you one," Boris told him. "Show you how it's done." With a few twists of the wrists, dollops of fruit, a dash of Bitters, he had made his cocktail, and successfully corralled Harley.

Once everyone was in calm spirits, I threw back the last of my drink and retreated to my room. After I washed up, I changed into pajamas. I sat on my bed, absorbing my surroundings. The cozy fireplace. The delicate pink decor. The luscious chocolate morsel on my pillow. Get rid of the evil, and this place would be amazing. How I'd love to see Jillian running down the halls, I thought, grabbing for the locket around my neck. Cripes, my necklace was gone. I wasn't sure if it fell off, or if I mindlessly put it away someplace.

ৠৎ৯ঌ

I searched the bedspread, the wooden floor, and my suitcase. No luck. I rummaged through the bathroom next, through my make-up case, and in the medicine cabinet, sporadically tossing out lotions and miniature bars of soap to the marbled floor. The necklace was not there, but I had made a curious discovery. The neat little row of miniature size shampoos had been covering a literal hole in the wall. I peeked into the hole, anticipating a grand reveal of the vacant room next door. Instead, I was met with darkness.

My nightstand lamp, minus its shade, served as the perfect beacon of light. Once I crumpled a bit of the surrounding drywall away, the light fit in nicely and still allowed a bit of space for snooping.

The decor was unexpected, wallpaper haphazardly torn from the walls, broken light fixtures, and a flooring full of debris. And more oil paintings. But, these were different. None of them featured chocolate, instead they were all of people. The kind of portraits with cobwebs and antiqued frames that you'd expect to see in century old abandoned houses. The kind of aged portraits that correlated to deceased relatives. Properly dressed ladies and gentlemen. Dignified standard poodles. And three children sitting on a porch stoop. Each of the painted eerie faces emitted a sadness. A mourning. Suddenly my insides felt empty.

I tilted the lamp base, allowing light to shine on the cornering wall. There was an antique dresser, acting as a pedestal for yet another picture. Only this one I recognized. It was my missing photo of Jillian. And next to it, the creepy doll. The creepy doll that just got a whole lot creepier. It's dark shallow eye sockets had been replaced with rays of light. Perhaps, a flash light?

Goosebumps swelled over my skin, as I followed the pair of glowing beams that highlighted a spot on the opposite wall. Words. Blood-curdling, toe-curling, horrid words in the all familiar deadly red paint.

Anna, do not be afraid. I will be waiting for you in heaven.

I forced a palm over my mouth, and did the *Oh my gosh-Oh my gosh-Dance* throughout the space. Of all the twisted things. This was beyond scary. Someone was taunting me. I ran out of my room to the room next door, jingled the doorknob and pounded on the door. Of course, it was locked. Of course, nobody was inside.

What did the words even mean? Was the killer threatening my family again? Or, was someone planning to kill us all, and then commit suicide? Maybe I was digging too deep. Perhaps, the words were meaningless, just there to mess with my mind and emotions. Weak victims are much easier prey. In that case, it was working. I dropped to my knees in front of the door, unable to hold back my tears.

After going through stages of anger, sadness, and helplessness, my buddy had come to my rescue. I wrapped my arms around Bonbon and wiped my eyes. "I'll deal with this mess later," I told her. For now, I had to solve my other dilemma, my missing locket. I wanted it back for sentimental reasons. But more pressing, the locket was engraved with Jillian's allergies, in case of an emergency. Not information I wanted in the killer's arsenal.

I remembered showing the necklace to Tessie earlier in the evening, so I figured I needed to explore the basement. As much as I didn't want to be wandering around this place alone, I had to push on, for Jillian's sake.

Everything was dark in the basement, except a crack of light shining on the floor, on the opposite end of the room. This was odd, because imagining the room layout in my mind, I recalled that space being occupied by the pool table.

Moving towards the light, I carefully maneuvered myself across the room until I was standing right in front of the Bells' oil painting. The light was coming from below. I slid my fingers over the dried strokes of paint, which easily slipped into a large groove. A slash in the canvas. A slash that was definitely not here the first time I viewed the art. Clearly, somebody didn't like this painting. I tugged on the outer frame that easily hinged open a panel, forming an entrance way to yet another secret room.

History taught me that bad things happen behind closed secret doors. But, I was desperate for clues.

A desk lamp dimly lit the office space. The room was filled with standard technology, file cabinets, and copy machines.

"Anybody here?" I called out timidly, not knowing what I would say if somebody answered my call. Silence. *Whewf,* I don't think the help would appreciate me snooping around Chandler's private workspace. Especially, Boris. Been there, done that, and this time he's liable to kick me out of the house.

I did a once over of the desk, casually rummaging over its contents. Pens, paper clips, a business card for Homer Chandler's *Nut House*, and Chandler's antique pipe in a pile of loose tobacco. I would have thought they would have locked it back up.

I opened up the laptop on the desk. Surprisingly, no password was needed. The last viewed page revealed an unflattering picture of Kiki with sagging eyes, hidden under blue stringy hair. I skimmed the accompanying report. Evidently, Kiki's anger issues had gotten her into some trouble over the years. Aggravated assault on a co-worker. Tire-slashing.

I clicked the other open tab. Official webpage for Chandler's Nut House. Looks like I stirred up some suspicion about Chandler's brother, Homer, at dinner the other night. I scrolled down the page to an unexpected photo. It was Frankie. Seems that our shy chauffeur used to work for Homer. That can't be good.

A red light blinking on the answering machine stole my attention. I pushed the button. Voices blared, "*Hey Winston, what's this that you're giving special treatment to Harley? Why does he get to buy privileged shares? We want our fair share man...*" It was Caesar's voice with Kiki's unmistakable laugh in the background. I remembered them making the call the day they found Winton's cellphone. Only the goofballs thought they were calling the lawyer's private office, not the basement.

My body jerked at the sound of a door closing in the main portion of the basement. Footsteps neared the office. I frantically pushed random buttons on the answering machine, but the message wouldn't shut off. In desperation, I yanked it by the chord and scooted to the other side of the desk. The footsteps got closer.

"Somebody in there?" said a man's voice, that I was struggling to recognize.

Peering under the desk, I could see shadows of feet in the hallway. I held my breath, crouching my body down as low as I could go, never taking my eyes off the silhouette cast in the doorway. Somebody had been doing some snooping in these private quarters, and I wanted them to think that their secret was secure.

As stealthy as I could, I maneuvered my body toward a cabinet on the farthest side of the wall. Perhaps if the individual entered the room, I could manage a peek at their identity, while holding on to mine. I crawled toward the wall, attempting to squeeze my body in between it and the cabinet. My hands inched over the velvety flooring, smoothing over individual strands of plush carpet. My fingers slid farther across the rug. Moisture meeting my fingertips signaled my body to stop. Fear trickled up my spine, thundering beats echoed in my head as I inspected the scarlet fluid on my palm. I got to my knees and peeked around the other side of the cabinet. Terror swept through my body. Without permission from my brain, my mouth let out an uncontrollable shriek, taking in the sight of poor Boris, his limp body and head resting in a pool of blood.

"What the hell?" said a voice suddenly hovering over me. "How did this happen?" asked Frankie.

Still on my knees, my body crunched up into a trembling ball, I sobbed, "I don't know. I just found him here." My body failed to move while my eyes assessed the crime scene. A broken bottle lay next to the still body, revealing its contents. *Bitters.*

"Move," he hollered, kicking glass chards away from Boris, then lifting the old man over his shoulder like a rag doll. "I need to get him to the hospital right away."

I cried uncontrollably, my stifled breaths merging into hyperventilation. I managed to vocalize, "I think it's too late." huh HUHHH huh HUHHH I tried desperately to get a hold of my breathing. My words spurted out, "You can't just take off with him," I said following him down the hall. "We need to call the police. We need to tell the others."

Frankie didn't slow. "Do whatever you want. But I'm getting this man out of here. I'll be back." And with that, he took off through the basement exterior door.

I needed to get help. Fast. As the office phone was now out of order, I raced up to the mansion foyer pleading for help. Remembering the rotary phone by the bedrooms, I flung on the lights and climbed up the stairs. Only the phone wasn't the first thing to grab my attention. I flicked the stupid box of chocolates behind the end table, picked up the receiver, and dialed 911. Nothing. I canceled and listened. No dial tone. I had used this phone before to call Jillian and never had a problem getting a line out. My fingers trembled as I repeated winding the numbers on the dial. "Come on, come on."

"Put the phone down," a voice said from behind.

I turned around. "Harley, you don't understand. It's Boris. He's been—"

Harley had dropped his dumb, surfer boy act. "Anna, drop the phone," he said to me, grabbing my wrist.

"Ouch. Let go of me."

Harley squeezed my arm tighter with one hand and yanked the phone away from me with the other. "Did you get through?"

I tried pulling away from him, ignoring his question.

He faced me now, grabbing both arms. "Did you get through to the police?"

"Let go of me," I said.

Brice ran into the hallway, dropping an armful of snacks onto the floor. "You at it again, Harley?" He grabbed him by the nape of his neck, jerking his back to the floor.

I said to Brice, "He killed Boris."

Harley lifted up his upper body from the floor. Brice stepped on his chest, pinning the man down.

Harley wheezed. "Boris, dead?"

Brice pushed his foot down on his ribs. "Don't play stupid, man." He asked me, "Where is he?"

Words sputtered frantically out of my mouth. "I found him in the office. In the basement. Then Frankie showed up out of nowhere and took off with his body. He said he was taking him to the hospital."

Harley struggled to get words out, "I didn't know about Boris— honest. I heard Anna scream, so I went to see what was wrong. When I found her on the phone, I panicked."

Brice said, "If you didn't know what happened, then why did you panic?"

"Don't you get it? If the police come here, it's all over. They will interrogate us all and we'll all be suspects for murder. On top of that, the public will find out about Chandler's death, and this mansion will be full of news reporters and photographers in a blink. Do it, but you'll only be screwing yourselves. Nobody will be seeing any money for a long time."

"Money?" I said. "Who in their right mind could possibly care about money right now?"

Harley snickered sarcastically. "You're here, aren't you?"

I hated to admit that he had a point. But, I was not about to debate my intentions with him. It was bad enough that I almost called the police. That natural reaction could have cost me my daughter.

"The phone doesn't work anyways," I said. "But, Frankie was taking Boris to the hospital. The hospital will notify the police."

Harley, still on his back, said, "You morons. Frankie's your guy. He's not going to any hack shack, he's going to ditch the body."

I looked at him dumbfounded.

"All this time you guys are pointing fingers at me. And that thug is hiding behind a pair of sunglasses, acting like he can't do any wrong."

Brice put his fingers through his hair, easing his foot off Harley's chest. "I don't know what to believe."

If this turns out to be true, I just watched as the murderer fled the scene. My frustration screamed out, "I can't take any more of this. I tallied on my fingers, "Paulie, Jasper, Caesar, and now, Boris. How many people do we have to watch die, before we come to our senses? If we stay, we might inherit a boat load of money. But, my bet is we're more likely to inherit a tombstone. All of us need to get out of this house."

Brice relaxed his hold on Harley, still towering over his body. "You're right, Anna. Obviously, someone's trying to get rid of us, one by one." He made it obvious that he was directing his stare at Harley. "But the moron didn't think it through. When he's the last one standing, isn't it going to be a bit obvious who killed us all?"

"It won't matter, because he's not a real heir," I blurted out.

"Good try," Harley said.

"It's true. Winston got the blood tests back."

Harley laughed. "Well, that's a convenient story, since nobody has seen the old man. Unless you can show proof, stay out of my business. Better yet, just stay out of my business."

∽⊙⊘⊙∾

Tessie came trotting down the hall. She hugged me, "You okay, shug?" I nodded in her arms. "But Tess, something terrible has happened. Boris is dead." Her face turned gravely white. I put an arm around her back and led her to the kitchen, settling her into a chair.

"No. This just can't be," she said. "He was just making me a drink at the bar." She looked at me. "Made one for you too."

"I know," I said. "It doesn't seem real. You sit here. I'm going to make you some tea."

She put her hand on top of mine. "No. Sit." She turned her head towards me. When her eyes met mine, she broke down.

I hugged her. "I'm so sorry, Tess. I know you knew him a long time."

"It's not just that," she said, wiping her eyes with a napkin. "He was family. I loved him."

206

My eyebrows raised. "You loved him?"

"No, not like that." Her eyes met mine again. "Anna, Boris was your granddaddy."

Huh? "What are you talking about? That doesn't make sense."

"Your grandfather was Ulysses *Boris* Chandler."

My head felt like a lit stick of dynamite, heat rising by the second. "You're trying to tell me that Boris-*the butler*, was actually the world-famous Chandler?"

She nodded.

"As in the Chandler that died a week ago and left me in his will?"

She kept nodding.

"Okay, do you hear what I'm saying? Because I'm not making any sense."

Tessie inhaled for several seconds, then pushed out a stream of air. "This whole thing was, a bit of *a sham*."

My chest rose up and down in double time, but I resisted the urge to interrupt.

"The part 'bout Chandler being your grandfather is true. The will even holds some merit. But up until tonight, Chandler was alive."

My mind raced back to the basement. The pictures on the sports' memorabilia wall showing Boris on the sidelines, the middle initial, 'B', on the monogrammed robe, and the recently smoked pipe in the basement. "So, Boris wasn't a butler at all?"

"No dear, Winston is the real butler."

"So, everyone is in on this? Am I the only fool that thought they were coming here for a will reading?"

"Of course not. None of the grandchildren know the truth. All the employees were sworn to secrecy, and in return got included in the will."

I stood up, recklessly combing my fingers through my hair. "We are all here, literally risking our lives for— a sham?" I draped my face with my palms. "Why then this big escapade?"

"It's complicated."

"Well then, it's a good thing that we've got all night."

"Fair enough. But, have a seat. We've got to keep our voices down."

I rejoined her at the table.

"It all started 'bout a year and a half ago. Chandler got lung cancer. His battle with cancer was a wakeup call. He knew he wasn't gonna live fer ever. And he'd be leavin' behind the factory. Why this business has been in the Chandler family fer generations. Problem was, the only family he knew was his brother, Homer. The two of them never got along. Probably stemmed from Homer's envy. After all, their daddy left the bigger business to Boris. And Homer, he got left with the nuts. Nothin' wrong with nuts. But, Homer never forgave Boris. On account of Boris wouldn't share the business. En why should he? Boris built up Chandler's Chocolates to where it is today. But Homer, that ol' mule, won't sell em not even one measly nut. Don't make no sense, right?"

"Cut to the important part. Why am I here? Why were any of us invited here?"

"Perdy simple. Yer blood. But, strangers. Boris had lots to lose. Wanted to see who he could trust and who had the heart. Smart too. Cause most these kin just wanna sell."

"So, he's a regular ol' Willy Wonka searching for his Charlie? It's still awful. You just can't play with peoples' minds and emotions like this. And what was he going to do when all of this training was over?"

"I'm not shore of his grand scheme, hun. All I know is that he didn't intend for it to unfold like this. Boris was a kind man. Little hard 'round the edges, but kind nonetheless."

"I can't believe you waited so long to tell me."

"Trust me, devil take my soul right now, I wanted to. Not even 'posed to be tellin' ya now. Chandler made us all sign off to keep our mouths shut. Ya know, only in some legal mumbo jumbo nice way of sayin' it. Anybody finds out I told ya, I'll lose my job."

"Sounds like blackmail to me."

"Forgive me."

"So, now that he's really dead, who are the real heirs?"

"I don't rightly know. Guess we find out when this thing's all over."

"Assuming we're still alive." I thought for a moment. "Wait, if this is all a hoax, no one is going to be arriving at the dock on the 13th day."

"That's really happenin'. As is the test. Frankie delivered it himself. I know that fer certain."

"The moment the truck driver was found, this whole thing should have been canceled," I said. "Cashmere wouldn't have gotten burned. People wouldn't have died. What on earth would possess the man to continue on with this devilish nonsense?" I was mad at Boris. I was sad about Boris. And I was more scared than ever. "Tess, we need to be honest with people. We need everyone to leave."

"You think those kids are going to believe me? Harley is not leaving without his pockets stuffed with cash."

"Well, then everyone but Harley leaves. He's not an heir remember. He won't see a penny."

"But, I thought you couldn't leave," said Tessie.

She was right. Which got me thinking. "Maybe Boris couldn't leave either." Someone had threatened my family. Someone had forced me to stay against my better judgement. If they had that control over me, they certainly could manipulate Boris as well. Pity pushed aside anger. Boris was a victim too. He may have started all of this, but the killer was finishing it with his or her own set of rules.

"I just can't believe he's really gone," I said. "Tess, I was the one that found him." My thoughts revisited the helpless old man laid out on the basement floor in pools of blood. "I never got to say goodbye to my grandfather. Never really even had the chance to say hello."

Tuxedo Truffle: Crisp, clean citrus flavors of mandarin and blood orange centered into a polished chocolate poppy seeded shell.

Chapter Six

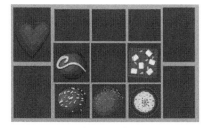

SIX untrusting souls prepared to sleep with one eye open.

*B*rice rounded everyone up in the parlor. "I think it's time we all get out of here," he said. "Whoever is behind this madness isn't going to stop until every person is out of *his* way."

Kiki nodded her head. "And how do you suppose we do that?" she said. "The phones are down."

Brice looked to Tessie, "Okay, so nobody is coming to us. Is there a car we can use?"

"Nope," she said. "Frankie has the Lincoln, and Winston has the keys to the stretch."

"Where is the old man?" said Harley, "I haven't see him all night."

Tessie and I shrugged off the question.

Brice said, "Okay then, here's the plan. If someone in this room is the killer, then none of us should be alone with him—"

"Or, her," said Harley.

Brice rolled his eyes. "Tonight, we stay together. Let's get some blankets, and we can all stay here."

There was no way in the world I was trusting Harley while I slept. "I don't think Tessie should be on the couch or floor," I said.

Brice agreed. "How about the girls stay together in your room, Tess?"

Tessie nodded.

"Brice, you can stay with us, too," I said, not wanting to leave him alone with Harley.

Harley shook his head. "Get over it, Anna. Don't keep blaming me, when you were at the scene of the crime."

Brice cut us off. "Anna, I'll be fine. Harley and I will bunk in Winston's room. That way, we can fill him in when he comes around. Nobody goes anywhere alone. Trust no one."

Before separating for the night, I spoke privately with Brice. He assured me that he would keep a close eye on Harley. We decided to meet up in the morning to come up with a plan out of here. Unless, of course, Winston came to our rescue first.

Tessie's room wasn't what I would call maid's quarters. And unlike the other rooms in the mansion, it didn't have a chocolate theme. The decor was antique elegance, with a subtle explosion of Grandma's garage sale. Chair rails and intricate crown molding traced the perimeter. Two queen canopied beds stood majestically, crowned with satin shammed pillows bordered with delicate laced edges. Victorian styled benches sat at the foot of each bed draped with hand-stitched patchwork quilts. An oversized chandelier hung between the beds, sparkling down upon dark mahogany furniture, every inch smothered with crochet doilies.

The farthest side of the suite was more personalized.

"Oh, you knit," I said to Tessie, noting a bag of yarn spilling onto the floor.

"I dabble," she said.

A rocking chair draped with an afghan in front of the fireplace was wearing through dark planks. An end table sat next to it holding a vintage radio and a touch-style Tiffany lamp. Seeing the lamp reminded me of the creepy light in the demolished room upstairs.

"Tess, do you know of anyone going in the vacant bedroom upstairs?"

She shook her head. "Can't find my upstairs' keys. Thought I misplaced em. But, now I'm startin' to wonder if someone stole em."

I walked over to the fireplace. The mantel held typical grandmother-like knick-knacks. The kind of things you see at a yard sale and wonder where they originated from. A wooden Dutch shoe, a gold pineapple that stored golden toothpicks, and a porcelain hand covered in assorted rings.

Kiki lugged her suitcases into the room. "It smells funny in here."

"It's Lavender," said Tessie. She opened several dresser drawers pulling out bars of Yardley soap and potpourri satchels. Perhaps, a bit overboard. But, still pleasant. How a grandmother's room should smell.

Kiki tossed her cosmetic bag on a bed. "I call this one."

Okay? I didn't need a bed. It wasn't worth fighting for it. Besides, I didn't plan on getting much sleep tonight, anyways.

The two of them got dressed for bed. I stayed in my jeans, sweatshirt, and sneakers, ready to make a run for it, if needed.

Tessie sat up in her bed. "Why this is like a regular old slumber party."

Kiki said, "Yeah, with someone on the loose, trying to murder us off one by one. How fun."

Tessie clapped twice, and the chandelier turned off. A couple minutes later, more clapping.

"I need to do some things," said Kiki. She sat up in her bed, filed her nails, smeared lotion onto her arms, and then started cleaning out her purse.

If I didn't know better, I'd think Kiki was scared. And human. Either that, or she wanted to ensure nobody was getting any rest. It was a standoff, but eventually, she fell asleep with the lights on.

I gave a quick clap, dimming the chandelier, and cozied up on a blanket next to the fire, quickly realizing that wood floors didn't make ideal beds. Sleep didn't come easy as I tried to centralize the roar of Kiki's snore. I said to myself, *the wave comes in, the wave goes out*, in rhythm to her breathing, hoping to fabricate a sea-side slumber. No luck, my mind would not believe Kiki's ocean impersonation. Old Tom and Jerry cartoons animated solutions in my head. Perhaps corking her nostrils with grapes? Or, attaching a vacuum nozzle to her nose to suck up the noise? My delusional brain really needed some rest. I laid there a long time, watching the transformation of blaring burning logs change into minute illuminations of scrawny exhausted timbers. Kiki coughed, finally giving a break to her rumbling snore, and I finally got my peaceful night's rest.

৵৹ৎ ৎ৹৵

I woke up in a Frankenstein paralysis, my stiffened bones struggling to straighten. My muscles ached. My back was wrenched. And my neck was kinked.

A quick glance let me know that the room was empty. Knowing Tessie, she couldn't stay out of the kitchen. Kiki abandoned ship, as well. But, her pungent perfume vapors lingered, letting me know she was primped for the day. So the buddy system was a success.

I encouraged my sore muscles to get up. It was day twelve, and I was ready to bail. The sooner we got going, the sooner we could figure a way out of here.

With a bit of effort, I rolled over. Ouch. And rolled on top of something. That was now poking me in the ribs. I pulled back the covers acknowledging an unwelcomed offering. That stinkin' box of chocolates. I've never hated chocolate so much in all of my life. I raised the top off the box. Just as suspected, another candy had been removed from the box, only this time somebody specifically wanted me to know about it. I studied the scarce chocolates in the box. Were one of these mine? Or was someone trying to tell me that I was next?

I pushed through aches and pains, darting to the staircase. I needed to warn the others. The only thing I knew for sure is that one of us was in immediate danger. Halfway down, a scream. The type of scream that ignites fire in every vessel of your body until it releases into your brain as a fireball of panic. I quick-stepped down the hall to discover the next casualty in this gruesome game. The charming parlor usually filled with scents of spiced tea and lemon curd, now felt empty and frigid, reeking of must and death.

Kiki, Tessie, and Brice hovered over the body. Could any of them be responsible? I couldn't fathom the thought.

Harley was sprawled out on the wooden floor, the chocolate-spattered machete pierced through his chest. A river of death flowed across the wooden planks, trickling its way down to a dead end. The liquid pooled over an aged, yellowed newspaper article. The caption under the photo read, *Troubled girl, a murderer?* Good heavens, the photo was of me.

I became aware of the chocolate box still in my hands, feeling the others' eyes burning upon me.

"I'm going to ask the question for everybody," said Brice. His eyes met mine. "Anna, did you do it?"

Heat rose to my head, feeling like an ant carcass underneath the wrath of a lad's magnifying glass on an August day. "Good heavens, I have no idea where that newspaper came from—"

He cut me off. "Yes or No? That's all I want to know."

"And this box, it was in my bed."

Kiki said, "What don't you understand? Yes, or no?"

"No. Of course not," I said, drowning in my own tears.

"That's good enough for me," said Brice.

Kiki said, "Well it's not good enough for me."

"She didn't do it," said Brice. "Let it go."

We all took a silent moment to absorb Harley's passing.

Harley's glazed over eyes closed the tunnel of his soul. Seeing the life literally draining out of somebody was hard enough. But, having others wonder if I could be the one responsible for his ending, was too much to take in. I studied the blood-soaked newspaper clipping. Somebody was setting me up. Perhaps, that's why the killer was forcing me to stay against my will. As a scape goat.

Ever since Caesar died, most of my suspicions had pointed to Harley. And with a quick twist of events, I was now the main suspect. Based on what? A fictitious newspaper article? Granted, the photo was of me. But, I had never seen it before in my life. I imagine with today's technology somebody could have fabricated such an item to appear weathered and worn. I had to give them props for that though, because the clipping was beyond convincing.

Brice covered Harley's body with a quilt.

This wasn't the plan. We were supposed to get out of this morbid hole first thing this morning. Not discover another corpse.

I said, "Enough is enough already. We need to get out of here and get the police."

"That's humorous coming from the girl with the box of chocolates in her hands," said Kiki.

Brice snapped, "Kiki, leave it alone already."

"No," said Kiki. "Look around. Four of us. One holding the forbidden candy box. Anna might as well have her hand on the trigger."

Kiki and Brice argued it out. Kiki blamed me. Brice blamed Frankie. And I was staying out of it. I didn't know what to believe any more. Every time I thought I'd figured things out, somebody else dies. We had to stop this. We had to escape. I just had to be careful about this. Once I left the property, I needed to secure Jillian's safety before involving the police. Meanwhile, I had to keep Kiki off my back.

I stepped in between Kiki and Brice. "We all have different opinions about what's going on here, except for the fact that we want to survive. So, let's get out of here."

"And how do you suggest we do that, Einstein?" Kiki asked me. "Tessie and I couldn't find spare keys to the limousine anywhere."

Brice sighed, "It doesn't matter anyways. I ran up to check out the entryway this morning. The gate is all padlocked up. We're trapped."

Tessie said, "There's an employee entrance."

"It's left unlocked?" asked Brice.

Tessie thought for a moment. "No padlocks. Some modern gizmo." She pursed her lips. "But ya need to be in the limousine to trigger it."

Brice asked Tessie? "Are the caterers or spa employees coming back today?"

She shook her head. "We were supposed to be exploring downtown Paris Falls today. Checkin' out Chandler's new shop."

We missed our window.

"So, we're back to square one," I said. "Stuck here for two more nights."

"Not if I can help it," said Brice. "I'm going to look for something to cut through those locks. Meanwhile, you girls lock yourselves in Tessie's room."

"I'm not staying with her," Kiki said, wide eyes on me.

"Whatever," said Brice. "Then lock yourself in your own room. Just stay safe."

I purposefully was the last person to leave the room. I tossed the chocolate box on the couch, trying to toss away with it the guilt I felt for something I didn't do.

⁂

Flaky Hawaiian Nut: Shell-shaped chocolate, imported from the Hawaiian Islands, featuring waves of rich chocolate, rolled in coconut flakes and sands of macadamia nuts.

Chapter Five

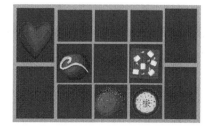

Five human heirs remained targets in a shooting gallery.

Tessie and I detoured to the kitchen, stockpiling leftover desserts from the cafe and a bag full of dry food from the pantry. One thing was sure, we weren't going to die of starvation.

We got Bonbon, and hunkered down in Tessie's room.

"I'm surprised you're still rooming with me," I said, while we barricaded the door with small furniture. "I thought everyone thought I was a mad killer."

"Do I look like a pony on a jackass farm?"

I bit my upper lip, not having a clue on how to respond.

"Of course, I do. Miss Piggy has checked into the looney bin. Yer as much of a killer as I am."

"Well then, who? Let's face it, there's not a lot of options left. I counted on my hand, "It's just you, me, Kiki, Brice and—" I thought for a moment. "There were five candies left. Who belonged to the fifth?"

"Frankie."

"When Frankie left last night, he told me that he would be back. I thought he meant like last night." I didn't want to upset Tessie, but I started to wonder about him. Evidence was stacking up against her star employee.

He had an affair with Kiki.

He used to work for Homer's Nuthouse.

He ran off with Boris' corpse.

And his candy was still in the box. When he left, he should have been eliminated from the competition, just like the others had been.

Tessie pondered. "And what happened to Winston?"

"He could have gone to Timbuktu, and been back by now," I said. "Why aren't those men sending us help?"

"Don't make a lick of sense," said Tessie.

Tessie put a hand over her heart, her eyes off in a daze. "Did you see Harley? Life plumb sucked out of em. We're dealin' with the devil alright. We're gonna die in here. I ain't never gonna meet my great grandbaby."

"Nonsense. Enough of this crazy talk. We're going to mush until Frankie or Winston gets back. Neither one of them are going to strand us here, with a killer."

"And if they never come back?"

"Then, we'll break down the flippin' gates. Now then," I scanned the room. "I give up, where is it?"

Tessie looked confused.

"I know you need your Dixie Hicks' fix."

Tessie pointed to an oil painting of a daffodil field.

I slid the painting on a track across the wall, revealing a television. "Clever."

"Just cause Boris liked to keep the mansion fit for an old fogie, doesn't mean I don't need my morning line-up."

She pulled back the lemon colored covers on her bed, then slipped inside the poster queen, draped with white sheer canopies tied off with gold silk roses.

I served her breakfast in bed, which consisted of our favorite leftover dessert from the caterer.

We sat in silence, feeding pain with gourmet desserts. After a while, my taste buds numbed, while my brain wondered off, staring through the painting on the wall. A sunny field of daffodils swept me off into a mental journey. I felt the breeze of the swaying stems. The sweetness of their delicate petals.

I walked over to the picture to have a closer look. My finger fell into the groove of the dried oil, its strokes pulling me into a peaceful trance. "This is a beautiful painting," I said to Tessie, admiring the golden daffodils with chins raised to the sun. An endless field of yellow flowers, was feast for a single minuscule butterfly. "It reminds me of my mama's garden. Daffodils. She had tons of them. I hadn't thought about them in so long."

"What do you remember about her?"

While I spoke, a force kept me drawn to the painting. Distant memories. I barely knew her, but I still had days full of sadness when I just missed her. "I don't really remember much about her. Sometimes, I don't know if the stories in my head are real, or dreams. But, I recall Mama taking me out to the daffodil beds, lifting me up in the sky. Twirling me around like a beautiful butterfly. Then, she put me down and told me that I could have a flower. Any one that I wanted. I knew they meant so much to her. I told her I was lucky to have such a pretty flower. And she told me, it was the flower that was the lucky one, to be picked by me. She ever so carefully snipped its stem, then I held it in my hands as if it was a fragile bubble, shielding it from the winds. Mama and I went inside for lunch. While she made sandwiches, I put the daffodil in an empty root beer bottle. She placed the flower on the table next to a plate of finger sandwiches. They were my favorite. Each with a layer of canned strawberry jam, a layer of butter, and a layer of apricot preserves. All cut nice and tidy into finger sandwiches.

I realized I had been rambling on. "Anyways. Silly boring story. Probably not even real."

"Are you kiddin'?" Her eyes were welled up. "Yer mama was blessed with you for such a short time. Yet, she taught you so much."

"What do you mean?"

"About loving the little things."

I thought back to my miserable childhood birthday party. "Tess, you were right. About those girls at my birthday party."

Her eyebrows raised.

"I *was* jealous of them. But, it was never about the money. I was jealous of the other girls because they had mothers. Mothers that dressed them in frilly dresses and lacy pinafores, and curled their hair into perfect locks. Mothers who draped their gals in strings of pearls and prim and proper gloves to show off their Southern etiquette. Mothers that did all those prissy things– that were not me."

It took me twenty years to realize, I was happy. Uncle Wiley didn't shove pretentiousness down my throat. He just let me be me. Not saying I didn't own hot rollers. And a couple dozen eyeliners. But then, those are just Southern gal staples. And I only bring out the big hair for special occasions.

I needed to see my uncle. I needed to thank him for all the things I resented him for growing up. He didn't ruin that birthday party. I did it. Because I forgot who I was. I wanted to be like everybody else, just so I'd fit in. But, what's the fun of that?

My finger's trail ended at the cornered signature, A.H. "All of the paintings in the mansion were painted by the same person. Did you know the artist?"

"Them pictures been on the walls fer years. Seems I recall Chandler havin' a contest of some sorts. Folks were 'sposed to send in photos showin' how Chandler's chocolates made them happy, or some nonsense like that. Turns out, the lady that won sent in a painting. Guess Chandler fancied her work. He mine as well have put her on the payroll, hirin' that gal to paint picture after picture. She hasn't painted any in years though, case you were interested."

"No, it wasn't that at all. You know the picture in the basement, of the little girl on the swing?"

"Course, that's the Bells' gal. Everyone knows the Bells' gal."

"As a young girl, I remember seeing a framed photograph almost identical to that one, on my uncle's dresser. Only the picture was in color and the little girl was holding a doll in her hands, not a sack of candy. Tess, I think the painting is of me— Anna *Bell*. I dropped the Bell in grade school."

She placed her hands on her hips. "For the love of Bisquick, are ya fer real?"

"As real as Kiki's dark roots."

"Then the woman, she was—"

"My mother. But how is that even possible?"

"I'll tell you how. Chandler." Tessie sprung up and paced rhythmically back and forth. "Why that makes me madder than a hornet. Why that lousy good fella, knowin' where she was all those years." She picked up Kiki's ponytail extension off the dresser, taking out her aggression on it. "He knew her. Every minute he spoke to her, was one minute more than I ever did. Why if he wasn't dead already— I would—" *rip* She shredded the hair piece. She ripped and tore at it. A hunk at a time. When nothing was left to it, she flopped on the bed, and her frustration transformed into tears.

I wrapped my arms around her. "I'm so sorry. I can't even imagine how you're feeling."

"I'm okay," she sniffled. She took in an exaggerated long breath and was instantly upright. "I just have to shake it off."

"Sometimes it's good to let things out."

"Well shore enough, that's what I just done did, and now I'm fine. Life's too short to spend it snivelin' in misery.

Nothin' we can do 'bout the past. Besides I got somethang that ol kook didn't have."

I shoved the mangled hair shreds under the pillow.

"I've got me a grand-baby— and a great grand-baby."

❧ ❧

Cabin fever was setting in. I tried to pass time with a nap, tricking my body into a relaxed state. My head sunk into the goose feather pillow, my eyelids released like blinds on a finished day, and my mind prepared for total relaxation.

"Buttocks!" Tessie hollered at the television. "No, you ninnies."

Ding! Survey says— buttocks. The number one answer.

"I knew it," she said victoriously.

And that would end my nap.

As Tessie enjoyed channel surfing, I gave up on sleep, opting for a soak in the tub with another round of dessert. I spent time with each confection, individually tasting them, exploring the textures and flavors of each one on my tongue, as if they were fine wines. My muscles rejoiced in the warm, bubbling water, finally on the trail to inner peace. I breathed in slowly and exhaled, leading myself in a relaxation exercise.

Bang Bang Bang

With one pound of the door, anxiety instantly surged back through my bones.

"I'll get it," said Tessie.

"No," I hollered with maternal force. "Don't get near that door." I wrapped a towel around my body and made my way to the entryway. I pushed the barricade a couple inches from the door and cracked the door open with the chain still attached.

"I need to talk to you," said Brice. "Can I come in?"

My eyes met his hands. "Why do you have a golf club?" I asked, suspiciously.

Brice looked at me as if I had gone goofy. "For protection," he said.

"And why are you running around, instead of being locked in your room?"

"I needed to talk to you. There aren't any working phones," he said, as if that was already obvious. His eyes met mine. "Are you okay, Anna?"

My trust was running so scarce, I was now accusing my allies. Panic attack, here I come. "Of course," I said. "Just give me a minute to get dressed."

Tessie was barely phased, enthralled by her game show. "Pick the box. Make a deal, you ninny," she hollered at the TV, watching a man dressed like a chicken contemplate his fortune.

"Hey, Tess. I'm going to step out to talk with Brice. Be sure that you lock the door behind me."

I actually got a coherent response from her, thanks to the feminine hygiene commercial. "Are ya off your rocker? It's not safe out there."

"I'll be fine. I'll be with Brice."

"He needs to be locked up too."

"I'll be right outside."

I rummaged through my suitcase, grabbing a t-shirt and squeezing it over my head.

"Anna, what en tarnation is that?"

"What?"

"On yer back."

"Oh that. Just an old scar." I lifted up the back of my shirt revealing a scar that traced a curvy line down my torso.

"Heavens to Betsy girl, that's a real doozie."

"It's from a car accident when I was young. This scar is a reminder of the last day I ever saw my Mom."

Tessie gasped.

"Sorry. I thought you knew."

"I knew Adeline died, but the car accident is news to me."

Brice knocked again. "Anna, you coming?"

"Just a minute." I slipped on a pair of jeans and fixed my shirt. I stepped into the hallway with him. "What's up?"

"I didn't want to worry Tessie, but I think our culprit is on the move."

My eyes squinted. "What do you mean?"

"I was out on my balcony, and I heard somebody behind the pool path. It sounded like something was being dragged or pushed. Kind of squeaky. Like something on wheels."

"We should check it out *in the morning*," I said.

"I already did, but whoever it was, was long gone. I took the path up the mountainside too. Nothing."

I let out a heavy sigh.

"I'm going back for another look around, but I wanted to check on everyone in the house first. Problem is, you and Tessie are the only ones in your room. I can't find Kiki, and Winston never showed up."

"Who in their right mind would be wandering about the property?"

"Exactly. You guys, lock your door behind me. I'll come back here and fill you in after I have another look around. Don't open your door for anyone. You hear?"

"No way, Brice. You shouldn't be wandering around out there alone. It's not safe."

"I'll be fine. He held up the golf club."

My eyebrows raised in doubt. That may not cut it. I'm not sure where the courageous stupidity came from, spewing from my mouth, "I'm coming with you." *I am?*

Brice agreed. "Only if you stand back. Even if I'm in danger. And if something happens to me, don't try to be a hero. Go get help."

I appreciated his confidence in me, but I don't think I was born with the hero gene. Crikey, what have I gotten myself into? I peeked through the door to Tessie. "We're just going for a walk. We'll be back soon."

Tessie argued. "But—"

"I'll be fine." Just after I throw up.

Without pause, I reopened the door. "Tess, don't forget, lock the door behind me."

I turned to face Brice. "Okay, lead the way."

We headed up the path up the mountainside. "I'm sorry I dragged you into this," he said. "Now that Ashton is gone, I just don't know who else to trust."

I reassured him with a smile. "Trust me, I know the feeling." We got to a fork in the path. Going left would take us up to the highest point of the mountain, where we had the engagement party.

"I already tried that path," he said, leading us down the opposite path, sending us deeper into the woods.

Meanwhile, my brain tried to make sense of things. Nobody would be out here by themselves, unless they were up to no good. But, who? Winston had left. Frankie had not returned. So, Kiki had to be the one wandering about— unless our culprit was someone else altogether. My terror conjured up images of horror flick villains. Freddie, Michael, and Jason. Oh my.

Mimicking Brice's golf club over his shoulder, I paused to pick up a broken tree limb, slinging it over my shoulder. Scholar recruit. Until killer takes a chainsaw to it.

We rounded the corner, meeting a splendid glass structure, blooming out of a garden of trees. This must be the greenhouse that the horticulturist was speaking about. The building was an aged work of intricate art, fine detail given to the cathedral architecture, like a glass-blown church, in the arms of Jack's magical vines.

We investigated the perimeter, pressing our faces to the window for a peek inside. Between the layers of dirt on the windows and an abundance of greenery stuffed into the building, it was impossible to get a clear look.

I pointed out a wheelbarrow parked in the entranceway of the greenhouse. Wheels, check. Squeaky, check.

Brice gave me a sudden shush. He tilted his head toward the building. Somebody was in there. We found a hiding spot outside where we could track the internal movement. With every attempt, we couldn't make out who was inside. Just a hint of a silhouette, here and there. Like looking through fogged up goggles filled with seaweed. Brice wanted to storm in and confront the mysterious person, but I appealed to him. I just didn't have a good feeling about this.

He agreed to wait it out. What goes in, must come out. As the sun began to set, a figure moved toward the greenhouse entrance way.

We moved closer to gain a better view, like stealthy spies meandering through obstacles in the night brush. Unfortunate for us, I wasn't as stealthy as I pretended to be. I ran plumb straight into a limb and fell back into a carnivorous bush of thorns, and some unmentionable words may have escaped my lips— rather loudly.

Our gig was up. "Who's out there?" said Kiki.

Kiki? Brice lunged in her direction, and I grabbed his leg. I whispered, "Let's check it out, *after* she leaves."

We scuttled away from the greenhouse, hearing footsteps behind us.

"Awe hell, she's following us," said Brice.

"*POW!*" A gunshot.

My hands shielded a worthless tent above my head. "Nope, she's hunting us."

Brice grabbed my hand, and literally drug me down the path that was barely visible in the moonlight.

POW! POW!

Crikey, I'm going to die.

He pulled me off the path, into the darkness of the woods. "Just stay down—"

POW! We ran deeper and deeper into the field of trees. It was nearly impossible to see, at the mercy of filtered moonbeams. But, the fading sound of gunshots let us know we were going in the right direction.

We sat hidden in the darkness. Only the sound of my escaping breath heaving out of my mouth remained. I focused, trying to contain it. Realizing, I was now holding my breath. I whispered, "Do you think we're good?"

"Just stay down," he told me.

I could do that. At least I thought I could. Until something scampered across my foot, encouraging me to run. I ran. I ran as fast as I could. Ignoring breaking twigs and growths of knotted roots below my stumbling steps. Ignoring insects' taunting screams. I ran. I needed to escape. Escape the forest. Escape the darkness. Escape the monster threatening my family. I allowed my tears to pour into the earth in between my reckless steps.

Brice's voice paused my sprint. I stopped, taking a moment to assess my surroundings. I had no idea which way I came from, or which way the mansion was. The only thing I knew for sure, is that I was somewhere I didn't want to be.

"Hey, where did you go?" said Brice.

I'll tell you where I went. Deeper into the woods. Deeper into a panic. And suddenly thrown into a scene from a B-rated horror flick. Dead-ending at the doorstep of a cabin. Those cliché types, that force you to scream at your television set. "Don't go in there, stupid." Because *stupid* always gets killed in the cabin in the woods.

I stepped onto the porch, calling out to him, like kids playing Marco Polo in the pool. Only, I didn't like this game. Haunting whispers of wind swept over my skin. Marco was giving me the heebie jeebies.

Atlas, Brice found me. "Awesome, you found a place to hide."

No. Not awesome.

With faint gunshots off in the distance, we were faced with the option of being a human target, or hiding in a shelter. Brice shined a pen shaped flashlight on the door.

"All this time, we've been stumbling in the deathly forest, you had a flashlight?"

"I didn't want to attract attention."

And now my eye roll wouldn't gather his attention in the dark.

Brice jiggled the door knob. Locked. But as luck, or bad luck would have it, the back door was open. *Yeah.*

I took a cowered step back, and allowed Brice to open the door. I followed him through the dark space, pushing spider webs out of my face and hair. It was clear, friend or foe, had not been through this doorway for quite some time. A spec of relief.

The floor felt a bit unsteady, creaking with every amount of pressure. The air was dead and frigid. Debris around every blind corner. My imagination filled in the blanks. Walls of chainsaws, axes, and rusted torture devices hung on the walls. I ducked my head to avoid the metal teeth of animal traps lurking above. I would never watch another horror movie as long as I lived. Which I prayed was longer than this dreadful evening.

A floodlight of moonbeams shined through a small window, highlighting a chunk of stairs. Brice led the way up the narrow steps. I held onto the railing with one hand and his shirt tail with the other. Because if the step underneath me crumbled, I was certain his shirt tail would save me.

"Slow down." I whispered, carefully maneuvering each step. Not moving forward until my toe felt the wall of the step before it. This was no time to be careless. Breathing in the musty air, swelled my nose. I did everything in my power to hold in a sneeze. A sneeze that I was sure would bust me through the wooden planks.

Atlas, a door that led to level ground. We followed the string of light through the hall, to the kitchen. Brice lit a gas lamp on the table, lighting up the rustic space. Rusted signs and uneven shelves of jars and cans scattered the walls. He shined the light on the adjoining space. Log-framed couches cornered a fireplace that climbed up the two-story wall. Chopped wood piled on either side of it. And a kettle hung in the hollowed pit. As I got closer, I could feel heat.

"Uh Brice, somebody has been here. Recently."

"I know," he said, showing me a half cup of coffee on the table. "I think we just found the killer's hide-out."

Hiding out in the killer's hide-out. Perfect. As in perfectly, stupid. My gut reaction was to run the holy dickens out of this creep hole. But, Brice convinced me that we had to take the opportunity to dig around. And by convinced, I mean he wasn't leaving until he looked around, and there was no way in heck, I was facing the deadly woods alone.

Brice picked up the lantern and handed me the mini flashlight.

In the kitchen, I found a cupboard of canned food, boxed and bars of chocolates, wine, and assorted bottles of liquor. I suppose these were the bare necessities.

Meanwhile, Brice found a cabinet of hunting rifles. No surprise, one was missing. "Hurry up," said Brice. "Let's see what else we can find. We'll grab these when we leave. Then, I'm going to take a detour back to that greenhouse."

I searched upstairs, feeling like one of those CSI agents on television lurking around in the dark with a flashlight. The first room was locked, but the second room was wide open.

The nightstand held a pipe, tobacco, and a photo of a newborn baby. Certainly, an unexpected find in such a man-cave of a cabin. I rummaged through a desk finding odd change, a tiny ring of keys, fishing lures, and *loose bullets*. Giving it more of that cabin of the killer charm. All the while chanting to myself, "You shouldn't be here, stupid." I pocketed the keys.

I leaned forward, digging to the back of the drawer, trying to retrieve a small box, inadvertently getting my hair caught on something on the wall. I slid my hand in between my hair and the board, knocking the whole dang-it thing behind the desk— my hair still attached.

Brice quick-stepped into the room. "Someone's here, we have to go."

My heart raced at an unnatural speed. "My hair is sorta stuck. To the wall." I pulled and yanked.

"Seriously," said Brice. "We're going to get caught."

Twenty loss hairs later, I freed myself from the dreaded thing. I reached behind the desk, retrieving what turned out to be a fallen corkboard. My hair must have gotten tangled on a thumbtack.

"Hurry up," he pushed.

"I'm coming." Trying to cover our tracks, I desperately scraped the cork-board over the wall, finally getting it to catch the nail.

"Now," said Brice. "Let's got out of here. And turn off that flashlight."

As I raised the flashlight from the desk, it shined over the corkboard. My hand filtered my whisper, "Oh my gosh." Various photos of the grandkids had been pinned on the board. Cashmere's face had a big red 'x' over it, creating a lump in my throat. Ditto for Caesar. Cripes. My photo and Brice's photo were on there, too. Only ours were circled with the red marker. We were next.

Brice tugged on my arm, and dragged me down the hall. As we fled down the stairs, the front door rattled. Somebody wanted in. Bad.

Thankfully, Brice was there to pull me out. He led me to the basement. My feet sped down the staircase, my bum taking the faster route, slid down the last few steps.

"Darn it," said Brice. "I wanted to get those rifles. We have no way of defending ourselves in the mansion."

"It's too risky to go back tonight," I said.

Brice agreed. "We'll have to try again tomorrow."

We? I wasn't going to worry about that just yet. At the moment, we needed to worry about finding our way back to the mansion. At least we had a lantern now, not that seeing the surrounding trees gave us any indication of which direction to go.

We picked a direction, and went with it.

"We need to find out who's hiding in that cabin," I said.

"Well, I doubt it's Kiki," Brice said. "How would she even know the cabin existed? Unless she's working with an employee."

"You think there are two people after us?"

"Get down," whispered Brice, shoving my back. "Somebody's in that brush."

No, not again. Truly my heart couldn't take any more.

An unexpected ally. "Bonbon, what in the world are you doing out here?" I said, scratching her head. She moved her head from my reach, and ran off. "Come here, girl. Where are you going?"

Brice and I chased behind her, a half mile later realizing that she had rescued us.

⊱⊰ ⊱⊰

Tessie sprung up. "Yawl scared the chickens outta me."

Brice said, "I just wanted to make sure Anna got back here safely. Lock the door behind me and drag the furniture in front of the door if you can." He looked at me, "Tomorrow, I'm going back for the rifles." I was sure not to volunteer this time around.

He said, "Until then, I'll be in Winston's room. You guys stay locked in this room. I'll come to get you at quarter to one. Then, we'll go meet the courier together."

"Quarter to one," I repeated, and closed the door.

Tessie scolded me like a teenager missing curfew. "Where in tarnation have you been? I've been worried sick."

I frantically locked the door, but my quivering hands couldn't needle the peg into the chain bolt.

Tessie studied my fingers and lowered her voice. "You're all shaken up, real good." She patted her hand on the mattress, prompting Bonbon to jump aboard. "Had to send out the hound to drag you youngins' back in."

"*You* sent her?"

"Indeed, I did." She scooted over, making a spot for me, "Now then, sit down and tell me what happened."

I sat down next to her, my legs dangling over the side.

"Child, you done got yourself all scratched up." She reached inside her apron pocket. "I got just the thing for ya—"

Good heavens, not again. "No. No gelled road kill."

"Your loss."

I filled Tessie in about the greenhouse, the shootings, and the mysterious cabin in the woods.

"Shore I know about that place," she said. "Used to spend time there as a teenager, with the boss's son," she said with a wink.

Yuck. I hated being a visual person.

"But, as far as I know, no one has used it for years. Back in the day, the men would come for a hunting and fishing weekend. Mrs. Chandler didn't care for that sort of thing, so the Chandler men built the cabin. Didn't do half bad for building it themselves. Never got electricity in there though. They said they wanted to keep things rustic, but I think they couldn't figure out that part. Any who, once Boris' daddy passed, there wasn't much need for the cabin. Boris didn't like to hunt, he was a softy that way. Had too much respect for the animals. These days, when we have guests, and he needs alone time, he goes to his retreat in the basement."

"Who else knows about the cabin?" I asked.

"I spose some of the employees could know 'bout it. It's not a secret. But, I tell ya, I haven't known anyone to stay out there in years."

A pounding at the door, made us jump.

"Who is it?" I asked.

"It's me. Kiki. Open the friggin' door!"

Tessie and I looked at each other. "Shh," Tessie said.

I whispered, "She already knows we're here."

Kiki's pounding got louder. "Please, open the door. Frankie is hurt."

Tessie and I mouthed in confusion. "Frankie?"

"It's a trick," I whispered to Tessie.

"Frankie left," Tessie told Kiki. "With Boris. Ya think, we're donkeys?"

"No, he came back," she plead. "We were having dinner, and then he got sick. Like really, *really* sick."

Without reservation, Tessie opened the door. I grabbed a lamp, just in case I needed a weapon.

Kiki was all gussied up in a piece of a dress, and enough war paint to make her glow in the dark. "We need to get him help, but the phones are disconnected. So, someone needs to drive him to the hospital."

I looked to Tessie, "Kiki, you know we don't have keys."

"Frankie has them," she said. "Anna, I need you to go to the greenhouse and help Frankie. He told me there was a phone in the kitchen. I'm going to go look for it."

I made my way to the greenhouse. If there was the minute chance that Frankie had returned and was deathly ill, we needed to save him.

✸❀ ❀✸

The greenhouse that boasted thriving growth and flourishing beauty in the sunset, oozed creepiness in the black of the night. The intertwining life that blossomed within, now stood eerily still inside, like vultures' shadows patiently waiting for a perished soul. Panes of glass layered with years of dirt, clouded any encouraging voices inside my head. I had been shot at this evening. I had run for my life. And now I may have returned for another lashing. Like a puppet. Kiki's puppet. But, *what if?* What if Frankie is truly in danger? I could never forgive myself if I chose to let someone die because I was too scared to save them. My pep talk, landed me in front of the greenhouse doorway.

Standing on the doorstep, I looked up at the mighty glass and steel exterior, focusing on the uppermost window, as if staring the monster in the eye. My fingers reached for the doorknob, threatening to invade its castle. I directed the flashlight to the door. Seeing my fingers shake, somehow made me more self-aware of my fear. Forcing control of the tremble, my hand clinched over the cold knob of rusted metal. The door screamed open, as if warning me to stay out.

"Hello?" I called out, my voice dissipating in the air. The temperature was noticeably warmer in here. The air humid.

I forced my steps forward into the space. "Frankie? You in here?"

Lighting my own steps, I found a trail of petals. At first, I thought it was just random debris on the floor. But, the petals slightly shriveled, still had some color. A trail seemed like a hint for a game of hide and seek. And I wasn't in the mood for a game. I just hoped it wasn't a trap. For me, or for Frankie.

I followed the path, out of the entryway, now into the heart of the three-story atrium. I stopped and listened. Water trickling. Random flutters up above. And music. Like a sad string quartet, echoing in the lobby of a funeral home. The kind of music that horrifies you in a dark, over-grown century old greenhouse. I erred on the side of caution, not following the music or the petals. I thought it best to first have a look around, as to not walk myself right into an ambush.

Although the vaulted space was huge, I felt claustrophobic. Layers upon layers of trees filled the space, all weaving in towards the focal point of the greenhouse, an enormous pond. Chutes of water trickled over rocks filling the basin. The walls of the reservoir where almost as tall as me. I lifted the flashlight overhead, sending beams up to the glistening rocks, following the flow into dark waters. The pond's surface was overtaken with shriveled leaves, algae-coated debris, and patches of fuzzy green carpet. Water so dark, it would drag you under the depths of the earth.

Cold chills flushed over my body. I wasn't sure if the clamminess was the result of nerves or the humidity. I followed the trail of petals around the perimeter of the water, through a tunnel of overgrown trees. Vining branches crept over every post, holding the structure hostage in the dark. The intertwining branches mimicked snakes, forcing an irrational sensation over my skin, as if turning my back on the vines would send them slithering over me. I shook it off. I sporadically called out Frankie's name, each time with no response. Just the sound of creepy music harmonizing with my rapid breaths of distress.

As my flashlight trailed over the line of petals, the fermented air, sweetened. Sweetened, as in cocoa. It was so intense, I knew it was real. The scent of chocolate consumed the surrounding space, getting stronger with every step. The tunnel of branches dead ended at the fragrant secret garden.

A table for two centered the space, garnished with votive candles and a sprinkle of petals. The table hosted a romantic display of food; a silver tray of cheeses, olives, and hard meats, two salads, and a half bottle of wine. Wow. Kiki was really telling the truth. Only, there was no sign of Frankie.

I couldn't wrap my mind around this whole scenario. Frankie knew we were in grave danger. Even if he was having an affair with Kiki, why would he come back unannounced to have a romantic dinner with her? There may be a romantic feast set before me, but not an ounce of logic to back it up.

I needed to determine what had happened here. Was Frankie ever here, or was this a set-up by Kiki? I needed to look for anything that would tie another person to this meal. I took a closer look at the table. Two bowls of mixed salad. Each bowl about half full. Only noticeable difference, someone ate the strawberries out of one of them. There were a pair of wine glasses, but only one had been used. I wiped a napkin around the rim. Lipstick. The tray of food in the center was picked at. But there was no way of telling how many people had eaten off it. Conclusion. There was no concrete evidence of a second person being here.

So then, why did Kiki send me here? I rummaged around the area for something, anything else. I found a tote bag. Inside there was a plastic food container, some rolled up plastic wrap, and a lighter. Obviously, the bag used to carry the dinner.

I had a seat at the table to gather my thoughts. I visualized Kiki putting together the food, packing it, and setting up the fake feast. Things didn't add up. What did she hope to accomplish?

Hold up. Kiki carried the dinner in the bag. So then, what did she need the wheelbarrow for? She wouldn't drag a cheese tray around in it. She had to move something else to the greenhouse. There must be something else in this building. Something, or *somebody*, much bigger.

I sprung up out of the chair, on the search for anything that looked out of place. Not an easy task, when every corner was blooming foliage. If she hid something in here, even semi-large in size, it would be near impossible to find with only a pen-sized flashlight.

My fingers raked through random piles of dirt, under shrubs, and over trails of vines. I lit up pathways and corners, and an occasional spider web. The plants and trees had formed a natural maze. I randomly chose a path, coming out at the bottom of a staircase. It was a metal staircase that climbed up the height of the pond's fountain.

The staircase was rusted, steps covered with decayed foliage and sprays of water. It was unlikely anyone had climbed up them in years. It wasn't my favorite option, but it was my best opportunity for a view. I sucked in a breath and started the climb. I held on tight with one hand, while navigating the flashlight with the other.

Several steps completed, hadn't gained me any vision. I needed to get above the treetops. I lowered my head, shoving overgrown branches out of my way. Each step higher, felt less steady. At first, I thought my quivering nerves were causing the tremble in the staircase. But, halfway up, when I ducked to avoid a flying animal, I realized it was the rusted metal deteriorating under my feet.

My steps felt uneasy, but I wasn't going to turn back now. I was almost to a clearing. My hands braced on to branches, while I pushed my head through a tree to reveal a view.

I directed light over the slimy surface of upper fountain rocks. Water had been traveling over the same path for quite some time. The pond from above didn't look any more appealing. With just trickles of water feeding into it, it lie almost still, the weak current sending lily pads crowding to one side. I wouldn't step a toe in there for a million bucks. No telling what could be living or dying in there at its mercy.

I ducked again, at another flying beast. In hindsight, it probably wasn't close at all. But, unexpected things flapping around in the dark trees was creepy. I targeted one with a beam of my flashlight, not sure if it was a bat or an owl, or a small pterodactyl. I lost my balance, but regained my footing, inadvertently finding something that didn't belong in the pond. Bobbing against the side, caught in a nook of rocks, a shiny object reflected off my flashlight.

Incoming! My light flashed on a glowing pair of eyes coming straight for me. The beast swooped by, brushing its piercing fangs over my cheek. My quick steps of agility, paired with my awkward defensive techniques, sent the entire structure moving to one side. As my fingers grasped the railings, the creature squawked, and my flashlight rolled down the stairs. Cripes. I was three stories high, in the dark, face to face with a rabid beast, that I was sure was out for my blood. This couldn't get any worse.

"Game over," said Kiki's voice. And things got worse. She shined her flashlight upon me, and then onto herself, highlighting her gun. "Now walk down slowly."

"Woah," I said, instinctively putting up my hands. "Are you mad?" In hindsight, that was a dumb question.

"Where's Frankie?" she said.

"You know he's not here. My bet is that he was never here."

"What did you do to him?" Kiki persisted, turning the tables, trying to make me look like the bad guy. "Don't make me come up after you." She started up the leaning staircase, forcing me to go higher. The stairs wobbling. This is it. One way or another, I'm going down.

There were two options. One, I fought Kiki who was armed with a rifle. Two, I dove into a shallow murky grave. I wasn't sure if I could even survive a jump from this height. I knew the water was several feet above the surface, but beyond that was not visible to the eye. Saturated with algae and debris, I'm not sure it would even be visible in the daylight.

Option three. *Run.* My steps fleeted down the stairs. I couldn't see where Kiki was through the branches, but I could hear the clunking of her shoes, and an occasional curse. Meanwhile, the staircase felt more uneasy with every step. If I fell from this height, I was done for.

"Okay Kiki, I surrender," I said.

"You're lying."

"Nope. I'm on my way down. Just stay put."

"Good," she said. "And don't pull anything funny, or I'll shoot."

She targeted me with the flashlight beam. As I climbed down the stairs, I stumbled over my missing flashlight and shoved it in my pocket. While climbing through the next canopy of trees, I could see her. And unfortunately, she wasn't bluffing. The rifle was aimed on me.

"Almost there," I said, my brain scrambling to come up with a plan. I didn't even have a weapon. I didn't have a chance. My steps slowed, hoping for a miracle. Someone bursting into the room, and saving my neck. Yes, I watched too many movies.

"Stop stalling," Kiki said, followed by the cock of the gun.

And then she shot. The crazy girl took a shot. An aviating stampede emerged from the treetops. Squawking. Squealing. Eyes glowing.

Between the movement of the incoming herd and our fleeing steps, the teetering staircase was going down. My brain went into survival mode. I pushed off the staircase, latching onto a nearby tree. With that push, the falling staircase gained momentum, smashing through the glass wall of the greenhouse.

I hugged onto the tree branch for dear life, but I was losing to gravity. Without my brain's permission, my body jumped. Mere milliseconds thrusting through the air, slowed in time. I anticipated the shock of cold water, followed by my bones shattering into a million pieces once I hit concrete. My feet absorbed a rigid landing, scraping slimy residue with the tip of my toes, my body consumed in a lukewarm stew of leaves, debris, and some hidden slimy vegetation underneath the surface.

Kiki's wails were off in the distant. Cursing. No telling how badly she was injured. No telling if she could get to me. The only thing I knew for sure, she wanted me dead.

My legs pushed through the dense water, struggling towards the edge, trying not to focus on the pond's contents. Something rubbed against my leg. I disregarded what I'd like to think of as a harmless fish, a harmless gigantic fish, and moved forward. My hands stretched out in front of me, filtering lily pads out of my path. Almost to the edge. Cripes. I could hear Kiki's footsteps nearing. Meanwhile, the fish-like creature was still in my path. Swim away gosh doggit. I bravely grasped my palms around its clammy flesh. And quickly retracted them. I dug the flashlight pen out of my pocket, vigorously flicking the on and off switch. The best I got out of the wet tool, was a flicker. Just enough to flash visibility to the gruesome body floating before me. I wanted to believe my eyes had fooled me. But, another flicker, reflected light off the metal headband. Poor Priscilla floating amongst the leaves.

A beam of light, from afar, shined over Priscilla's face. Over two swollen, bruised holes on her neck. And then the distant light shined the light over my face. I couldn't see Kiki in the dark. I couldn't tell if she was still armed. But, with some distance in between us, I made a run for it. Out of the pond, out of the greenhouse, and through the woods. Without a working flashlight, I was at the mercy of the clouded moonlight. I pushed my body through bushes and trees, losing Kiki in the process.

Once back to the room, Tessie and I drug every single piece of furniture in front of the door.

I was shaking. I was trembling. I was sure I was having a panic attack. Tessie wrapped a quilt around me, then made me a hot toddy. I downed it in one gulp.

"Another," I said. I was never a big drinker, but I had to do something to calm my nerves. She made me a double. Or a triple. And I was out.

⁂

My brain was awakening after a deep sleep. I prayed that I would be opening my eyes to my modest full-sized bed, surrounded by an avalanche of pillows. Milton would be climbing onto my chest and nuzzling up to my neck with a good morning purr. Molly would be barking and jumping circles around my bed, offering an overexcited greeting. We'd stroll into the kitchen, put the liquid caffeine onto brew and moments later would be greeted by a barefooted

Jillian and Bob the bunny. Jillian would have a seat at the kitchen bar, with half-open eyes and mumble, "How 'bout a cup of Joe, mam?" I'd place a warm cup of hot cocoa in front of her and ask if she wanted one lump, or two. After her response, I'd plop two fluffy marshmallows into her mug. Then she'd signal me over for a secret. "I gotta tip for ya mam," she'd tell me, and give me 'two pennies'— a kiss on each cheek, 'a nickel'— a peck on the nose, and a 'buck and a quarter'— a bear hug.

I sucked in a deep breath and opened my eyes to reality, a hundred miles from home, spotting a vile sight on the nightstand. The chocolate box. With one less chocolate in play, Frankie's game was over. And the worst part, the room was still barricaded up, from the inside.

⚬ఴ❃ ❃ఴ⚬

Rocky Shaded Road: Hard chocolate almond crunch shell, with a hidden soft ganache center, sweetened with whipped swirls of muted marshmallow flavor.

Chapter Four

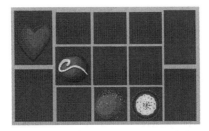

FOUR prisoners were trapped behind chocolate bars.

I sprang out of bed.

"Morning, Grandbaby," said Tessie.

I put my arms up in a standard karate defense mode, as if Tessie was going to sock me one. Not that I knew karate. "Don't grand-baby me. Where did that box come from?" I asked, backing up from her.

"What in heaven's tarnation is wrong with you, gal? It was sitting outside our door last night. You were so shaken up, I didn't want to upset you anymore."

"Oh." I felt a bit foolish then. I lowered my combat arms, and had a seat on the bed, holding my cheeks. "I'm sorry. Emotionally, I'm spent."

"I know, hun." Tessie went over to the end table stacked with our rations. "Let me get ya somethang to eat. That will make ya feel better."

It was day 13. I thought this would be the day I would be relieved. The day that would finally put all the misery behind us. But, it wasn't over. There were four of us left, which in Killer's eyes, was three too many. The plan was to stay put until quarter to one. But honestly, I didn't like the odds. With Kiki potentially armed, Tessie and I were sitting ducks while we waited for Brice.

The problem was that there was no safe place to hide. She could be watching at any time. And without car keys, we weren't escaping.

"Tessie, you can't think of any other place there might be spare keys?"

She sighed deeply considering my question. "Not unless you know where Winston is."

"Where's that note from him?"

Tessie pointed at the note on the desk. I studied it for obvious clues. But, it just looked like a note. It's not like I could dust it for fingerprints like on tv. Hmmm, tv. I retrieved my mental arsenal of television crime show techniques. I picked up the paper, and studied it again, now with the eyes of a star investigator. I felt it for engraving. Held it up to light. Held it up to the mirror. I even stole the lemon from Tessie's tea, to reveal possible invisible text. Nope, no secret message. Guess that's why I was a waitress, and not a detective, real or fake. The only paper I dealt with was food orders and receipts. Wait. Receipts. I wrote personal messages on my customer receipts, with my signature thank you and a happy face.

Once again, I studied the note. This time focusing on the penmanship. Gotcha! The writer of this note also had a signature mark. A double underline. On the note from Winston, the words, *be safe*, were double underlined. I retrieved the pinky present from my suitcase. Just what I thought. The threatening note ended with the same double underline. Winston never wrote a message to Tessie, the killer did.

So then, where was Winston? I thought about the last place Tessie or I saw him. The spa.

I knew Tessie wouldn't let me leave without a fight. So, I waited for her to go in the bathroom. Because frankly, she was never quick in the bathroom.

I knocked on the door, "I'll be right back. Re-stack the barricade when you come out." I ignored the resulting Southern profanities and made a run for it.

A few minutes later, I was tugging at the doors to the spa. Locked doors. I looked for witnesses. Witnesses? Crikey, I'm a criminal. I drove a branch through the glass panel next to the door, and unlocked it.

My steps slowed, as I walked the chocolate corridor, approaching the room that held my spackled secrets. A peer into the ajar door raised prickles on the back of my neck. This space in near darkness, turned my insides, inside-out. The once welcoming candles and fragrant coal pit were extinguished for the day, the only hint of light was an exit sign that dimly glowed onto a stack of sheets and towels piled atop the massage table.

Dismantling the pile confirmed my worst fear. Earlier that week, I had not witnessed Winston's deep tissue massage— I had witnessed his murder.

I stepped out of the room. Curling up to the wall. Hands grasping. Tears pouring. Trying to find escape from this nightmare. I let it out. I let it out hard. I didn't want to stay here any longer. But, I had a dreaded mission to complete. I needed to get the keys out of his pocket.

Against my desires, I returned to the room, trying to avoid eye contact with the corpse lying before me. Nothing prepares you to see a lifeless face. No emotion. No soul. I said my condolences and spoke useless apologies.

I took a deep breath, closed my eyes, and pulled the sheet off of Winston's body in one quick motion. I peered out my single eye peeking through my fingers. Cripes. He's still naked. I jumped up and down in circles, squealing. And quickly slapped the sheet back over him. I pulled back to reveal his face. "I'm so sorry, Winston." And tucked him back in.

Okay, find the stinking pants, Anna. And get the bloody hell out of here. It wasn't hard to locate them lying on the floor. I picked up the trousers and shook them out, as I wasn't sticking my fingers inside of anything. I snatched up the keys off the floor and made a sprint to the limousine.

⋅⊙⟨⟩⊙⋅

I scurried out the side entry to the parking area. The sky was darkening, and the wind was picking up. Trying to find the right key with my hair blowing in my eyes and my fingers trembling, was like trying to catch a catfish with your bare hands. Finally, success. I scooted into the driver's seat, pulled on the door to slam it shut, with unexpected resistance.

"Where do you think you're going?" said Kiki. With my focus on the keys, I hadn't even seen her coming.

"Leave me alone," I yelled, fighting her for control of the door. She squeezed her body in between the door jam, and flashed a kitchen knife. "Move over."

No, no, no. I was so close.

"Did I stutter? Move!" she said.

As I scooted over to the passenger seat, I managed to knock the knife out of her hand. But, it was too late. She slammed the door shut, and all the doors automatically locked.

"Now let's get out of here." She screeched out of the lot, overturned the wheel, surely leaving doughnut skids in our wake.

Her adrenaline weighted heavy on the gas pedal.

Part of me wanted to tell her to slow down, but the smart part of me knew better. I had to get out of here. Because one way or another, I was going to die. The glove compartment. It would not surprise me if Frankie kept a weapon in there. I tried to nonchalantly open the compartment's door.

"What are you doing over there?"

Gig was up. I had to work fast. With one good jerk, the glove door released, spewing its contents all over the floor. I mumbled, "Looking for a map?" Just great. My head in between my knees, trying to shuffle through the random articles. Meanwhile, Kiki's swerving was making me ill.

Cigarettes, car maintenance records. An unwrapped chocolate ball covered with gold dust? It was obviously not a random item thrown into a glove box. This chocolate was placed here, for my benefit. Without hesitation, I broke open the confection to reveal a fragrant peachy cream. Peaches. Georgia. My heart bellowed in my ribcage. Tessie.

Kiki, you just made this a little bit more personal. My hands rummaged through odds and ends scattered about the floor, searching for a weapon. Finding a screwdriver.

"Stop the van," I said in the most serious demon-like voice that had ever escaped my lips.

Kiki turned her head towards me, finding the screwdriver threatening her throat. I wasn't a violent person, and wasn't sure I could carry out a threat. But, she didn't know that.

"Unlock the door."

She obliged, then slammed on the brakes.

My head jolted into the dashboard. I lost hold of the screwdriver, but was able to break free.

I took a quick glance around at my surroundings. Nothing. Nobody. Just trees rustling in the wind. Kiki got out of the car, racing after me. "Anna, come back here."

I stared into her eyes filled with darkness. At that silent moment, I realized that she was going to kill me. I took off running, not having a plan. We had to be close to the entrance gates of the property, but it was hard to tell on the windy road. Either, I took my chances that Brice was able to open the gates, and I would be able to flag down a driver on the desolate road before Kiki caught me, or I hiked it back to the mansion.

Guess I was going back to the mansion. I sprinted with all my might, my jelly legs, instantly questioning my decision. The wind had intensified, orange clay swirled around us like a dusty tornado.

Kiki chased after me. "Stop. I just want to talk to you."

Of course you do, Killer.

I wasn't letting up. Er, my will was not giving up, but my legs were cursing me. Kiki gained on me. I pushed my legs as fast as they would go, moving on pure adrenaline.

"Anna, just give up."

I glanced back at her, oblivious to a pothole in my path, falling to my knees. I strained to get up and she pounced on top of me, like a cheetah capturing a gazelle. Forced on my stomach, my legs flailed wildly, my screams muffled in the earth. It didn't matter though, because nobody was around to hear me.

Kiki pinned down my wrists. "Listen to me."

But, I didn't want to listen. I just wanted to get away from her. My cheek rested on the dirt, while terror rambled from my mouth, "I don't care about the money. Just please don't kill me. My daughter needs a mom—"

She smacked my cheek. I didn't feel a thing. I kept on kicking.

"Moron," she yelled at me, pushing down on my wrists harder with all her body weight. "If I was going to kill you, this would be an opportune time. Right now."

My ears heard her words, but my brain listened to her actions.

She raised up from my wrists, sitting up to a kneeling position on my legs, muffling my pleas with her palm. With my hand free, I pulled at her arm. With zero effect. She had the leverage.

"What the heck?" Kiki said, while pulling up the back of my shirt. Her finger traced over my scar. She talked softer now, "I don't believe it. It's you."

"Yes, it's me. Now get the heck off me." But, she didn't.

"You don't understand. I was there; the day you got this scar." Her head dropped to my back. "I thought you died. Anna, I'm your sister."

"Sister, really?" I laughed at her desperate attempt. "I don't know what kind of angle you're trying to work now. But, you most definitely weren't around the day of the car accident. And you're not my sister. In fact, you're not anything to me. So, get the heck off me, crazy woman."

Kiki laughed sarcastically. "There's the same spoiled brat I knew. Just like all those years ago when you were mom's chosen one. Sitting on your little prima donna swing. Shoving candy into your face. Everyone thought you were so precious. But, I didn't. I knew you for the little piece of trash that you were."

Kiki released body pressure. I struggled to get on my feet. This insanity was centered around the picture of a little girl?

I said, "So, you were the one that tore up the Bells' painting in Chandler's basement?"

"I always hated that picture of you. I always hated you." Tears ran down her face. I took her weak moment, to break away, and ran like heck back towards the mansion.

My legs raced. My mind raced. The car accident. It was just me and my mom. I didn't have any siblings. The girl was crazy. Trying to mess with my mind. I dug into my soul, recalling my earliest childhood memories. They were all after the accident. Truth is, I didn't remember the accident itself. But, if I had a sister, she would be living with me. Uncle Wiley would have taken her in too.

I continued running, more like forced jogging, occasionally turning back to check on Kiki. She was out of sight. Nothing made sense. Not her actions, not her words. Before this trip, I had no knowledge of my connection to

Chandler, Tessie, and the handful of oddball cousins. Who's to say I didn't have some deranged, murderous sister out there too, who hates me because I was in an old chocolate ad?

I kept my jogging pace as long as I could, pausing occasionally, resting my palms on my thighs while I attempted to catch my breath. By the time I made it back to the mansion, the limousine had returned to the lot, and the red head with the insane agenda, was nowhere in sight. I had to warn Tessie. I resumed my marathon, tearing through the mansion halls. Feeling the emptiness of its walls. The walls that now contained more dead souls, than alive.

⟡⟡⟡

I approached her door and pulled out my key, devastated to realize I didn't need it. *She didn't lock the door.* I cursed to myself, pushing into the room.

"Tessie," I screamed in desperation, searching in the bathroom and in the closets. "Oh no," I cradled my head in my palms, facing the box of chocolates sitting eerily upon her bedspread. I flicked it open, confirming Tessie's fate. Kiki must have snuck in here while I was at the spa.

My eyes flooded with guilt and sorrow. I should have never left her alone. While wiping my tears, my vision expanded beyond the chocolate box to the nightstand holding a silver tray of gourmet desserts. Bananas' Foster, a slice of cake, a dish of pudding; all went untouched. But one glass dish was toppled on its side. Ruby raspberry sauces oozed over the table onto the floor, next to a spoon, resembling a pool of blood.

Oh my gosh, she poisoned her. I picked up the fallen dish and instinctively smelt it. Realizing, I didn't know what I was smelling for. I set the dish on the tray, and noticed a note next to it. A note written in the horrid red paint. A note—from me?

Grandma, stay put. The police are on their way.

That explains why she ate it. But, how had Kiki known that I was her grandchild? And furthermore, why would Tessie have trusted a note from anyone?

Who am I kidding? I would have fallen for it, too. Because it's what we wanted to hear more than anything. That this nightmare was over.

My emotions took over. Tessie didn't deserve this. Nobody deserved this. I tried to compose myself. There was still hope. Tessie wasn't here, so she could be alive. I had no idea where she was, but if she was too weak to hold a spoon to her mouth, her time was limited. I needed to find her quickly. Clues. Focus on the clues.

A struggle definitely took place in front of the fireplace. A vase was smashed on the floor in front of it. The logs held remnants of the flowers and a puddle of water sat below it. The flowers were barely burnt, still in whole. Obvious conclusion, someone threw the vase of flowers as a weapon, and it landed in the fire. I prayed that that someone was Tessie.

On the floor, next to Tessie's rocker, I found a floral scarf. It was tied in knots and ooh, reeked. Perhaps this is what poison smelt like? My eyes teared up visualizing my poor grandmother with a scarf tied over her face, gasping for air. Maybe Kiki force-fed her the poisoned dessert?

No matter the method, Tessie's life was in jeopardy. If I didn't find her soon, I'd lose her forever.

୬ଓ୧ ୨ଡ଼୭

Southern Peach Cordial: Ripened sweet and sour peachy

cream with a fine dusting of antiqued gold.

Chapter Three

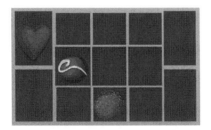

THREE cliffhangers grasped branches of truth from their hollowed family tree.

I winced away from the new empty space in the chocolate box. Staring at the chocolate box of terror wasn't going to help anybody. It was 12:10. In less than an hour, dead or alive, it would all be over.

Since dead wasn't an option, I couldn't sit here waiting for Brice. He wasn't supposed to meet me for over a half an hour. Tessie could be dead by then.

I wandered around the surrounding hall. No leads. No sounds. Where did I go from here? I needed to get help, but how? Kiki had the keys for the car. I couldn't leave by foot. The phone lines were dead. *Phones.* At the beginning of this dreaded experience, we all turned in our cellphones. But, where are they? I thought about the tiny keys that I had found in the desk in the cabin. Perhaps, they were for a safe or a file cabinet. It was a long-shot, but my best bet was the office in the basement.

My path veered towards the basement, down the stairs. I cautiously pushed open the door to the secret office. Praying I didn't find any body. Not dead, or alive. Because either way, I was guessing, it wasn't going to be pretty.

The good news was that I was alone. The bad news, was that somebody, without a key, had beat me to it. The drawers had been forced open, and the contents spewed throughout the space. I randomly tried any electronics I could get my hands on, with a desperate try for a connection. Laptop, phone, fax machine. No surprise, everything was dead. But, a ripped paper stuck in the fax machine printer got my attention. I unjammed the paper, and skimmed the contents of what was left of the page. Someone had sold out to Chandler's archenemy, his brother, Homer. One of the heirs was willing to do the one thing Boris would never do. Merge the companies. The receipt was proof of a hefty bank transfer to Homer's account. But, what did it all matter now? The last thing I cared about right now was money. Lives were at stake.

I swallowed hard. According to the chocolate box, there were only two of us, Brice and myself, left standing in Kiki's way.

Best case scenario, Brice had retrieved a rifle from the cabin, and is locked away safely in his room. Worst case scenario. Nope, not going there. Staying positive.

Without thought, I ran over the stained carpet, where poor Boris bled. My anger kicked at the deadly weapon, the broken bottle of Bitters. Bitters. I thought back to Frankie; if only I had collected one hundred Sweet Bitter Bonker Bars to redeem a free life. Yeah, if only life was a game, and not an uncontrolled reality of doom. I made my way to the hallway, cringing with each squeaking shoe sticking over the wooden floor. I had to ignore my emotions and push forward.

Time was not on my side. The courier would arrive in less than 35 minutes. Thirty-five minutes for Kiki to take us down. I needed to get to Brice.

I headed to the outside corridor, towards the poolside guest suites. Brice had been staying in Winston's room the past couple of nights. Hopefully, he was still there. Right now, Brice and I were targets, our breaths ticking on the stopwatch. My legs pushed faster. My heart beat louder.

The scent of rain saturated my breath, clouds darkening overhead. Stepping into the hallway was like walking into a wind tunnel. The swirling wind howled, as if warning me, sending goose bumps over my skin. I pushed against the invisible turbulent wall, not gaining much yardage, like a turtle trying to paddle up a waterfall. My steps ever so slowly approached the guest suite that Brice had been staying in.

There was no breaking into this room. The door was already wide open and evidence of suffering on the ground. My heart throbbed like a time bomb, my body anticipating the explosion at any moment. I stepped through the doorway, cautiously taking in my surroundings, preparing myself to enter a crime scene. Bloody footprints led from the entryway out into the hallway.

There was no time for emotion. I must search for clues. My head felt like I was on the teacup ride at Disneyland. I forced control of the spinning walls before me, taking in a mental inventory. A shattered television. The phone receiver and base recklessly hanging off the nightstand. Splattered scarlet stains on the bedspread and carpet. Definite signs of struggle and injuries; no signs of Brice's body. Kiki was a tough one. Still, it was hard to rationalize how her weasel-like stature could take on a lion, in his own den. Unless that is, she still had the shotgun.

My head hurt. There was only one thing I knew to be certain. *I was next.* How I just wanted the insanity to end.

I took a closer look at the footprints that trailed from the bed to the entryway. One set of them, shaped in a blobbed egg and dotted pattern. Like the bottom of a high-heeled shoe. No surprise, as that was Kiki's standard footwear. Alongside of the prints was a trio of crimson-lined tracks, as if something was being rolled on three wheels. My guess, the wheelbarrow. I followed the diminishing tracks down the cement hallway that led to the path up the mountainside.

Do I follow the bloody trail up the mountainside, or go directly to the dock to meet the courier? Kiki couldn't be in both places. Although, she could target me in either. If I was down on the dock, she could pick me off from the top of the mountain. Assuming she was a good shot. And I was assuming everything right now.

As it stood, I was defenseless. I scoured Winston's room, finding a walking stick. Not the best weapon. But, better than nothing.

I started the climb up the path, meanwhile my brain scrambled to make sense of things. Last night Kiki was shooting at me. Today, she had an open target and let me flee. And on top of it all, she tried to convince me that I was her sister. Maybe it's all part of her game. A really twisted game. Maybe I was the last one on her list. Or, she was keeping me alive to frame me for all the murders.

My legs hiked on autopilot, while my mind conjured a running list of victims. All the brutal tragedies. But, something didn't connect. I got to a fork in the path. My brain told me to continue up the mountainside. But, my gut took me on a detour, bringing me to the front door of the cabin.

I pounded on the door. "Tessie, are you in there?" I frantically banged. "Tessie?" I wailed. I peered in the front window. All was still.

"I know what's going on." I paused, "Do you know how I know?"

I retrieved my waitress pad from my bag and scanned my notes.

I yelled as I paced in front of the door, "Jasper drowned in a vat of chocolate. Caesar dropped to his death on a chocolate themed ride." I kicked at the door and yelled louder. "Harley stabbed with the cocoa pod machete. See, I get it. *Chocolate.* The killer sent me a message through a recipe. Death by chocolate. Only something is out of place." I went around to the kitchen window, stumbling over a pair of muddy boots. Make that *two* pairs of boots. One quite large, the other significantly smaller. I thought I had finally solved this puzzle. Only now I had found an extra puzzle piece.

I wasn't sure about the time, except for the fact, that I was almost out of it. I abandoned the cabin, and my chocolate theory, resuming my climb up the mountainside, the ticking of the clock beating heavy in my chest.

The sidewalk ended at the height of the mountain. The portion of cliff in front of me was not passable, barricaded with a wall of trees and prickly shrubs. I walked along the clay area, parallel to the edge, blasted by intensified wind currents. It was difficult to look down to the ground, each attempt greeted by bursts of spitting dirt granules. I picked up on a sparse trace of the lined track that was quickly eroding in the wind. I followed the path along the curvy terrain, all the while, visually searching through bushes and tall grasses along the cliff's edge. The tracks disappeared at a rocky area, forming a clearing amongst the lush border. Hopefully, I could get a view of the dock from here.

Cripes, the boat had arrived. And, it was empty. I wasn't sure what Kiki had in store for the courier, but I don't think it involved the messenger leaving here alive.

ა৪ৎ ৩ৎৡ

I walked a bit further, devastated to notice the trio of wheel prints this close to the edge. I braved my body toward the cliff's edge, praying that it didn't double for a diving board. My body pushed forward, terrified of what lurked below. I inched closer, climbing upon a boulder, instantly feeling as if somebody was rubbing an ice cube up my spine. I had been lured here.

I pulled myself toward the final boulder above me, exposed to the open air. My fingers struggled to push hair out of my eyes, unveiling the boulder's function, a new pedestal for that horrid coffin of chocolates. Feeling defeated, I stood on the cliff's edge, shouting mad as heck for the world to hear me, "You win." My eyes unwillingly lowered down to the ground, revealing my worst fear. Amidst the brush, I could make out the remnants of the smashed wheelbarrow. Of course, Kiki couldn't carry Brice's body; she needed the wheels to transport it.

Rain set in, drops scarce, but the size of elephant tears. I set the walking stick down momentarily, using my hands to shield my eyes from the sudden gust of dirt and spray. I opened them, not believing the sight before me. I sprung up, my eyes welling with tears as I embraced my cousin. "Brice, thank goodness, you're alive."

His airy white button-down shirt flowing in the wind, gave him an angelic presence. Brice smiled, apparently equally relieved. "I've been searching all over for you Anna. Are you okay?"

"Yes, but the courier has already arrived. And we need to find Tessie. She's been poisoned. And—"

Brice embraced me again. "Easy girl. Slow down and tell me exactly what happened."

I breathed heavy, forcing my words out in a quick stream, "There is no time. That's what I'm trying to tell you. It's a trap up here." I pointed to the box of chocolates.

"I know," said Brice. "It's Kiki."

"I think she's coming," I said, pointing at movement in the nearby brush. "We're too late," I said. "We need to run."

Kiki came sprinting towards us. Face flushed. Mascara bleeding down her cheeks in the rain. "Anna, get away from him."

"Get away from *him*?"

She ran closer to us. "Anna, it's him. Brice is the killer."

Was this girl for real? "An hour ago, you had a knife to my throat."

"I thought you were the killer," she said. "Last night, Frankie sent me to the kitchen to find an emergency cell phone. But, I found this instead." She pulled on her necklace, holding out my missing locket of Jillian.

"Where did you get that?"

"I told you. I found it in the kitchen. I thought you were the one that poisoned Frankie."

"Good try, Kiki. But, you were shooting at me and Brice by the greenhouse, *before* your so-called dinner date."

"That wasn't me. It was Frankie."

Brice stood in front of me, arms sprawled out, like a human shield. "Enough with the lies, Kiki. Anna didn't poison anyone. And Frankie didn't hurt anyone."

"You're right," said Kiki. "But, you did." She forced her eyes on me. "Anna, get away from that psycho."

The psycho protecting me from you?

"We need to get away from her," said Brice.

"He's the killer," said Kiki. "Trust me."

I was being pulled like a rope in a game of tug-o-war.

Brice grabbed my hand. "Anna, come on, before she tries to finish us off."

My mind felt like somebody just pushed the pause button on the whole world around me. *Why is he wearing a leather glove on his hand?* He released my palm, transferring a red smudge onto my skin. At first, I thought it to be blood. But, it was thicker and more vibrant, and downright terrifying. It was the killer's ink, the infamous red paint. The red paint on Tessie's note. The red paint from the amusement park caution sign. And the same red paint used on the theatre curtain that looked like a toddler penned it. Nope, the painter wasn't a child. And wasn't drunk. But he did have a bad arm, causing him to write the over-sized letters carelessly or with his non-dominate hand.

I didn't want to believe it. But, my cousin, who I'd grown to adore, had clearly deceived me, and now my life depended on me playing along. "You're right Brice, let's get out of here."

But Brice wasn't moving. He spoke eerily calm. "It's been Kiki from the start. She was the one who killed Jasper, you know? She was mad at him over those stupid shoes, and she was going to make him pay for it. Lucky thing she got in a tour group with him that day at the factory, made it a cinch to push him off the catwalk."

"I did no such thing," said Kiki. "Anna, you have to believe me." And I did.

Brice continued, "And Caesar, my poor pal. She encouraged him to ride that death trap, how very naughty of her."

"No Brice, you were the one that egged Harley and me on, telling us to get the coward to ride the ride," said Kiki. "How did you know it would be him that got killed and not one of us?"

Brice snickered. "Actually, I frayed the chords on both bucket seats. But, gravity was on your side. Think of a roach and a maggot hanging from flimsy strands of a spider web. The roach is going to make its fall first." He put his fingers to his mouth. "Oopsie. Did I just confess?"

His words paralyzed me, my body trapped in a cage of cold, steel fear. I muttered, "Why, Brice? Why did you hurt all those innocent people?"

Brice laughed sarcastically. "So, by *innocent* people, are you referring to the gardener, who was a thief? The gambling felon that was hitting on my girlfriend? The lawyer that was a fraud? Or, the innocent surfer dude that killed his wife?" He shook his head in disappointment. "You see, those were the bad guys. I'm the good guy. And I got screwed."

I held my temples. "It just doesn't make sense."

He let out a breath. "Okay, it doesn't matter what I admit to you; ultimately the evidence will all tie back to Kiki. Off the record, I'll come clean. It's funny, because before I got to the mansion, I had no intentions of knocking anybody off. I just wanted what was supposed to be mine."

I pursed my lips, "The money."

"Come to find out Chandler's will was a bunch of crap. You can't make people compete for an inheritance. On top of that, none of those people deserved a penny."

I didn't agree with him, but I knew better than to argue my opinion.

He tallied on his fingers, "The Wellingtons, Harley and Priscilla. And your buddies, Cashmere and Caesar. None of them were even related to Chandler."

"So, you were the one that researched the grandkids," I said.

Kiki mumbled, "I told you those papers weren't mine."

Brice smiled proudly.

"What about the employees?" I asked. "What did you have against them getting a shot at the money?"

"Seriously? That's like saying a fry cook should inherit McDonalds."

Um no, not really the same thing. It was difficult for me to comprehend his thought process. "But we're talking about peoples' lives here, Brice. Nobody deserved to die."

"Nobody had to get hurt. The first morning, I warned everyone, in big red letters, on the theatre curtain, but nobody took me seriously. So, I needed a new plan. It was when I went up to take a shower in my suite that things started falling into place. I turned on the faucet, then left the bathroom to get a towel. And that's when I found the gardener snooping in my room. I kept quiet because I wanted to see what he was up to. That S.O.B. went rummaging through Ashton's suitcase and shoved her jewelry in his pocket. With that dumb act, Jasper became the sacrificial lamb."

As Brice confessed, I searched Kiki's face for some type of comfort. A gesture. Eye contact. Something to show me that we were in this together. But, she had the emotion of a manikin.

Brice continued, "I thought knocking off the gardener would show everyone that I meant business; but guess what? The idiots stayed."

"So that's why you killed Caesar," I said.

"First off, that guy had it coming. Putting his grubby paws on Ashton. Secondly, I didn't kill him, I was just trying to generate a good scare. As I said, I frayed one rope on each swing. It wasn't my fault he busted through both ropes. Blame his blubber."

"What about the others? Why hurt them?"

"They're all greedy bastards. As you see, I tried to get everyone to leave, time and time again. But, nothing was more important to them than their precious money. So, I had to take matters into my own hands and force them to leave, one by one. Being a nice guy, I gave each of them the opportunity to survive— if they received medical treatment in time. Of course, no guarantees."

"Where's Tessie?"

"Well, let's just say her times a tickin'."

I had to find her before it was too late. I turned to run. Kiki sprang up to follow my lead.

"Nuh, uh, uh," he nodded his head side to side. I pivoted back to find the barrel of the rifle pointed at us. "Good news, I got the gun." His voice took on a creepy tone. "Where are you girls off to? The family fun is just beginning. Time for us three genuine heirs to bond." He motioned the gun toward the boulders on the cliff's edge. "Sit."

Without hesitation, Kiki and I took a seat on the cold rocks, now face to face with the gun's barrel.

"Just let us go," said Kiki. "You can have the money."

He smiled in a way that made my goosebumps swell. "Finally, somebody's thinking. But, it's too late for that."

"Please don't do this, Brice," I said. "I have child. She needs me."

"Oh, she's young, she'll bounce back. Besides she'll have her uncle."

"Uncle Wiley is like a grandfather to her. He can't mother her."

"No silly. Not that old geezer, her *uncle*." He put the rifle down, and fished his wallet out of his pocket. "See. My niece."

He flashed me a photo of Jillian in front of our house. With an instant surge of nausea, the back of my hand raised involuntarily to my mouth. Not only was he a psychopath, but he was delusional, and he had been stalking my family.

"She's not your niece."

"Of course, she is, *sis*."

He kicked Kiki's shin. "Right, *Katherine*?"

I said to Kiki, "What's he talking about?"

Kiki swallowed hard. "I tried to tell you before. You and I are sisters." Her face slumped to the ground, as if to avoid eye contact with me. "Katherine Herrington is my real name, and Brice, well, he's our younger brother."

I took hold of Kiki's shoulders, "That's a lie."

"It's true. We were all separated after the accident."

"Why would we be separated?"

Brice snickered. "Yeah, Katherine. Tell her why."

"I'm sorry, Anna," said Kiki. "But I couldn't stand that picture of you."

"Again, with the stinking picture? I was four years old, for goodness sakes."

Kiki went on, "It ate me alive. The way everyone poured praise over sweet little Bells."

"Bells?"

"You don't even remember? That's what mom called you. It was the only name I ever knew you by. You were everything to her. Once you came along, I was invisible."

Mom? I examined Kiki's eyes, always a different color, this time pure green, just as Brice's— just like Jillian's. We were the three children in the old photo, sitting on the porch stoop. We were the three children depicted in the Chandler's advertisement paintings. Three pictures, three children.

Kiki continued, "Before you were born, life was good. Mama was married to her true love, a military doctor, and I was their pride and joy. Life was perfect, until Daddy died overseas. Mama remarried a couple years later to a loser. Any guesses?"

I bit my lip.

"Rusty Clementine. Your winner of a dad. Stayed around long enough to bring me a little sister and clean us out dry. And if things couldn't get worse, Mama married again on the rebound. This time I got a brother, and some bruises. Life was hell."

Brice said, "A trip down miserable, memory lane. Enough, save it for Dr. Phil."

Two weeks ago, I thought life was rough. I was a single mom serving coffee and pie in a dive. End of story. I wish I had never learned about this new family. Family— Yes, family. Perhaps, I could use this to my advantage. "Brice, we're your sisters. We have so much time to catch up on. You don't want to hurt your family."

"Awe Anna," he said, gently rubbing the side of my cheek with his gloved hand, sprouting prickles on the back of my neck. "I don't want to hurt you. You're my good sister."

He pointed the gun at Kiki, "And this one is my evil sister."

"Brice, please," Kiki pleaded.

Brice said to her, "Oh, don't worry sis, I'm not planning on hurting you either."

My head was spinning. "So then, what do you want us for?" I asked in between bursts of tears.

"Don't cry," Brice said. "It will be over in seconds, you won't even know what hit you. Although, you will know *who*." His eyes locked again on Kiki. "Go ahead my little red herring, give her a push."

I gaped over the edge at the stirring waters, crashing on jagged rocks below. The underbelly of the rumbling, flashing skies above resembled a witch casting spells upon her wildly churning brew, spewing murky foam into the air.

"Are you nuts?" I asked, already knowing the answer.

"Come on," he encouraged her. "Finish things off. Just one little push. Just like you did twenty-five years ago." He pulled a woman's shoe from the brush, pinching its narrow heel in his fingertips. "Watch how easy it is," he said while releasing his grasp.

We watched the minuscule shoe get swallowed into the mouth of the famished waters.

"What are you guys talking about?" I asked.

Kiki sobbed. "I thought she was dead. It was her ghost I thought I saw in the window at the mansion. Probably because some moron left that creepy crying baby doll outside of my room."

"Ghosts? Sounds like a haunted conscious to me." said Brice.

"You're not going to get away with this," I told him. "The police will tie the evidence back to you."

Brice put an arm around my shoulder facing me towards the water. "They can't peg it on me, a victim." He pointed below. "Look, I died. There's the wheelbarrow that held my mutilated body, crashed horrifically to the rocky waters, my body swept off into the depths of the lake, never found again. Quite tragic, really." He placed his other arm around Kiki. "Nope, this here, is our girl of the hour. Katherine left her bloody footprints in my room." He scrunched his nose. "Those heels pinch in the front by the way."

Kiki said, "They'll know it's a scam when they test your DNA."

"Oh that, don't you worry. All our loose ends are tied. By the way, kudos to whoever arranged for us to have the blood test. I just stole my own vials and splattered them around the room."

"You can't frame me for murder," said Kiki.

"Ooh you're right, that would be an unforgivable thing for somebody to do," he said with heavy sincerity. "Surely, that sinner's soul would burn in hell for eternity— to do such a horrific thing like that."

Brice's mood instantly changed, as if he just dug this beastly being from a dark troubled place in his soul. His tone was no longer playful, his eyes filled with anger and his voice flat and serious. "Tell her what you did to her mama, Katherine. Go on, tell her."

"My mother, was tragically killed in a car crash," I said. "The same crash that scarred me." I looked to Kiki. "You saw it. Tell him you saw the scar on my back," I persisted.

Brice laughed it off. "Oh silly, little girl. Is this what big sister told you? That mother died in a car accident? Think, Anna. Remember that old newspaper clipping back at the house? That picture wasn't of you, it was our Katherine. As a kid, she looked just like you. She's been changing her appearance her whole life, just to lose the resemblance."

I kept glancing over to Kiki, waiting for her to argue his words. But, she never did.

Brice said, "But you haven't heard the best part. When you were just four years old, your sister had so much hatred for you, that she pushed you out the window. Do you remember, we lived in a two-story house?"

I didn't respond, just gazed through him with numb expression.

"Don't worry, I was just a toddler, I don't remember either. Evidently, you took quite the tumble and got really mangled." He mimicked a zombie, twisting his arms into a pretzel, tongue hanging out of his mouth. "Everyone believed you were going to die. Problem is, big sis didn't own up to her attempt to kill little sis, and she told the police that her mother did it. Our mama, the saint, wasn't going to rat out her little bitch of a daughter. Instead, she went off to prison thinking her precious Annabell was dying. She couldn't live with the grief and the pain knowing the world thought she murdered her own child." Brice broke down, falling to his knees. "And mommy—mommy killed herself!"

"What? Kiki, tell me this isn't true." But, she wouldn't even look at me.

"So, thanks to Katherine's hatred for her princess sister, the three of us loving siblings got separated. Anna, your dad was out of the picture, so you went off to live a cushy life with your uncle in Mayberry. Katherine got sent off to a foster home. Only she wasn't so smart there either. She bragged to the foster parent's daughter about what she did to you." He sympathetically squeezed my hand. "Long story short, the parents told the police, she got sent off to a juvie house and made new, fun friends. Bet if Chandler did his homework, he wouldn't have put her in the will."

Kiki burst out, "I was fifteen for crying out loud. Those court files were sealed."

"Let's just say, money talks." Brice looked back to me. "Oh, I almost forgot to tell you my prize. I got sent off to live with my dear old, alcoholic, druggy convict of a dad. You remember him, huh Katherine? He told me that my mama abandoned me. I suffered my whole childhood, never having enough to eat, left alone most of the time, which I suppose was better than taking licks and bruises from my old man. That's why I became an athlete, so I could be strong and stand up to him. But, life lesson. A quarter back will always get tackled by a linebacker." He stepped closer to Kiki. "FYI, now you know why my arm is so messed up. That drunken loser broke it when I was a teen. When I injured it again on the field, it took me out of the game for good." He whacked the gun's barrel on the side of Kiki's head. "And it was all thanks to you."

I tried to reason with him, "Let us live and we'll let you have the money. Think about it, if everyone thinks you're dead, you can't collect."

"Nope the dead guy won't get a penny. But, his widow will."

I looked at him dumbfounded.

"You know? My wife, Ashton." He laughed. "Surprise, we were married all along. But, once I realized that fact made her a threat, I undid that. Funny thing is, she was never even in the will. You all are so easy to manipulate. She didn't have her wedding rings because the gardener had stolen them. I was the first one to take jewelry out of the pile of stolen goods. No one even noticed the rings."

"The whole engagement was a sham?"

"We got married at the courthouse, so Ashton's fantasies about the wedding were real. And now thanks to your sacrifices, we can make that happen."

"See? You don't want to do this. Life is good. You're happily married, a famous actor—"

He laughed sarcastically. "Are you flipping kidding me? Famous actor? I'm a joke and you know it."

"Okay, so Deputy Dude wasn't the most dignified job, but you can get a different role."

He shoved his wrist with the scar into my face. "See this? This is what rejection does to a person. Those Hollywood idiots telling me that I've been type casted. That nobody will ever take me serious."

I gasped. "You tried to take your life?"

"And now I find out it's all because of what this wench did."

"Brice, I get that your angry. But, you don't have to do this anymore."

Brice shook his head. "Actually, I do. Just a couple more steps. He pulled a folded envelope from the back waistband of his pants. I'll plant two tests in the courier's boat, one for me, and one for Katherine. Then, Katherine will take the fall for the murders, Ashton will collect the inheritance, and my wife and I will disappear off of the grid for a life of Easy Street."

I was afraid I knew where this left me. I pleaded with him. "What do you want from us?"

"Justice. We need to finish off what Katherine started twenty-five years ago." He poked a finger at my chest. "Seems we have one more loose end." He spoke nonchalantly as if talking about plans for a summer's day picnic, "Katherine needs to push you off of the cliff, plummeting you to your tragic death. Then, an anonymous call will tip off the police, who will in turn lock Katherine up for life, hopefully not giving her the death penalty. We want her to think about what she did for a long, long time.

Brice continued, "Now, I know what you're thinking. What if Katherine runs?" He scratched his head in thought. "I've contemplated this one, too. But, don't worry, she can run, but she can't get too far on this property. The dogs will eventually sniff her out. Imagine a pack of Doberman Pinchers; ravenous, barking with rage, saliva escaping through their pink-stained fangs, on the hunt for the criminal's flesh." He squeezed Kiki's thigh. Yes, they will like you a lot. It's a shame that Cashmere and Frankie got away, and missed out on the party. Oh well, they'll have to read about all the gruesome details in the paper. He scowled at Kiki with disappointment. "They'll be so shocked to hear how naughty you've been."

I tried to keep him talking. As long as he was immersed in speaking, I gained time to figure out how to stop myself from becoming fish-chum. I took on a complimentary tone, "Using the box of Chandler's chocolates was clever."

"Yeah, I thought so too. Kept everyone on their toes. Kind of like my tribute to Gramps for making this whole experience possible. Why, before I got the letter about the inheritance, I didn't even know I had sisters, let alone all of the other grizzly details. Guess money's good for something. Too bad Gramps didn't use his money too, and dig up the real story first." He set down the gun and picked up the chocolate box. "Here, let's make this extra special. You guys can eat your own chocolates before you're eliminated from the game. That's the least I can do for my sisters."

We played along as to not anger him.

Brice held out the box to Kiki. "Katherine, you can pick first since you gave me the idea to use the box of candy, after you choked down the chocolate that belonged to the dead guy. You know the driver that died of a heart attack?" He shoved the box to her chest. "So, which one do you think is yours?"

She pulled a confection glazed in a shimmering red candy coating.

"Let me do the honors." He read, "Ginger Snapped. Well, ain't that the truth? He rubbed his palms together. "Ooh, this is so exciting. We're like siblings on Christmas morning."

༄ༀ ༀ༄

Ginger Snapped: Red Velvet tart overflowing with full-bodied spiced flavor, dressed in a seductive layer of bitter chocolate.

Chapter Two

TWO estranged sisters bonded through fear and insanity.

I stared blankly at the duo of chocolates, sitting rather lonely-like in the box.

"Okay Anna, your turn. Which one do you think it is? I'll make you a deal. If you choose correctly, I'll let you live five more minutes."

I didn't want to play this malicious game.

"Come on gal. Times a tickin'. Choose!"

I eyed each of the candies, desperately trying to pick up on clues. One was sort of a rounded shape, maybe that of a football? The other heart-shaped. "Okay, I think the football shaped one is yours, and the heart one is mine."

"Oops, too bad. The heart shaped one was mine, a symbol of my love to my bride." Brice revealed the other candy, which bowed out on the bottom. "This should have been a cinch, sis."

A bell. A Chandler's Classic Bell, just like from my childhood. How could I have not recognized it in the box? I can't believe it had been spelt out in front of me all along.

Brice smashed the chocolate into my lips. "Even though you're a loser, you can still eat your chocolate."

As much as I wanted to spit the candy at him, I resisted.

He plastered on a pretentious pout. "Oh well, guess it's time then. I'll save the chocolate heart for my niece, Jillian."

It was so hard not to explode out in rage. I could feel every muscle of my body tense up.

"A young child needs a lot of love from family, after losing her mother. But, don't worry. I'll be there for her."

My insides were trying to get out, and attack this lunatic. "Why are you doing this to me?" I said. "What did I ever do to you?" My eyes met his. I looked past the anger. Past the insanity. And found the hurt. "Oh my gosh. You blame me, too."

His eyes narrowed. "Anna, don't you get it? She chose you. Mama died for you, instead of living for me." He pulled a scrap of paper from his pocket and handed it to me. "I've read this every day since the moment I found it."

It was a piece of a photocopied letter, stamped *Exhibit B.*
"*My Darling Annabell,*
Do not be afraid. I will be waiting for you in heaven."

That explains those words. Those awful, cringeworthy words. I spoke through tears of sadness, anger, and guilt. "I'm so sorry, Brice." And I truly was. "Mama was in a painful place. She wasn't thinking rationally. But together, we need to move forward—"

He took a deep breath. "You're right. Enough small talk. Mama's been waiting a long time for you." He wiped his cheek with the back of his glove.

Meanwhile, Kiki sat in silence, slumped over, head in palms.

I grasped at straws, trying a different approach to gain time. "Brice, I'm still amazed that you were able to fool us all. You have to tell me how you pulled it all off."

"Yeah, I was brilliant. So, I'll fill you in, just because you're the good sister." He stood up tall, hands on hips. "So, let's see, I already told you how—" He put his fingers in quotes. "*Katherine*" got rid of Jasper and Caesar. Next on the chopping block was Cashmere. He was boasting about this grand chocolate dessert he was making for our engagement dinner. Fact is, pretty boy lit himself on fire. *Mostly.* That guy always soaks himself in cologne. So, I may have spritzed the outside of his jacket for him. Let's just say when I was done, he was pretty flammable. Somehow his lighter vanished, but thankfully Kiki generously offered hers up. Unfortunate for her, the police confiscated it, as evidence in a possible crime.

He tallied on his fingers, "Let's see then, who was next? So exciting, right?"

I didn't want him to lose focus. I helped him, still dragging out my time, trying to figure out how to get a hold of the rifle on the ground in front of me.

"Next was Priscilla, right?"

You already know what happened to her. He put his fingers in quotes again. "Frankie" left her an invitation to come to his room for a surprise. She found Kiki's bikini, and curiosity sent her to open up the picnic basket. Surprise! A recently discovered species from the island of Cacau. I read it right on the glass tank in that Brazilian restaurant by the hotel. They should probably put locks on the animal displays, or someone is liable to get hurt. Maybe Priscilla will be lucky enough to be the first documented kill of the Cacau snake. Honestly, I didn't think the poison was potent enough to kill an adult. But, I guess Priscilla was more on the frail child-size of the scale. I tried to get her some fresh water to wake her. You know in the pond? But, she wouldn't budge."

"So, what happened next?" I asked trying to sound eager.

"You took a pampered rest, while helpless Winston got his neck broken."

I swallowed the lump in my throat.

"Of course, I hadn't planned on killing him. But, he knew too much. I had no choice."

My current agenda was to keep Brice talking. But, it was so difficult listening to his words. I focused, trying to keep him on track. Meanwhile, I pushed the rifle with my toe, ever so slowly inching it closer to me. "What about Harley? Why did you kill him?"

"I didn't." He snickered. "Surfer dude caught me hiding the chocolate box in my bag. He came at me like a bull, and my reflex was to grab the closest weapon to defend myself. I held up the machete and he just charged right into it."

We're going with suicide? I could hear Kiki's deep moans next to me, her sulking face hidden in her palms. I hoped she had observed my footwork with the rifle, through the cracks in her fingers. The gun was almost in reach, but I wanted to be careful about this. It might be our only chance to escape.

"So then, what really happened the night you and I staked out the greenhouse?" I looked to Kiki, "Why were you shooting at us?"

Kiki didn't budge.

"So clueless, sis," said Brice. "It was Frankie."

My face scrunched. "Frankie shot at us?"

"Correction. He shot at *me*. I saw his face when you ran sniveling off into the woods." He shook his head. "I can't believe that weasel almost messed up my plan that night. I slipped him and Kiki notes, inviting them to the greenhouse for a romantic dinner for two."

I said to Kiki, "So, the affair was real?"

She finally spoke, "No. I just wanted to get information from Frankie about the test. But, he got sick before we even got through the salad."

Brice smiled. A cocky smile. As if he were proud. "Guess lover boy didn't care for the secret ingredient. Flowers. If you listened to Florence, you would have learned that Cosmos are poisonous."

"But, I didn't get sick," said Kiki.

"You're welcome, sis. I added strawberries to the poisoned salad. I heard you refuse the chocolate covered strawberries at the candy shop because of your allergy."

Brice mumbled to himself. "I wonder if the big duffus survived the poisoning? Ah, no worries, even if he made it, he knows better than to squeal. He wouldn't put his family's safety over the worthless people here."

So, he threatened him too.

"What about Tess—"

Kiki interrupted, "Remember, when we first met at the mansion, Anna? You and Cashmere went on forever talking about your cats."

Why in the heck was she talking about this now? Brice scowled at her, but allowed her to ramble, perhaps letting her take a moment for her *last words* to me. I bit my lip.

"Well, my cat's name is Stiletto."

I crunched my eyebrows in confusion.

Kiki continued, "I wanted to let you know we had something in common."

I really didn't know what this had to do with anything. Maybe this was her way of making peace with me?

Brice interrupted, "Awe this is touching, watching my big sisters make up."

Kiki's pupils shifted to the rock next to me. "I think you would like *Stiletto.*"

It finally clicked. In an instant, Brice anticipating my move, reached down to grab the rifle as I grabbed the blood stained, patent pump from the rock next to me. Before he had a chance to settle the rifle on his shoulder, I forced the

pointy heel of the shoe to his forehead and made a run for
it.

Kiki ran ahead, glancing back at me. "Limo!"

I nodded my head in agreement. The two of us sprinted
down the mountainside towards the parking lot.

Brice held his gushing head, hollering, "Hey girls,
need these?" He shook a key ring in his fingertips.

"Shoot," I ran as quick as I could, trying desperately to
keep up with Kiki, swerving in and out of the forest of
trees. I hollered ahead, "The boat."

Kiki's path veered toward the water. The sound of Brice's
thundering footsteps let me know he was not far behind.
We ran forever. Eventually, I made it to flat ground. But,
the rocks and gravel were almost impossible to run over.

I followed Kiki's sporadic steps away from the rocks,
through small brush.

POW!

Good grief, he was shooting at us. By some miracle, I
made my way to the dock. Brice was right on my tail. I
wasn't sure if I would make it to the boat before he caught
up to me. As I approached a small bait shed, I took a
moment to try the doorknob. Against all odds, it was
locked. Kiki had already made her way to the boat. The
shelter was hopeless, so I made a run for it. I leapt into the
watercraft, realizing Brice's course had slowed. He must
have seen me trying to get into the fishing shed, because he
paused as he pounded on its door. How could he not see us?

Kiki turned the starter key on the boat. Nothing.

"Try again," I said.

She turned it repeatedly. "The flipping thing is dead."

Set up, once again.

The boat swayed ferociously in the water, but had only
drifted a couple of feet from the dock. By now, Brice had

reached our boarding location. "Oh no, are you poor little girls having some trouble? Let me help you."

We desperately paddled our arms in the water, our efforts rather meaningless.

Brice detached a loose timber from the side of the dock, stretching it out toward the boat. "Here, this should help you." Crouching down, with his arm outstretched, he was just able to grab a hold of the boat with the makeshift oar and pulled the boat back towards the dock. He jumped aboard. "Hey, why did you guys run off so fast?"

Water poured from the skies. Violent winds stirred the lake into swelling waves. My eyes contemplated the wild water splashing against the side of the boat. Would I survive a chance in the frigid waters? And even if I did, I was pretty certain that a former professional football player could out swim me, bad shoulder and all.

Confusing to me, he tossed the timber to Kiki. "Here, sis."

Kiki caught it with two hands.

"That should do the trick," Brice said to her.

Kiki wasted no time using the weapon to her advantage. She cocked the plank over her head, and swung it out at him like a baseball player in the last inning, with two strikes under his belt.

Brice clinched the wood in his gloved palms. "No silly, you're not supposed to swing it at *me*. Why you could have accidentally hurt your baby brother." He easily pulled the plank away from her. "All right, since you already put your fingerprints on the murder weapon, I suppose I could help you out and do your dirty work for you." He raised the beam in my direction.

I pleaded with him, "Brice, you don't want to do this."

He paused as if in thought. "I didn't want to be the one to do this to you." He swiped his glove over the blood dribbling down his cheek, gushing down from his split forehead. "But, that's when you were the good sister. I think Katherine has been a bad influence on you."

A lifetime raced in front of my eyes. Only it wasn't my life, it was Jillian's. Her first day of school, her first lost tooth, birthdays, dance recitals... I had to survive.

"Anna, jump!" said Kiki.

In a blink of an eye, the wooden plank came crashing down, my body scarcely missing its blunt force. I found myself submersed in the icy water with my overworked, jelly legs kicking wildly like a beetle on its back.

POW! A gunshot out of nowhere collapsed Brice's body in the boat.

Kiki bobbing in the water, pointed up towards the mountain. "Over there," she said to me.

A figure stood on the mountain, frozen in position, pointing the gun at the vessel. Kiki, a stronger athlete than myself, had already almost made her way to the shore. I fought the current, grasping onto the side of the dock. Meanwhile, the man, still in armed position, had moved down to the dock.

I gasped. "Boris."

He flinched in my direction and quickly turned back to the boat.

I smiled to myself. "I knew it. I knew you were still alive."

A strained voice in the wind broke off my words, "Hey old man, you missed," said Brice, while holding his blood-soaked thigh.

"I don't miss, lad. Now, you just sit still, so I don't have to put a pop in the other leg."

The sound of sirens fought through the thunderous downpour. Flashing lights came crashing through the sheets of rain. It didn't take long for Brice's boat to be surrounded.

Meanwhile, Kiki helped me up on the dock.

Boris nodded over to us. "You girls, get inside and get warm."

While we walked, I asked her, "Are you okay?"

"Yeah. Listen," she looked away from me. "I'm not good at this. But, I'm sorry."

I stopped walking and squeezed her tight. "I know," I said.

As our shivering bodies trenched down the dock, we heard shuffling inside of the bait shed, followed by some Southern profanities barely auditory over the sounds of the sirens.

A smile bigger than the size of my head grew on my face. "Tessie, you can come out now."

"Heavens to Betsie, mercy me, I went and got myself stuck. Just like Ethyl Rogers when she lost her earring—"

I circled the shack, finding Tessie straddling the open-aired window with one leg hanging outside, and one inside. Kiki and I released the poor woman's dress that was snagged on a fishing hook and helped her down.

"I was just fixin' to make my big move," Tessie said. "Was gonna give that boy the what for."

I put my arms around her. "You did good." I squeezed her so tight, she squeaked. Which was a polite southern expression for— never mind. I studied her face, full of mischievous life. "But, how did you escape?"

A smile appeared on the leisure lady's face. "Anna, thanks to you bringin' me food bedside, I shore enough knew that dessert trio like the underside of a Scottish three-testicled oxen. And just the same too. When I saw me that dessert platter, I was in awe, but I knew there was just one too many. Problem was, Brice saw me dump the poisoned dessert to the ground."

I swallowed. "So, what happened?"

"Next thing I knew, he was tying me up in my rocking chair. Then, that lousy man tossed the flowers in the fireplace. Ya know, the poison ones from Florence? The fumes from those burning plants, would kill me in a few measly minutes."

"So, how did you escape?"

"Well, Brice had tied my hands up—" She demonstrated with her hands behind her back. "Real tight like, with my scarf."

I remembered picking up that scarf in the room. "That scarf reeked of poison. I thought he tried to kill you by tying it around your face."

"Nope." She got a devilish grin.

I can't believe what I'm about to say. "Mabel's Pickled Possum Jam saved your life, didn't it?"

She pulled a small jar from her apron pocket, "Always carry it with me. Loosened my wrists up real good. My hands slipped right out. Then I tossed the vase of water into the fire. And came down here to wait."

Tessie was back in all her glory. "Now then," I said to the two ladies. "It appears that introductions are in order. Tessie, I'd like you to meet Katherine." I took Tessie's hand in placed it in Kiki's palm. "Katherine, I'd like you to meet your *grandmother*."

⊶⊜ ⊜⊷

Chandler's Classic Bell: Malted bell, covered by a layer of pure chocolate, oozing simple sweetness in its chewy caramel center.

Chapter One

ONE big, happy dysfunctional family was reunited.

*I*t was the first time I had been back to the Chandler mansion, since the murders a month ago. As for Brice, he's locked away. Hopefully, for good. I thought about sending him a box of chocolates.

We sat around the table in the gazebo overlooking the pond. I was eager to reunite with the others, resolve some lingering questions, and see Cashmere and Frankie on their feet.

Cashmere was still healing. After the fire incident, he was taken to Chandler's personal wing of the local hospital. He had quite a bit of scarring on his arm, but thankfully, no permanent damage. The staff took great care of him, but as to Mr. Chandler's orders, had no communication outside of the hospital staff.

Frankie was fine. The night he was poisoned, he managed to drive himself to the hospital. Obviously, he didn't eat enough to cause death, just enough to make him deathly sick.

Boris, substituting his tuxedo for khakis and an apron, flipped meat patties over the open flame. Nothing like a juicy grilled hunk of beef to say *Happy Easter*.

Turns out Brice had been right about one thing. Chandler's only child was Adeline. Leaving Kiki, aka Katherine, Brice, and myself as the only true grandchildren.

Chandler confessed that the whole will was a scam. A little obvious, when the deceased stood there in front of us explaining that he was still alive. Chandler never actually called it a *scam*, rather an exercise in character that offered business opportunities. He insisted that the fine print of the will justified his explanation. The words, "In the event of my," went a long way.

So, everyone wanted to know, why the big ploy, *er exercise,* to begin with? Chandler's Chocolate had been facing some financial troubles breaking ground on the billion-dollar amusement park and luxury hotel. Grandpa was in fact worried about his own health and fate, but as equally concerned about the fate of his empire. He did his homework, digging up information on his grandkids, challenging their hands in the family business. At the same time, he took the opportunity to gather up a few extra "potential heirs" that met specific criteria. Each had a parent that had been adopted, each was loaded, and by the status of their financial portfolios, each explored investments. And thus, possessed one of humans' primal instincts. The rich, wanted to be richer. Making them all the perfect, greedy Veruca Salt candidates to purchase millions of dollars of Chandler Chocolate shares. With their stock investments, these handful of wealthy individuals made a hefty dent in the project's debts.

Unbeknownst to Brice, he had been the biggest contributor. Ashton, intending to sell out to Ulysses brother, had unintentionally donated Brice's entire life savings to H.O.M.E.R., short for, Helping Old Man's Early Retirement. An account set up by Chandler's real lawyers, strictly for donations, not to be confused with his actual brother, Homer. Yep, the one that owned the Nut House. Chandler and Winston had planted business cards for his HOMER fundraising organization all throughout the mansion. And as greed would have it, Ashton took the bait.

I questioned Chandler's ethics. It was bad enough for him to bring his grandkids into this whole escapade, but worse to let these others think they had shot at the fortune, stealing their money right underneath their noses.

He straightened me out, real quick. "Truth is, if one of those kids were better candidates than my own flesh and blood, I would have written them in the will on the spot. But, no worries. Most of them were schmucks."

I've got a question for you," said Boris. "How was it that you knew I was still alive?"

"Well for starters, everyone else's accident or death had a chocolate factor. You know, death by chocolate. You were supposedly knocked over the head with a bottle of Bitters. It didn't sink in though until I went back to the basement to look for a phone. I mistakenly stepped in your pool of so called blood. Oddly, it was still damp a couple days later, the color was off, and was too sticky.

Boris nodded his head. "Well, well. It appears we have us a detective in the family."

I said, "Not to mention Frankie's subtle clue. Collect one hundred Sweet Bitter Bonker bars–"

Frankie finished, "...and get a free life." We hit knuckles. Awkwardly. Because quite frankly, I wasn't a knuckle-knockin' kind of gal.

I smiled at him. "And here I thought you were just a pro at that video game."

"He outta be, said Boris. "He created it. Can you believe this genius use to work at my brother's Nut House? I know talent when I see it."

Game developer? So much for my detective skills.

Boris and Frankie also filled in the blanks about the cabin in the woods. They both had stayed on property, while they tried to target the killer. Boris explained the mysterious cork-board. "Frankie and I were trying to figure out who was behind all this tragedy. I had circled the photos of my grandchildren."

I hadn't noticed Kiki's photo, so it was probable that it had fallen behind the desk when my hair got stuck on the thumbtack. "Why didn't you call the police and end it all?" I said.

Boris nervously massaged his mustache. "Brice had all of you hostage. He realized I was alive the night you both broke into the cabin. I was locked in the first bedroom, but he easily picked the lock. He threatened to kill you instantly if I made a sound. Minute later, you were gone." I was hoping Frankie would come through and take him down that night, little did I know he was in the process of being poisoned."

Boris plated the last of the hamburgers and joined us at the table. "Fire is still hot, if anybody wants to toast some marshmallows."

Cashmere snickered, "Your grandfather knows your weakness, Anna. Just try not to get them in your hair this time."

It was a holiday, I deserved a guilt-free pass. But watching the marshmallow darken on the stick, stirred up too many painful memories. I tossed the whole thing into the flames and then reached into my purse for more kindling wood. My old faithful waitress notepad. I read the preprinted portion of the bottom of a receipt, *Thank you and have a nice day*, and added it to the fire. No more waitressing. No more sleuthing. It was time to start a new chapter in this life.

Boris gave me a curious expression. Being face to face with my newfound Grandfather evoked millions of questions in my brain that now felt like a frozen smoothie in a blender. Numb and spinning at the same time. Most of them concerned my mother. But, this wasn't the time for it. Easter was hardly the appropriate time for a Q & A session regarding deceit, affairs, and murder. We would have much time in the future for explanations and family counseling. Of course, in the meantime there was much reconciliation to be done. Tessie was mighty angered at Chandler for keeping my mom, the artist, a secret from her. His excuse was that he was trying to protect both ladies. He felt a parental need to watch over Adeline, and give her work, after he learned that she was single for the third time and unemployed. She really had had hard luck with men. He actually invented the contest solely for her, desperately delivering her individual contest entry forms in the mail, on her doorstep, and on her windshield. When she finally entered, she miraculously won the contest the next day. Evidently, she didn't read the fine print. Odds of winning, 1 in 1. And lucky for Chandler, she actually painted a pretty picture.

Boris also gave explanation for the money given to my father, Rusty. Without revealing his relation, Boris had set up a Chandler's donation fund for Kiki, Brice, and myself. As we were minors, our legal guardians held the financial control. Which unfortunately meant, none of us kids ever saw a dime, or even knew the fund existed. Initially, I didn't understand why my Uncle Wiley had kept the truth from me. But, I realized, just as always, he was trying to protect me. He knew I would have sought out my father and siblings long ago. And he knew they were bad news. My father taking off with the money, leaving me behind, was the best thing he'd ever done for me.

As for my current relationship with Kiki, well, we're trying to make it work. I still have a lot of forgiving to find in my heart. And ironically, she has a lot of forgiving to do, as well. Kiki had spent her whole life resenting me. When in truth, she missed her parents. And she missed being loved.

I watched her take a bite of her hamburger speckled with blue cheese, cheddar cheese, and bacon oozing out the buns onto her mini-skirted lap. I self-consciously wiped my own mouth and opted to take a stroll along the porch, settling in a comfortable rocking chair. I sipped my icy rose-tinted lemonade, gazing through the ribbons of blooming miniature roses. My eyes smiled in the distance, watching my Jillian, hand in hand with her Grandmother, feeding hamburger buns to the ducks in the pond. Yes, this I could get used to.

Three glasses of lemonade later, Jillian was off playing with Bonbon, and Tessie had joined me at the rocking chairs.

"The daffodils are in bloom in the garden," Tessie said. "Thought you might want to show them to Jillie."

I smiled and poured Tessie a glass of lemonade. "This day couldn't get any better. I just can't believe it's really happening."

"It's all thanks to you." She took a long sip of her drink. "Why the way you done figured thangs out, yer a regular ol' Agatha."

"Thank you. Being compared to the queen of mysteries is quite a compliment," I said.

"Huh? Ol' Agatha Krimpets don't like no mysteries. Not shore she even reads. But, she's got that magical voodoo sense, just like ya."

I would have stopped the woman from talking, but I was curious enough to see where this was going.

"Like that night Ethyl was stuck 'tween the tub and the toilet for eighteen hours lookin' for er earring." Tessie's voice got soft and sort of creepy in an old southern woman not so scary sort of way. "It was a dark and stormy night, an Ol' Agatha was sitting at home knittin' knickers, when all of a sudden, lightning struck. Now Agatha she had her a metal hip and when the lightning struck, she got zapped, screamed, and peed her pants. Sherlock got spooked and bit her in the ear!"

"Sherlock? As in Holmes?"

"As in Tapioca. They only carry it at The Thrifty Pickle. And it is go-ood," she sang. "Sherlock's got bigger squishy balls than them other brands. And when it comes to Tapioca, it's all about the size of the balls. Especially when ya only got one set of choppers. Don't wanna get em stuck in yer choppers. That's what happens when ya get as old as Ol' Agatha."

"And exactly how old is, Old Agatha?"

"Nobody quite knows. I'm guessin' 117. Give er take a decade. Any who, where was I? It was a dark and stormy night..."

"You said that. You were at the part where the Tapioca bit Agatha's ear."

"Well that don't make a lick of sense. Sherlock's a cat named after tapioca. Are ya even payin' attention?"

Like it mattered.

"So, Sherlock got spooked, and bit Agatha's ear." She leaned in toward me and whispered dramatically, "The left one! That very same ear that Ethyl was missin' an earring from. Five minutes later Ethyl heard someone knockin' at the door. And do you know who it was?"

"Agatha?"

"See I done told ya you was good at this."

"So this 117 year old woman drives?"

"And why not? She still got one good eye. That gal ain't gonna let cataracts stop 'er."

"Continue." Please, so we can get this over with.

"So Agatha was there at Ethyl's house. Outta all the houses she could of picked, she picked Ethyl's house to borrow er a pork chop."

I pursed my lips in question, but was careful to not ask for details.

"She needed the pork chop on accounta her ear wouldn't stop bleedin. Her—

I finished her sentence, "Left ear."

"Yer just showin off now. If it wasn't for Agatha's sixth sense, Ethyl might still be laying there."

Good golly, is it over?

Cashmere called for us, "It's time." I had no idea what it was time for, but I was in.

We went inside and followed the pitter patter of little feet, and big feet, up the stairs. Tessie took the lead, with the whole procession behind her, pausing on the landing to the second floor. Tessie prompted my baby, "Okay Jillie, crack er open."

Jillian split open the halves of a plastic golden egg. Expecting candy or treats, she frowned at the ordinary key that rest inside. A key that was just like the one given to me at the diner.

"Okay hun, ready for yer surprise?" Tessie asked. "Let's see what treasure that key unlocks."

Treasure? Now you had the lass's attention. We followed Tessie past the Raspberry Room. She paused at the room of ruins next to it.

"All right gal, give that key a whirl."

Jillian inserted the key into the bronzed door knob. Tessie gave it a twist, unveiling a delightful renovated bedroom fit for a candy princess. The room sang pink. The bubblegum color was accented with lime and brown stripes and squished polka dots. Above the bed was a familiar picture. The one of Jillian in the broken frame transferred onto oil canvas. Only in this one, her rain boots seemed to be jumping into sweet puddles of rich chocolate and her fuchsia umbrella repelled brightly colored candies shooting them into the pink powdered sky. The corner was signed, G.T. In dancing, polka dotted letters, it read, "Jillie Beans."

"They come in raspberry, mint and fudge," squealed Grandma Tessie, holding out a shiny sack of jelly bean shaped licorice covered in chocolate. "Just in time for Easter. They're a hit."

Jillian was right at home, already playing with her miniature play oven, mixing cookies. Chocolate, no doubt.

Tears poured from my eyes, "I just can't believe it."

"Sorry, I snagged your photo, gal," Tessie said to me.

"I didn't know you could paint." I grabbed her and squeezed her tight.

And then the room became silent. My ears perked up like a puppy hearing the word *cookie*. I heard a tiny tin melody. My head wrenched back, pulling away from Tessie's hold. I walked over to the white Chester drawers with sweet swirled brass knobs. Atop its surface sat a twirling carousel, miniature lights twinkling around chocolate bunnies, chasing shiny butterflies. I listened closely and smiled. *Here Comes Peter Cottontail.* Yes, it was just like the merry go round at the amusement park.

Jillian squeezed in between my arms, her emerald eyes widened in delight. She pointed at the treasure. "Bob."

I embraced her sweet little soul. "Yes sweetie, here comes *Bob*, the Easter Bunny."

"Sorry about lying to you about the wine," Cashmere said to me. "I was just trying to surprise you, not give you reason to suspect me of murder."

"You're the best," I told him. I gazed around the room. "That goes for all of you." Yeah, we were just one big happy family— Uncle Cashmere, Grandpa Chandler and Grandma Tess.

Tessie pulled something from the toy box. "Kiki dear, I got somethin' to show ya." She gave the fluffy pig a squeeze and it snorted. "Why it sure enough sounds just like ya, gal."

As for Tessie and Kiki, they were mending their path towards a beautiful relationship that would someday emerge into the best of friendships — when pigs fly, and drink afternoon tea.

⁂

Solid Heart: Solid hunk of nuts, hidden inside a devilishly dark heart.

Life After Chocolate

*E*ven though yours truly aced the Chandler's Chocolate assessment; the mansion, the factory, and the endless supply of chocolate, didn't belong to me, just yet. Which was fine by me. I was looking forward to making up lost time with my grandparents.

Meanwhile, Grandpa wanted me to get better acquainted with the business. Although I didn't agree with his tactics, I did accept his proposition for hire. If this business was going to stay in the family, I was going to keep it honest. He was impressed by my big ideas and thought he could use my talents as an honest way to schmooze, (I told him *encourage* was a more honest word than schmooze), potential shareholders into investing money into the company and giving his customers back what they wanted most— good, clean chocolate fun.

In exchange for a top position in the company, Grandpa had one condition. As I was next in line for his factory, he wanted to keep his "investment" safe. So, he came up with a plan to hide me in plain sight. A new identity. A new name. A month ago, I would have resisted. But, I now realized that it was my name that had started this whole domino effect of devastation. It had all stemmed from that haunting Bells' advertisement twenty-five years ago. It was time I let Annabell go.

Grandpa Chandler presented his fresh marketing approach to the shareholder's board. Dang gummit, it was me. I was the whole marketing plan in a nutshell.

Chandler spoke to the board, "Introducing the Chandler's Chocolate official event coordinator. She has Southern Charm. She has French style. She has the grace of a royal duchess."

I searched behind me for the French gal and the Princess puff. Nada. I'm sunk.

Chandler proudly continued, "From the heart of Paris Falls, I introduce the new face of Chandler's Chocolates— (insert fancy French accent), Miss Agatha Chocolats."

The End

90777776R00183

Made in the USA
Columbia, SC
07 March 2018